OUTSTANDING PRAISE FOR THE NOVELS
OF ELLEN MARIE WISEMAN!

THE PLUM TREE

"Ellen Marie Wiseman's provocative and realistic images of a small German village are exquisite. *The Plum Tree* will find good company on the shelves of those who appreciated *Skeletons at the Feast*, by Chris Bohjalian, *Sarah's Key*, by Tatiana de Rosnay, and *Night*, by Elie Wiesel."
—*New York Journal of Books*

"The meticulous hand-crafted detail and emotional intensity of *The Plum Tree* immersed me in Germany during its darkest hours and the ordeals its citizens had to face. A must-read for WWII Fiction aficionados—and any reader who loves a transporting story."
—Jenna Blum, *New York Times* bestselling author of *Those Who Save Us*

"Wiseman eschews the genre's usual military conflicts in favor of the slow, inexorable pressure of daily life during wartime, lending an intimate and compelling poignancy to this intriguing debut."
—*Publishers Weekly*

"Ellen Marie Wiseman weaves a story of intrigue, terror, and love from a perspective not often seen in Holocaust novels."
—*Jewish Book World*

WHAT SHE LEFT BEHIND

"A great coming-of-age story."
—*School Library Journal*

"A real page-turner."
—*Historical Novel Society*

"The author has once again delved into the lives of teenage girls, albeit in different circumstances than her first work, yet with the same insight, nuance, and raw emotion readers can appreciate and enjoy."
—*New York Journal of Books*

"A great read!"
—*The San Francisco Book Review*

Please turn the page for more outstanding praise!

P9-DDL-630

COAL RIVER

"Wiseman offers heartbreaking and historically accurate depictions. . . . The richly developed coal town acts as a separate, complex character; readers will want to look away even as they're drawn into a powerful quest for purpose and redemption . . . a powerful story."
—*Publishers Weekly*

"This book will attract readers of historical fiction and those looking for strong female characters."
—*VOYA Magazine*

"Heartrending and strongly drawn."
—*Booklist*

"Ellen Marie Wiseman takes readers deep into the politics and hidden atrocities of a 20th-century Pennsylvania mining town."
—BookPage.com

THE LIFE SHE WAS GIVEN

"Wiseman has crafted a can't-put-it-down novel of family secrets involving two young girls who only seek to be loved. Perfect for book clubs and readers who admired Sara Gruen's *Like Water for Elephants*."
—*Library Journal, Starred Review*

"Wiseman has created two equally enticing story lines that gradually reveal the commonalities between them. This well-crafted novel provides rewards throughout."
—*Publishers Weekly*

"Wiseman excels at creating an atmosphere . . . Her characters are all vividly drawn and complex, especially Lilly's abusive mother, Coralline. But at the heart of Wiseman's tale of loss and redemption are Lilly and Julia, connected in spirit by their determination to overcome years of pain and sorrow. Fans of Karen White and Sara Gruen will be drawn in by the drama and mystery of Wiseman's novel."
—*BookPage*

The Orphan Collector

Books by Ellen Marie Wiseman

THE PLUM TREE

WHAT SHE LEFT BEHIND

COAL RIVER

THE LIFE SHE WAS GIVEN

THE ORPHAN COLLECTOR

Published by Kensington Publishing Corporation

THE ORPHAN COLLECTOR

ELLEN MARIE WISEMAN

KENSINGTON BOOKS
www.kensingtonbooks.com

This book is a work of fiction. Names, characters, and incidents either are products of the author's imagination or are used fictitiously. Any resemblance to actual persons living or dead, or events or locales, is entirely coincidental.

KENSINGTON BOOKS are published by
Kensington Publishing Corp.
119 West 40th Street
New York, NY 10018

Copyright © 2020 by Ellen Marie Wiseman

All rights reserved. No part of this book may be reproduced in any form or by any means without the prior written consent of the Publisher, excepting brief quotes used in reviews.

To the extent that the image or images on the cover of this book depict a person or persons, such person or persons are merely models, and are not intended to portray any character or characters featured in the book.

All Kensington titles, imprints, and distributed lines are available at special quantity discounts for bulk purchases for sales promotion, premiums, fund-raising, educational, or institutional use.

Special book excerpts or customized printings can also be created to fit specific needs. For details, write or phone the office of the Kensington Sales Manager: Kensington Publishing Corp., 119 West 40th Street, New York, NY 10018. Attn. Sales Department. Phone: 1-800-221-2647.

Kensington and the K logo Reg. U.S. Pat. & TM Off.

ISBN-13: 978-1-4967-1587-6 (ebook)
ISBN-10: 1-4967-1587-X (ebook)
Kensington Electronic Edition: August 2020

ISBN-13: 978-1-4967-1586-9
ISBN-10: 1-4967-1586-1
First Kensington Trade Paperback Printing: August 2020

ISBN-13: 978-1-4967-3467-9 (signed edition)
ISBN-10: 1-4967-3467-X (signed edition)

10 9 8 7 6 5 4 3 2 1

Printed in the United States of America

For my beloved family
I treasure each and every one of you

CHAPTER ONE

PIA

September 28, 1918

The deadly virus stole unnoticed through the crowded cobblestone streets of Philadelphia on a sunny September day, unseen and unheard amidst the jubilant chaos of the Liberty Loan parade and the patriotic marches of John Philip Sousa. More than 200,000 men, women, and children waved American flags and jostled one another for prime viewing space along the two-mile route, while the people behind shouted encouragement over shoulders and past faces to the bands, Boy Scouts, women's auxiliaries, marines, sailors, and soldiers in the street. Planes flew overhead, draft horses pulled eight-inch howitzers, military groups performed bayonet drills, church bells clanged, and police whistles blew; old friends hugged and shook hands, couples kissed, and children shared candy and soda. Unaware that the lethal illness had escaped the Naval Yard, the eager spectators had no idea that the local hospitals had admitted over two hundred people the previous day, or that numerous infectious disease experts had pressured the mayor to cancel the event. Not that it would have mattered. They were there to support the troops, buy war bonds, and show their patriotism during a time of war. Victory in Europe—and keeping the Huns out of America—was first and foremost on their minds.

Many of the onlookers had heard about the flu hitting Boston and New York, but the director of laboratories at the Phipps Institute of Philadelphia had just announced he'd identified the cause of the specific influenza causing so much trouble—Pfeiffer's bacillus—and the local newspapers said influenza posed no danger because it was as old as history and usually accompanied by foul air, fog, and plagues of insects. None of those things were happening in Philadelphia. Therefore, it stood to reason that as long as everyone did what the Board of Health advised—kept their feet dry, stayed warm, ate more onions, and kept their bowels and windows open—they'd be fine.

But thirteen-year-old Pia Lange knew something was wrong. And not because her best friend, Finn Duffy, had told her about the dead sailors his older brother had seen outside a local pub. Not because of the posters on telephone poles and buildings that read: "When obliged to cough or sneeze, always place a handkerchief, paper napkin, or fabric of some kind before the face," or "Cover your mouth! Influenza Is Spread by Droplets Sprayed from Nose and Mouth!"

Pia knew something was wrong because the minute she had followed her mother—who was pushing Pia's twin brothers in a wicker baby pram—onto the packed parade route, a sense of unease had come over her, like the thick air before a summer thunderstorm or the swirling discomfort in her belly right before she got sick. Feeling distraught in crowds was nothing new to her—she would never forget the panic she'd felt the first time she walked the busy streets of Philadelphia, or when Finn had dragged her to the maiden launch of a warship from Hog Island, where President Wilson and thirty thousand people were in attendance, and the water was filled with tugboats, steamboats, and barges decorated with American flags.

But this was different. Something she couldn't name seemed to push against her from all sides, something heavy and invisible and threatening. At first she thought it was the heat and the congested sidewalks, but then she recognized the familiar sinking sensation she had grown up trying to avoid, and the sudden, overwhelming awareness that something was horribly wrong. She felt like the little girl she had once been, the little girl who hid behind Mutti's apron when company came, unable to explain why she always wanted to play alone. The little girl who didn't want to shake hands or hug, or sit on anyone's lap. The little girl who was grateful to be left out of kickball and jump rope, while at the same time it broke her heart.

Looking up at the boys in worn jackets and patched trousers clambering up streetlamps to get a better view of the parade, she wished she could join them to escape the crush of the growing throng. The boys shouted and laughed and waved their newsboy caps, hanging like monkeys below giant American flags. More than anything she wanted to be like them too, carefree and unaware that anything was wrong. But that was impossible. No matter how hard she tried, she'd never be like everyone else.

When she looked back down at the sidewalk, her mother had disappeared. She opened her mouth to shout for her, then bit her tongue. She wasn't supposed to call her Mutti anymore—not out loud, anyway. Speaking German in public was no longer allowed. Her parents would always be Mutti and Vater in her head, no matter what the law said, but she didn't dare draw attention by calling her that in a crowd. Standing on her tiptoes to see over shoulders and backs, she spotted the top of Mutti's faded brown hat a few yards away and hurried to catch up to her, stopping short and moving sideways to avoid bumping into people on the way.

Finally behind Mutti again, she wiped the sweat from her upper lip and breathed a sigh of relief. The last thing she needed was to get lost in the city. Bunching her shoulders to make herself smaller, she stayed as close to Mutti as possible, weaving and ducking to avoid the sea of bare arms and hands all around her, wishing her mother would slow down. If only she could crawl into the baby pram with her twin brothers and hide beneath their blankets. She had known coming to the parade would be difficult, but she hadn't expected this.

As far back as she could remember she'd been extraordinarily shy; Mutti said few people could hold her when she was a baby because she'd cry like the world was coming to an end. And she used to think being bashful was the same for everyone; that it was something you could feel, like a fever or stomachache or scratchy throat.

Sometimes she wondered what would have happened if Mutti hadn't been there to protect her from men wanting to pinch her cheeks, and little old ladies waggling their fingers at her to prove they were harmless. But gradually those feelings had changed, even more so in the last couple of months. She'd started to notice other sensations when she touched someone's bare skin, like a dull pain in her head or chest, or a strange discomfort in an arm or leg. It didn't happen every time, but often enough to make her wonder if something was wrong with her. Now, whenever she went to the dry goods store or vegetable market, she took the streets—dodging horses, wagons, bicycles, and automobiles—to avoid the congested sidewalks. And handing coins to the peddlers nearly gave her the vapors, so she dropped them on the counter more often than not. Unfortunately there was nothing she could do about any of it. Telling Mutti—or anyone else, for that matter—was out of the question, especially after hearing about her great-aunt Lottie, who spent the second half of her life locked in an insane asylum in Germany because she saw things that weren't there. No matter how confused or scared Pia got, she wasn't willing to take the chance of getting locked up too.

Now, following Mutti along the packed sidewalks, her worst fears that something was wrong were confirmed when a man in a linen suit and straw gambler cut across the flow of pedestrians and bumped into her, laughing at first, then apologizing when he realized what he'd done. Having been taught to always smile and be polite, she forced a smile—she was so good at it that it sometimes frightened her—but then the man pinched her cheek and a sharp pain stabbed her chest, like her heart had been split in two. She shuddered and looked down at herself, certain a knife would be sticking out of her rib cage. But there was no knife, no blood trickling down the front of her flour-sack dress. The thin bodice was smooth and spotless, as clean as it had been that morning when she first put it on. She stepped backward to get away from the man, but he was already gone, the pain disappearing with him. The strength of it left her shaky and weak.

Then a small, cool hand latched on to hers and her chest constricted, tightening with every breath. She swore she heard her lungs rattle, but couldn't be sure with all the noise. She yanked her hand away and looked down. A little girl in a white ruffled dress gazed up at her, smiling—until she realized Pia was a stranger. Then fear crumpled her face and she searched the crowd with frantic eyes before running off, calling for her mother. When she was gone, Pia could breathe normally again.

How Pia longed to be back in Hazleton, Pennsylvania, where open spaces were filled with blue skies, swaths of wildflowers, and herds of deer, instead of miles of pavement, side-by-side buildings, and hordes of people. In Philadelphia, she couldn't walk ten feet without bumping into someone, and every sight, sound, and smell seemed menacing and foreign. The neighborhood alleys were strewn with garbage and sewage, and the biggest rats she'd ever seen crawled in nooks and crannies, scampering between walls and passageways. Trolleys and wagons and motorcars fought for space on every street, and more people than she had ever seen at one time seemed to crowd every sidewalk. The city reminded her of a clogged beehive, teeming with people instead of insects. Even the row houses were full to overflowing, with multiple families squeezed into two and three rooms. Certainly there had been hardships in the mining village back in Hazleton—the walls of their shack were paper-thin, everything from their clothes to their kitchen table seemed covered in coal dust, and worst of all, Vater's job digging for coal was dangerous and grueling—but it didn't make her any less homesick. She was glad her father had found less dangerous work in the city a little over a year ago, but she missed the chickens in the yard and the neighbor's hound dog sleeping under their front porch. She missed taking the dirt path to Widow Wilcox's shack to learn how to read and write. She missed the mountain trails and the grass outside their front door. Vater said she missed Hazleton because she longed for the rolling hills and green fields of Bavaria. And when she reminded him she was only four years old when they boarded the ship to America, he laughed and said Germany was in her blood, like her fondness for sweets and his love for her mother.

Thinking of her father, her eyes burned. If he were here with them now, she could hold his wide, weathered hand in hers and lean against his tall, muscular frame. He'd squeeze her fingers twice, in quick succession like he always did, which meant "I love you"; then she'd squeeze his back and they'd smile at each other, delighted with their little secret. No one would guess by looking at Vater that he was tenderhearted and always whistling, singing, and making jokes; instead they tended to hurry out of his path because of his imposing presence and piano-wide shoulders. With him by her side, she could have moved through the crowd nearly untouched. But that was impossible because he'd enlisted in the army three months ago, along with two of his German-American friends, to prove their loyalty to the United States. Now he was somewhere in France, and she had no idea when he was coming home. Like Mutti said through her tears when he left, moving to the city to keep him safe had done no good at all.

Suddenly a woman in a Lady Liberty costume pushed between Pia and her mother, jarring her from her thoughts. When the woman's bare forearm brushed her hand, Pia held her breath, waiting for the strange sensations to start. But to her relief, she felt nothing. She relaxed her tight shoulders and exhaled, trying to calm down. She only had to get through the next hour or so. That was it. Then she could go home, to their rooms on Shunk Alley in the Fifth Ward, where no one but her loved ones could reach her.

Then Mutti stopped to talk to a woman from the greengrocers' and a pair of clammy hands clamped over Pia's eyes. Someone snickered in her ear. A sharp pain instantly twisted near her rib cage, making her hot and dizzy. She yanked the hands away from her face and spun around. It was Tommy Costa, the freckle-faced boy who teased her during school recess, and two of his friends, Angelo DiPrizzi and Skip Turner. They laughed and stuck out their tongues at her, then ran away. The discomfort in her ribs went with them.

By the time Mutti chose a spot to watch the parade, Pia was shaking. She'd begged her mother to let her stay home, even promising to straighten up their two-room apartment while she and the twins were gone. But despite knowing how Pia felt about large gatherings, Mutti insisted.

"Going to the parade is the only way to prove we are loyal Americans," Mutti said in heavily accented English. "It's hard enough after President Wilson said all German citizens are alien enemies. I follow the new laws. I sign the papers they want me to sign refusing my German citizenship. I do the fingerprinting. But I have no money to buy Liberty loans or make a donation to the Red Cross. I have to feed you and your brothers. So we must go to the parade. All of us. Even your father fighting in the war is not enough to keep the neighbors happy."

"But it won't matter if I'm with you or not," Pia said. "Everyone will see you there, and the twins will enjoy it. I could make dinner and have it ready when you return."

"*Nein,*" her mother said. As soon as the word came out of her mouth, worry flickered across her face. "I mean, no. You must come with us. The radio and newspapers tell everyone to be watchful of their German-American neighbors and to report to the authorities. Before your father left, a woman shouted at me, saying he stole a real American's job. She spit and said to go back where I came from. I am not leaving you home alone."

Pia knew Mutti was right; she'd suffered enough bullying at school to know everything she said was true. Rumors were flying that German spies were poisoning food, and German-Americans were secretly hoarding arms. Some Germans had even been sent to jail or internment camps. The city was plastered with posters showing Germans standing over dead bodies and ads directing people to buy war bonds to "Beat back the Hun!" Churches with German congregations had been painted yellow, German-language newspapers were shut down, and schoolchildren were forced to sign pledges promising not to use any foreign language whatsoever. As if that weren't enough, a special police group called the Home Guard, originally formed to patrol the streets with guns to ensure adequate protection of important points in the city—the Water Works and pumping station, the electric light distributing plant, the telephone service, and various power stations at manufacturing plants—now also patrolled the south end of the city to keep an eye on German immigrants. Some companies refused to employ Germans, so Mutti lost her job at the textile mill. And because she needed a permit to withdraw money from the bank, what little cash they had left was kept under a floorboard inside a bedroom cubby. Even sauerkraut and hamburgers were renamed "liberty cabbage" and "liberty sandwiches."

But knowing Mutti was right didn't make going to the parade any easier.

Three days after the parade, while her schoolmates laughed and played hopscotch and jump rope during recess, Pia sat alone in her usual spot, on a flat rock near the back fence of the schoolyard, pretending to read. The air was pale, as gray as smoke, and the breeze carried a slight chill. Luckily, she'd remembered to bring her sweater, especially since the school windows were being kept open to ward off the grippe. Her three-quarter-length dress had long sleeves and her cotton stockings were thick, but the flour-sack material of her skirt and bodice was worn and thin. She put the book down, pulled her sleeves over her fists, and tried to stop shivering. Was she trembling because of the cold, or because she couldn't stop thinking about what she'd seen and heard since the Liberty Loan parade?

Mrs. Schmidt had told Mutti that within seventy-two hours of the parade, every bed in each of the city's thirty-one hospitals was filled with victims of a new illness called the Spanish influenza, and the hospitals were starting to refuse patients. By day four, the illness had infected over six hundred Philadelphians, and killed well over a hundred in one day. Pia overheard the teachers talking about a shortage of doctors and nurses because of the war, and that poorhouses and churches were being used as temporary hospitals. More posters went up that read "Spitting Equals Death," and the police arrested anyone who disobeyed. Another poster showed a man in a suit standing next to the outline of a clawed demon rising from what appeared to be a pool of saliva on the sidewalk, with the words "Halt the Epidemic! Stop Spitting, Everybody!" And because everyone was wearing pouches of garlic or camphor balls in cheesecloth around their necks, the streets were filled with a foul, peculiar odor that she couldn't help thinking was the smell of death. Most frightening of all, she heard that those who fell sick were often dead by nightfall; their faces turned black and blue, blood gushing from their mouth, nose, ears, and even their eyes.

She'd been having nightmares too, filled with ghastly images of the parade spectators flashing in her mind like the jerky moving pictures in a penny arcade—each face with black lips and purple cheeks, and blood coming from their mouths and eyes. Every time it happened she woke up in a sweat, her arms and legs tangled in the sheets, her stomach and chest sore and aching. Just thinking about it made her queasy. The stench wafting up from the garlic tied around her neck didn't help.

She took the putrid necklace off and laid it in the grass, then lifted her chin and took a deep breath, inhaling the familiar scents of fall—a mixture of moist earth, sunburnt leaves, and chimney smoke. But despite the fact that the air smelled significantly better than the strong odor of garlic, it still reminded her of her first dreadful day in her new school last year. She could still hear the voices of her mother and new teacher.

"Did you see the letter I send in to school, Mrs. Derry?" Mutti had said.

"Yes, Mrs. Lange, I received the note. But I'm not sure I understand it."

"Forgive me, I only wish to make sure . . ." Mutti said, hesitating. "My Pia is, how do you say, delicate? She does not like crowds, or anyone touching her. I am not sure why. . . ." Her mother started wringing her hands. "But she is a normal girl and smart. Please. Can you be sure the other children—"

"Mrs. Lange, I don't see how—"

"Pia needs to learn. She needs to be at school. I don't want her to . . ."

"All right, Mrs. Lange," Mrs. Derry said. "Yes, I'll do my best. But children come into contact with each other while playing all the time, especially during recess. It's part of learning. Sometimes I won't be able to stop it from happening."

"Yes, I understand," Mutti said. "But if Pia doesn't want . . . if one of the other children does not know to leave her alone . . . please . . ."

Mrs. Derry put a hand on her mother's arm, looked at her with pity-filled eyes, and said, "Don't worry, I'll take care of her. And I'll let the other teachers know too."

Mutti nodded and gave her a tired smile, then said goodbye to Pia and left.

After that first day, for the most part, Mrs. Derry and the rest of the teachers had done little to look out for Pia. And the memory of that encounter—her mother wringing her hands and trying to communicate her odd concerns to a confused Mrs. Derry while Pia cringed at her side and the other kids watched—recurred to her every time she stepped foot in the classroom. While the other children played Duck, Duck, Goose or Ring-Around-the-Rosy, Pia stood off to the side, sad and relieved at the same time. Inevitably, when the teachers weren't looking, some of the kids taunted and poked her, calling her names like freak girl or scaredy-cat. And now, because of the war, they called her a Hun.

Thankfully she'd met Finn before school started, while he could form his own opinion without the influence of the other kids. It was the day after she and her family had moved in, when Mutti sent her out to sit on the stoop with strict instructions not to wander off while she and Vater talked—about what, Pia wasn't sure. She'd been homesick and near tears, frightened to discover that the jumble of trash-strewn alleys and cobblestone streets and closely built row houses made her feel trapped, and wondering how she'd ever get used to living there, when he approached from across the alley. She tried to ignore him, hoping he was headed for the entrance behind her, but he stopped at the bottom of the steps, swept his copper-colored bangs out of his eyes, and gave her a friendly grin.

"Yer a new lass around here, aren't ye?" he said in a heavy Irish brogue. "I'm Finn Duffy, your neighbor from across the way." He pointed at the shabby building across from hers, a four-story brick with narrow windows and a black fire escape.

She nodded and forced a smile. She didn't feel like talking but didn't want to be rude either. "Yes," she said. "We moved in yesterday."

"Nice to meet you, um . . . What did you say yer name was?"

"Oh, sorry," she said. "I'm Pia Lange."

"Well, nice to meet ye, Pia Lange. Can I interest you in a game of marbles?" He pulled a cloth sack from the pocket of his threadbare trousers.

She shook her head. "No, thank you."

"Would ye mind if I sit with you, then?" he said. "You look rather lonesome, if you don't mind me saying so."

She thought about telling him she wanted to be left alone, but didn't want to start off by making enemies. Instead she nodded and moved over to make room, gathering her pleated skirt beneath her legs and sitting on her hands. He smiled and sat beside her, a polite distance away. To her relief, he kept quiet, almost as if he knew she didn't feel like making conversation. Together they sat lost in their own thoughts, watching three colored girls with braids and pigtails play hopscotch across the way. One held a rag doll under her arm, the doll's limp head flopping up and down with every jump. A group of ruddy-cheeked boys in patched pants and worn shoes kicked a can along the cobblestones, shouting at each other to pass the can their way. Snippets of laughter, conversation, and the tinny music of a phonograph drifted down from open windows, along with the smell of fried onions and baking bread. Line after line of laundry hung damp and unmoving in the humid air above their heads, crisscrossing the row of buildings like layers of circus flags. People of all colors and ages and sizes spilled out onto the fire escapes, some sitting on overturned washtubs and kettles, all looking for relief from the heat.

An old colored woman in a dirty scarf and laceless boots limped past, humming and pulling a wooden cart filled with rags and old bottles. She skirted around two boys of about seven or eight playing cards on their knees in front of a stone building three doors down. One of the boys glanced over his shoulder at her, then jumped to his feet, grabbed something from her cart, and ran, laughing, back to his friend. The old woman kept going, oblivious to the fact that she had been robbed. The second boy gathered up the cards and did the same; then they both started to run away.

Finn shot to his feet and chased after them, cutting them off before they disappeared down a side alley. He yelled something Pia couldn't make out, then grabbed them by the ears and dragged them back to the old woman. After returning her things to the cart, the boys hurried away, rubbing their ears and scowling back at him, muttering under their breath. The old woman stopped and looked around, finally aware that something was amiss. When she saw Finn, she shooed him away and swatted at him with a thin, gnarled hand. He laughed and made his way back to Pia, shrugging and lifting his palms in the air.

Pia couldn't help but smile. "Do you know her?" she said.

"I don't," he said, catching his breath. He sat back on the stoop beside her and wiped the sweat from his brow. "But I see her every day, selling rags and bottles on the corner. I know the lads, though, and they're always causin' a ruckus."

"They didn't look very happy with you," she said.

"I suppose they're not," he said. "But they won't cause trouble for me."

"Well," she said. "It was very nice of you to stop them and make them return what they took."

He gave her a sideways grin. "Why, isn't that grand? Ye think I'm nice. Thank you, Pia Lange."

Heat crawled up her face. She nodded because she didn't know what to say, then went back to watching the girls play hopscotch. Did he really think what she said was grand, or was he making fun of her? His smile made her think he appreciated the compliment, so she told herself that was the case. Not that it mattered. Once he found out she was German he'd probably never speak to her again.

He sat forward, his elbows on his knees, and watched the girls play hopscotch too. "We came from Ireland three years ago," he said. "How long have you been in the States?"

"Since I was four," she said.

He raised his eyebrows at her. "That long?"

She nodded.

"Livin' here in Philly the entire time?"

She shook her head. "We came here from Hazleton, Pennsylvania. Vater . . . I mean, my father worked in the coal mines."

He forced a hard breath between his teeth. "That's a bloody hard way to make a living."

She nodded. At least he didn't react to the German word. Or maybe he didn't notice.

"This city can be a mite overwhelming when you first arrive," he said. "But you'll get used to it. My da was the one who wanted to come, but he never got to see it."

"Why not?"

"He didn't survive the voyage."

"I'm sorry."

"Aye, I appreciate it. My mam has been having a hard time of it since then, so my older brothers and I have been taking care of her and my granddad. Then the army took one of my brothers six months ago, and my other brother had to start working double shifts at the textile mill. I'm ready to take a job, but Mam insists I finish my schoolin' first. Things were hard in Dublin, but I'm not sure they're much better here. It makes ye long for home, even when you know leaving was the right thing to do."

She really looked at him then, at his kind face and hazel eyes. It was almost as if he were reading her mind.

From that day on, they were fast friends. He didn't care that she and her family were German, or ask her to explain why she didn't want to play cat's cradle or any other game that might involve close contact. After he sent her a note on the clothesline between their fourth-floor apartments that said, *'Twas nice to meet ye, lass!* they started sending each other messages on Sunday nights when the line was empty—but only if the windows weren't frozen shut and they were able to find scraps of paper not set aside for the war effort. The notes were silly and meaningless, just hello or a funny joke or a drawing, but it was their little secret. One of the few things Pia didn't have to share with anyone else.

Once school started and they discovered they were in the same classroom despite him being a grade ahead, he offered to sit with her at recess, but she said she'd rather not have the added attention. While he played kickball and marbles with the other boys, he always looked over to offer a smile or a wave. And that small gesture made everything easier.

Most days she didn't mind sitting alone. But today was different. She wished he'd stop playing ball and come sit with her, even if it was just for a few minutes. Because no matter how hard she tried, she couldn't stop thinking about the flu, and was constantly distracted by an overwhelming feeling of worry and dread. When a group of girls skipping rope began to chant a new rhyme, chills shivered up her spine.

> *There was a little girl, and she had a little bird,*
> *And she called it by the pretty name of Enza;*
> *But one day it flew away, but it didn't go to stay,*
> *For when she raised the window, in-flu-enza.*

"What are you staring at, scaredy-cat?"

Pia looked up to see who had spoken, unaware she'd been staring. A thin girl with brown pigtails glared down at her, a disgusted look on her face. It was Mary Helen Burrows, the girl everyone liked or feared, depending on which day you asked, and whether or not Mary Helen was within earshot. No one had ever seen her get into an actual brawl, but permanent anger knitted her brows, and bruises marked her arms and legs. Two other girls stood behind her, Beverly Hansom and Selma Jones, their arms crossed over their chests.

"I wasn't staring at anything," Pia said, reaching for her book.

"I'm telling you, Mary Helen," Beverly said. "She was staring at us, like she was coming up with some nasty German scheme or somethin'."

Mary Helen knocked the book out of Pia's hand. "You spying on us?"

Pia shook her head. "No, I was just—"

"What's going on?" someone said. "Are you all right, Pia?" It was Finn. He was out of breath, his face red and his hair disheveled.

"Your girlfriend was giving us the stink-eye," Mary Helen said.

"She's not my girlfriend," Finn said.

"Shut up, Mary Helen," Pia said.

Mary Helen ignored her and glared at Finn. "I just wanna know one thing. What would your mother think if she knew you were friends with a filthy Hun, 'specially with your older brother over there fighting to keep you safe?"

Pia bounced to her feet. "Take that back!"

Mary Helen's head snapped around and she gaped at Pia, shocked to hear her standing up for herself. "What'd you say?"

"I said take it back!"

Mary Helen held up her bony fists. "You want a fat lip to go with that stink-eye, scaredy-cat?"

"Jaysus," Finn said. "In the name of all that's holy, shut up, Mary Helen. You're not gonna fight."

"Oh yeah?" Mary Helen said. Suddenly her hand shot out and grabbed the front of Pia's dress. She yanked Pia forward and pushed her contorted face into hers, the stench of garlic and onions wafting from the bag around her neck almost making Pia gag. Thinking only of escape, Pia grabbed Mary Helen's wrist with both hands and tried to pull her off. A quick stab of pain twisted in her chest, sharp and immediate, and she gasped, unable to get air. She let go of Mary Helen's wrist and tried to step away, suddenly disoriented and dizzy. Finn pried Mary Helen's fist from Pia's dress, moved Pia behind him, and stood between them. Pia sat down hard on the ground and tried to catch her breath.

One of the teachers hurried over. "What in heaven's name is going on over here?" she said. It was Miss Herrick. She towered above them, willowy as a flower stem.

"Nothing, ma'am," Mary Helen said. "You must be balled up. We were just playing a game."

"Well, it doesn't look like a game to me," Miss Herrick said. "You and your friends run along now, Mary Helen, and leave Pia alone."

Mary Helen harrumphed, but did as she was told. The other girls followed, their faces pinched.

"Are you all right, Pia?" Miss Herrick said. She bent down to help her up, reaching for her arm.

"Don't touch me," Pia said, louder than intended.

Miss Herrick gasped and clapped a hand to her chest.

Pia instantly regretted her outburst. The last thing she needed was to get in trouble at school. Mutti would never understand. She got up and brushed off her dress. "I'm sorry, Miss Herrick," she said. "I didn't mean to be rude. I was frightened, that's all."

Miss Herrick sighed. "That's understandable, I suppose. I know Mary Helen likes to start trouble, and everyone is feeling anxious these days, but are you sure you're all right? You look like you've just seen a ghost."

Pia mustered a weak smile. "I'm fine. Thank you, Miss Herrick." She wasn't anywhere near fine, but how could she explain to the teacher what she'd felt when she grabbed Mary Helen's wrist? She'd think she was crazy.

The next day, Mary Helen was absent from school and Selma Jones fainted while unpacking her sandwich during lunch. Miss Herrick rushed over to Selma and shook her while the class watched, mouths agape, but Selma didn't move. Miss Herrick ran out into the hall yelling, and two teachers carried Selma away. Beverly Hansom's mother pulled her out of class shortly afterward, scurrying into the room and wrapping a protective arm around her daughter, her face pale. On the playground that afternoon, the teachers spoke in hushed voices behind their hands, their brows lined with worry. Rumors flew that Mary Helen and Selma had the flu and Mary Helen was already dead.

After the last lesson of the day, Pia hurried out of the building and started for home, her books held to her chest, her head down. Normally she would have waited for Finn on the school steps, but she had to get away from there. She needed to go back to her family's rooms, where she could close the door and hide from everyone and everything. A block from the school, a Red Cross ambulance sped by, and a man on a bench was reading a newspaper with the headline: ALL CITIZENS ORDERED TO WEAR GAUZE MASKS IN PUBLIC. On the streetlamp above him, an advertisement for masks read: "Obey the laws and wear the gauze, protect your jaws from septic paws."

Deciding she didn't want to walk the rest of the way alone, she ducked into a landing to wait for Finn, away from the congested sidewalks, and leaned against the doorframe, wishing she could disappear. Everyone seemed to be in a hurry. Two women with scarves over their mouths darted by arm in arm, walking as fast as they could without running. A gray-haired couple wearing gauze masks and carrying suitcases rushed out of a building and hailed a cab, the old man practically pushing other pedestrians aside with his cane. Even the motorcars and horse-drawn wagons seemed to go by faster than normal. A strange awareness seemed to fill the air, like the lightheartedness on the day before Christmas, or the shared excitement she'd felt before the fireworks display on her first Independence Day in Philadelphia. Except this awareness felt ominous and full of menace, like the sensation she felt at the parade, but ten times worse. And now everyone could feel it.

When Finn came walking down the block, her shoulders dropped in relief. She stepped out of the landing onto the sidewalk in front of him.

"Hey," he said, surprised. "Why didn't you wait for me?"

"I did," she said. "I'm right here, aren't I?" She started walking and he fell in beside her.

"Ye are, but I didn't know where you were. I thought . . ."

"You thought what?"

He shrugged and shoved his hands in his pockets. "Everyone's getting sick. Remember we heard Tommy Costa and his family left town?"

She nodded.

"Aye, well, his best pal, Skip, said he died last night."

Pia stopped in her tracks. Tommy was the boy who had put his hands over her eyes at the parade. "Was it the flu?"

"I can't think of anything else that'd take him that quick."

She hugged her books to her chest and started walking again. Tommy and Mary Helen were young and strong. How could they be dead from influenza? How could Selma Jones be fine one day and fainting the next? And why had she felt pain when she'd touched them? Was it the flu she'd felt? No. She couldn't feel sickness in another person. It had to be a coincidence. Or maybe her shyness really was starting to become a physical ailment. More than anything, she wanted to tell Finn what was going on, to ask him what he thought. But she couldn't. Not yet.

At the end of the fourth block, they turned left into Jacob's Alley, a cart path lined with bakers, shoe cobblers, tailors, and cigar makers working out of storefronts in brick houses, their families' apartments above. Some of the homes had been turned into boardinghouses, or rented-out rooms to sailors. Crepe ribbons hung from several doorknobs, black and gray and white, swirling in the afternoon breeze. Some doors were marked with signs that read: "QUARANTINE INFLUENZA: Keep out of this house." At the end of the alley, a woman in a black dress came out of the silversmith's shop and tied a piece of white crepe to the doorknob, sobbing uncontrollably.

Pia couldn't help staring, new tremors of fear climbing up her back. She knew what the different colors of crepe meant; she'd seen enough of it in the mining village after cave-ins and explosions, and during the wave of tuberculosis that hit the village when she was seven. Black meant the death of an adult; gray an elderly person; white a child. She and Finn looked at each other. A silent alarm passed between them and they started walking faster. When they turned the corner onto Lombard Street, they slowed. Dozens of policemen, all wearing gauze masks, patrolled the sidewalks, telling people to keep moving. A line of people snaked out the door of the pharmacy, holding empty glass bottles and barely speaking. Their faces were drawn by worry, their eyes hollowed out by fear. Some of these anxious souls wore white masks and kept their distance from others and the pedestrians pushing by on the sidewalk, newspapers held over their mouths. A sign in the pharmacy window read: "Formaldehyde tablets. Melt under your tongue. Proven to kill germs and prevent infection and contagion. Fifty tablets for fifty cents."

"What kind of medicine do you think they're waiting for?" Pia asked Finn.

"Anything they can get, I suppose," he said. "But whiskey, mostly."

In the window of a sporting goods store next door, an advertisement for phonographs read: "This machine is guaranteed to drive away Spanish flu. Stay at home. Keep away from crowds and theaters. Doctor's Orders. Hear the new October records on your new phonograph and you'll never know you had to stay in nights or miss gasless Sundays." Across the road, people holding sacks and baskets crowded around a truck with a sign that said: "Eat More Onions,

One of the Best Preventatives for Influenza." A gathering of colored people stood to one side, waiting to see if there would be any onions left over for them.

Seeing the onion truck, Pia thought of what Mutti had said that morning—they were short on supplies and she needed to go to the market but didn't want to have to take the twins, so she might wait until Pia came home from school. Hopefully Mutti had stayed home. Pia needed to tell her it wasn't a good idea to go out, not until things returned to normal.

A streetcar rattled past and stopped a few yards away. Two men in black bowlers hurried toward it, one wearing a mask. The conductor, also wearing a mask, came to the door and pointed at one of the men.

"You're not getting on without a mask," the conductor said. He let the other man on, then blocked the maskless man from boarding.

Anger hardened the man's face. "I have a meeting and I can't be late," he said. "I insist you allow me to get on."

"Sorry," the conductor said. "Those are the rules."

A policeman approached, one hand on his billy club. "You heard him," he said to the man. "No mask, no ride."

The man cussed and stomped away. The policeman waved the trolley on, but before the conductor could climb back up, a woman screamed and the passengers scrambled out the door onto the street, nearly knocking the conductor over and running in all directions. Pia and Finn stopped to watch. The policeman clambered up the trolley steps, then jumped back down. Two more policemen appeared and spoke to him. One hurried away while the other turned to face the gathering crowd.

"Stay clear!" he shouted. "We're sending for the coroner!"

When Pia saw why the passengers were in such a hurry to get off the trolley, she gasped and put a hand over her mouth. A man sat slumped over in his seat, his forehead against the window, a stained mask ripped and dangling from his chin, his face a strange mixture of gray, blue, and red. Blood spilled from his eyes and mouth and nose, smearing the glass with dark clots. Horror knotted in Pia's stomach. She started walking again, as fast as her shaking legs could carry her. Finn followed.

"Finn?" she said, breathing hard.

"Aye?"

"I'm scared."

"I know."

"Aren't you?"

"I am."

They strode in silence for another few minutes, then Finn said, "Have you gotten any more letters from your father?"

If she hadn't been so terrified, she would have smiled at him. As usual, he was trying to distract her from her distress. That was Finn, always thinking about other people. She wanted to hug him, now more than ever, but at the same time, now more than ever, she was afraid to touch anyone. "No," she said. "We haven't heard anything from him in weeks."

"Ye will soon, I bet."

She nodded. "Mutti . . . I mean, my mother says we should, any day now. I wish he was here now." Her chest tightened and she blinked back a sudden flood of tears. If Vater were here now, maybe he'd know what to do. Maybe he'd take them out of the city, away from what was happening. Because for as far back as she could remember, he'd always been their protector. Like that time a sudden lightning storm hit while they were on a Sunday picnic and he'd herded her and Mutti into a cave. Or when she accidentally knocked a hornets' nest out from under the front porch and he picked her up, covered her with his jacket, and raced her inside their shack. He wouldn't have been able to do anything about the flu, but just having him here would have made her feel safer.

Finn glanced at her with concern. "Try not to worry too much, lass. It takes a long time for a letter to get across that great ocean."

She nodded again, thankful for Finn's kindness but unable to speak around the burning lump in her throat.

After turning left on Broad Street, they made their way toward the congested maze of alleys and gritty blocks of row houses they called home—the section of Philadelphia labeled the Bloody Fifth Ward because of the area's violent reputation. In the last week alone, two men on their block had been murdered—one shot and the other stabbed—and a colored man was beaten and left for dead in an alley behind a warehouse on the corner. Other than the ever-present Home Guard, whose job was to spy on German immigrants, it seemed like the only time the police came into the neighborhood was to raid the speakeasies, arrest women for vagrancy and "night walking," and apprehend men for gambling, assaults, and drunkenness. Some people said crime had heightened because of the growing number of immigrants and colored who'd moved in looking for work since the start of the war, but Finn said the streets of the Fifth Ward had always been dangerous. He told her stories about a colored rights advocate being murdered, a church being torched, and a number of homes being destroyed during race riots. Pia and her family had only been there a few months when a policeman was shot and killed during a heated race for Select Councilmen, when eighteen men called the Frog Hollow Gang came all the way down from New York to attack one of the candidates.

Had her parents been aware of the dangers of a large city when they'd decided to move here? Did they know and decide to come anyway? She wasn't even allowed to go outside after dark anymore, which made her all the more homesick for the mountains, where she used to watch fireflies in the switch grass and search for the Big Dipper in the stars. And there was no Spanish flu back in Hazleton, she'd bet. She couldn't help thinking how different her life would be if they'd never come to Philadelphia.

But then she and Finn turned off the main street into Shunk Alley, and something strange happened. Whether it was the group of boys playing stickball or the little girls having a pretend tea party on a building stoop, she wasn't sure, but for some reason, her fear seemed to lessen. No one was wearing masks or running from a dead man on a trolley. No signs on doors warned of quarantine. No new posters had been put up. Everything looked normal. When they reached the steps outside her row house, she loosened the grip on her schoolbooks, and a sense of calm washed over her. Maybe the flu wouldn't reach their little part of the city.

Then the sound of a woman sobbing floated down from an open window.

Finn glanced up at the window, then gazed at her, his forehead furrowed. Clearly he was wondering the same thing. Had the flu already reached Shunk Alley? He opened his mouth to say something when his mother yelled down from the fire escape outside their apartment.

"Finn, come quick! It's yer brother!"

He shot Pia a worried look, then turned to leave. "I'll see ye later, lass," he said over his shoulder. "Take care of yourself, all right?"

Before she could respond, he sprinted across the street and went inside. She fixed her eyes on the door after it closed, shivering. His parting words felt weighed down with apprehension and misery, like an omen or a warning. Would she ever see him again? Dread fell over her shoulders like a heavy blanket. She suddenly wished she had told him what happened with Tommy Costa and Mary Helen, how she had felt something strange when they touched her. He couldn't have done anything to help, but maybe sharing her secret would have made her feel less alone.

Behind her, someone called her name. She jumped and spun around, almost dropping her books. Mutti stood in the open doorway of their building, scrubbing a calloused hand on her apron, the telltale sign that she was worried. Pia had seen her do it a thousand times—every day when Vater left to work in the mines; when the Black Maria came into the village carrying the injured and dead after a mining accident; when Vater said they were moving to Philadelphia; when she thought she might miscarry the twins the same way she'd miscarried three other babies; when Vater left for the war.

"Hurry, Pia," Mutti said, gesturing frantically. "Come inside."

Pia's heart skipped a beat. Had something happened to Vater? Or the twins? No. That wasn't it. Fear darkened her mother's eyes, not sorrow.

"What is it?" Pia said, running up the steps and hurrying inside. "What's wrong?"

Mutti closed the door behind her, giving it a little extra push after it was shut, as if trying to keep something from slipping inside. "The churches and schools are to be closed," she said. "All places for gathering, even the factories and moving picture houses, will not be open. No funerals are to be allowed either. Many people are getting sick, so everyone is to stay home." She moved across the dim foyer, scrubbing her hand on her apron. Pia followed.

"How do you know everything is being closed?" Pia said. "Who told you?" They didn't own a radio and hadn't gotten the newspaper since Vater left because Mutti couldn't read.

"Frau Metzger heard it at the butcher shop," Mutti said. "And Mrs. Schmidt heard it on the radio." She stopped and pointed toward the front door, her face a curious mixture of anger and fear. "Those mothers still letting their children outside? They are *Verruckt!*" She spun her finger near her temple. "You must stay inside until this is over, you understand?"

Pia nodded and put a finger to her lips.

"What?" Mutti said. "Why are you shushing me?"

"You were speaking German," Pia whispered.

Mutti gasped and put a hand over her mouth. Then she glanced at Pia's neck and her eyes went wide. "Where is your garlic?"

Pia felt for the rank necklace, only then remembering she had taken it off and laid it on the grass during recess, like she'd done the day before when Mary Helen came over to pick a fight. "I must have lost it," she said.

"You must be more careful, Pia," Mutti said. "Mrs. Schmidt was very kind to give us the garlic and I have no more."

"I'm sorry. It was an accident."

Mutti threw her hands up in exasperation, then started down the hall toward the back of the building. "Come help with the water, *bitte,*" she said, too upset to realize she was speaking German again. "The twins will wake up again soon."

Pia followed her mother down the hall, squinting as her eyes adjusted to the deepening gloom. Except for the front apartments on each floor, which had the only windows in the building, the hallways and the rest of the rooms were shrouded in darkness, even in the middle of the day. She tried not to think about their little shack back in Hazleton, with windows on three walls to let in the sunshine and mountain breezes. Thankfully, though, her family lived in one of the front apartments, with a window in the main room to let in natural light. She couldn't imagine what it was like living in the back and middle of the row house, where the only light came from candles or lanterns. Not to mention no fresh air to ward off the flu. With that thought, frightening images formed in her mind of the people in the back apartments, sick and dying in the dark, where no one would find them for days.

Clenching her jaw, she pushed the gruesome thoughts away and followed Mutti through the back door and outside, into the fenced backyard that housed the water pump and outhouse. Mutti picked up one of two buckets and put it beneath the cast-iron spout. Pia set her books on the back step and pumped the handle, grateful to be getting water now instead of being sent to fetch it after supper. She hated coming down to the backyard alone, especially to use the outhouse. Sharing outhouses and water pumps with other families was nothing new—they had done it in the mining village—but the fences and closeness of the surrounding buildings made her feel like a pig in a pen, vulnerable to whomever else was in there at the same time. Like Mrs. Nagy, who kept asking questions in Hungarian, then stared at her waiting for an answer, as if Pia could speak the language. And especially old Mr. Hill, who rattled the outhouse handle when it was occupied and started pulling down his pants before shutting the door when it was his turn. Sometimes he talked to her until she came out of the outhouse, then grinned like they were best friends. He always shook his head and chuckled, making excuses about being old and senile, but she could see the cunning in his eyes. He knew exactly what he was doing.

When they finished filling the two buckets, Pia picked up her books and helped Mutti carry the water inside, down the shadowy hallway and up the narrow stairs, their hard-soled shoes crunching on dirt and plaster. What seemed like a hundred thick odors layered the floors of the row house—boiled cabbage, fried potatoes, warm curry, simmered tomatoes, sautéed sausage, roasted garlic, baked bread—each one more fragrant than the one before. Despite her fear and unease, Pia's stomach growled with hunger. It had been over six hours since her breakfast of rye bread and hot tea, and there hadn't been enough food to pack a lunch.

On the third floor, Mrs. Ferrelli was outside her door, tying a piece of black crepe to the handle, her face red, her cheeks wet with tears. Dark streaks and maroon blotches stained the front of her yellow dress, striping the swell of her pregnant belly.

No, Pia thought. *Not Mr. Ferrelli.* He was too young and too strong, a broad-shouldered brick mason who filled the halls with laughter and had been hoping to see the birth of his first child before reporting for the draft. Not to mention he and his wife were one of their few English-speaking neighbors who weren't afraid to be friends with Germans. How could the flu kill someone like him?

Mutti came to a halt and Pia stopped beside her, not knowing what to do or say. The bucket handle dug into her fingers. She felt awful for Mrs. Ferrelli and her baby, but more than anything, she wanted to keep going, to get to the safety of their rooms.

"I'm very sorry for you," Mutti said.

"I'm sorry too," Pia said.

Mrs. Ferrelli murmured a quiet thank you.

"Was it flu?" Mutti said.

Mrs. Ferrelli nodded, her face contorting with grief, then hurried back inside.

Mutti glanced at Pia with tears in her eyes.

"Did you know he was sick?" Pia said.

Mutti shook her head, her free hand scrubbing her apron, then rushed up the last flight of stairs. Pia followed her up the steps, across the hall, and inside their apartment, closing the door behind them. At last, she was home. The dark-walled space consisted of two rooms—a combination kitchen/living room, and a windowless bedroom no bigger than the chicken coop they'd had back in the mining village. An oil lantern cast a dim light over the necessities of life that filled every square inch of space. Rough-hewn shelves lined with graying eyelet doilies held a crock of silverware, a stack of white plates, baking tins, a mismatched assortment of cups and glasses, baby bottles, a clay pitcher, and a mantel clock. Frying pans hung from hooks above a narrow wooden table with three mismatched chairs that had been repaired and strengthened with twine and pieces of wood. Baskets, a metal tub, and empty pails sat stacked beneath the table, along with a bucket of cleaning rags and a short broom. Across from the table, a chipped enamel teakettle and matching pot sat simmering on a coal stove with a crooked pipe that leaked smoke at every joint. A cloth calendar hung on the wall above a metal washbasin sitting on wooden crates, and clean diapers hung from clotheslines strung across the ceiling. The only decorations were a blue bud vase and a faded embroidered table-cloth that had belonged to Pia's late *oma*. To the left of the stove, Pia's narrow bed sat beneath the only window, lengthwise along a wall covered with newspapers to keep out the cold. Drapes made out of flour sacks fluttered above the peeling sill.

Remembering how crowded it had been when they'd shared the rooms with her paternal aunt and uncle for ten months after they arrived in Philadelphia—Mutti and Vater on the narrow kitchen bed, Pia sleeping on the floor—she knew how lucky she was to have an entire bed to herself. Eventually her luck would change, either when the landlord found out her aunt and uncle had moved to New York and he needed room for more tenants, or when the twins got too big to sleep with Mutti. But for now, she relished being able to stretch out and turn over on the horsehair mattress.

Thinking about it now, she couldn't wait to go to bed later. Exhaustion weighed her down, making her lungs and limbs feel heavy and slow, every thought and movement an effort. She couldn't wait to eat, then escape into sleep, so she could stop thinking about the little girl who grabbed her hand during the parade, and Mary Helen and Tommy Costa, Mr. Ferrelli, and the man in the trolley. She wanted to stop thinking about the trolley man's bloody face, and the flu, and the horrible things happening in the city, and in this very building. It was too much. Then she remembered Finn's brother and prayed he wasn't sick too, even though in her heart of hearts she knew the truth. Hopefully Finn would send her a note saying she was wrong, if she heard from him at all.

After setting her water bucket next to Mutti's near the washba-sin, Pia put her books on her bed, the familiar aroma of vinegar, boiled potatoes, and the sharp tang of lye soap wrapping her in an invisible cocoon of home and safety. She wanted to close the window to keep the comforting smells in and whatever was happening in the city out. It made no sense, of course—fresh air was supposed to ward off influenza—but the urge to shut out the disease and fear-filled air everyone else was breathing outweighed any common sense. She knelt on the bed and put her hands on the sash, ready to pull it down.

"What are you doing?" Mutti said.

"It's chilly in here," Pia said. "May I close the window?"

"We will shut it when the boys wake up," Mutti said. "The fresh air is good. We need to keep it open when they are sleeping." She went over to the table, picked up a spoon, and held it out to Pia. "Mrs. Schmidt brought this over. To keep away the flu."

Before getting off the bed, Pia glanced over at Finn's window. It was open, but no one looked out. She got down and went over to her mother. "What is it?"

"A sugar cube soaking in . . ." Mutti furrowed her brow. "I cannot think of the word. Kar . . . karo . . ."

"Kerosene?"

Mutti nodded. "*Ja.* I took one and gave one to the boys too, with a little water. This is for you."

Pia made a face. Back in Hazleton, they ate violets and drank sassafras tea to keep sickness away, not kerosene. But no violets or sassafras trees grew in the Fifth Ward, or anywhere in the city as far as she knew. Knowing she had no choice, she took the spoon and put the sugar cube in her mouth. It tasted sweet and oily at the same time, as if she were eating a piece of candy rolled in tar. Trying not to gag, she chewed and swallowed as fast as she could. Mutti gave her a ladle of water from the bucket, but it didn't help. The inside of her mouth tasted like mud and lantern oil. She grimaced and wiped her lips with the back of her hand.

"That was awful," she cried.

Mutti put a finger to her lips. "Shh, don't wake your brothers. They have not been happy all day." She took the spoon and put it in the washbasin, then sat down at the table and picked up a darning egg from her mending basket.

"They probably didn't like the medicine," Pia said.

"Medicine is not meant to taste good," Mutti said.

Hoping supper would get rid of the horrible taste in her mouth, Pia went over to the coal stove and lifted the lid on the simmering pot. Potato soup. Again. Due to the war, they were supposed to sacrifice by having wheatless Wednesdays and meatless Mondays, but she couldn't remember the last time they'd had meat at all. Maybe it was Easter, or Christmas. Vater had tacked the newspaper articles on the wall before he left, to remind them to keep sacrificing while he was gone. As if they had a choice.

If you eat—THESE—you eat no wheat/CONTAINS NO WHEAT:
Oatmeal, potatoes, rice, hominy, barley, and 100 percent substitute
bread.

100 percent breads:
Corn pone, muffins, and biscuits, all kinds of bread made only
from corn, oats, barley, and all other wheat substitutes.

Don't waste ice. Don't waste ammonia.
A ton of ice waived may mean one pound of ammonia saved. One
pound of ammonia saved may mean twenty hand grenades. Twenty
hand grenades may win a battle.

Potatoes are a splendid food. Excellent for your body. Delicious
when well cooked.
What they do for your body: They are good fuel. They furnish
starch, which burns in your muscles to let you work, much as the gaso-
line burns in an automobile engine to make it go. One medium-size
potato gives you as much starch as two slices of bread. When you have
potatoes for a meal, you need less bread. Potatoes can save wheat.
They give you salts like other vegetables. You need the salts to build
and renew all the parts of your body and keep it in order. You can even
use potatoes in cake!

If only we could get muffins and biscuits and meat, Pia thought. She glanced at her mother, who was picking up a tattered sock and scrubbing one hand on her apron. Her flour-sack blouse hung loose on her shoulders, exposing her thin neck and jutting collarbones, and her brown skirt hung like a faded tent over her legs. Her jawline and cheekbones stood out in sharp angles in her pale face, and her waist-length blond hair, which Pia used to love to brush and Mutti now wore in a loose braid, looked limp and dull. Pia wasn't sure how much longer her mother could keep nursing the twins without eating more, but Mutti refused to spend what little money they had on formula when she could feed her babies for free, and she didn't want to use the jars of Mellin's Infant Food on the shelf until absolutely necessary, even though doctors said Mellin's mixed with cow's milk was superior to mother's milk. But they only had water to mix it with, anyway.

Pia wanted to look for a job to bring in more money, but Mutti hoped the war would be over soon, Vater would return, and things would go back to normal. In the meantime, Pia was only thirteen and needed to stay in school as long as possible, especially because the laws for Germans seemed to change every day, and there was no way of knowing how much longer she'd be allowed to attend. Finn had offered to teach her how to steal food at the open-air market, but she refused. Mutti would never eat stolen food, not to mention the trouble she'd be in if she got caught. The first time she saw Finn stuff a brisket under his jacket, she'd been shocked—and asked him afterward how taking meat was any different from robbing bottles and rags from the old colored woman. He said the boys who did that were trying to cause trouble by stealing from someone who already had nothing, but he was trying to help his family survive. Like him and everyone else unlucky enough to live in the Fifth Ward, she'd been dealt an unpredictable lot in life, he said, and someday she might need to slip a loaf of bread beneath her shirt to stay alive. Having been taught that taking something that didn't belong to her was wrong, no matter what, she hadn't been convinced. But she had to admit she was beginning to understand. Desperation was a powerful thing. Now she wished she'd listened to him. She supposed she could still try stealing if things got any worse; then she remembered she was too scared to leave the house.

"Did you go to the market this morning?" she asked her mother.

Mutti shook her head. "I was waiting for you to stay with the boys. Then Mrs. Schmidt told me everything was closing and I should stay home."

Just then, one of the twins started crying in the other room. Mutti sighed and pushed herself up from her chair, her hands on her knees, her face contorting in pain.

"What's wrong?" Pia said. "Did you hurt yourself?"

Mutti shook her head. "*Nein*, I am only getting old."

Pia frowned. At thirty-two, Mutti wasn't *that* old. "Stay there," she said. "I'll get the boys."

Her mother sat back down and sighed. "*Danke.*"

Opening the door a crack, Pia peeked inside the bedroom. Maybe whoever was crying would fall back asleep. The lantern light from the kitchen fell over a wooden washstand, a dresser with mismatched handles and crooked drawers, and her parents' rusty iron bed filling half the room. Near the head of the bed, a floor-level cubby and open closet took up one wall. The twins lay on the bedcovers in cotton gowns and day caps, their rattles and swaddling blankets on the floor. One was on his back with the toes of his foot in his mouth, the other on his stomach, red-faced and howling. Their names were Oliver and Maxwell, Ollie and Max for short—good American names, according to Mutti, who wanted Pia to change her name to Polly or Peg after the war started. But Pia liked being named after her great-grandmother, even though some of her schoolmates used it as another reason to pick on her, and in the end, Vater said she could keep it. Max was the one howling.

She entered the bedroom, lit the lantern on the dresser, picked up the rattles and blankets, and stood by the bed, waiting to see what the twins would do when they saw her. Max noticed her first. He stopped crying and gave her a teary-eyed grin, his drool-covered lips still quivering. She wrapped one of the blankets around him, scooped him up, and sat on the edge of the bed, cradling him in one arm. He grabbed a handful of her hair, and Ollie cooed up at her from the bed, then stuck his toes back in his mouth. Then she remembered something and stiffened. What if she felt something strange when she held her brothers? What if her chest hurt or her lungs burned? Touching family had never troubled her before, but that was before the parade and the flu, before Mary Helen and Tommy Costa. She took Max's tiny hand in hers, held her breath, and waited. To her relief, she felt nothing but his warm body against hers, and the silky soft skin of his little fingers and palm. She exhaled, her breath shuddering in her chest, and wiped the tears from his face.

"What's the matter, little one?" she said in a soft, singsong voice.

"Did you think we left you home all alone? Don't you know we'd never do that?" She kissed his forehead. "Never, ever, ever."

Max grinned up at her again, bubbles of spit forming between his lips.

Unlike everyone else, she could always tell her brothers apart. Even Vater joked about hanging numbers around their necks so he would know who was who. Looking at their white-blond hair and cobalt blue eyes—traits inherited from Mutti—it would be easy to get them confused. But Pia knew Max's face was the slightest bit thinner than Ollie's, his button nose a tad flatter on the end. His dimples were deeper too.

She'd never forget the day four months ago when the twins were born, the tense minutes after Ollie's appearance when Mutti continued to groan and hold her still-bulging stomach. Vater sent Pia to get Mrs. Schmidt, but by the time she returned, a second baby had arrived, much to everyone's surprise. Mrs. Schmidt, holding a jar of lard to "lubricate the parts of passage," seemed unfazed.

"I knew you were having more than one when you said the kicking felt like the baby was wearing hobnailed boots," she said proudly.

While Mrs. Schmidt helped Mutti remove her soiled skirt and get cleaned up, Pia swaddled the newborn twins and studied their tiny faces, grateful and amazed to finally have two brand-new brothers. From that day on, telling them apart had been easy.

"I know who you are," Pia said to Max now, as she cradled him on the edge of her parents' bed. "Yes, I do." She bent down and kissed Ollie's forehead. "You too, Ollie boy."

Ollie smiled, chuckling around the toes in his mouth.

Pia picked up one of their rattles and held it out for him, trying to get him to let go of his foot. Vater had carved the rattles out of wood before he left for the war, sanding them over and over until every spot was smooth and soft. He used twine threaded through holes to hold four brass bells on each side, and carved each boy's initials on the handles. The sound they made when shook reminded Pia of sleigh bells at Christmas.

Ollie was more interested in playing with his feet. She put the rattle down and noticed Max was falling back asleep, his long dark lashes like feathers against his pale cheeks. She rocked him in her arms and sang a lullaby in a soft voice. Ollie lay still and listened, then let go of his toes, put his thumb in his mouth, and gazed up at her with sleepy eyes. Within minutes they were both napping again. She covered Ollie with the other blanket, then stood and carefully laid Max next to him. After waiting a few seconds to make sure they'd stay asleep, she turned the knob on the oil lantern and the thick wick receded, reducing the flame. Then she tiptoed out of the room, giving them one last look before letting the door latch slip quietly back into place.

When she turned around, her mother was still at the table, her head in her hands, her mending forgotten in her lap. A knot of fear twisted in Pia's stomach.

"What is it, Mutti?" Pia said. "What's wrong?"

Mutti looked up. "Oh, *liebchen*," she said. "Nothing. I'm only tired."

Her words did little to lessen Pia's alarm. She studied her mother's face, worried she wasn't telling the truth. It wasn't like her to complain about being tired. Or anything else, for that matter. "Did you eat today?"

Mutti nodded. "*Kartoffelpfannkuchen*, a potato pancake, and applesauce."

"That's not enough," Pia said. "Why don't you have something to eat and take a nap while the twins are sleeping? I can work on the mending."

To Pia's surprise, Mutti nodded, put the mending on the table, and stood. "*Ja*, I think I will lie down for a little bit." She went over to Pia's bed, moved her schoolbooks to the floor, and got under the blanket. "The soup is almost finished," she said. "Be careful not to let it burn." She took a deep breath, then exhaled with a shuddering sigh.

Pia dug her nails into her palms. Mutti never lay down in the afternoon. She went over to the bed and knelt beside her. "Are you sure you're feeling all right? Maybe I should get Mrs. Schmidt."

Mutti gave her a weak smile. "Do not worry, *liebchen*, I'm fine," she said. "Remember I said the twins were fussing today. They were awake all night too. I'm only tired from that." She closed her eyes. "And Mrs. Schmidt is not here."

"What do you mean? Where is she?"

"On the train to her mother's house. In Pittsburgh."

"Maybe I should go look for a doctor, then," Pia said. The thought of leaving and going into the city again terrified her, but she'd do it for Mutti. Then she remembered what her teachers said about the shortage of doctors and nurses because of the war—that those left behind were overwhelmed and the hospitals were full—and a cold block of fear settled in her chest.

Mutti opened her eyes and looked at her, her face serious. "I am not sick, Pia. I only need to rest, just for a few minutes. Then I will feel better."

Pia sighed. She prayed Mutti was right, but she hated feeling so helpless. "Then let me close the window so you don't get chilled."

Mutti turned on her side and pulled the blanket up to her chin. "*Nein*, fresh air is good to keep away the flu."

Pia lifted her hand to check her mother's forehead for fever, then froze. What if she felt pain in her chest or became short of breath when she touched her? What would she do then? Mrs. Schmidt was gone and the hospitals were full. Chewing her lip, she went over to the table, picked up the darning egg with trembling fingers, and dropped it into a sock. Maybe she *should* feel her mother's forehead. The sooner she knew if she was getting sick, the sooner she could try to find some kind of help. Maybe someone else in the building would know what to do. Maybe they'd have whiskey or some other kind of medicine. If only Mrs. Schmidt were still there.

After a little while, she put down the mending, went over to the foot of the bed, and gazed down at Mutti. She was sound asleep, her mouth hanging open, thin strands of hair stuck to her cheeks and lips. Exhaustion clung to her features, aging her beyond her years. Pia took a deep breath and let it out slowly. What should she do? She looked out the window toward Finn's apartment. If only she could send him a note to ask for help. But undershirts and baby-wear filled the clothesline. She couldn't take them off without waking Mutti. Who knew if he'd answer in time, anyway? She thought about hurrying across the alley and knocking on his door, but what if the twins woke up and Mutti didn't hear them? Not to mention she didn't want to go out in the hall, let alone outside.

As if roused by her thoughts, the twins started crying. Mutti opened her eyes and started to sit up.

"Stay there," Pia said. "I'll get them."

"*Nein*," Mutti said. "They are hungry and I have too much to do." She moved to the edge of the bed and stood, her hands on the small of her back as she straightened, and started toward the bedroom. "Please take some soft potatoes from the soup for their supper."

"Yes, Mutti," Pia said.

"And close the window. It may be too cold for them."

Pia pulled the window sash all the way down, then went over to the stove. She took a slotted spoon from the kitchen shelf, fished several floury potatoes out of the soup, and put them in a bowl. Mutti came out of the bedroom with Ollie and Max, laid them on the bed, unpinned two clean diapers from the ceiling clothesline, and started to change them. She smiled and kissed the boys' faces, laughing when they babbled and cooed.

"You are the best little boys in the world," she said, cooing back at them. "And the most handsome too. Are you hungry? *Ja?* Your sister is getting your dinner ready for you."

Pia mashed the potatoes in the bowl and softened them with a little broth, one eye on her mother. Maybe she'd been wrong to worry. Maybe Mutti really was just tired and the short nap had helped. In any case, she was acting normal now. Fear seeped out of Pia's chest and relief loosened her shoulders.

Mutti picked Ollie up and kissed him on the cheek, then put him back down on the mattress. She made a move to pick Max up, then hesitated, put a hand to her head, and sat down hard on the edge of the bed. Red blotches bloomed on her pale face.

Pia put down the soup bowl and rushed to her side. "What is it, Mutti?" she said.

Mutti closed her eyes and moaned. "I'm not sure," she said. "I . . . I'm feeling a little dizzy."

Panic flared in Pia's chest again, beating against her rib cage like stone wings. "I'll go try to find a doctor."

"*Nein*," Mutti said. "You are not leaving. It's not safe."

"But what if . . ." Pia hesitated, trying to keep her voice from trembling. "What if you're getting sick?"

"I'm all right. I am not coughing or too hot, only tired. Besides, there is no money for a doctor. And they don't want to help a German, anyway."

"Is there anyone else in the building like Mrs. Schmidt? Someone who might know what to do?"

Mutti shook her head. "Our neighbors have their own troubles right now. I only need to sleep. It is the best medicine." She pushed herself off the bed and stood. "Will you take care of the boys for a few hours while I lie down in the bedroom?"

"Yes, of course. And I'll bring you some soup."

Mutti nodded and started toward the bedroom, walking slowly. Pia followed, struggling to stay calm. For as long as she could remember, her mother had never complained about not feeling well, not even after having the twins, when Mrs. Schmidt instructed her to spend two weeks in bed. Not even when she had a horrible headache that seemed to last for weeks, or when she broke her big toe. Mutti always kept quiet and kept going as best she could. She never gave up or gave in. To hear her say she didn't feel well sent a flood of terror through Pia's bones. Mutti sat on the edge of the bed and Pia knelt down, unbuttoned her boots, and pulled them off.

"*Danke*," Mutti said, lying back on the pillow. Pia covered her with a blanket, wondering what else she should do.

Out in the other room, Ollie and Max started crying.

"*Bitte*, feed the boys and let me rest," Mutti said, shooing her away with one hand. "I will be much better when I wake up."

"Will you promise to call me if you need anything?"

"*Ja*, now go."

Pia started out of the room, then stopped at the door and turned. "And tell me if you start feeling worse?"

"*Ja, ja,*" Mutti said. She laid her forearm across her forehead, her pale wrist turned up, and closed her eyes.

"Promise?" Pia said.

"*Ja*, Pia."

With growing dread, Pia left the room and closed the door. Hopefully Mutti was right; she was only overworked and exhausted. It made sense, with the twins waking up several times a night to nurse, then barely sleeping during the day. Still, Pia couldn't help fearing the worst. She prayed she was wrong.

After feeding Max and Ollie mashed potatoes softened with broth, she put them on a blanket in the middle of the floor with their rattles, then filled a bowl with soup and slowly opened the bedroom door, trying not to make any noise. A slice of weak light fell across Mutti's pale face. She was sound asleep again, her mouth agape.

"Mutti?" Pia said in a quiet voice. "I brought you some soup." She went over to the bed and looked down at her. "Mutti?"

Mutti didn't blink or move. Pia thought about waking her, but decided to let her rest. The few minutes she'd gotten earlier probably weren't enough. She needed an entire night of uninterrupted sleep, then maybe she'd be back to her old self by morning. Pia left the bedroom, quietly closed the door, took the soup over to the table, and sat down. From the blanket on the floor, the boys watched her eat, grinning and gurgling, and reaching for each other's hands and faces. She would take care of them tonight. She would mix a jar of Mellin's Infant Food with water and feed them that so Mutti wouldn't have to wake up and nurse. They weren't used to drinking from bottles, but if they were hungry enough, they'd figure it out.

When she was done with her soup, she got up, knelt on her bed, opened the window, and, working fast, pulled the clothes off the line and piled them beside her. The undershirts and nightdresses were still damp from the fall air, but she'd hang them up again inside, when she had time. When everything was off the line, she closed the window and stacked the laundry on the kitchen chairs, then took her math book out from beneath her bed and tore out the first page, which was blank, except for the title and copyright. Damaging a schoolbook would likely get her in trouble, but there was no other paper in the house, and this was an emergency. She found a pencil, sat down at the table again, and wrote to Finn.

*Are you all right? What's wrong with your
brother? Mutti might be getting sick and I don't know
what to do. I have no medicine or whiskey. She says I
shouldn't leave the house to find a doctor, and I don't
really want to, anyway. Please help. I'm scared.*

She folded the paper, crawled up on her bed again, opened the
window partway, fastened the note to the line with a clothespin,
and sent it across the alley. The pulley squeaked while the clothesline lurched and paused, lurched and paused, until finally the
note reached the ledge outside Finn's window. Afraid to blink, she
watched to see if he would reach out and take it, but no one came to
the open window, or looked out. She glanced over her shoulder at
her brothers, content and playing on the blanket, then pushed the
window open all the way and leaned out as far as she dared. Praying
Mutti wouldn't hear, she called out, "Finn!"

No answer.

"Hey, Finn! Are you over there? It's me, Pia!"

Still no answer.

She pulled the sash down and watched for a few more minutes,
but no one came to the window. Looking out over the eerily silent Fifth Ward, a cold eddy of loneliness began to swirl inside her
chest. The sun blazed on the distant horizon, casting a yellow glow
over the cool fall evening, the perfect weather for a brisk walk or
a rousing game of stickball. But no children played in the alley below. No delivery wagons rattled along the cobblestones. No women
gossiped on the front stoops or called their children in from open
windows. A hollow draft of fear swept through her. It felt like the
end of the world.

While Mutti slept and Pia took care of her brothers, panic
gripped the city. The director of the Philadelphia General Hospital
pleaded for volunteers to relieve nurses who had collapsed from
overwork. Doctors and nurses started dying, three one day, two
another, four the next. Undertakers ran out of embalming fluid
and coffins, and masked policemen guarded what coffins were left.
Gravediggers were either ill, overcharging people, or refusing to

bury influenza victims. The director of the city jail offered prisoners to help dig graves, but withdrew the offer when he realized there were no healthy guards to watch them. Thirty-three policemen had already died. The citizens of Philadelphia began whispering the word *plague*.

Meanwhile, *The Philadelphia Inquirer* scorned the closing of public places:

What are the authorities trying to do? Scare everyone to death? What is to be gained by shutting up well-ventilated churches and theaters and letting people press into trolley cars? What then should a man do to prevent panic and fear? Live a calm life. Do not discuss influenza. Worry is useless. Talk of cheerful things instead of disease.

For Pia, getting the twins to drink formula out of bottles proved to be more difficult than she thought. By the time the first feeding was over, all three of them were exhausted. When her brothers finally collapsed into a restless sleep on her bed, it was after midnight. She edged off the mattress, moving slowly and quietly, and peeked into the dark bedroom, surprised her mother hadn't heard the boys' frustrated cries. Mutti was still sound asleep, her breath like sandpaper against wood. Pia tiptoed into the room, stood by the bed, and, with trembling fingers, reached out to feel her mother's forehead. As soon as her hand touched Mutti's clammy skin, heat lit up her face and neck, and an invisible weight pressed against her chest. She yanked her hand away and the frightening sensations disappeared. Tears filled Pia's eyes. *No. Mutti can't be sick. She just can't be.*

Turning toward the dresser, she quietly opened the bottom drawer, took out a sweater, and laid it over her mother's chest and shoulders, pulling it and the blanket up beneath her chin. She didn't know what else to do.

Queasy with fear, she crept out of the room and closed the door. The thought of leaving the safety of their apartment, going out into the city in the middle of the night to search for a doctor, not knowing if anyone would even help, terrified her. And who would take care of the babies while she was gone? Mutti might be too sick to watch them. And the boys probably shouldn't be near her, anyway.

Paralyzed by indecision, she turned down the lantern and lay in her bed, the boys' small bodies snuggled between her and the wall. She needed to organize her thoughts and gather her courage. The sun would be up in a few hours. Then she could ask a neighbor to watch the twins. Mutti always said everything looked less frightening in the light. She hoped so, because right now she was scared to death. Knowing she couldn't sleep, she tried to come up with a plan.

When her frantic dreams ended, she opened her eyes, confused and trying to remember what day it was. An eerie, grayish glow filtered in under the flour-sack drapes. She turned her head and looked up. A jagged water stain colored the gray ceiling paper like a small yellow lake, making her think of the spring runoff near the culm banks in Hazleton. Then she remembered—the schools and churches and all public meeting places had been closed. And Mutti might be sick with the flu. The twins still lay between her and the wall. She sat up with a start and nearly fell off the edge of the bed, then blinked and looked around, trying to figure out how long she'd slept. She got up on her knees and pulled aside the drapes.

It was dawn.

And her note to Finn still dangled on the clothesline.

Ollie turned toward her, kicking his legs and starting to fuss. Max was starting to wake up too. She picked Ollie up and bounced him on her hip, her eyes fixed on Finn's window.

"Shh, Ollie boy," she said, patting his back. "Everything's going to be all right."

She watched Finn's window for another few seconds. No one moved behind the glass. Had they taken his brother to the hospital? Or were they all sick? Ollie started to wail, his face turning red, his small hands in fists.

"I know," she said to him. "You want your mommy. Have you had enough of me?" She got down from the bed, snuggled his cheek against hers, and moved toward the bedroom. "All right, all right. I'll take you to your *mutti*." Then she stopped and glanced over her shoulder at Max. "Stay right there, good boy. I'll be right back."

Max blinked and grinned at her, still half asleep, while Ollie howled in her ear, loud enough to wake the people next door. She started toward the bedroom again, a growing surge of fear coursing through her, making her chest hurt. Surely Mutti could hear Ollie crying. Why hadn't she come out to see what was wrong?

Pia knocked lightly on the door. "Mutti? Are you up?"

No answer.

"Mutti?"

Pia opened the door and entered slowly, keeping her eyes down in case her mother was dressing. "I'm sorry to wake you, but Ollie's hungry. I fed him some Mellin's a while ago, but—" Then she looked up and went rigid.

Mutti lay on her side in the bed, her clawed hands frozen at her throat, her mouth agape as if stuck mid-scream. A dark fluid ran from her nose and mouth and eyes, red and crusty and black, and her skin was the color of a bruise. The coppery smell of warm blood filled the thick air.

"Mutti?" Pia managed.

No response.

"Mutti?"

Realization, sudden and horrible, struck Pia. Her legs turned to water and she bent over, gagging and almost dropping Ollie. She grabbed the iron footboard to stay upright. The floor seemed to tilt beneath her feet.

Ollie wailed louder, filling the room.

Pia fell to her knees, her heartbeat thrashing in her ears. *No. This can't be happening. It can't be.* Dizzy and hyperventilating, she edged around to the side of the bed, the wood floor like a rasp on her bare knees, her shaking arms struggling to hold on to her baby brother.

"Mutti," she cried. "Get up! You can't leave us! You can't!" She held her breath and reached out with trembling fingers, as if one touch would shatter her mother like glass. "Please, Mutti. Wake up!" Her fingertips grazed the sleeve of Mutti's sweater, and she drew back, her stomach turning over. She didn't need to touch her mother's skin to know something was horribly wrong. She didn't want to touch her and feel *death*. Grabbing the side of the damp mattress, she pulled herself to her feet, put a hand on Mutti's shoulder, and shook her. Mutti's body wobbled back and forth, like a life-size doll lying on a shelf.

A scream built up in Pia's throat, but she clamped her teeth against it. She fell to her knees again and let Ollie slide to the floor, her arms too weak to hold him. He lay on his back, his face red, and cried harder. In the other room, Max started wailing too. Pia buried her face in her hands and squeezed her eyes shut, hoping the image of her dead mother would be gone when she opened them. *This can't be true! It can't be! Mutti is not dead. She's not!*

She dropped her hands to the floor to keep from collapsing and opened her eyes. Her mother was still there, on the bed, covered in blood. Pia moaned and slumped to the floor, her legs and arms vibrating out of control, her breath coming in short, shallow gasps. Violent sobs burst from her throat one after the other, before she could catch her next mouthful of air. Each wail wrenched the strength from her body. Ollie howled beside her, oblivious to the fact that his mother was dead and his life had been changed forever. He reached for Pia's arm, clutching her sleeve in his small fist. She picked him up and hugged him to her chest, her shoulders convulsing, her mind screaming in terror and grief.

More than anything, she wanted to lose consciousness, to faint and escape into nothingness, where pain and fear couldn't reach her. But she had to take care of the boys. She had to go out to the other room and get Max, who was crying even harder now. When she trusted herself to stand, she staggered to her feet, still hugging Ollie, and stumbled out to the kitchen. She hefted Max onto her other hip and carried her brothers back into the bedroom on quivering legs, then slid down the wall opposite the bed, dizzy and out of breath. Her body felt like kindling, her nerves stripped and sparking, ready to burst into flames at any second. Her mind raced and her stomach churned, overwhelmed with grief and horror and disbelief. How could Mutti be dead? Dead? She rarely caught cold. How could she catch the flu? She kept her feet dry. She stayed warm. She even ate sugar cubes soaked in kerosene.

Pia stared at her mother, bile rising in the back of her throat, the babies howling in her arms. What were she and the twins going to do without her? Who was going to take care of them now? Pia wailed with her brothers, fighting the urge to scream and vomit, the black manacle of grief closing around her shattered heart and locking into place with a horrible, sickening thud.

CHAPTER TWO

BERNICE

October 11, 1918

For what seemed like the thousandth time in the past few days, twenty-year-old Bernice Groves stared out the third-floor window of her row house on Shunk Alley in the Fifth Ward, trying to figure out how to kill herself. She thought about jumping out the window, but worried the fall would only break her legs, not end her life. Slitting her wrists with a kitchen knife was an option, but she hated the sight of blood. She could swallow the rat poison her husband had brought home before he was drafted, but she didn't want to die writhing in agony. Her death needed to be as quick and painless as possible. Maybe that made her a coward, but she didn't care. There was no one left to notice, anyway. Then her eyes traveled to the clotheslines between the buildings, crisscrossing the alley like the threads of a giant spiderweb. Braiding several lengths of it together might make a rope strong enough to hold her weight so she could hang herself. But how would she get that much? She couldn't very well go door to door asking her neighbors to loan out their clotheslines. Not that they would answer their doors, anyway. Since the epidemic started—Had it been a week? Ten days? Fourteen?—no one dared let anyone but family into their homes, and sometimes not even them.

No children played in the alley below, no women hurried out to run errands, no men whistled or smoked on their way home from work. Even the laundry lines hung empty. The only living things she'd seen over the past few days were a street sweeper sprinkling some kind of powder along the cobblestones and a brown dog sniffing two sheet-wrapped bodies across the way before dashing down the alley, his nose to the ground. More often than not, she wondered if she was the last person alive on earth.

It was easy to understand why the man who lived upstairs, Mr. Werkner, had shot his wife and two children before putting a gun to his own head instead of letting the flu decide their fate. While the rest of the city waited in fear and bodies piled up outside the morgues and cemeteries, he had taken matters into his own hands. She would have done the same thing if she'd known a week ago what she knew now. And if she had a gun.

Hopefully she already had the flu and would be dead soon, anyway. Then she would be with her husband and son. Except she didn't want to wait that long. She wanted to die *now*, to escape this wretched grief, this horrible, heavy ache in her chest. She couldn't stand the agony another minute. The Bible said taking your own life was a sin, but surely God would understand that a mother couldn't live without her child. Surely He would understand why she longed to be reunited with her son in heaven. Everything she knew to be good was gone. Everything she knew to be true and absolute and fair about the world had been destroyed.

Maybe she should just stop eating. Not that she had been eating much, anyway. How could she think about food when her baby boy was dead? How could she swallow a bite of doughy bread with sweet jam, or soothe her dry throat with hot tea with honey? How could she do any of those things when Wallis would never taste a strawberry or an egg, eat an apple or a warm piece of johnnycake? It seemed blasphemous to even think about eating when he couldn't, as if she were betraying him.

A loaf of bread wrapped in cheesecloth sat untouched in her dresser drawer, along with a pound of lard, a few strips of cooked bacon, and a dozen eggs in the larder, three boxes of cereal, several jars of pears and tomatoes, and a half-dozen cans of beans and carrots on the kitchen shelves. She thought about leaving the food out-side her neighbors' doors, but couldn't find the strength or desire to pack it up and take it out. And despite her revulsion at the thought of eating, every now and then the desperate gnaw of hunger grew unbearable, as if her stomach were eating itself from the inside out. She tried to ignore it by lying down and hoping she would pass out or starve to death, but an involuntary will to survive always seemed to win and she'd tear into a box of cornflakes, disgusted and crying and hating herself as she shoved them into her mouth. Then, with her hunger abated, she'd make a vow to start starving herself all over again, and beg Wallis to forgive her for being so weak.

Thinking about her beautiful baby boy, her burning eyes filled and she looked over at him. A week ago, he'd been the picture of health, giggling and babbling and reaching for her with his chubby little hands. Then he woke up with a fever and a cough, refusing to nurse. After two days of trying every recommended cure for the flu—onion syrup, chloride of lime, whiskey, Mrs. Winslow's Soothing Syrup—she bundled him up and ran what seemed like a hundred blocks to the nearest emergency hospital—the local poor-house, which had been converted after the epidemic started. Crying the whole way, she prayed that the good Lord would save her only child. She'd already lost her husband to war. How much misery was one person supposed to endure?

But when she reached the hospital, she'd slowed. Every type of vehicle she could imagine crowded the street—trucks and cars and wagons and carts, all of them bringing the sick, the dying, and the dead. Even police cars were bringing in victims. What looked like thousands of people—some wearing yarmulkes and dark clothes, others in babushka scarves and colorful skirts—swarmed the building, trying to get inside. Some sat or lay on the ground wrapped in blankets, while others were half-naked and soaked in sweat, moaning, coughing, and struggling to breathe. A number of them were already dead, their faces as purple as plums, their mouths and noses and eyes caked with dark blood. A colored man stumbled in front of her toward the hospital, begging to be let in, and a white man pushed him backward, telling him to go some-where else. The colored man collapsed on the sidewalk, then lay there, lifeless. Masked policemen did their best to keep order, while nuns in white aprons prayed over the living and the dead. Beneath a canopy on the sidewalk, Red Cross workers handed out masks and sewed burial shrouds. A chorus of voices cried out for water and prayed in what seemed like a dozen different languages—English, Russian, Italian, Yiddish, Polish, German.

She fought her way through the crowd, clasping Wallis to her chest. "Please," she cried out. "Please let me through! I need help! My son is sick!"

"Hey," someone shouted. "Get in line!"

"Wait your turn," a woman yelled.

Bernice ignored them and kept going, pushing and shoving her way through. A policeman and a nun stood guard at the hospital entrance, both wearing gauze masks. When Bernice reached them, the policeman stepped between her and the nun.

"Please," Bernice said, trying to catch her breath. "You have to help me. My boy is sick."

"I'm sorry, dear," the nun said. "We've run out of room."

"But he's just a baby," Bernice wailed. "My only child!"

"I understand," the nun said. "But there are other mothers with children here too."

Bernice looked around, tears blurring her vision. A young, dark-haired woman wearing a scarf over her mouth knelt on the sidewalk beside a pale, coughing toddler, her eyes filled with fear. Another woman held a young girl on her hip, swaying back and forth, trying to comfort her child. The little girl's legs dangled skinny and limp against her mother's skirt, and her skin was tinged a strange, bluish gray. A thousand faces stared back at Bernice, some gasping for air, others weary with pain, all knotted in terror.

Bernice gazed up at the nun. "Why aren't you helping us?" she cried. "What's wrong with you?"

"All of our beds and even the hallways are full," the nun said. "We're crowded to the doors, and most of our doctors and nurses are overseas. We've put a call out for volunteers, but I'm afraid we're overwhelmed. I'm so sorry, dear, but you must get in line."

Just then, a man carrying a little boy ran up the steps with a wad of money in his hand. He begged the nun to take his son inside, but the policeman pushed him back, threatening to arrest him for bribery.

Seizing the opportunity, Bernice darted around the policeman and started for the entrance, shoving the nun to one side with her shoulder. Suddenly a woman in a peasant skirt appeared out of nowhere, blocking her way. A feverish-looking toddler slumped in the cloth sling strapped around her chest.

"*Volte!*" the woman said. "*Você tem que esperar como todo mundo!*"

Bernice tried forcing her way past, but the woman stood her ground, snarling and pushing her back with rough hands. A broad-shouldered man came to the woman's rescue and got between them, his arms out to keep Bernice at a distance.

"*Não toque nela!*" he shouted.

Bernice didn't understand his words, but menace filled his voice. She tried to get around them again, but the policeman gripped her by the shoulders and pulled her backward.

"Come on, lady," he said. "You can't go in yet."

The immigrant couple kept yelling at her, pointing their fingers and shaking their fists.

"What about them?" Bernice shouted. "You can't let them in either!"

The policeman ignored her. She struggled to get away from him, twisting and pulling and bending, but it was no use.

"Who do you think you are, trying to stop me from getting help?" she screamed at the couple. "You don't even belong here!"

The woman shouted something else, and the nun ushered her and the man away from the door. "It's all right," she said to them. "Please, calm down. We're not letting anyone in ahead of you."

The policeman turned Bernice around and took her down the steps, one hand gripping her arm, the other putting pressure on her back—almost pushing, but not quite. At the bottom of the stairs, he let go and went back to his post. She gazed down at her sweet little Wallis, gasping for air and struggling to stay alive in her arms. How could they make him wait in line behind people who should have been looking for help from their own kind? She'd tried minding her own business when it came to the strangers who had invaded her city, but this was too much. Between a German stealing her father's job and this, she was done being civil.

She turned and looked up at the nun and policeman again. "What are you doing?" she cried. "Half these people are foreigners. They shouldn't be trying to get help from doctors meant to help Americans. It's not right!"

"We're here to help everyone," the nun said. "I'm sorry, but you'll have to wait like everyone else."

Above the din of the wailing, pleading crowd, Bernice heard her heart break. No one was going to help her boy. No one was going to give him medicine or ease his pain. Not until they'd helped the hordes of people who didn't belong here. It didn't make sense. The immigrants should have been turned away, not her son. On legs that felt like stone, she turned and staggered through the frightened swarm of tormented and dying people. She would take Wallis home. She would take him home and they would die together.

Except she didn't die. She didn't even get a fever. She didn't have a cough or as much as a tickle in her throat. The only thing she had was a headache, which always happened when she was distraught.

Wallis, on the other hand, had died the next morning.

She'd never forget the last minutes and seconds of her baby boy struggling in her arms, the fear and panic in his innocent eyes, the way he'd gripped her finger in his little hand as he fought for air and life. After a while, his face changed and grew gray, then got darker and darker. Blood seeped from his nose and rimmed the lower lids of his eyes. Then, with one final gasp, his tiny body shuddered and went slack. His hand loosened around her finger, and his eyelids drifted partway closed. She held him in her arms and stared at his face for what seemed like forever, then got up, laid him in his crib, and collapsed on the floor, shrieking over and over until she tasted blood. When she finally stopped screaming, the world started to close in around her like a curtain being drawn. Certain she was dying of a broken heart, she welcomed the relief. Finally she would be at peace, blessed with the knowledge that she would be with her husband and son. She felt like she was floating in a pool of liquid silver, and a smile played around her lips. Then everything went black.

She had no idea how much time passed before she came to, but the room was getting dark, the grayish light of dusk sliding down the bedroom wall. At first she thought she had fallen asleep and it was all a horrible nightmare; then she bolted upright and looked over at the crib, her heart roaring in her chest. Wallis lay where she had left him, wrapped in his favorite blue blanket, his face the color of a storm cloud, his nose and mouth smeared with dried blood, his eyes swollen shut.

Dead.

Her son was dead.

She covered her face with clawed hands, her mouth twisting in agony, her mind screaming. *He can't be dead! Not my baby! Not my little boy!* She pounded the floor with her fists, cursing God and howling, then crumpled forward, still on her knees, slumped over like a rag doll. She cupped her swollen bosom in her hands, her throbbing breasts engorged with milk her son would never drink, her own body betraying her with a painful reminder of all she had lost. She squeezed her breasts and screeched in pain, punishing herself for letting Wallis get sick. She had seen the signs and read the warnings. She should have stayed home until the danger was over instead of going to the parade. She should have kept Wallis safe, away from the man selling balloons and the mobs of immigrants on the sidewalks. She should have shoved the dark-skinned boy away from Wallis's buggy and told him to keep his filthy fingers away from her son when he had dropped his miniature flag on Wallis's blanket and reached in to pick it up without asking. It was her fault. Her fault Wallis got sick and died.

Then, after a few minutes of anguished sobbing, she pushed herself up on her hands and knees, swayed upright, and sat on the bed, her mind reeling. How was her heart still beating? Her lungs still drawing air? She picked up her son with gentle hands and kissed his cold forehead, his tiny lips, his miniature fingers, and prayed that her bleeding, shattered heart would kill her and put an end to her suffering. Then she lay on her side on the mattress and cradled him to her chest, hoping her mind would shut down and release her from the pain. She closed her eyes and willed her lungs to quit working, her blood to stop moving through her veins. She cursed God for taking her child, for deserting her in her hour of need. Then she begged Him to take her too. Her prayers went unanswered.

That was three days ago.

Now Wallis lay like a stone in his crib while she stared out the window, trying to figure out how to end her life. The radio said the city's funeral homes were overwhelmed, but she wouldn't have been able to bring herself to take him to the undertaker anyway, to hand over his tiny body to be embalmed, to be laid in a tiny casket and buried in the cold, hard earth. She couldn't part with him. Ever. The only thing she wanted to do was to join him.

Down in the alley, a woman in a red babushka and tiered skirt pushed a wicker pram with wobbly wheels past the row houses. Then she stopped, lifted a baby from the buggy, and entered one of the buildings across the way. Bernice clenched her jaw in frustration. What was that immigrant woman doing out there when the city was under quarantine? And with a baby no less! Was she crazy or just plain ignorant?

Seeing the woman made her think of the immigrants at the hospital, trying to get help from doctors meant for Americans instead of turning to the witches and wizards they believed could heal them through some kind of sorcery. Wallis might have lived if it hadn't been for them. Then again, it seemed like the entire neighborhood had been taken over by migrants and Negroes since the war started, all of them looking for work in the shipyard and munitions factory. They weren't like her and her family, whose relatives had lived in South Philly since the 1830s, when her grandfather had moved here from Canada to work as a stonemason. Now the entire city was teeming with large ghettos housing every type of foreigner she could think of, and they were stealing jobs from real Americans, like her late father, who had worked at the shipyard for over forty years until a German who lived across the way, Mr. Lange, was hired to replace him. Just six days after he was let go, her father had died—liver failure, the doctors said. But losing his job to a foreigner was what killed him.

Like they'd done outside the hospital, the newcomers crowded around the market stands in their odd clothes, holding up checkout lines because they couldn't speak English. Bernice could hear her father's voice now: "This is America, they need to learn our language or go back where they came from!" Even the editor of the newspaper had expressed his opposition to *"the flood of undesirables from the darker sections of the Old World who are arriving in the United States with no conception of American ideas."*

As if that wasn't bad enough, the heavy aromas of their peculiar cuisine stank up the hallways—boiled lamb, paprika, curry, and peppered cabbage—and children of all colors filled the alleys and streets, shouting and playing games in strange languages. Even the number of homeless had increased since the waves of peasants arrived. She wouldn't have been surprised to learn the flu started with them. After all, everyone knew migrants brought disease across the nation's ports and borders—the Irish brought cholera, the Jews brought tuberculosis, the Italians brought polio, and the Chinese brought bubonic plaque. She and some of the other women in her prayer group had often discussed the personal hygiene habits, unhealthy tendencies, and questionable morals of foreign-born people. And they all agreed the "Don't Spit" signs should have been printed in all languages, not just English.

Why weren't *their* children dying? Why had her son, a true American, gotten sick and passed away? It wasn't fair.

As soon as the thought crossed her mind, a rush of guilt twisted in her chest. She had seen the immigrant mothers at the hospital with their sick children. She had seen the anguish on Mr. and Mrs. Yankovich's pale faces when they brought out their dead daughter, how Mrs. Yankovich had nearly collapsed and her husband had held her up. She had seen the white crepe on the Costas' door after little Tommy died. Deep down, she knew all mothers loved their children and grieved the same way, no matter their nationality, race, or religion. And yet . . . and yet it seemed as though the newcomers always had three or four offspring to replace the children they lost. She only had one. And he was gone.

No one was immune to getting sick.

Except, it seemed, for her.

After the lady in the babushka disappeared into the row house, a low, lone voice echoed between the brick buildings, and the dry creak of wagon wheels drew closer and closer. Bernice craned her neck out the window to see. Two men on a horse-drawn wagon moved along the alley toward her building, both wearing masks.

"Bring out your dead!" one of them called out. His voice sounded weary, yet indifferent, like a newspaper hawker on an empty street corner.

Bernice pulled her head back inside to watch. She couldn't help but remember the stories she'd heard about the yellow fever, when the rush to get victims in the grave had resulted in some people being buried alive. Was that happening during this epidemic too? According to radio newscasts, there'd been over five thousand flu deaths since the parade. Embalming students and morticians had come from hundreds of miles away to help take care of the victims, but it wasn't enough. In the last newspaper she'd read before Wallis got sick, the daily notices of death from the flu filled an entire page—along with those killed and missing in the war—seven columns of small print with a repetitive litany: Cecil Newman of pneumonia, age twenty-one; Mavis Rivers of influenza, age twenty-six; William Flint of influenza, age fifteen. Another article stated trucks were being used to carry bodies from the morgue to potter's field. Corpses were tagged for later identification before being buried in a trench dug by a steam shovel, and the men filling in the mass graves were falling sick. On the radio, the Pennsylvania Council of National Defense explained: *"It is doubtful that the city of Philadelphia has, at any time in its history, been confronted by a more serious situation than that presented in connection with the care and burial of the dead during the recent epidemic."* With everything going on, people being buried alive was certainly a possibility. Just the thought of it made her shiver.

Down in the alley, the driver slowed the horses, pulled to a stop outside one of the row houses, and tied the reins to the wagon. Three bodies wrapped in dirty, bloodstained sheets lay in the wagon bed. The driver and the other man climbed down, went over to the front stoop, lifted a sheet-draped body from beside the steps, and piled it on the back with the others. Then they returned to the steps and picked up another body, this one smaller than the first. With the wagon loaded, they climbed back on and moved closer to Bernice's building, continuing the call for people to bring out their dead.

She would not hand Wallis over to those men. They couldn't take her baby. She wouldn't let them. Then she realized they had no idea she was there, watching from her third-floor window. They didn't know her boy was dead. And she needed to keep it that way. Otherwise, they might put him on that horrible wagon, and once they got a good look at her, they'd force her to go to an asylum.

She had seen her reflection in the cracked mirror above the washbasin. It was that of a stranger, with dull eyes and tangled hair, sunken cheekbones and sallow skin. She looked like a woman insane. They'd think she was sick and needed help. But she didn't want help. There was nothing they could do for her, anyway. She wanted to die. She wanted to be with her husband and son. She shrank back when the men passed beneath her window, but not before catching sight of a small, pale hand sticking out of the bloody pile of sheet-wrapped bodies in the wagon bed.

The men stopped two more times to load dead bodies, then drove along the alley as if it were a normal routine, like delivering milk or lighting the streetlamps. Finally they turned the corner and disappeared, the low, indifferent voice calling for people to bring out their dead echoing once more in the empty alley before growing fainter and fainter. Then the afternoon went silent and Bernice was alone again.

Seeing the men in the wagon made her think of her older brother, Daniel, how he used to shut her in a storage crate and tell her their parents were getting rid of her. He'd say the postman was coming to pick her up to mail her to a different family, or the nuns were coming to take her to an orphanage. He said orphans slept on wooden planks in cold attics, and the only thing they got to eat was cold gruel. If they were bad, the nuns beat them or locked them in closets, and sometimes forgot to let them out. The first time he did it Bernice was five years old, and she stayed in the box for hours, crying and waiting to be taken away. She finally snitched on him when she turned eight, but her mother refused to believe her precious son would do anything so horrible. Instead, she accused Bernice of making up stories and sent her to bed without supper. Then, finally, her father caught Daniel sitting on top of the crate while she wept inside, and punished him with a belt. After that, Daniel never did it again. But from that day on, after their mother blew out their bedroom lantern every night, he whispered across the room in a menacing voice that the nuns were still coming to get her. Or he crept across the floor in the dark and grabbed her ankles, scaring her so badly she nearly wet the bed. For years she didn't dare fall asleep until she heard him snoring. Sometimes he asked if she could taste the rat poison in her oatmeal, or left a noose lying between her sheets. When he died of typhoid at thirteen, she was inconsolable. No one knew she was crying tears of relief.

Suddenly a flash of movement caught her attention, pulling her from her thoughts. The door in the row house across the alley opened partway and someone peeked out, a small, pinched face looking up and down the street. It looked like a young girl, with blond braids and a red scarf over her nose and mouth. After checking both ways, the girl came out and stood on the stoop, her shoulders hunched as if trying to make herself smaller. She wore an oversize coat with baggy pockets over her long dress and carried what looked like an empty sack in one hand.

Bernice couldn't be sure, but it looked like Mr. and Mrs. Lange's daughter, the one with the bluest eyes she'd ever seen and the odd-sounding name. What was it? Gia? Pia? Yes, that was it. Pia. She remembered because she'd heard the Duffy boy calling out to her as she sat reading on the steps one day. At first she thought he was yelling in a different language, but then the girl waved and went to greet him. That's when Bernice realized the strange word was a name. Another time at a vegetable stand, she'd heard Mrs. Lange talking to the same girl and realized it was her daughter. Neither of them paid any attention to her, but Bernice had noticed the striking color of Pia's eyes, like the deep cobalt of a blue jay's wing. At the time Bernice had been only weeks away from giving birth to Wallis and had almost stopped to admire Mrs. Lange's new twins—but she kept going because Mr. Lange had taken her father's job. Not to mention she couldn't let the neighbors see her talking to Germans. She'd wondered briefly if she'd temporarily lost her mind, then reminded herself the twins were only babies, too young to be swayed by German views and behaviors. She couldn't fault herself for being drawn to their sweet, newborn faces.

Now she couldn't imagine why Pia was leaving the safety of their row house during a citywide quarantine. Where was her mother? And what about her brothers, those beautiful twin boys? Mrs. Lange had to be out of her mind to allow her young daughter to venture out at a time like this. Pia couldn't have been more than twelve or thirteen. Even if Mrs. Lange couldn't read the newspaper and didn't own a radio, she had to know people were getting sick and dying. She had to know it wasn't safe for Pia to leave their apartment. The thought briefly crossed her mind that the Germans had started the epidemic and Pia and her family were immune, but she pushed it away. Mr. and Mrs. Bach and their four daughters were German too, and every last one of them was dead.

In spite of her anger with Mr. Lange for stealing her father's job, and the fact that they were German, Bernice could tell that normally, Mrs. Lange was a good mother. If there was a chill in the air, the twins and Pia always wore warm coats and knitted hats. Whenever she came out of the building with the twins, Mrs. Lange kissed them both before putting them in their pram, then smiled and talked to them while pushing them down the sidewalk. She caressed Pia's cheek with a gentle hand and kissed her forehead when seeing her off to school. So why would Mrs. Lange risk her daughter's life by letting her go outside during a flu epidemic?

Then Bernice had another thought. One that made her blood run cold.

Maybe Mrs. Lange was dead.

Maybe the twins were dead too.

No. Not those beautiful baby boys!

Nausea stirred in Bernice's stomach, and the room seemed to spin around her. She grasped the back of a kitchen chair to steady herself, and fixed watery eyes on the body of her dead son. How was it possible that babies were getting sick and dying? How was such a horrendous nightmare allowed? And where was the God she knew and loved? The Lange boys were a little older than Wallis, but just as innocent and pure, even if they were German. Pulling her gaze back to the window, she tried to focus. Pia was hurrying along the alley with her head down, occasionally glancing over her shoulder and looking around as if worried she might be seen.

Bernice couldn't imagine where she was headed. Maybe she was going to try to find medicine but hadn't heard that the pharmacies had run out of everything but whiskey—now that the saloons were closed, it was the only place you could get it. Maybe she was going to the hospital to look for help. But if the boys were sick, Mrs. Lange should have gone instead of sending her young daughter. It wasn't right. Unless Mrs. Lange was sick too.

Then Pia climbed the steps of the next building and went inside. What was she doing?

CHAPTER THREE

PIA

While the dead backed up at mortuaries and pressed into undertakers' living quarters, hospital morgues overflowed into corridors, corpses at the city morgue spilled into the street, and Pia
struggled to keep herself and her brothers alive inside the dim,
cramped rooms of their apartment on Shunk Alley. Before making the decision to leave, she had suffered eight days of increas-
ing anxiety, with no idea when—or if—it would be safe to go out
again. She did her best to make sure their meager supplies would
last as long as possible by rationing the Mellin's Infant Food and
adding spoonsful of porridge, soft boiled eggs, cooked potatoes,
and mashed carrots to the boys' diet. Wishing she'd paid more
attention when Mutti made their meals, Pia tried to duplicate her
lentil soup, but the lentils turned out either half-cooked or too
mushy, and the soup tasted like chalk mixed with paste. She forced
herself to eat it anyway, so she could save the rest of the food for
the twins. She hated the taste of her mother's Postum but drank
that too, despite the fact that she didn't even like real coffee. It
didn't matter if her stomach cramped with hunger or she longed
for something to drink besides fake coffee and water, Ollie and
Max came first. Anything that could be made soft enough, she fed

to them. Anything that was hard or distasteful, like crusts of bread or lentil soup, she kept for herself.

When she wasn't busy feeding, changing, or trying to get the twins to sleep, she checked out the window to see if people were coming outside yet, if the nightmare was going to end. She hoped against hope to see her father in his uniform, returning home from the war in time to save them. But he was never there. Every so often neighbors hurried out of their homes, their pale faces lined by sorrow and fear, to leave bodies wrapped in sheets on the steps. Otherwise, the alley was empty. She wondered briefly if she should put Mutti outside, but didn't think she could carry her down three flights of stairs on her own. Besides, she didn't want to leave her out on the street. It wouldn't seem right. For reasons she couldn't explain, it felt better having her mother there, in the apartment with them.

Remembering the wakes she'd attended in Hazleton, she'd done her best to honor Mutti by carefully brushing her hair out of her face, sweeping it back on the pillow, and decorating the pillowslip with paper flowers made out of pages torn from her schoolbook. She didn't care if she got in trouble for damaging the book. Who knew if she'd ever return to school, anyway? After that, she covered Mutti with an extra blanket so she wouldn't be cold, then tried closing Mutti's mouth and washing the blood off her face with a wet rag, but gave up because she had to press too hard.

Every morning, she checked the clothesline for a message from Finn, but her note still hung outside his window, damp and tattered from the October wind and rain. The sight of it made her shiver. If it weren't for the occasional muffled voices and bump and scrape of furniture on the other side of the tenement walls, she'd have thought she and her brothers were the last people left alive. Sometimes, when she heard muted anguished wails and sobbing, she imagined the flu taking them all one by one, until no one was left in the city.

Grief and despair nearly swallowed her.

By day four she stopped looking for a note from Finn. And when she opened the bedroom door to look for warmer clothes for her brothers, she recoiled and clamped a hand over her mouth.

She'd never smelled anything so horrible—a pungent combination of dead animal, the inside of an outhouse on a hot day, and the strange, cloying scent of old perfume. Vater had found a dead rat rotting under the stove the day they'd moved into the apartment, and that had made Pia gag, but this was worse.

She stood frozen in the bedroom doorway, holding her breath and fighting the urge to vomit; at the same time, she couldn't pull her eyes away from the sight of Mutti on the bed. Her body had started to bloat, the thin skin of her face stretching as if about to burst. Somehow, more blood foamed from her eyes and nose and mouth. Forcing herself to enter the room, Pia grabbed the rest of the boys' clothes from the dresser, hurried back out, closed the door, and leaned against it, breathing hard. But the horrible smell seemed to cling to her, gluing itself to her hair and caking the inside of her nostrils. She threw the clothes on the table, hurried over to the wash bucket, scrubbed her hands and face with the last sliver of Ivory soap, and ran her soapy fingers through her hair. It didn't help. She grabbed diapers and rags from the clotheslines above the stove and shoved them under the bottom of the door, tears burning in her eyes.

"I'm sorry, Mutti," she said. "I know it's not your fault."

The first time she saw men with carts picking up bodies, she'd thought about calling out the window to ask if they had any news, if things were getting back to normal or the doctors had found a cure for the flu. Then she realized drawing attention to herself was a bad idea. The men might call the authorities. Then the police would come, find Mutti dead, and take her brothers away. She'd probably never see them again. No, she couldn't let that happen. It didn't matter that she was only thirteen, she would take care of Ollie and Max until their father came home. She had to. There was no other choice.

Despite her best efforts to keep her brothers clean, dry, and fed, it seemed like they cried day and night. On the rare occasion they were asleep at the same time, she rushed down to the fenced yard to get water and use the outhouse, praying the boys wouldn't wake up or start crawling while she was away, and that she wouldn't run into anyone, especially old Mr. Hill. Mutti used to carry the twins down the four flights in cloth slings strapped to her waist, then carry them back up again—along with two buckets full of water. But Pia didn't think she was strong enough. Plus, taking the twins would have slowed her down. Sometimes she used the mop pail as a toilet so she wouldn't have to leave, emptying it in the outhouse when she went down to the yard, but when it came to getting water, she didn't have a choice. And they needed lots of it—to mix with the Mellin's, to soften food, to wash dishes and baby bottoms and diapers. Loads and loads of diapers. She used as little Borax in the washtub as possible, but they were running out of that too.

Whether Ollie and Max cried more because they missed Mutti or because the sudden change from breast milk to Mellin's and real food upset their bellies, she wasn't sure. But there was nothing she could do about it, anyway. Maybe they sensed that their lives, like hers, had been horribly and forever changed. Maybe they were getting sick. No. She refused to think that way. If they hadn't caught the flu by now, she convinced herself, they probably wouldn't. Besides, they couldn't get sick. She wouldn't let them. And yet, when she picked them up to change or feed or comfort them, she held her breath, terrified she'd feel the same thing she felt when she touched Mutti the day before she died. So far she'd felt nothing worrisome, but the fear sat like a boulder in her stomach, heavy and solid and unmoving.

If only she could send a telegram to her aunt and uncle in New York. Maybe they would come to Philadelphia to get them. She doubted anyone on Shunk Alley owned a telephone, and she wasn't sure where the nearest one might be. But her aunt and uncle probably didn't have one anyway, and she didn't know their number if they did. Their return address was on letters sent to Mutti and Vater, but she didn't dare go to the post office twenty blocks away. She couldn't leave the boys that long, and she couldn't take them with her. If the post office was even open.

When the eggs and fresh vegetables ran out on the sixth day, she fed Ollie and Max old bread soaked in water and canned applesauce from apples bought at the farmer's market last fall. Two days later, she gave them the last of the porridge for breakfast, then sat on the bed to watch them nap, fighting against the weight of despair. Even in sleep, misery pinched the twins' faces and furrowed the smooth skin of their small brows. Their eyes darted back and forth beneath their lids, chasing bad dreams. Seeing them that way broke her heart—struggling to find comfort, not knowing or understanding why their stomachs hurt or where their mother had gone. She missed Mutti too, more than she would ever have thought possible. She could almost feel her brothers' pain, their intense aching for Mutti's gentle snuggles and warm kisses, her lavender-and-lye-scented skin, her soft hair that always smelled of baking bread. Grief twisted in Pia's chest and she hung her head.

Through everything their family had endured, the move from Germany when she was four, the seemingly endless journey across the Atlantic Ocean—which Pia barely remembered—the transition into a new country and new home, the worry of Vater working in the mines and going off to war, it was Mutti who was the constant source of comfort. No matter where they were or what was happening, she was the thread to everything familiar and normal, from food in their stomachs to clean clothes and warm baths. Certainly Vater worked hard to take care of them while still making sure he had time for fun—he took her swimming in the creek back in Hazleton in the summer, taught her how to whistle and skip rocks across the culm ponds, and showed her how to identify edible mushrooms in the woods—but Mutti was the one who put soap on beestings and scraped knees, the one who sat on the edge of the bed when Pia couldn't sleep, and traced a gentle finger across her forehead and cheeks to help her relax, the one who put bonnets on the twins to protect them from the sun. Mutti was the one who knew when they were hungry and tired, or just needed an extra hug.

According to Vater, Mutti even calmed his fears about following his brother to America after the construction company he worked for in Germany collapsed, and convinced him they'd be fine when they found out they had two more mouths to feed so soon after they started their new life in Philadelphia. She kept the family organized and strong, while always making sure they knew they were loved. How would Pia ever survive without her? Who was going to help her get through the ups and downs of life? Who was going to teach her about being a woman and a wife? If Pia lived that long.

One of Mutti's favorite sayings was, "We may not have it all together, but together we have it all." Except they weren't all together anymore. And now they never would be. Mutti was gone, and Pia had no idea if, or when, Vater would come back. Between that and everyone dying of the flu, the world felt like it was coming to an end. Everything Pia knew and relied on had disappeared. What was she supposed to do now? She was only thirteen. How was she going to take care of the twins when, and if, this nightmare was over? How would she keep them safe and fed until Vater returned? She had no job. No money. Then she remembered what Mutti always said whenever she felt confused or unsure, "Just do the next thing." Whether it was getting dressed in the morning or doing chores and homework, the best way to move through a complicated situation was to decide what needed to be done next and just do it.

With that thought, Pia noticed how dirty her dress was, stained with formula and baby spit and something that looked like gravy. She couldn't remember the last time she'd changed. Or even what day it was. Before the flu, she used to put on a clean outfit every Monday, unless she'd spilled something on the one she was wearing or somehow got a tear. Not that she had a lot of dresses to choose from—two made from flour sacks and one made out of a printed sheet, along with two skirts and a cotton blouse—but everything was always clean and in good repair, even her leggings and undergarments. And to think she'd been sleeping in her clothes.

She glanced around the room, the beginnings of panic shuddering in her chest. Empty Mellin's jars littered the counter next to a bowl filled with moldy potato and carrot peels. A half-dozen soiled diapers floated in the washtub with the last of the Borax, like gray islands in a muddy sea. A kettle crusted with soup sat on the stove, which was splattered with bits of dried food and baby formula, and the coal bucket stood empty. Stacks of dirty bowls and cups sat on the table, leaning this way and that. She'd stopped washing dishes three days ago, too exhausted to keep fetching water. Mutti would have been appalled.

Between the horrible odor coming out of the bedroom and the stench of dirty diapers and old soup, she felt like she was suffocating. She climbed on a chair and searched the shelves for something to help cover the smell. Maybe she'd find some herbs from Mrs. Schmidt, a leftover sprig of lavender or sage she could crush and spread around the room. She felt in the jars and cups, looked behind plates and bowls and pots, but found nothing.

Then her fingers landed on something long and hard behind the mantel clock. She pulled it out. It was one of Vater's cigars. She got down from the chair, grabbed the box of matches next to the stove, put the cigar in a saucer on the table, and lit one end. Smoke curled from the brown paper and the cigar started to burn, filling the air with the familiar smell of tobacco and reminders of Vater. Tears filled her eyes. What would he think if he knew what his family was going through? That his wife was dead and his daughter was trying to keep his sons alive? Surely he would curse himself for leaving.

She took a deep breath and tried to think. What should she do next? Her father wasn't going to return in time to help. She didn't even know if he was alive. It was up to her to save Ollie and Max. But the last of the Mellin's Infant Food was already in their bottles, the bread and eggs had been used up, the last jar of applesauce was nearly empty, and the potatoes and carrots had been cooked and eaten. The coal stove stood empty, the last embers nothing but gray ash. Everything was gone.

She went to the end of the bed to look out the window. Dark clouds scuttled across the gray morning sky, and her note to Finn still hung on the clothesline, shuddering in the breeze. No one walked in the alley below, but four more bodies covered in bloody sheets had appeared sometime during the night. Hunger cramped her stomach and she gritted her teeth. She had to find food. It was either that or they'd starve. She'd steal if she had to—anything to keep them alive. But the twins had to stay here. It wasn't safe for them out there, not to mention she wouldn't be able to carry much food if she had to carry them too, and she couldn't push a baby pram up and down the stairs. She wouldn't go far, just to the neighbors to see if they could spare anything. If that didn't work, she'd try the next row house. The problem was that Ollie and Max were starting to push themselves up on their knees and getting ready to crawl.

She looked around the room and imagined all sorts of accidents waiting to happen if she left—Ollie pulling himself up on the table leg and toppling it over, or pulling the tablecloth off along with the dishes on top. Max getting his head stuck between a chair and the bed. She couldn't leave them on her bed because they might fall off. If only there were some place small and safe to put them, like a crate or a crib with a lid. Then she remembered the cubby in her parents' bedroom, where they hid money beneath a loose floorboard. Ollie and Max would be safe in there, and they wouldn't be able to open the door. She could put blankets inside and leave bottles too, even though they were only just starting to hold them. They might cry, but at least they wouldn't be able to crawl around and get hurt. It would be scary for them to be shut in such a small, dark space, even for a few minutes, but it was better than letting them starve. And they'd have each other. She tried to think back to when she was their age, if she could remember anything unpleasant. She couldn't recall anything—scary or otherwise. They wouldn't remember being shut in a cubby. And she wouldn't be gone long.

But she had to do it now, before she changed her mind.

She went over to the table and picked up the cigar. The paper had stopped burning, and the tobacco was going out. Remembering how Vater used to smoke, she put it to her lips and inhaled to get it going again. The harsh smoke burned her throat and she coughed, the gritty taste of ash coating her tongue and cheeks. She clamped a hand over her mouth so she wouldn't wake the boys, trying not to cough too loud. When she finally stopped choking, she closed her eyes, held her breath, and waved the smoke toward her hair and dress, covering herself in the smell. Then she put the cigar down and pulled the diapers and rags out from underneath the bedroom door. She hadn't been in there in days—how many she wasn't sure—but the stench was worse than ever, even on this side of the door.

On shaking legs, she took a deep breath and fixed her eyes on the floor, then rushed into the bedroom, hurried past the bed, and knelt in front of the cubby. She opened the door and took the money out from under the loose floorboard, then examined the walls, floor, and ceiling of the cubby for splinters or nails. The wood was smooth and sliver-free. Her lungs felt ready to burst, so she exhaled, put her hands over her nose and mouth, and, trying not to gag, took another deep breath. Then she got up to rummage in the closet for Mutti's winter coat, which would hang on her like a tent—it was too big on Mutti—but had deep pockets to carry food. When she found the coat, she held part of it over her nose and mouth and, powerless to stop herself, turned to look at the bed. Mutti's body had deflated, the bloat mostly gone. Bloody green blotches covered her skin, and her tongue protruded from her yawning mouth.

Bile surged in the back of Pia's throat and she ran out of the room, shut the door, and put the diapers and rags back under it, gagging and trying not to throw up. Now she understood why people were putting their loved ones out on the street. She laid the coat over a chair and wiped her arm across her mouth, trying to control her roiling stomach. Sweat broke out on her forehead. When she could breathe again without gagging, she pulled the money from her pocket and counted it. Three dollars. More than likely the markets and vendor stands were closed too, and the nearest one was ten blocks away anyway, but maybe she could buy food from one of her neighbors.

Trying not to wake the twins, she pulled two grocery sacks from a wicker basket beneath the table and put them in the coat pockets. Then she took the pillow from her bed, picked up the boys' rattles and bottles, and stood looking at Ollie and Max, dreading what she had to do next. Just the thought of it nauseated her. She took Mutti's red scarf from the hook next to the front door, held it over the burning cigar for a minute, then tied it over her nose and mouth. It wasn't perfect, but it would help.

She held the pillow in the cigar smoke too, then took a deep breath, went back into the bedroom, and put it on the floor of the cubby, pushing it down along the edges and the corners to make a soft bed. After leaving the bottles and rattles on the pillow, she went to get the boys, trying to decide which one to move first. Max slept more soundly, but Ollie usually slept longer.

Moving slowly, she swaddled Ollie's blanket around him, lifted him from the bed, lowered the scarf from over her mouth, and lightly kissed his tiny, soft head. He squirmed and started to wake, then whimpered and went back to sleep, snuggling against her chest. She carried him into the bedroom and carefully laid him on the pillow inside the cubby.

"Damn it," she whispered.

He took up more room than she'd thought. Maybe the twins wouldn't fit in there together. For a second, she wavered, but then her stomach cramped again and she knew. She had to do it. A few hours of discomfort was better than letting her brothers starve to death.

Moving as fast as she could without running, she tiptoed back into the other room and picked up Max. His legs were pedaling and he was starting to wake. She swaddled him tighter in his blanket, kissed his forehead, and rocked him back and forth, humming softly. After a few moments, he quieted and went back to sleep. She breathed a sigh of relief. There was no way she could put the boys in the cubby if they were awake. She just couldn't. It would be too hard.

She pulled her blanket off the bed and took Max into the bedroom, relieved to find Ollie still asleep. She knelt and laid Max beside him, placing them back-to-back. Ollie squirmed and she reached in and patted his side, holding her breath and praying he wouldn't wake up. Finally, he put his thumb in his mouth and settled. She took her arm out of the cubby, put her hand on the door, and stared into the gloomy space, tears blurring her vision.

"I'm sorry," she whispered. "I promise, I'll be right back." She started closing the door, watching the twins until the last second. "Just keep sleeping and you'll never even know I was gone." Then the latch clicked shut and she sat frozen on her knees, her heart thumping in her chest, waiting to see what would happen. If one of the boys woke up, she wasn't sure what she would do. But no crying came from inside the cubby, no whimpering or wailing or panicked shrieks. Ollie and Max were still sleeping. They would be all right. They had to be.

With tears streaming down her face, she stood and looked at her mother on the bed, praying she'd understand why she had to do this. Surely Mutti would've done the same thing if it meant life or death for her children.

"I'll be back," Pia whispered. "I promise. Keep them safe for me."

Swallowing her sobs, she bit her lip and rushed out of the bedroom. She had to leave before she changed her mind. Not only because she felt terrible about putting her brothers in the cubby, but also because she was scared—terrified really—of what she might find outside their safe rooms, where everyone seemed to be dead or dying. She took off the scarf, then realized she needed a mask, like the ones the policemen and other people had been wearing the day the schools and churches closed, and retied the scarf around her nose and mouth. It would have to do. She put on her mother's oversize coat, thrust her arms into the wool sleeves, and tied the belt around her waist. The bottom hem hung to her ankles and the sleeves hung past her wrists, but between its large pockets and the grocery sacks, she'd be able to carry home plenty of food. She went to the front door and started to turn the knob. Then she heard it.

A baby's soft cry.

She stared at the bedroom door, trying not to breathe. The only thing she heard was the sound of her blood rushing through her veins and her pulse slamming inside her temples. Maybe she had imagined it. Then the cry grew louder. Pia cringed. It sounded like Ollie. Tears flooded her eyes and her heart thrashed in her chest. She yanked open the door and ran out of the apartment.

CHAPTER FOUR

BERNICE

Keeping an eye on the front door of the row house next to the Langes', Bernice watched to see if Pia would come back out. If she'd gone to a neighbor's to pick up something, more than likely she'd be quick about it. But what could possibly be important enough for Pia to leave the safety of her home? And if it was something for the babies, how could Mrs. Lange think it was acceptable to risk one child's life for another? Bernice wondered again if Mrs. Lange was dead. And if so, who was taking care of those precious twin boys?

After what felt like forever, Pia was nowhere to be seen. Bernice couldn't take it any longer. She had to know why Pia left and, most of all, if the twins were all right. She just had to. Without giving it another thought, she spun around, grabbed her coat, and hurried out of the apartment.

Squinting in the dank hallway, she walked as fast as she could without running. The aroma of fried onions filled the dim corridor, along with an underlying stench of something that reminded her of rotten meat. She nearly tripped over a rusted bucket, then gave a wide berth to a lumpy seed sack crumpled against one wall. It was tied shut at one end and covered in maggots and flies. She couldn't imagine what was inside. Two black ribbons hung from the door handle of the apartment at the top of the stairs, the rooms that belonged to the widow, Mrs. Duffy, and her sons.

That's what you get for being a know-nothing drunkard, she thought. *You should have stuck with your own kind, instead of coming here to cause trouble with the rest of the bog-jumpers.* Her thoughts were unchristian, but she didn't care. Mrs. Duffy was lazy and trying. She let her sons yell out the windows, and she sang loud, strange songs in the hallways in her heavy Irish brogue, using words no one understood. She showed too much cleavage and came home late at night, her face flush with alcohol, her hair a mess. Bernice couldn't count the number of times she'd peeked out her door after midnight to watch Mrs. Duffy fumble with her key in the hall, mumbling and unaware she was being watched. It wasn't right for a mother to behave that way. Bernice wasn't sure who the ribbons on the Duffys' door were for, but one thing was clear: Mrs. Duffy had paid for her sins.

As soon as the thought crossed her mind, she cringed. *If Mrs. Duffy was punished for her sins, what about me? What did I do to deserve losing my husband and son?* She gripped the staircase railing to keep from falling and went down the dark steps, around and around and around, like the dizzying notions inside her head. She was a moral woman and loving mother. She was fair-minded and kind, and she had been a virtuous wife to her husband. She hadn't done anything to deserve losing him or Wallis. The flu took whomever it wanted. By the time she reached the bottom floor, she was woozy and breathless, and one of her headaches had started. She stopped in the foyer and rubbed her temples, trying to focus on the task at hand. She needed to find out why Pia had left her building, and if the twins were still alive. She wasn't sure what she would do if the babies were dead from the flu, but she had to know one way or another. Then she had another thought. What if Mrs. Lange answered the door and wanted to know what she was doing there? How would she explain herself? Anger churned at the bottom of her rib cage again. If Mrs. Lange was there, Bernice would let her know in no uncertain terms that she was crazy and careless for letting her daughter outside at a time like this. If Pia were her child, she'd have kept her home, where she was safe.

Crossing the foyer, she grabbed the handle of the front door, ready to march across the street and give Mrs. Lange a piece of her mind. Then she hesitated. She needed to make sure the coast was clear and Pia wasn't on her way back. She opened the front door a crack and peered out, checking left and right. The streets were empty. She hurried down the steps, across the cobblestones, and up the steps of the Langes' building. Their rooms were in the front of the house, to the left of the fire escape. She knew because she'd seen Mrs. Lange hanging blankets and pillows over the sill. Germans were always hanging things outside—rugs, curtains, clothes—even in the winter. She didn't understand it.

When she stepped inside the foyer, she clamped a hand over her mouth and nose. The Langes' row house smelled worse than hers, as if it'd been closed up for years. But there was no time to waste wondering why. She climbed the stairs as quickly as possible, rapped her knuckles on the Langes' door, and looked up and down the hallway. She was vibrating with nerves, every sense on high alert. If she heard someone coming into the building and up the stairs, she would scurry into the shadows at the end of the hall, then wait and see who it was. If it turned out to be Pia, she'd go home and try to forget about the twins. If she could.

She knocked again, leaned close to the door, and said as loudly as she dared, "Mrs. Lange? Are you in there?"

No answer.

"Mrs. Lange?"

No sound came from the other side. No talking or banging dishes. No radio played. She put an ear to the wood and held her breath, listening. And then she heard it.

Babies crying.

CHAPTER FIVE

PIA

Originally, Pia had planned on searching for food in her own build-ing first, to ask the neighbors if they could spare a few potatoes or one or two eggs, hoping she could remember who had seemed friendly, who hadn't scowled at Mutti or told the police they were German. Because the closer to her apartment she stayed, the sooner she could return home. But after hearing Ollie start to fuss before she left, she knew if she stayed in her building, no matter what floor she was on or how far away, she would hear her brothers cry. And if she could hear them cry, she'd go back. She'd go back, take them out of the cubby, and promise never to leave them again. And that was something she couldn't do. Not until she found what they needed. Not until she could bring Ollie and Max something to eat and drink. She had to be strong. There was no other choice.

Now, she stood in the first-floor hallway of the row house next door, trying to decide where to start. Inky shadows filled the halls, growing darker toward the back of the building. Crepe ribbons—some gray, some white, some black—hung from all but one door. Maybe she'd picked the wrong building to begin her search. She went up the first flight of steps to check the second floor. No crepe hung in the hall. She stopped at the apartment nearest the staircase.

If no one answered, she would see if it was locked. If the handle turned and the door opened, she would go inside. It would be all right to enter if the apartment was unlocked. And take food if no one was home. That's what she told herself, anyway. She knocked on the peeling wood and waited. Hushed voices and muffled movements filtered through the door, and someone shushed everyone to be quiet. She tilted her head, trying to listen.

"Hello?" she said. "I'm looking for food for my brothers. They're babies, only a few months old. Do you have anything to spare?"

A gruff voice called out, "Go away!"

"Please," she said. "I can pay. I have money. Just a loaf of bread or tin of broth is all I need."

"No!" the voice called out again. "Leave us alone!"

Pia sighed and moved down the hall, her shoulders bunched, her jaw clenched. She stopped in front of another door and listened. No sounds came from the other side, no whispering or crying or talking. She knocked and waited. Still nothing. She knocked again and tried the handle. It was locked.

"Is anyone there?" she said.

No answer.

A sudden image flashed in her mind: the people inside dead and rotting, sitting and lying in their chairs and beds, the table set for dinner, the coal stove empty and cold. A chill passed through her and she shivered. Why else would they not answer the door? They wouldn't be out and about in the city at a time like this. Unless they were doing the same thing she was doing, searching for food and supplies. But they wouldn't all leave at the same time, would they?

She pushed the gruesome images from her head and moved toward an apartment at the back of the building. If no one answered and it was unlocked, she would go inside, but the rooms had no windows, meaning it would be dark and hard to see. Still, she had to try. She knocked on the door, berating herself for not bringing a lantern. Then she reminded herself that a lantern would have been one more thing to carry. And with all the horrible things that had been going on—her mother dying; taking care of the twins alone; so many other people passing away all at once, maybe even

Finn—she could barely remember what day it was, let alone re-member to bring a lantern.

No one answered. She tried the handle. It was locked. Maybe she was wasting her time. Maybe she should search somewhere be-side the Fifth Ward, where everyone had so little to begin with, let alone anything to spare. Not to mention it seemed like people were too scared to answer their doors. She couldn't blame them. But the longer she looked for help where she wouldn't find it, the longer her brothers would be shut in the cubby. Maybe the flu hadn't spread to other parts of the city yet. Or maybe the churches were handing out food.

Refusing to give up completely before leaving, she decided to try a different floor. She climbed the second staircase and stopped at an apartment toward the front of the building, where the rooms had windows. She knocked and waited. No one answered or shuf-fled toward the other side of the door. No one yelled at her to go away. She knocked again, harder this time, then turned the knob. It was unlocked. She gave the door a gentle push. It swung open and a swirl of rank air sent a piece of crumpled paper over the cracked threshold. She clamped a hand over her scarf, instantly recognizing the stench of decaying flesh.

A weak shaft of daylight reached across the floor, illuminating the gloomy interior of a room nearly identical to her home, from the coal stove to the rough-hewn shelves filled with dishes to the bedroom door. Taking a step inside, she had to fight the urge to run into the back room and look for her brothers, to kiss them and hug them and make sure they were all right. Even the narrow iron bed under the window looked the same.

The only things missing were Mutti's vase and Oma's tablecloth. Her heartbeat picked up speed. Had someone taken their things? What if Ollie and Max were gone too? She shook her head. No. This wasn't home. The table was bigger, with wooden stools around it instead of chairs. And a fringed rug with a strange design covered the floor, not layers of threadbare throw rugs.

Trying to remind herself where she was and what she was doing there, she struggled to stay calm. She was in the row house next door, searching for food for her brothers. She needed to keep going so she could get back to them as soon as possible. Then the room seemed to rotate and she put a hand on the wall to steady herself. Sweat broke out on her forehead. Confusion and panic jittered inside her head. Except for the fear of finding dead bodies and the guilt over leaving Ollie and Max, she had felt fine a minute ago. Maybe that, combined with the worry of not finding food, was too overwhelming. Then her stomach clenched with hunger and she remembered she hadn't eaten since yesterday. When, or if, she found food, she needed to eat something straightaway. She wouldn't be able to take anything back to Ollie and Max if she passed out from hunger. Gritting her teeth, she waited for her head to stop spinning.

Dead bodies or no dead bodies, she had to search the apartment for food. She had no choice. She edged in farther, ready to run if anyone appeared. And then she saw a pair of brown buckle boots on the floor, one pointed up, the other flopped on its side. Above the boots, beige stockings covered a pair of swollen ankles.

Pia chewed her lip. A clear path led to the kitchen area. If she kept her eyes straight ahead, she'd be fine. She could make it past whoever lay on the floor. She steeled herself and moved forward, her arms and hands tight to her body. Except. Except. She had to look.

The remains of a blond woman lay shriveled on the rug, her head propped crookedly against a coal bucket. Black blood caked her hands and face, and her eyes had sunken into her skull. Maggots crawled around her swollen mouth and nose. Pia looked away, toward the kitchen, but it was too late. She pulled the scarf down from her face, bent over, and threw up what little she had in her stomach, then dry-heaved until there was nothing left but bile. When she could breathe again without gagging, she wiped her mouth on her coat sleeve, put the scarf back up, and stumbled toward the stove, praying she would find something, anything, to eat.

Moving dishes and plates out of the way, she searched the shelves for a jar of applesauce or can of beans, trying not to make too much noise. More than anything, she needed to find some Mellin's Infant Food. Suddenly another wave of dizziness swept over her. She grabbed the shelf to keep from falling and knocked off a flowered teacup. It hit the floor and shattered everywhere, tiny shards of porcelain flying over the hardwood planks. She froze, terrified someone else might be in the apartment, or a neighbor might hear and wonder what was going on. She let go of the shelf and waited, unnerved by the sudden silence.

A faint groaning came from the other room.

She turned toward it, her heartbeat thudding in her ears.

Another groan.

She edged over to the door and peeked around the frame. A man lay on the bed in a fetal position, his face swollen and black, his chest rising and falling in shallow, shuddering breaths. Beside him on the floor, a baby and little girl lay on a pile of soiled blankets, both of them dead. The man locked red, weepy eyes on Pia, then moaned and lifted a blue hand, reaching out with blood-caked fingers. She started to tremble, the urge to run like fire in her chest.

"I'm sorry," she whispered. "I can't help you."

Seeing the dead family, hopelessness fell over her like a shroud, weighing her down with despair. Tears filled her eyes and her lungs felt heavy, her blood like lead. Part of her wanted to give up and give in, to go home and lay down with Ollie and Max, to let the flu or starvation take them, whichever came first. Because what was the sense in surviving if everyone else was dead?

The other part of her refused to give up, couldn't begin to imagine letting her brothers die. She didn't know what was going to happen to any of them, if and when this nightmare ever came to an end, but she couldn't and wouldn't stop fighting. She loved Ollie and Max too much. And how would she face Mutti and Vater again, in heaven or otherwise, if she didn't try?

She turned back to the kitchen on watery legs, desperate to find food so she could get out of there. Then she noticed a squat cupboard next to the stove, partly concealed behind a worn paisley curtain. She hurried over to it, fell to her knees, and yanked the curtain aside. A jar of Mellin's sat on the top shelf, along with a can of black-eyed peas and something wrapped in brown paper. She put the Mellin's and peas in her coat pocket and tore open the paper. Inside were two slices of bread. She pulled one out, lowered her scarf, and took a bite.

The crust was stale and hard, but it was the best thing she'd ever tasted. She swallowed and took another bite, then did a quick search of the rest of the kitchen. Finding nothing more, she took a wide berth around the dead woman and headed for the front door.

In the bedroom, the man went on groaning.

CHAPTER SIX

BERNICE

Standing in the hallway outside the Langes' apartment, Bernice couldn't decide what to do. The twins were still crying inside, and no one was answering the door. She knocked a third time.

"Mrs. Lange?" she said again. "Are you in there?"

Still no answer.

"It's Bernice Groves, your neighbor from across the street. I saw your daughter leave the building and wanted to make sure you're all right." She hesitated and tried to think of something else to say. Flu or no flu, she was probably the last person Mrs. Lange wanted to see at her door. "I know we've had a few cross words between us," she said, "but at times like this we need to look out for each other."

The babies' wails seemed to grow more frantic.

Bernice felt like screaming. She had to get inside. Even if it meant breaking down the door. She knocked again, frustration pounding inside her head, then tried the handle. To her astonishment, it turned and the latch clicked open. She gasped, surprised and angry at the same time. What kind of mother leaves an apartment unlocked with two babies inside? Then she remembered Pia was the one who had left the building. Maybe she forgot to use her key. That, at least, would be understandable. She was just a young girl, likely frightened by the horrible things that had been happening. Bernice was a grown woman and *she* was horrified. And even though they were too young to understand, Pia's brothers could probably sense something was wrong and were scared too. Thinking of the twins, a flood of maternal instinct surged through her and she pushed the door open and hurried inside.

The smell of rotting flesh instantly filled her nostrils, making her gag. She clamped a hand over her nose and mouth, and looked around the dim apartment. Flour-sack curtains swelled out from a half-open window above a crumpled bed, then blew in again when she closed the door. Baby clothes hung, haphazard and crooked, from clotheslines draped along the ceiling—clothespins clamped to a sleeve here, a leg there, the collar of a nightdress somewhere else. Dirty dishes filled the table, and a washtub full of soiled diapers sat next to the stove. Either Mrs. Lange wasn't as hardworking and orderly as the rest of the Germans, or Pia had been living there on her own.

And somehow, even though she was inside the apartment now, the babies' cries still sounded distant and muffled, like they were coming from somewhere else. Had she broken into the wrong place? She held her breath and listened, unable to tell now if it was one baby or two. Maybe it was a neighbor's baby and she'd imagined the entire thing. Then she noticed the diapers and rags stuffed under the door to the other room, and her heart sank.

No. God. Please. Not the twins.

She moved toward the door, her stomach twisting. She clenched her jaw, turned the handle, and slowly pushed the door open.

A weak shaft of light revealed a plank wall and two framed black-and-white photographs above a leaning dresser. The photographs were of Mr. and Mrs. Lange, smiling on their wedding day, him in a dark suit and her in a lace veil and simple white gown. Bernice held her breath and edged inside, letting her eyes adjust to the gloom. What was left of Mrs. Lange lay on the bed, a gray blanket pulled up to her chin, a blood-spattered pillow beneath her head. Flies and maggots crawled on her eyes and in her nostrils. Bernice gasped and looked away, then forced herself to look again, to see if the twins lay beside her. A half circle of paper flowers surrounded

Mrs. Lange's hair, and something that looked like baby powder covered the blanket and pillow. But no dead boys lay with her. No infant corpses with their eyes swollen shut. She scanned the cramped
space to see if the twins were in the bedroom at all. Somewhere, the
babies went on crying.

The idea that she was hearing things crossed her mind, and
she considered for a brief moment that she had gone insane. Her
headache pounded with every beat of her heart, as if there were a
sledgehammer inside her brain. She glanced at Mrs. Lange again.
Did she hear the cries too? Did she, as she lay lost in death, hear
her sons calling out for her, desperate for her loving arms and milky
breasts? Was her poor soul being tortured, unable to understand
why she couldn't see or find her boys? Maybe her ghost was in this
room, feeling helpless and confused and lost, searching frantically
for her babies.

Bernice swayed on watery legs. She knew exactly how Mrs.
Lange felt. But for the first time, she was grateful Wallis had left
this earth before her. If she had died first, there would have been
no one to look after him, no one to love him like she did. And he
might have starved in their rooms all alone. Then she had another
thought. Maybe the twins really were dead and she was hearing
their ghosts. Or maybe the agony of losing Wallis had driven her
over the edge. She shook her head. No, the cries were real. She
was certain of it. If the boys had passed, they would have been in
this room, in bed with their mother. She squinted at the mattress
again, studying the blanket. It lay flat on both sides of Mrs. Lange's
corpse. Nothing moved beneath it. She went to the open closet, her
hand over her mouth and nose, and reached blindly between worn
sweaters, dresses, trousers, and a ratty jacket. She knelt to search
the bottom of the closet. A pair of women's boots sat on the floor,
and two hatboxes leaned against the back wall. Finding nothing
there, she peered under the bed frame. No babies lay crying and
squirming beneath the mattress. No hungry boys in diapers and
cotton bonnets gazed back with frightened eyes. Still on her knees,
she looked under the dresser, under the washstand, under the legs
of a chair. Then she saw it.

A small, squat door between the bed and closet.

The door was the same dark color as the walls, except for the small, round doorknob and latch, which were painted red. Bernice scrambled over to it on her hands and knees, grabbed the doorknob with shaking fingers, and yanked it open. If she had been standing when she saw what was inside, she would have sunk to the floor in disbelief.

One of the twins lay on top of a blanket and pillow, howling and kicking and shaking his tiny fists. The other was wedged in a corner, half sitting, half lying down, his red face wet with tears. Both wore long-sleeved nightdresses, sweaters, bonnets, and booties. Two bottles lay leaking on the blanket beside two wooden rattles. Bernice pulled out the first baby and hugged him to her chest.

"Oh my God," she cried. "Oh my God. You poor things."

The baby whimpered and shuddered against her, his crying momentarily quieted. His skin felt clammy, and his diaper felt heavy and wet, the stench of it filling her nose. With her free hand, she reached in for the other twin. She didn't want to put the first one down, but couldn't get enough leverage to bring the other one out without hurting him. Trying not to panic, she wiped her flooding eyes so she could see better, then gently tugged the blanket out from beneath his bottom, quickly wrapped it around the first baby, and laid him on the floor. As soon as she reached in with both hands for the second twin, the first one started howling again.

"Shhh," she said. "Don't cry. I'm right here."

With the second baby safely out of the cubby, she scooped the first one into her arms and stood on wobbly legs, both boys clutched to her chest. They whimpered and cried, exhausted and trembling, while she quaked with rage, unable to grasp how Pia could do such a horrible thing. And to her own brothers, no less! She knew people had abandoned sick family members during the epidemic because they didn't know what else to do, but other than being hungry and dirty and scared, the twins looked fairly healthy, considering what they'd endured. Leaving them alone was unforgivable. Apparently what everyone said about Germans being heartless was true.

She bounced the boys gently up and down, holding them close to her chest. "There, there," she said, her voice quivering. "No need to cry. You're all right now. Don't worry, I'll take care of you."

CHAPTER SEVEN

PIA

After discovering two more corpses in the row house next door, and more apartments either locked or occupied by people who told her to go away or refused to answer, Pia decided to try more prosperous neighborhoods, where people had extra to begin with. Maybe she'd discover an open market or street peddler along the way. One thing was certain—leaving her brothers was torture and she didn't want to do it again until absolutely necessary. She needed to find enough food to last until Vater came home or this nightmare was over. If it was ever over. And the food she'd found so far—the jar of Mellin's, a can of black-eyed peas, and two slices of bread—wasn't nearly enough. As much as she dreaded wandering farther away from home, she wouldn't find what she was looking for among the poorest of the poor.

After leaving Shunk Alley, she moved west on Delancey, then turned north, walking fast. No motorcars or wagons traveled along the cobblestones. No one walked along the sidewalks. A trolley rattled by, but only a few masked passengers rode in the seats, sitting far away from one another. The feeling that she and her brothers were some of the last people alive in the city grew stronger with every step. Normally the thoroughfares were so crowded she couldn't walk two feet without bumping into shoppers or children or businessmen or bicyclists. Now crepe ribbons hung from doors, silent and swirling in the morning breeze, and sheet-wrapped corpses lay outside what seemed like every other building. The only sounds were her shoes on the cobblestones and the tinny voice of a radio somewhere, floating out into the empty streets. The farther she walked, the harder a cold slab of fear pressed against her chest, making it hard to breathe.

She'd planned on staying on the sidewalks, close to front doors and banisters in case she needed to hide—from whom, she wasn't sure—but the stench of dead bodies was unbearable. Instead she walked in the middle of the road, trying not to think about what was under the bloody sheets, or Mutti, or the blond woman with maggots on her face. She tried not to think about the fact that only days ago those people had been watching a grand parade, celebrating and having fun with their spouses and children and friends, unaware that death was waiting right around the corner. Now they were covered with flies and rotting on the sidewalk, like the fish sold at the seaport, and the dead pigs hanging behind the butcher's shop. At least the fish were on ice. And the pigs were cut up and cooked before maggots crawled on their faces. The gorge rose in her throat, and she wrapped her arms around herself, blinking back tears and trying not to be sick.

Announcements with black lettering on buildings and telephone poles read: ALL SHOWS AND CHURCHES ARE ORDERED CLOSED TO FIGHT THE EPIDEMIC. CASES IN THE STATE 100,000. STATE AND CITY HEALTH BOARDS MAY TAKE MORE DRASTIC STEPS—COMPLAIN THAT FAILURE OF PHYSICIANS TO REPORT CASES HANDICAPS THEM IN THEIR WORK—DEMAND FOR PHYSICIANS GREATLY EXCEEDS THE SUPPLY.

Ignoring the screaming voice in her head telling her to turn around and go home, she made her way toward Third Street looking for a sign to point her in the right direction. Every now and then a moving curtain caught her eye, but when she looked up at the window, the curtain dropped back into place. On one hand, she worried someone might try to rob her—not that she had anything worth stealing, but people were desperate. She knew because she was too. On the other hand, seeing moving curtains gave her a small measure of comfort. At least she wasn't alone. Other people were hiding in their apartments too, trying to survive. She thought about going inside one of the houses to ask for help, but knew she'd likely be turned away. And she needed to stop wasting time in the poor sections of Philadelphia. If she knocked on the right doors in a different part of the city, maybe some rich woman, after hearing her story, would offer a loaf of bread or jar of fruit. Maybe a caring mother would share a tin of cow's milk or a jar of Mellin's Infant Food. She prayed someone would, anyway.

Then she came to Pine Street and slowed. Men with guns guarded what looked like hundreds of homemade coffins stacked outside the fence around the cemetery of St. Peter's Church. Next to the coffins beneath a row of sycamore trees, haphazard piles of bloody corpses lay beneath dirty sheets and swarms of flies. More men, in masks and filthy clothes, picked up the bodies and carried them into the cemetery, where another group was digging what looked like a massive grave. Some of the men were wearing what looked like prison uniforms, while others were wearing school vests and trousers. Another wave of nausea washed over Pia, making her dizzy. Hoping no one noticed her, she dropped her eyes and kept going.

When she reached the end of the block it started to rain, a dreary gray drizzle pitting the greasy tops of brown puddles. The wind picked up, carrying with it the chill of the coming winter. She blinked against the cold and wrapped her arms around herself, suddenly freezing despite Mutti's heavy winter coat. She was quickly becoming exhausted too, as if her legs had turned to cement. It shouldn't have come as a surprise that everything she'd been seeing and feeling and doing was starting to wear her out, that trying to stay strong for the boys and refusing to give in to panic was tiring. But how much fear and worry was someone her age supposed to bear? And who was going to take care of her when, or if, this was over? As soon as the thoughts crossed her mind, she scolded herself for being selfish. Finding food for Ollie and Max was all that mattered. Not how she felt. Not how scared she was. Not how much she missed her parents. Only a few more blocks and she'd be nearing South Street, the much-traveled route that, along with the Schuylkill River, claimed to separate the city's rich from the poor.

By the time she reached Lombard Street, a thin sheen of sweat had formed on her forehead and upper lip. She wiped her face with the sleeve of Mutti's coat, then stopped and took it off, yanking on the collar and cuffs, suddenly desperate to remove it. She put the coat over her arm and trudged on. Why was she so hot? Being cold was understandable—it was October and the raindrops felt like ice. But somehow, rather abruptly, the air had turned heavy and warm and damp, like it did in the middle of summer. She slowed, her heart racing, and stopped on the edge of the road. Mutti's coat felt like it weighed a hundred pounds.

Footsteps sounded behind her and she spun around. A man stumbled toward her, his eyes and nose bleeding, his mouth gasping for air. He reached for her with bloody, clawed hands.

"Help me," he said in a ragged voice.

She turned and ran. When she glanced over her shoulder to see if he was following her, he had collapsed on the sidewalk, his legs and arms splayed out at odd angles. She ran a little farther, then stopped and put her hands on her knees, trying to catch her breath. Strands of wet hair hung in her eyes. Then she coughed, hard, and pain exploded in her throat and lungs. She put a hand to her chest. *No.* She couldn't be getting sick. She just couldn't. Maybe it was a cold. Maybe she was exhausted from worry and grief and lack of food and sleep. Whatever it was, she was determined to ignore it and keep going.

She straightened and looked back at the man. He lay motionless on the sidewalk, a growing puddle of blood around his head. Ignoring her burning throat, she swallowed her terror and started walking again. Just two more blocks and she'd find what she was looking for. Then she'd be able to go home. She'd be able to feed the boys, have something to eat, and they'd all curl up on her bed to sleep. They'd wait for this to be over and for Vater to return from the war, together and safe in their rooms. Then everything would return to normal. Except . . .

Mutti, she thought, and her eyes filled. Her legs went weak and she sat down hard on the curb. The buildings across the way seemed to waver, like they did in the summer when heat rose off the cobblestones. Except it wasn't summer. It was October. And it was raining. She put her head in her hands. Her chest felt heavy and her throat felt raw, as if she'd swallowed broken glass. Her temples pounded with each hard thud of her heart. She closed her eyes. She needed to rest. For just a minute. Then she'd be fine.

Suddenly remembering she hadn't eaten anything but a mouthful of bread since yesterday, she reached into the coat pocket for the bread from the dead woman's apartment. She unwrapped it and took a bite. This time it tasted like paper, and her teeth hurt when she chewed. Swallowing felt like razor blades going down her throat. She took another bite anyway. She had to keep up her strength. Then she coughed again. And again. And again. She couldn't stop. She spit out the bread, staggered to her feet, and bent over at the waist, gagging and trying to breathe. Panic exploded in her mind. She had to turn around. She had to go home. She had to get Ollie and Max out of the cubby.

Finally, after a few minutes of coughing so hard she thought she'd pass out, she could breathe again. She picked up Mutti's coat from the sidewalk, then half walked, half staggered to the other side of the street to avoid the collapsed man, and turned toward home. The only food she had was the Mellin's, the can of black-eyed peas, and the rest of the bread. It would have to do for now. Maybe she could go out again after she got some rest. Maybe things would get better in the meantime. Maybe people would stop dying and those left behind would come out of their homes.

It was a relief, in a way, to be going home, to know she would be letting her brothers out of the cubby. Her heart lurched when she pictured them, red-faced and crying in the dark space, scared and wondering where they were and what had happened. Would they ever forgive her for what she'd done? Would they remember tomorrow? She tried to walk faster.

Then something happened—she wasn't quite sure what. It seemed like she fell, except she was still upright. The world started to spin, around and around like a carousel. She crumpled to the ground in what seemed like slow motion and her cheek collided with the street, tiny stones and gravel cutting her skin. Pain exploded in her useless limbs; the muscles in her neck loosened and tightened as her lungs screamed for air. Terror twisted in her mind and dizziness overwhelmed her as she felt herself sinking deeper and deeper into darkness, suddenly blind, deaf, and mute. Her last thought was of Vater finding the twins in the cubby, their small white bodies skeletal and cold.

Then the world disappeared.

CHAPTER EIGHT

BERNICE

Clutching the twins in her arms, Bernice glanced over at their dead mother on the bed, a sliver of fear crawling up her spine. Had Mrs. Lange's eyelids been open a few minutes ago? Was she watching her? Bernice told herself to stop being silly, that she must have been imagining things. She took the twins out of the bedroom, laid them on the bed below the window, then closed the window and the bedroom door. As soon as she put the boys down, they started howling again, their faces trembling and red, their legs quivering.

Bernice yanked off her coat, threw it over a chair, and grabbed a clean washrag, diapers, and nightdresses from the clothesline. Working fast, she wet the washrag in a bucket, took off the boys' soiled clothes and diapers, and cleaned them up as best she could. They kept on crying.

"I know, I know," she said. "You're cold and hungry and scared. But you'll feel better in a minute, I promise."

After getting the boys dressed again, she sat between them on the bed and scooted back so she could lean against the wall. She moved the twins next to her, one on each side, then unbuttoned her blouse, pushed aside the frilly edge of her camisole, and lifted one of them to her engorged breast, his feet toward the wall. He nuzzled her areola, then stopped crying and latched on, nursing greedily. A sharp pain shot across her nipple and she arched her back, sucking air between her teeth, then lifted the other baby to her free breast. He immediately started drinking. After a few moments, the pain began to throb and ease, throb and ease, pulled from her body with every gush of her copious milk.

Tears spilled down her cheeks and she closed her eyes, fresh grief threatening to swallow her whole. Every ounce of her body ached for Wallis, for his small mouth at her nipple, his soft hand in hers as he nursed. It seemed like only yesterday she'd marveled at his tiny, perfect fingernails and pink skin, had stroked the downy hair on his small head. Now he was dead. Dead. He'd never drink her milk again. It felt like a knife in her chest.

Then she had another thought. Did babies nurse from their mothers in heaven? Would Wallis still need her when they were reunited in God's kingdom? She couldn't wait to find out, and prayed the day would come sooner rather than later. Then fear tightened her throat. She had cursed God so many times after her son died. Had almost killed herself. There was no guarantee she was bound for heaven now. She shook her aching head. No. She couldn't think that way. Knowing she would see Wallis again after she died was the only thing that kept her sane.

She opened her eyes and looked down at the twins, heartbroken that they weren't Wallis, at the same time astonished and grateful to be feeding these small strangers. Surely she was saving them from certain starvation. Surely God would look on it as a favorable act. Maybe He had allowed her to notice Pia on the street so He could lead her to the twins. Maybe He was giving her a chance to redeem herself, to prove she was a good Christian. Normally she hated when people said everything happened for a reason. Because what reason could there possibly be for her husband to be shot in the head during a war? What reason could there be for allowing Wallis, a perfectly innocent baby, to get sick and die? There were no reasons for such horrible things. But maybe, sometimes, good things did happen for a reason. Maybe she was meant to save these boys.

The twins were falling asleep, their mouths suckling slower and slower as exhaustion overtook them. With their light hair and pale skin, they reminded her so much of Wallis it filled her with agony. At the same time she loved swaddling and holding their little bodies, touching their baby-soft cheeks and velvety hair. They were beautiful babies, as close to perfect as she'd ever seen, besides Wallis, of course. You'd never know they were German. If she were being honest, it would have been a toss-up between them and her son if they'd been entered in the state fair "Better Baby" contest.

For the life of her, she'd never understand how Pia could have abandoned them. Even if she planned on coming back, clearly she was too young and irresponsible to take care of them properly. She had proved as much by putting them in the cubby in the first place, not to mention leaving them alone in there—in an unlocked apartment, no less! If Bernice hadn't found them, who knew what might have happened? Then she had another thought. Maybe losing her mother and being left to take care of her brothers had proved to be too much for Pia. Maybe she'd suffered a breakdown of some sort and hoped they wouldn't be found until she was long gone. Bernice had heard of husbands abandoning wives on their sickbeds, mothers abandoning sick children after being instructed by doctors to stop feeding them, and children leaving their doomed parents. But it was difficult for her to imagine anyone deserting innocent babies, for any reason. Then again, it seemed anything was possible in this day and age. Immigrants had taken over the city, and foreign languages could be heard throughout the streets. Her husband and son were gone, and the flu had become an epidemic, killing off the population of Philadelphia one by one by one. Everything was out of control, and she was helpless to change any of it.

Until now. She could right this grievous wrong.

It would be easy for her to pass the twins off as her own. And after everything she'd been through, no one could fault her for taking them. Their mother was dead, their sister had abandoned them, and the odds of their father returning from the war were poor. The newspaper listings of those killed in action, along with the new flu cases and deaths, had grown every day. Even if the twins had family back in Germany, it would be impossible to locate a relative in that war-torn country. She could take good care of the boys and, more importantly, bring them up properly, free from the sway of their barbaric, backward heritage.

When the twins finished nursing, she laid them on the bed and slid slowly off the mattress, careful not to wake them. If she was going to do this, she needed to hurry. She yanked the rest of the clean diapers and baby clothes off the clothesline, piled them on the table, then held her breath and went in the bedroom. Starting with the dresser and doing her best to pay no heed to Mrs. Lange, she searched for more baby clothes, but found none. Two small coats hung in the closet. She took them, and the rattles and bottles from the cubby, then hurried out of the room.

Back in the kitchen, she searched the cupboard and shelves for more bottles and food, but found nothing. Above the washbasin, a drawing of a blond girl holding hands with two little boys in a field of flowers hung on the wall. A yellow sun peeked out from behind puffy clouds and, in the bottom left-hand corner, careful cursive words that read:

To Ollie and Max. Love, your big sister, Pia

A stab of guilt twisted in Bernice's chest. Maybe Pia really was coming back. Maybe she'd left to get food and hadn't abandoned her brothers. Maybe, now that they were fed and dry, they'd be all right until she returned. Bernice chewed her lip, her hands in fists at her sides. Maybe she should leave the boys here. Maybe it wasn't her place to take them from their big sister. And what if their father returned from the war? She picked up her coat and started toward the door, then stopped. No, if Pia came back and found them gone, it would serve her right. They were just babies and never should have been left alone, no matter what. And they certainly shouldn't have been locked in that cold, dark cubby. It was horrible and cruel and neglectful. Bernice pressed her fingers over her temples, trying to decide what to do. Her head was pounding. Was she trying to justify taking them? No. That wasn't it. They never should have been abandoned. They needed her. And she needed them.

She turned around, put down her coat, and got back to work gathering the twins' things. Putting the soiled clothes and blankets in a sack and rinsing out the bottles from the cubby, her disgust and anger grew. Pia should have asked a neighbor for help or taken the boys to the Red Cross—anything but what she'd done. The babies deserved better.

Suddenly someone knocked on the front door. Bernice jumped and almost dropped a bottle.

"Hello?" a woman's muffled voice said. "Is anyone home?" She knocked again.

Bernice went rigid, her eyes fixed on the unlocked door. She glanced at the twins, praying they wouldn't wake up. The woman knocked again, louder this time. Bernice held her breath.

"I'm with the Visiting Nurse Society of Philadelphia," the woman said. "We're going door to door to see if anyone needs help. Are you in there?"

Then the handle turned and the door edged open. Bernice swore under her breath, put down the bottle, grabbed an apron hanging next to the washbasin, slipped it over her head, and rushed to the door, tying the apron strings behind her back. Only half pretending to be out of breath, she pulled the door open.

"I'm sorry," she said. "I was scrubbing the bedroom floor and didn't hear you knock."

The nurse gazed at Bernice, her chestnut eyes filled with concern above a gauze mask. Wearing a long, military-style jacket, hat, and high button-up boots, she carried what looked like a doctor's bag in one gloved hand. The edge of a dark skirt and white apron hung below her jacket hem.

"I'm sorry to interrupt you," the nurse said. "But how are you faring? Is anyone in your home sick?"

Bernice shook her head. "No."

"That's good to hear," the nurse said. "But if you want to stay well, you should always wear a mask when you answer the door."

Bernice nodded and pulled up the bottom of the apron she was wearing, holding it over her nose and mouth.

"And you really shouldn't leave your door unlocked," the nurse said.

"Oh. Yes, I know. I just came up from getting water and forgot."

The nurse peered over Bernice's shoulder, trying to see inside. "Do you have this apartment all to yourself?"

Unable to tell if the nurse could see the twins on the bed, Bernice said, "It's just me and my boys."

The nurse furrowed her brow and put a gloved hand over her mask. "Has someone passed in there?"

Bernice clenched her jaw, cursing silently. If she said no, the nurse might insist on coming inside to check. She looked down at the floor, trying to buy time, then sniffed and wiped her eyes. "Sadly, yes," she said, hoping she sounded sincere. "My beloved sister. We lost her a while ago, but I didn't know what to do with . . . with her. I've seen the men on the wagons gathering bodies, but I couldn't carry her outside by myself. And I couldn't leave the babies."

"I'm so sorry," the nurse said. "I'll send someone to pick up your sister as soon as I can."

Bernice started to say no, then realized it didn't matter. She'd be gone by the time someone came to get Mrs. Lange. "Thank you. I appreciate that more than you know."

"I'm here to help however I can," the nurse said. "How old are your sons?"

"Four months."

"Twins?"

"Yes, ma'am."

"And your husband? Is he in the military?"

Bernice nodded.

"Well, be sure to keep your boys at home until the worst of this is over," the nurse said. "And if you start feeling sick, let someone know. People are dying faster than we thought possible and I've found a number of children left to fend for themselves. You don't want that to happen to your boys. Just this morning I found a three-year-old who'd been alone in his apartment for several days. His parents passed and no one knew. He doesn't have the flu, but he was half-starved. Sadly, I'm not sure he's going to survive."

Bernice gasped, shocked by the knowledge that more babies were being left alone. It made her feel ill. "Oh my word," she said. "What are you doing with the children you find?" As soon as the words left her mouth, she berated herself for continuing the conversation. She needed the nurse to leave.

"We do what we can. First, we ask the neighbors if the family had any nearby relatives or close friends, someone who might be willing to take in the children. If no one can be found to take care of them, we take them to an orphanage. Unfortunately, the city's orphanages are getting overcrowded due to the epidemic."

Bernice shivered, remembering the stories her brother used to tell her about evil nuns and cold gruel in orphanages. "Oh dear," she said. "The poor things. Well, thank you again for stopping by."

"You're welcome," the nurse said. "Take care of yourself and those boys now. And stay inside until this is over, all right?"

Bernice nodded and the nurse turned to leave, giving her a friendly wave. Bernice closed the door and leaned against it, breathing a sigh of relief. She tried to remember everything she'd said and done, if somehow she'd given herself away or acted nervous. She didn't think she had. The nurse had no reason to suspect her, anyway. Still, she had to admit she was surprised by how easily she'd lied about being the twins' mother. But then again, she *was* their mother now, and mothers would do anything to protect their children, even lie, cheat, or steal. When her racing heart slowed, she went to the window and looked out, waiting for the nurse to leave the building. After what seemed like forever, the nurse skittered down the steps, hurried along the alley, and disappeared into the next row house. Bernice watched for another minute to make sure the nurse wasn't coming out again and Pia wasn't on her way back, then quickly gathered the twins' belongings and put them in the center of a blanket on the floor. When she was certain she had everything, she tied the corners of the blanket together to make a sack, then stood over the boys on the bed.

"Now, which one of you is Ollie and which one is Max?" she said in a quiet voice. Then she waited for a sign, for one of the twins to move or make a noise. Whoever stirred first, she decided, was Ollie. But they kept on sleeping, the only movement the rise and fall of their tiny chests. "Well, it doesn't matter. I'm giving you new names, anyway."

She thought about looking in on Mrs. Lange one last time, to tell her she'd take good care of the babies and maybe say a prayer for her. Knowing how devastated she would have been if someone had taken Wallis, it felt like the right thing to do. Then she remembered Mrs. Lange was German—who knew what strange religion she followed, if any. Not to mention Mr. Lange had stolen Bernice's father's job. He might as well have killed him with his bare hands. And the twins would have died if Bernice hadn't found them. Now they would have a loving home and caring mother who would bring them up right and teach them the American way. She didn't owe Mrs. Lange an apology or a promise or a prayer. If anything, Mrs. Lange should be grateful she was willing to take in her sons. A lesser person would have left them to starve.

With a baby boy on each hip and the makeshift sack of diapers and clothes and bottles tied around her shoulders, Bernice huffed up the last flight of stairs to her apartment, sweat covering her face and running down her back. More than anything she wanted to stop and take off her coat, but she needed to get inside her apartment before someone saw her. With every step the boys felt heavier, the loaded sack ready to topple her backward down the steps. When she reached the top, she stood for a second to rest, then trudged down the hall to her door, her muscles throbbing. The twins, silent and teary-eyed, looked around in bewilderment, too weary and frightened to protest or cry.

"Don't worry," she whispered to them. "You're going to be just fine. Better than fine, now that you're with me."

Then she remembered her key was in her coat pocket. In order to retrieve it, she'd need to put down one of the twins. Silently scolding herself for not carrying the key in her hand, she bent over and gently placed one of the boys on the floor, on his back. He looked up at her and blinked, then started to cry.

"I know, I know," she whispered. "I'm hurrying as fast as I can."

When she found the key, she put it in the lock, opened the door, and put the other boy inside on the rug. Like his brother, he immediately began to fuss.

"Shhh," she said. "We're almost there." She let the sack slide off her shoulders onto the floor, then stepped back into the hall to retrieve the first boy. When she picked him up, he stopped crying. She started to go back inside, then froze. Someone was at the top of the stairs.

It was the nurse who had stopped by the Langes' apartment.

"What's going on here?" the nurse said, and headed toward her.

Bernice hurried the rest of the way back inside and started to close the door with her free hand, but the nurse put her foot against it.

"What are you doing over here?" the nurse said, holding the door open with her arm and leg. "I thought we agreed it was too dangerous to take your sons out."

Bernice released the door. "Oh, it's you," she said, pretending to be surprised and praying the nurse couldn't see the panic in her eyes. "You scared the daylights out of me. I'm checking on a friend. I know it's not safe, but I made a promise."

Hearing his brother crying inside the apartment, the twin in her arms started to whimper.

The nurse set down her bag and offered to take him. "Here," she said. "Let me help you."

Bernice turned to one side, pulling him out of her reach. "No," she said, louder than she intended. "I can manage."

The nurse furrowed her brow. "Are you sure you're feeling all right? Your face is quite flushed."

"Yes, I'm fine," Bernice said. "I'm just overheated from carrying the boys up the stairs. Now, if you don't mind, I need to . . ."

The nurse looked past her with narrowed eyes. "Is there a dead body in there?"

Bernice took a step back and started to close the door again, but the heel of her boot caught on the makeshift sack of baby clothes and, thinking she'd stepped on the other boy, she overcorrected, lost her balance, and started to fall. The nurse leapt forward to catch the baby before she dropped him. But Bernice grabbed the door with her free hand, catching herself, and pulled him out of her reach again. She tried to block her from entering but it was too late. The nurse was inside.

Before Bernice could react, the nurse picked up the twin on the rug and gently bounced him up and down, patting his back, her eyes scanning the room. When she saw Wallis's crib in the corner, she started toward it. "Whose child is this?" she said.

Bernice swallowed the sour taste of fear in the back of her

throat. "It's my friend's baby. I tried to convince her to take him to the funeral home, but she refused. He was her only child and she's extremely distraught. Understandably, of course. That's why I promised to stop by again, to make sure she was all right."

The nurse looked in the crib, then turned back to Bernice. "Oh, the poor dear," she said. "Perhaps I can help. Where is she?"

Bernice glanced at the closed bedroom door. "She must be sleeping. I don't want to wake her."

"I thought you came over here to check on her? How can you find out if she's all right if you don't go in there?"

"I will," Bernice said. "It's just—"

"Why don't you take your boys back home and let me take care of your friend," the nurse said. She moved the twin, who had fallen asleep on her shoulder, to the cradle of her arm, and gazed down at him. Then she looked up at Bernice, her eyes smiling. "That's what I'm here for, remember?"

Bernice shook her head. "Thank you, but I made a promise and I intend to keep it."

"All right," the nurse said. "Then I'll watch the babies while you check on her." She unbuttoned her jacket, shrugged it off one shoulder, switched the sleeping twin to her other arm, let the jacket fall to the floor, then lay him on top of it. When she straightened, she reached for the other twin.

Bernice's heart beat so hard and loud she swore the nurse could hear it. What could she say to make the nosy nurse leave? Nothing came to her. If she tried to kick her out, she'd wonder why. Even if she could force her out, she might come back with the police. Then who knew what would happen. But what if she went into the bedroom and saw the empty bed? What if she insisted on helping her back to the Langes' apartment after she checked on her "friend"? Playing along was Bernice's only choice. She handed the other baby to the nurse, took off her coat, and hung it over a chair. A frantic trembling came from somewhere deep inside her body, as if she'd eaten spoiled food.

The nurse slowly strolled around the room, patting the other twin's back and trying to get him to sleep. "Go ahead," she said to Bernice. "We'll be fine." Then she stopped at the table to look at the photographs on the shelf above it—the only two pictures Bernice owned, one of her and her husband on their wedding day, him in a chair and her standing with one hand on his shoulder, and one of her holding Wallis in his christening gown.

Sweat broke out on Bernice's upper lip. "After he falls asleep you can go," she said, trying to distract her. "I'm sure there are other people who need you more than we do."

"I don't mind," the nurse said, still studying the pictures. After what seemed like forever, she turned, confusion lining her brow. "You and the woman in these photographs bear an awfully strong resemblance to each other."

Bernice dug her nails into her palms. "I know," she said. "Everyone says my sister and I look like twins."

The nurse's brows shot up. "Are you saying this is your sister's apartment?"

Silently cursing herself, Bernice nodded.

"I thought you were checking on a friend?" the nurse said.

Bernice made her eyes go wide. "Is that what I said?" She put a hand to her chest, feigning embarrassment. "Good heavens. I must be having the vapors. After everything that's been happening I can't seem to think straight. I meant to say I was checking on my sister."

The nurse's forehead furrowed. "But you said your sister was dead. I was going to send someone to your apartment to pick up her body, remember?" She glanced at the makeshift sack Bernice had tripped over, and the folded diapers and baby nightdresses spilling out onto the floor. "And why did you bring clothes and diapers with you if you're only staying long enough to check on someone?"

Bernice clenched her jaw, the deep trembling of fear turning into shakes of anger. This nosy nurse needed to leave. Where was she when Wallis got sick? Where was she when he couldn't breathe? No nurse came around to help then. No nurse knocked on her door to offer medicine or comfort or advice then. No nurse stopped by to ask how they were faring. "I have more than one sister," Bernice said, struggling to conceal her frustration. "And I brought extra diapers in case she needed me to stay longer than I planned."

The nurse looked doubtful. "Why don't you see if your sister is awake?" she said. "I'd like to talk to her, if she doesn't mind." The baby in her arms had fallen asleep, so she laid him on the jacket with his brother, then regarded Bernice with suspicion. "I'll wait."

Shaken into silence by rage and fear, Bernice turned and went over to the bedroom door. She rapped on it lightly as if someone were inside, then opened it and went in. She had to get rid of the nurse but had no idea how. She closed the door and sat on her bed, making the rusty springs creak. She froze with the sound, certain the nurse could hear everything. Then she had an idea.

"How are you feeling?" she said quietly.

She lowered her voice and mumbled, "Tired."

"There's a nurse here. She wants to talk to you."

She groaned and, in the low voice, said, "Send her away. I don't want to see anyone."

"Are you sure? Maybe it would help."

"I don't need help," she said, pretending to weep. "I need my baby."

"I know. I'm sorry."

She moved on the mattress to make the springs creak again, as if someone was rolling over or sitting up, then said in a frightened voice, "Don't let her take him. I need him here, just a little while longer."

"I won't, I promise," Bernice said. "Why don't you rest while I make you something to eat?"

"I'm not hungry."

"But you need to keep up your strength. I'll wake you when the food is ready."

After a moment, she stood, ran her clammy hands over her skirt, raked her fingers through her hair, and prayed the nurse believed her little act. If the nurse insisted on seeing for herself that someone else was in the bedroom, Bernice would have to come up with another excuse. She had no idea what the excuse would be, but no matter what, she wasn't going to lose the twins because of some nosy nurse who couldn't mind her own business.

She took a deep breath and let it out slowly, then backed out of the bedroom, quietly closed the door, and turned to face the woman. To her surprise, the nurse was holding herself up with both hands on the kitchen table, her face blotchy, her lips blue. Her throat rattled as she gasped for air and stared at Bernice with frightened eyes.

"I'm having trouble breathing," the nurse said. "I think I'm getting sick." She pulled out a kitchen chair and sat down hard.

A strange mixture of relief and panic swept over Bernice. The nurse didn't care who was in the bedroom anymore. She didn't care about anything but surviving the flu. But she couldn't die here. "You need to leave," Bernice said.

The nurse put her head in her hands. "I know. I'll go. But I . . . please . . . I just need a few minutes." She started to cough. "I need something to drink. Please. I don't care what."

Cursing under her breath, Bernice took a glass from the shelf and turned toward the washbasin.

"Please hurry," the nurse said behind her.

If giving the nurse a drink would make her leave, Bernice was glad to do it. She felt bad for her, of course; she clearly had the flu and might die. And maybe she had a husband and children at home. But Bernice had her own problems. The last thing she needed was someone meddling in her affairs or dying in her apartment. Then alarms sounded in her head. What if the nurse left and sent someone else back to check on them? What if she sent someone to the Langes' and they found Pia there, distraught and looking for her missing brothers? They might put two and two together and discover what Bernice had done. She started to fill the glass, frantic and trying to figure out what to do, then noticed the container of rat poison on the cupboard below the washbasin. And her half-empty teacup from earlier that morning sitting next to the basin. "I'm out of clean water," she said. "Would a little cold tea help?"

"Anything," the nurse said. "Please. My throat . . ." She coughed, hard and loud. "It's burning."

Bernice glanced over her shoulder at the nurse. She was still sitting with her head down, trying to stifle her cough. She seemed dreadfully sick. Sometimes people died within a few hours of contracting the flu; there was no harm helping it along. Bernice sprinkled a little rat poison in the teacup, put the container in the cupboard again, gave the tea a good stir, and delivered it to the nurse.

The nurse took it with shaking hands and drank it down. "Thank you," she said, gasping.

"You're welcome," Bernice said, and stepped back.

The nurse pushed herself up from the table, then sank back down in the chair again. "Oh my word," she said. Her eyes, frightened and staring, turned red at the rims. The skin on her face started to turn blue. She tried to stand. Her legs gave out and she collapsed on the floor, hitting her head hard on the wood. Bernice had no idea if rat poison worked that quickly or if the nurse was overcome by the flu, but she told herself it was the latter. Surely the poison didn't help, but Bernice wouldn't take the blame. The nurse was going to die anyway. Bernice had to do what was best for the twins. That was all that mattered now.

The nurse gaped up at her, clawing at her throat, her mouth open, sucking in air. Bernice stepped around her, picked up the teacup, rinsed it out, put it next to the washbasin, and went over to the twins. Trying not to wake them, she knelt and picked them up. They squirmed and opened their eyes but didn't cry. She carried them into the bedroom, laid them on their stomachs on her bed, closed the door, and covered them with a blanket. Then she sat on the edge of the mattress and rubbed their backs, humming softly. One of the boys turned on his side and looked up at her, his small forehead furrowed. In the other room, the nurse went on coughing and choking.

"It's all right," Bernice said in a quiet voice. "I'm right here. Now be a good boy and go back to sleep. I'll feed you supper soon."

Rubbing the boys' backs, she softly sang Wallis's favorite song, "Row, Row, Row Your Boat" over and over and over. Finally, the twin who'd been wide-awake turned on his side, his watery blue eyes slowly closing. The other lay sound asleep, his mouth half-open, spit bubbles forming on his lips.

When both boys were napping again, Bernice kissed their heads, got up, and stood over the bed. While putting them to sleep, she'd come to the realization that everyone in the building had seen Wallis and knew she had one son, not two. More than likely some of her neighbors knew Mrs. Lange also, and if and when the epidemic came to an end, they would recognize the twins. If she was going to keep the boys, there was only one way to protect her new family. They had to leave. And soon.

But before she could decide how to proceed, she needed to get organized. And she needed to eat. For the first time since Wallis passed away, she was genuinely hungry. She tiptoed out of the bedroom and quietly closed the door.

The nurse still lay on the floor next to the table, her breathing shallow and fast. Blood dripped from her mouth and nose. She gaped up at Bernice with wide, terror-filled eyes and croaked, "Help me."

"I'm sorry," Bernice said. "But I can't. You shouldn't have come in here."

Moving the scattered diapers and baby clothes she'd taken from the Langes' apartment out of the way, she opened the front door and looked left and right. The neighbors' doors were closed. No one peered out to see what was going on. No one clambered up the stairs. She grabbed the nurse's bag, brought it inside, and locked the door. Then she went to the larder, found a leftover piece of cooked bacon, sat down at the table, and ate it. When she was done, she wiped her hands on Mrs. Lange's apron, having forgotten she was still wearing it until now. Then she went over to the nurse, who was barely conscious, knelt at her feet, and started taking off her boots.

CHAPTER NINE

PIA

At first, Pia became aware of a thin line of pale light seeping under her eyelids and a high-pitched ringing in her ears. Her body felt bruised and beaten, her arms and legs immobile, her head split open. She tried opening her eyes all the way, but her lids felt stuck together, as if someone had covered them with glue. Then she realized she was lying on something hard. Not her mattress. Her bed at home was soft, with random lumps of knotted horsehair. Her throbbing head rested on a pillow, but whatever she was lying on was stiff and narrow, like a board against her hips and back. The outside of her right shoulder pressed against another board, and so did the bottoms of her bare feet.

She was in a casket.

Terror plowed through her and she tried to scream. Nothing but a dry squeak came from her throat. She thrust her hands up to push against the casket lid, certain she was on the edge of madness, but her trembling arms flailed in open air. She scraped the hard crust from her eyes and forced them open, squinting against a blurry, bright light. At first she thought she'd gone blind, confused because she'd always imagined blindness to be dark, not light. Then a curved ceiling slowly came into focus, soaring above her like an alabaster sky. Was she awake at her own funeral? Was she about to see someone looking down at her as she lay in an open casket for one final goodbye?

She lifted her arms to look at her hands. They seemed to float, ghost white, against the alabaster ceiling. Blood caked her finger-nails and knuckles. Then she noticed her heart, thundering in her chest. If she were dead, it wouldn't be beating. If she were dead, her pain would be gone, not leaking out of her like a bad smell. She opened her mouth and took a deep breath. Her lungs felt like they were on fire. Then she started to cough, every bark like a knife in her ribs. Her throat involuntarily opened and her lungs desperately sucked in air, then forced it out again and again and again until she nearly choked. When she could breathe again without coughing, she held a hand over her mouth, a flood of relief washing through her. She was alive.

She struggled to push herself up on her elbows, but her arms gave way and she collapsed back on the pillow. She turned her head to look around, taking slow, shallow breaths so she wouldn't start coughing again. A piece of painted wood blocked her view on one side, and a white sheet hung above that, like a curtain. She turned the other way. A second sheet hung on the other side, reaching down to the floor. A water pitcher, a drinking glass, and an enamel basin sat on a stool between her and the second sheet. She lifted her head and gazed down at herself. A thin blanket mottled with brown spots covered her from the waist down, and dark stains peppered the front of her white nightdress. Her feet rested against a narrow footboard, above which more white sheets hung a few feet away, like a line of sideways flags. Above them, a row of arched, stained-glass windows stretched toward the ceiling. It all looked familiar and strange at the same time, like she'd visited it in a dream or another lifetime. Then it came to her.

She was in a church. And she was lying inside a box pew.

But how did she get there? And why?

Finally, her thrashing heart slowed, and the ringing in her ears disappeared. Mumbled words and low groans filled the air, like the distant moans and shouts of injured miners returning home after a cave-in. Somewhere, a woman was crying. A person nearby gasped for air, each breath gurgling like a clogged gutter. It seemed to be coming from the other side of the curtain. Then the sweet, sickening smell of rotting flesh filled her nostrils and she remembered.

People were dying of the flu.

Mutti was dead.

And Ollie and Max were shut in the bedroom cubby.

She bolted upright and yanked off the blanket, a flood of panic filling her with a sudden surge of strength. She had to get out of there and go home. She had to get back to her brothers. Then she turned to drop her feet off the edge of the pew and her head swam, dark and heavy, nearly toppling her. She closed her eyes, gripped the edge of the seat with both hands, and took a deep breath, clenching her teeth against the pain in every inch of her body. When she felt steady enough to open her eyes again, she pushed herself up on quivering arms. Her chest felt like stone, her legs like jelly. She wiped the sweat from her upper lip with the back of her wrist and started out of the box pew.

Patients on cots lined the center aisle of the church, their faces blue and bleeding. A nurse wearing a gauze mask and bloodstained apron and shoes tied a brown tag to a man's toe, despite the fact that he was still gasping for air. Another nurse wound him in a sheet. The next patient called out for help, blood gushing from her open mouth. She, too, had a toe tag. Pia gazed down the line at the scores of patients, alive and dead, all wrapped in winding sheets, some still writhing in pain, all with tags dangling from their toes like holiday gift cards. The overwhelming sensation of being surrounded by the dead and dying was almost too much to bear. It felt like a boulder in the middle of her chest, crushing her lungs, like the sensation she'd had at the Liberty Loan parade, except a thousand times worse. She looked down at her feet. A brown tag hung from her big toe. She bent over to yank if off but stumbled sideways and fell, hitting the floor with a bone-jarring thud, the wind knocked from her lungs. She didn't think she could get back up. Slowly she pushed herself into a sitting position, trying to ignore the pain in her elbow and hip, and yanked off the tag. Another wave of dizziness hit her and she put her head in her hands, praying for the feeling to pass. Every second it took her to get out of there and go home was another sec-

ond in the cubby for Ollie and Max. She had to get back to them.
She had to get back to them now. After what seemed like forever,
the world stopped spinning. She reached for the arm of the pew
and pulled herself up, determined not to let anything stop her, not
even the flu.

"What on earth are you doing?" a female voice said. "Get back
in bed this instant."

A nurse in a blood-spattered apron and a white mask rushed
into the box pew and steered her back to the makeshift bed. Pia
tried to resist, but it was no use. She was too weak. Her muscles
quivered and her lungs ached with each labored breath. Maybe if
she lay down again for just a little while longer, her strength would
return. Maybe the nurse would give her something to eat—a biscuit
or some soup, something to give her a little energy. Then she would
go home to Ollie and Max. They had to be so scared and hungry.
Just thinking about them in the cubby made her knees give out.

Somewhere in the back of her mind, as the nurse guided her
back down on the pillow, she realized that the part of her that
dreaded another person's touch seemed to have disappeared. Either
that or it was masked by her own suffering.

She tried to speak. "I have to go home," she said, her voice hoarse
and raspy. "My brothers are—"

"You're not going anywhere," the nurse said. "You're not well."
She covered Pia with the blanket.

"Where am I?"

"You're in St. Peter's Church. The hospitals are full. Now what's
your name?"

"Pia Lange."

"And how old are you?"

"Thirteen."

"Well, Pia, the undertakers found you on Lombard Street. They
thought you were dead, but you started moaning and thrashing
about. You're lucky they brought you here instead of throwing you
on the wagon with the corpses. They saved your life. But you need
to stay in bed."

Pia tried to sit up again but couldn't. "You don't understand,"
she said. "I need to get back to my brothers. They're all alone!"

"Shh," the nurse said. "I'm sure your brothers are fine. Right now you need to calm down and do as I say." She picked up the water pitcher, filled the glass, and helped Pia lift her head to take a drink. Pia took several big sips—she hadn't realized how thirsty she was until the cool water soothed her parched throat. Then she lay back down, her arms and legs shaking.

"But Ollie and Max are only four months old," she said. Her teeth chattered and her voice trembled. "My father is in the army and my mother died and I . . ." The words caught in her throat and she couldn't go on. Her mind screamed at her to get up and leave, to push the nurse out of the way and run out of the church. But she couldn't find the strength to sit up again, let alone stand or run. Her body felt strange and thick and heavy, like it belonged to someone else.

The nurse pulled the blanket up under her chin. "There, there," she said. "I know you're scared and upset. But I think you're going to be all right. You've made it through the worst of it. Not everyone has been so lucky." She took a wet rag from the enamel basin, wrung it out, and dabbed the sweat from Pia's forehead.

"What do you mean I made it through the worst of it?" Pia said. "How long have I been here?"

"Six days."

Pia drew in a sharp breath, her panic turning into horror. "No," she cried. "That can't be. I . . ." She tried to get up again, triggering another coughing fit, each forceful hack jolting her body like a plank of wood slammed against her back. When it was over, she collapsed on the pew, exhausted and shaking.

The nurse looked at her with pity-filled eyes. "I'm afraid it is, sweetheart. I know because I've been taking care of you since they brought you in. Now, please, do as I say or you're going to get worse again."

"No," she cried. "I have to go home. I have to help my brothers!"

"I'm sorry," the nurse said. "But you can't leave yet. You're still sick."

Pia rolled on her side, her stomach twisting and dry heaving. Nothing came up but bloody mucus and bile. The thought of Ollie and Max trapped in the cubby, probably dying, with no one to hold and comfort them, no one to wrap them in a warm blanket or kiss their cheeks and tell them everything was going to be all right, was more than she could bear. She wished the undertakers had let her die.

The nurse rubbed her back and shoulder. "Oh dear," she said. "Try to calm down and breathe normally. You're getting yourself all upset and it's not good for you. I'm sure your neighbors are taking care of your brothers. Or maybe one of the visiting nurses picked them up. Either way, I'm sure they'll be fine."

Pia swallowed over and over, trying to stop gagging and coughing. When she could finally speak again, she said, "What . . . what nurses?"

"The Visiting Nurse Society sent people into the city to see if they can help citizens in their homes. Trained nurses, nursing students, anyone who has ever acted as a caregiver, really, has been called to service. I'm sure they'll take care of your brothers." She paused, her eyes growing glassy. "Don't worry, sweetheart. This will all be over soon, then you can go home and—"

Dizziness descended on Pia again. "But . . . but you don't understand. I . . . I . . ."

"You what?" the nurse said in a gentle voice.

Pia struggled to speak without retching. "They're . . . they're in my parents' bedroom. We ran out of food and I . . . I left to find them something to eat. I put them . . . I put them . . ." A sob escaped her throat and she couldn't finish.

The nurse's eyes widened slightly, but her expression remained calm and professional. "Try not to worry. I'm sure someone found them."

Pia buried her face in her hands, shoulders convulsing. Why hadn't she taken Ollie and Max with her when she went to look for food? Why hadn't she put them in their buggy or strapped them to her hips with a scarf or blanket—anything to keep them safe? Then, when she collapsed, the undertakers would have found them and at least they would be alive. No matter what happened after that, or where they were taken, at least they wouldn't have starved to death in a dark cubby, cold and alone and terrified.

Oh God! What have I done?

She dragged her hands from her face and gaped at the nurse, more desperate than she'd ever felt in her life. If something happened to Ollie and Max, she'd never forgive herself. "Do you think there's a chance they're still alive? After six days? Do you think they might have survived? Please, I'm begging you. Tell me yes. Please."

The shadow of understanding darkened the nurse's features, but she kept her composure. "Like I said, I'm sure they're fine," she said. "Someone is probably taking good care of them as we speak."

"Can you send someone to 408 Shunk Alley, apartment 4C?" Pia reached under the blanket with trembling fingers, searching for her dress pocket. "I'll give you the key. Please, you have to help them." But her pocket was gone. Then she remembered she was in a nightdress.

"Where's my dress?" she cried. "What did you do with it?"

"We had to get rid of it. I'm sorry, but it was filthy and—"

"But the key. It was in my pocket. How will anyone get inside without the . . ." Then she remembered. She'd run out the door because her brothers had been crying. She'd run out the door. And she never locked it. Her head started spinning again. She moaned and fell back on the bed. "The door is unlocked," she said. "Please, send someone, anyone. I need to know if . . . if . . ."

"Everything is going to be all right," the nurse said. "Don't you see? It's a good thing the door was unlocked so one of your neighbors could go in and get your brothers."

"No, please. They won't know where to look. You have to send someone. You have to tell them—"

"All right, all right," the nurse said. "I'll see what I can do. If I can't find anyone to go, I'll do it myself when my shift is over. But please, in the meantime you need to rest."

"You . . . you would do that for me?"

"Of course," the nurse said, giving her a slight smile. "I have a little brother too. His name is Johnny."

Pia tried to return the smile to show her gratitude but felt herself slipping away, her strength and emotions spent. "Thank you," she said in a weak voice.

"You're welcome," the nurse said. "Now get some sleep. It's the best thing for you."

Pia closed her eyes, but didn't think she could sleep. Part of her wanted to lose consciousness, to tumble into complete unawareness, to escape the mind-numbing horror of what she'd done. The other part begged God for the strength to get up and run home, to save her brothers before it was too late. Then she had another thought. What if the nurse had told her what she wanted to hear so she'd stop begging for help? What if she said she'd send someone to check on the twins just so she'd rest? More than anything, Pia wanted to make her promise she'd go to the apartment, but she couldn't find the will to ask.

"If they move you into recovery and I'm not there when you wake up," the nurse said in a soft voice, "my name's Carla. Carla Miller." Then she put a hand on Pia's forearm and gave it a little squeeze.

This time, Pia's chest constricted at the woman's touch, but it was hard to tell if the pain was coming from the nurse or her own struggling lungs. Then Carla removed her hand and the sensation disappeared.

If she was going to help Ollie and Max, she had to do it soon.

Red and yellow leaves swirled against the backdrop of a baby-blue sky outside the window, falling past the glass in what seemed like slow motion. Relief fell over Pia like a soft blanket, and she closed her eyes again. She was home in bed, tucked under the window in her family's snug rooms. It had been nothing but a bad dream—chasing Mutti through the crowded sidewalks at the Liberty Loan parade, losing her to the flu, leaving the twins. Then bits and pieces flickered in her mind like a slow-motion picture show— vague memories of sponge baths and people standing over her, of nurses wiping her brow and spoonfuls of broth, of fevers and toe tags and blood. She opened her eyes again and looked down at herself, her heart racing. She was still wearing a hospital gown, and a white blanket covered her from the waist down. The stench of human sweat, urine, and vomit filled her nostrils. She bolted upright and looked around.

She was on a low cot in a dim, stone-walled room lined with bookshelves and framed photographs of priests, churches, and groups of smiling nuns. A wooden cross hung between a second window and an arched door with a wrought-iron latch. Scattered around the room like playing cards, men, women, and children lay on cots beneath white sheets, either asleep or unconscious, she couldn't tell which. An elderly man with a grizzled beard snored next to her on his cot, his thin-lipped mouth open wide. Opposite her, a boy of about fifteen rested on his side with his hands tucked beneath his pillow. On the other side of the boy, a woman with snarled hair and black rings under her eyes wept in a fetal position, her sheet bunched in her hands.

A cold eddy of fear opened up in Pia's chest. How much time had passed since she'd woken up in the box pew and asked Nurse Carla to help Ollie and Max? Had it been ten minutes or ten days? She swung her legs over the edge of the cot, wrapped the sheet around her shoulders, and pushed herself up. Her ribs were sore from coughing, but she could breathe without pain. She took a small step, testing her legs. Her muscles felt weak, but they held her up.

She started to take another step, but the door latch rattled and clunked, and a nun wearing a mask came into the room. Pia went back to her cot and sat down. The nun pushed the door shut, then surveyed the patients, a ring of iron keys dangling from her hand. When she saw Pia sitting up, she made her way toward her, winding her way through the cots. Pia's heart beat faster. Maybe the nun had news about her brothers.

The woman with the snarled hair grabbed the nun's habit as she passed. "Help me," she cried. "Please!"

The nun stopped and turned toward her, gently pulling her habit from the woman's grip. "What is it, dear?" she said. "What do you need?"

"I can't find my daughter," the woman said. "I brought her here with a fever. Then I got sick and now I don't know where she is."

The nun looked around. "She's not in this room?"

The woman shook her head violently. "No," she wailed. "I've already lost my mother, my sister, and two nieces. My daughter is all I have left. You have to help me find her!"

The nun crossed herself and put a hand on the woman's head.

"I'm sorry, dear, but only those recovering are being kept here in the parish house."

The woman screamed and collapsed back on the bed, her fingers like claws over her face.

The nun crossed herself again. "May the Lord give you strength, dear," she said, "and bless and keep you. I'm sure there's a special jeweled crown waiting for your family in heaven. I'll pray for you. And your daughter too." Then she left the sobbing woman and approached Pia. "I'm glad to see you're awake, my child. How are you feeling?" Her brown eyes looked weary above her mask.

Pia swallowed and tried to find her voice. "Much better. I'm sure I'm strong enough to go home now."

"That's good to hear," the nun said. "Because we'd already decided you were probably well enough to leave. Truth be told, we need to make room for more patients."

One of the other patients stirred and moaned, the white sheet over their cot flailing like a restless ghost. The boy opposite her opened his eyes and blinked, then gazed at her and the nun, watching silently, his face pale and drawn. He reminded her of Finn. And Ollie and Max. Her chest tightened.

"How long have I been here?" she said.

"Two days," the nun said.

Pia gripped the edge of the cot, bile surging in her throat. *Eight days.* Ollie and Max never could have survived eight days without food and water. She clenched her jaw, trying to control the dizzying wave of nausea that swept over her. If the nun thought she was still sick, she might make her stay longer.

"There was a nurse," she said, doing her best to keep her voice steady. "Her name was Carla. She promised to check on someone for me."

The nun furrowed her brow. "I'm sorry to have to tell you this, my child," she said. "But Nurse Carla, bless her sweet soul, went to be with our Lord two days ago."

Pia blinked back a flood of tears. "Do you know if she found my brothers?"

The nun shook her head. "I'm afraid she didn't say anything about that. Her passing was rather sudden, as happens in some cases. Now, please, lie down and rest. You've got to keep up your strength for the days ahead."

Pia's vision began to close in on her, like a curtain being drawn. Fighting against it, she struggled to stay upright, again wishing the flu had taken her so she wouldn't have to face this horror. Maybe surviving was her punishment. She wanted to scream and throw up and die, but she couldn't let the nun see her distress. She had to go home to Ollie and Max, to see if they were . . . if they were . . . She couldn't finish the thought. It was too horrible, too dreadful to even consider. She had to get back to them. She had to hold them in her arms. She had to kiss their small faces. If her worst fears were true, she had to make sure that their bodies, and Mutti's, were taken care of properly. She owed them that much, at least. After that, she didn't care what happened to her.

"Mother Joe has sent someone to collect you," the nun continued. "I must say, it's not an easy feat to find someone willing to travel about the city these days. And because a number of our nuns have gone to the West Philadelphia Home for Backward Children to care for the youngsters there after the staff fled, we don't have anyone to spare. But as usual, with God's help, Mother Joe seems to manage the impossible."

Pia wiped her brow with a trembling hand. "I don't need anyone to pick me up," she said. "I know my way home."

The nun frowned, her mask crinkling below pity-filled eyes. "I'm sorry, my child," she said. "But you're not going home. We're sending you to St. Vincent's Orphan Asylum. The city's orphanages have been flooded since the outbreak, so you should thank the good Lord they're willing to take you in."

The blood drained from Pia's face. "No," she said. "I'm not going there. I'm going home. I have to go home."

"I'm afraid that's impossible," the nun said. "Before she passed, Nurse Carla made a note about your mother succumbing to the flu and your father being overseas. You have our deepest sympathies, dear, but you can't go home."

"But my father might have returned while I was here," Pia said. "He's probably looking for me right now. And . . ." She dropped her eyes to the floor, her chin trembling. What if Vater had found Ollie and Max? What if they were alive and well, wondering what had happened to her? Or what if he opened the cubby and found them . . . She couldn't say it. Either way, how would she ever face him again? He'd never forgive her for what she'd done. And she wouldn't blame him. "Please, I'm begging you. Let me go home. My brothers need me."

"I'm sorry, but the decision has been made," the nun said. "I'm sure someone is looking after your brothers, a neighbor perhaps, and there's no telling when, or if, your father will return. We can't let you end up on the streets. It wouldn't be right."

"But I have relatives in New York," Pia said. "If you send them a telegram, I'm sure they'll take me in." She wasn't sure of anything, but she had to try.

"Do you know their address?"

Pia tried to picture the return address on the envelopes from her aunt and uncle. It had been a while since they'd heard from them, so only part of it came to her. "It's Mr. and Mrs. Hugi Lange, Orchard Street, New York, New York."

The nun creased her brow. "I don't think that's enough information, but I'll see what I can do. In the meantime, I'll bring you something to eat. Then, like it or not, you'll be sent to St. Vincent's straightaway."

"Don't you need to write it down?" Pia said.

"Write what down, my child?"

"The address."

"Oh. Yes. I mean, no, I'll remember it."

Pia didn't believe her, and she couldn't understand why she wasn't more willing to help. "I'm their niece. I'm sure they'll take me in."

The nun suddenly seemed very tall, a black statue in the murky room with her veil adding a few inches to her height. She stared down at her, rolling the key ring back and forth between her finger and thumb. "Being sent to St. Vincent's is going to be difficult," she said. "But it's for the best. It might not feel that way right now, but some day you'll thank us. They'll take good care of you there. And

I'll pray for you, my child. May the Lord give you strength, and bless you and keep you." Before Pia could respond, she turned and left the room, locking the massive door behind her.

Pia felt like she was suffocating. Panic squeezed the air from her chest. The smell of urine and vomit stung her nose, and the grieving woman's sobs grated in her ears. She gazed up at the window, her only chance for escape. A thick grid of painted wood separated the glass into separate panes, and the window was fixed into the stone wall. There was no way to open or break it. She lay down on the cot, turned toward the cold wall, and covered up with the sheet. She had to come up with a plan to get out of there, and soon. After a few minutes of coming up with impossible ideas that wouldn't work, she turned over to look at the boy on the bed. Maybe he could help her. Maybe she could tell him her story, part of it, anyway, and when the nun came back, he could distract her so Pia could run out the door. Surely he'd understand why she didn't want to go to an orphanage.

She started to get up, to reach over and wake him, but the key rattled in the lock and the door opened. It was the nun again, with a curly-haired woman in a black hat and patched coat. The woman regarded Pia and the other patients with owlish eyes, one hand clasped over her gauze mask, the other carrying a gunnysack.

The nun shut the door and locked it, slipped the key ring beneath her scapular, and started toward Pia. "There's no need to be afraid," she said to the woman. "Everyone here has recovered from the flu."

Looking around, the woman followed on high alert, as if someone might attack her at any second. When they reached Pia's cot, she stood off to the side, several steps behind the nun. Soot and dried mud covered her boots, and the brim of her hat was ripped and ragged.

"Miss O'Malley arrived sooner than I expected," the nun said. "So I'm afraid we won't have time to feed you before you go."

Pia didn't care about being fed. She wouldn't have been able to eat, anyway. "What about the telegram you were going to send to my aunt and uncle?" she said.

"I'll do it as soon as I'm able, my child," the nun said. "And if I hear back from them, I'll let Mother Joe at St. Vincent's know. Now get up and get moving."

Pia rose from the cot on trembling legs. Miss O'Malley watched her with a furrowed brow, as if she were a wild animal about to lunge or run off at any second.

The nun regarded Miss O'Malley. "I'm sure she won't give you any trouble." Then she looked at Pia. "Will you, my child?"

Pia shook her head.

"I ain't worried," Miss O'Malley said.

"Come along, then," the nun said to Pia. "We can't very well send you outdoors in your convalescing gown." She turned and started toward the exit. Miss O'Malley and Pia followed.

After leading them out of the room, the nun locked the door behind them and marched down a short hallway that smelled of mold and rotten wood. Near the end, she unlocked a narrow door and held it open. "You can change in here," she said to Pia. The paneled room was small, no bigger than a closet, with a washbasin, a cushioned bench, and a simple white cross hanging on one wall.

Miss O'Malley dropped the gunnysack at Pia's feet. "If the clothes don't fit ye, don't blame me."

Pia picked it up, opened it, and pulled out a blue cotton dress, undergarments, and a pair of scuffed ankle boots with frayed laces. She took everything into the small room and waited for the nun to close the door.

"Have you forgotten your manners, my child?" the nun said. "The polite thing to do would be to thank Miss O'Malley for your new clothes."

Pia forced a smile. "Thank you, ma'am," she said to Miss O'Malley.

Miss O'Malley nodded once, her face pinched.

Inside the room, Pia pulled off her hospital gown, put on the undergarments, and slipped the dress over her head. It was stiff and scratchy, but after breathing in nothing but the rank odors of human fear, dried blood, and urine for so long, it smelled wonderful, like lilacs and laundry starch. She pushed her feet into the boots and tied the laces, the hard leather pinching her toes. After buttoning the blouse of the dress, she took a deep breath, gathered her courage, and went back out in the hall.

"Let's get going, then," Miss O'Malley said. Evidently she wanted to get out of there almost as badly as Pia did.

From the hallway, the nun led them into an octagon-shaped room with an arched roof, white walls, wrought-iron candelabras, and an oversize painting of the Last Supper. A thick red rug lay over the floor like a pool of blood, and the wet odor of damp stone, mildew, and dead flowers filled the air. From there they went through another wooden door, down a set of stone steps, and into a stone-walled passageway lined with narrow doors. The thought briefly crossed Pia's mind that, even if she'd been able to escape, finding her way out of the parish house would have been difficult. At the other end of the hall, weak sunlight illuminated a miniature stained-glass window in another wide wooden door. Pia had to fight the urge to push past the women and run toward it.

Pulling a ring of keys from beneath her habit, the nun unlocked the door and held it open. Miss O'Malley exited, went down a set of stone steps into a narrow alley between the parish house and another building, then turned and waited.

"Good day, Miss O'Malley," the nun said. "Bless you for helping in this hour of need. May the good Lord watch over and keep you."

Miss O'Malley nodded. "Yer welcome, Sister."

Pia wrapped her arms around herself and followed her down the steps. A light frost covered the cobblestones and iced the vines carpeting the wall of the other building. Despite the cold, the fresh air felt wonderful on her skin. She looked up and down the alley, trying to get her bearings.

On one end, a trio of clay pipes climbed up the side of the parish house, jutting out into the alley like an afterthought. Between that and a decorative outcropping of brick on the adjacent building, it was impossible to see what lay beyond. At the other end of the alley, a faint slice of sunlight lit up the stone façade of St. Peter's bell tower across the road. Pia's breathing grew shallow. Home was only blocks away. But she had to wait. She couldn't run yet.

"I'll pray for you, my child," the nun said to her. "Do as you're told and you'll be fine. May God bless and be with you."

Pia nodded and started in the direction of the church, ignoring the pinch of her too-small boots and the fact that Miss O'Malley hadn't said which way they were going.

"Come back here," Miss O'Malley snapped. "You're going the wrong way. I've got a driver and carriage waiting out back. Now hurry up." She started in the other direction.

Pia stopped and looked back to see if the nun was still at the top of the stairs. The parish door clunked shut and the key turned in the lock. She turned and started toward Miss O'Malley, moving slow, her head down to hide her anxious eyes. Miss O'Malley glanced over her shoulder to make sure she was coming, then slipped between the clay pipes and the bricks on the adjacent building, slapping away the frost-covered vines that brushed against her face. Pia thought about turning and running then, but Miss O'Malley had stopped on the other side of the opening and stood waiting for her to come through.

Had she just missed her only opportunity to escape? No. She had to have a plan. She couldn't just run off. Not yet anyway. She went through the narrow opening, trying to think. If she got into the wagon with Miss O'Malley, who knew how far it would take her from home? She clenched her fists and followed her out of the alley into the street, blinking against the bright sky. It seemed like forever since she'd been outside. A barrel-chested driver in a ragged coat slouched in the front seat of a square-boxed buggy, a cigar in his mouth, the horse's reins at his feet. When he saw Miss O'Malley, he sat up, snuffed the cigar out on the top of his boot, pulled his mask up over his mouth, and picked up the reins, the axles creaking with his every move.

Miss O'Malley climbed into the wagon beside the driver, eyed Pia, and jerked her head toward the back. "What are ye waitin' for?" she said. "Get in."

A knot of fear snarled in Pia's stomach. Her legs refused to budge, and her feet felt rooted to the sidewalk. She stared at Miss O'Malley, her breath coming faster and faster.

When Miss O'Malley realized what Pia was about to do, her eyes went wide. Before she could react, Pia spun around and bolted back through the opening into the alley. Miss O'Malley yelped like a strangled dog, then yelled at the driver, "Don't just sit there! Get after her!"

Pia kept going without looking back. Had Miss O'Malley clambered down from the wagon to give chase, her legs tangling in her skirt, her face white, or had she stayed seated beside the driver?

"Yes, ma'am," the driver said. "Giddyup!"

A whip cracked, axles squealed, and hooves pounded on the cobblestones.

Racing to the other end of the alley as fast as her still-weak legs could carry her, her lungs throbbing in protest, the frigid air whistling in her throat, Pia started to cough. But she kept going—across the cobblestone street and the frosty grass of the churchyard, around the piles of coffins next to the cemetery and into the next road. A colored woman in a blue scarf scurried toward her along the narrow sidewalk, clasping a lumpy flour sack to her chest. When she saw Pia, she turned and went in the other direction. The clatter of wagon wheels and horse hooves echoed through the maze of buildings and empty thoroughfares, getting closer and closer.

Halfway down the next block, Pia ducked into a dim alley and kept running. She tripped and fell twice, her strength nearly spent, but scrambled to her feet and kept going. Pain flared briefly in her ankle, but she ignored it and hobbled a few steps before finding her stride again. After what seemed like forever, the alley opened up and she nearly fell, bursting into a cluster of yards behind a block of row houses. She stopped to catch her breath, her heartbeat thudding in her ears. Panic bristled along her body. She was trapped. She glanced over her shoulder. Maybe she should turn back. No—Miss O'Malley and the driver could be waiting at the other end of the alley. She had to find a way out.

She scanned the houses for an open door or window, or an entrance to another alley. There were none.

Across the way, in a muddy courtyard, a woman with a long braid and ragged coat pumped water into a bucket, her breath billowing out in the cold. Pia raced toward her, climbing over fences and trampling through gardens, stumbling through backyards and wet chicken runs. When the woman saw her, she startled, grabbed her bucket, and ran into the back door of a row house.

At the water pump, Pia fell to her knees, panting. She worked the handle once and put her mouth under the faucet, the icy water soothing her irritated throat. She wiped her chin on her sleeve, then stood on trembling, mud-covered legs and glanced over her shoulder. No one was coming out of the alley. No one had followed her into the yards. She eyed the back door of the row house, praying the woman had left it unlocked. If her guesses were right, the front of the building came out on Delancey Street, and her building would be on the next block over. But she would need to cross Third Street to get there. Then she'd be six houses away from home. Six houses away from Ollie and Max. Six houses away from finding out if . . . if . . .

Her knees went weak and she grabbed the water pump to stay upright. She had to stop thinking and keep going. She had to put one foot in front of the other and get home. Maybe Nurse Carla had sent someone to check on her brothers before she died and they'd been taken to a hospital or orphanage. Maybe Vater had returned and was taking care of them. She had to believe it was one or the other. Otherwise she wouldn't have the strength to go on.

When she let go of the water pump, the cold metal pulled at her skin. Swearing under her breath, she shook her hand to numb the pain, then hurried to the back of the row house and tried the door. To her relief, the latch clicked and the door came loose of its frame. She slowly opened it and slipped inside.

Darkness permeated the first-floor hall, inky shadows veiling the far corners. The sound of her blood rushing through her veins filled her ears. She waited for her eyes to adjust, then edged forward, her shoulders hunched, ready to run if someone came out of their rooms. A weak light at the other end led her to the front door.

Bracing herself, she opened the front door a crack and peered out. A horse-drawn wagon driven by an old man moved along the edge of the road in the other direction. Miss O'Malley and the driver were nowhere to be seen, and no one else was on the road. No other horses, no wagons, no motorcars, no people. She breathed a sigh of relief. She was right; it was Delancey Street.

She started out the door, then froze. Hooves pounded along cobblestones on what sounded like the next street over. It was impossible to tell if they were getting closer or moving farther away. She shut the door, crouched in the shrouded hall, and tried to listen, but all she could hear was her thudding heartbeat and labored breathing. Maybe if she opened the door a crack, she'd be able to hear better. She stood and grabbed the handle.

Behind her, another door creaked. She turned and peered into the darkness. A dim light spilled out of an apartment, and a man in a ripped undershirt and dirty trousers came into the hall, cursing under his breath. When he saw Pia, he staggered toward her and grinned. His gray, crooked teeth were too big for his mouth.

"Who's there?" he said in a raspy voice.

Pia started to open the door, then stopped. Miss O'Malley and the driver could be out front. She edged toward a corner of the hall, dusty cobwebs brushing across her face.

"Are you lost?" the man said.

She shook her head.

"Don't be afraid," he said. "I won't hurt you." He gestured toward his door. "Why don't you come inside and I'll fix you somethin' to eat. I could use the company."

"I'm waiting for my father," she said. "He'll be here any minute."

He moved closer. "Your father, eh?"

She nodded.

"If I didn't know any better, I'd say you were lying to me. Now, why do you suppose that is?"

"I don't know," Pia said, moving toward the front door.

Suddenly he was in front of her, grabbing her wrist. The metallic tang of whiskey and the ashy musk of cigarettes filled her nostrils. And then she felt it—a stabbing pain beneath her rib cage. She nearly doubled over in agony. Whatever was wrong with him, it didn't feel like the flu. She yanked her arm from his grasp, tore open the front door, looked up and down the street, and ran out of the row house. When she reached the opposite side, she stopped and leaned against a brick building, listening for the wagon she'd heard earlier and trying to catch her breath. She peered around the corner, down Third Street. A block away, Miss O'Malley leaned out of the wagon to talk to a person on the sidewalk. The wagon was facing the other direction. The person shook their head, Miss O'Malley straightened, and the wagon started moving again. Pia dashed across Third Street and didn't stop running until she reached Shunk Alley. When she turned down it, she slowed.

Laundry hung here and there on clotheslines above her head, but no children played on the cobblestones. No mothers pushed bundled babies in prams. No men smoked on stoops. She started walking faster, her heart about to burst. She was almost there. Almost home. An image of Vater flashed in her mind, Ollie and Max swaddled in his arms. He was smiling, but his eyes were glassy and sad. ·

A sudden falling sensation swept over her and she nearly stumbled. She gritted her teeth and trudged forward, stopping every now and then to remind herself to breathe. The cobblestones and gray sky reeled in front of her. Nausea churned in her stomach. Maybe she should turn around. Maybe she should go back and turn herself in to Miss O'Malley. Maybe going to an orphanage was what she deserved. No, she had to face what she'd done, no matter what. She owed it to Ollie and Max. Then she was there. In front of her house. She looked up, hoping to see someone in the window. No one looked out. She glanced over at Finn's apartment. Her note was still there, soggy and limp and torn, dangling from the empty clothesline.

She walked up the front steps and into the dim foyer on watery legs. In what felt like slow motion, she climbed the stairs to the fourth floor. The smell of boiled cabbage and fried onions filled the halls, giving her a tiny measure of hope that some of her neighbors were still alive. Maybe one of them had heard her brothers' cries and saved them. Maybe Nurse Carla had been right. Maybe it was a good thing she'd left the door unlocked.

She went down the familiar hall and stopped in front of her door, realizing for the first time that she'd thought she'd never see it again. Certain she was going to collapse, she took a deep breath, grabbed the handle, and turned it.

The door was locked.

No. It couldn't be.

Unless . . . unless . . .

She pounded on the door. "Vater?" she cried. "It's me, Pia! Let me in!"

No sound came from the other side. No footsteps or shuffling feet. No babies crying or laughing. She pounded harder and rattled the handle, tears flooding her eyes.

"Vater, please! Let me in! If you're sleeping, you have to wake up!"

She put her forehead against the wood and rested her palms on the door, breathing hard. If no one would answer, she'd break it down. It was her only choice. She couldn't wait another second. She dropped her hands and started to step backward, bracing herself and getting ready to shove her shoulder into the door. Then the handle turned. The hinges creaked and the door inched open. A wedge of pale cheek became visible, a brown eye looking out through the dark crack. A child.

"Who are you?" Pia said. "And what are you doing in our apartment?"

The door opened wider. A black-haired boy blinked up at her with wide chestnut eyes. He looked to be around six years old, with milky cheeks and an innocent smile. For a second, she thought she'd knocked on the wrong door. She glanced down the hall and checked the number again. Yes, this was right. This was 4C, her family's apartment.

"What are you doing in there?" she said again.

No response.

She brushed past him into the apartment. Then she froze, shocked by what she was seeing. A dark-haired woman in a yellow dress and worn apron gaped at her from the coal stove, a wooden spoon in her hand, a startled look on her face. A thin man with a scraggy beard sat on her bed in his undershirt and drawers, his bare feet hanging over the edge. On the mattress beside him, a baby held a cloth doll to its mouth.

Ollie!

She raced over to the bed, then stopped in her tracks. The baby was older than the twins. And it was a girl. Pia looked frantically around the apartment. Had she stopped at the wrong house? The wrong floor? A ratty blanket hung over the window, casting murky shadows across the room. A straw mattress lay on the floor next to the table, which was shoved in a corner, not centered on the wall, where Mutti liked it. Then lantern light flickered off Mutti's blue vase in the middle of Oma's embroidered tablecloth and she knew. She was right. This was her home.

She frowned at the woman. "Who are you and what are you doing here? Where are my brothers?"

The woman furrowed her brow. *"Ki vagy te és mit csinálsz itt?"*

Pia couldn't understand what she was saying. It sounded like Hungarian—the language Mrs. Nagy used when she cornered Pia in the backyard—but she wasn't sure. And she didn't care. She bolted past the woman toward the open bedroom door.

The man jumped up and grabbed her by the arm, shaking his head. *"Mit gondolsz, hová mész?"*

Pia fought to escape, but it was no use. He was too strong.

"My brothers are in there," she cried, trying to get away.

The man shook his head again, harder this time. *"Mit akarsz?"* Fear and anger distorted his face. At the same time, sympathy flickered in his red-rimmed eyes.

She stopped struggling and tried to catch her breath. There was no escaping his strong grasp. And she wouldn't get anywhere by acting crazy and being aggressive. He was hurting her arm, but at least she was wearing long sleeves so she wouldn't feel anything that might be wrong with him. "Do you speak English?" she said, panting.

He shook his head again.

She pointed at the bedroom door, fighting the urge to scream at him. "My brothers," she said. Then she pointed at herself. "My baby brothers. I need to see if they're in there." She pointed at the door again.

The man and woman stared at her, confused.

She pretended to rock a baby in her arms, then pointed at the bedroom a third time, a question on her face. Finally, the man let go. He gestured toward the bedroom and shook his head again.

Pia's eyes filled. What was he saying? That Ollie and Max were gone? That he had no idea what she was talking about? Either way she wasn't going to wait another second. Before he could stop her, she fled into the bedroom. Two children looked up from the bed, a boy and a pale-faced girl, their eyes wide with surprise. One had a rag doll, the other a wooden top. Mutti's decayed corpse was gone. Pia fell to her knees in front of the cubby and, with shaking hands and trembling fingers, undid the latch and yanked open the door.

No babies lay inside the bedroom cubby. No rattles or milky bottles waited in the cramped, dark space. No twin skeletal bodies resting side by side. Ollie and Max were gone.

Agony seized Pia's chest, as if a giant hand had reached into her rib cage and yanked out her heart. She moaned and collapsed on the floor, fear and grief and horror and relief crashing over her in waves. It was all she could do not to be sick. Her limbs vibrated out of control, and violent sobs tore from her throat, each howl stealing the air from her lungs and the strength from her body. She wanted to die.

She lay that way for what felt like forever, until she could finally breathe again without gagging. Then she pushed herself into a sitting position and leaned against the wall, her legs like water, her arms like ice. She needed to compose herself so she could figure out what to do next. She needed to find out what happened to Ollie and Max. Hopefully someone, maybe a neighbor, had found them before it was too late. Or maybe this family, these strangers living in her home, had taken her brothers' small bodies to the morgue. Either way, one thing was certain. Whatever had happened was her fault.

The strangers stood gaping at her from the foot of Mutti's bed. The woman was on the verge of tears, her hand over her bosom, the baby girl on her hip. The little boy leaned against his father's legs and stared at Pia out of the corners of his eyes, his face fraught with fear. The man looked helpless and confused.

Pia made a rocking motion with her arms again, her chin trembling. She pointed at herself, then at the cubby, a question on her face. She made the rocking motion again, pointed at the family, and held up her palms. The man shook his head. Then, finally, understanding transformed the woman. She handed the baby to the man and disappeared into the other room. Pia got up and followed her on wobbly legs. The man and boy stepped back, giving her a wide berth. At the kitchen table, the woman riffled through the thin pages of what looked like a Bible. When she found what she was looking for, she turned, startled at first to see Pia behind her. Smiling warily, she handed her a piece of folded white paper. Pia took it with trembling fingers and opened it. In scrawling cursive it read:

May God forgive you for what you've done.

Pia dropped the note. The room spun and she swayed and started to crumble. The woman took her by the elbow and backed her toward a chair. Reaching blindly for the seat, Pia lowered herself into it. She leaned forward and put her head in her hands, struggling to make sense of it all. Someone had found Ollie and Max. But who? And when? Before it was too late? Or after? One thing was certain, it wasn't the strangers who had taken over her family's apartment. It was someone who spoke English.

The woman cleared her throat, and Pia took her hands away from her face. The woman picked up the note, pointed at the bedroom and the note, over and over again.

Pia nodded. "You found it in the cubby," she said. "Yes. I know."

The woman smiled and tried to say more, using small words and gesturing, but Pia still didn't understand.

Pia made a writing motion, then lifted her hands, palms up, and shrugged. "But who wrote it?"

The woman frowned and shook her head. Pia had no idea if she understood.

She stood and headed toward the front door, one hand on the wall to keep from collapsing. The woman followed, shaking the note and saying something incomprehensible. Pia stopped and looked around at what used to be her home. It all seemed like a bad dream. Her home was gone. Her family was gone. And she had no idea how to find Ollie and Max, or if they were even alive. She didn't know where to go or what she would do when she walked out the door, but one way or another, she had to find out what happened to her brothers.

Then she had an idea. She pointed at the note in the woman's hand and made a writing motion. The woman furrowed her brow again. Pia pointed at herself and made the writing motion again. The woman smiled, held up a finger, went to the shelves beside the stove, and rummaged around behind a nutmeg-colored creamer and matching sugar bowl. When she found what she was looking for, she went back to Pia and handed her a stubby pencil. Pia took it and wrote on the back of the note.

> *Dear Vater, I'm sorry to tell you this, but Mutti passed away from the flu. I tried to take care of Ollie and Max, but I got sick too. I'm looking for them now. Please wait for me. I'll be back, I promise.*
> *Love, Pia*

After handing the paper and pencil back to the woman, she patted her heart and held her hand above her head to indicate someone tall. Then she pointed at the note and pretended to give it to someone. She repeated the gestures again, hoping the woman would understand. Finally, the woman nodded. But then she held up a finger again, as if telling Pia to wait. Pia had no idea why but did as she was asked.

The woman went over to a wicker basket at the foot of the bed, removed something from it, returned to Pia, and held it out. Pia gasped.

It was a homemade rattle.

Pia took it and examined the handle. On the bottom was a perfectly carved O.

A burning lump formed in her throat. "This was Ollie's," she said, her voice high and tight. "Where did you find it?" She pointed toward the bedroom. "In the cubby?"

The woman nodded.

"Only one?" Pia said. She pointed at the rattle and held up one finger, then did it again and held up two.

The woman held up one finger and nodded.

Pia clasped the rattle to her chest, a fresh flood of tears filling her eyes. Was the rattle left behind by mistake, or because it didn't matter?

The woman gave her a sad smile, her head tilted to one side. Then she pretended to eat something and gestured toward the stove.

Pia shook her head. "Thank you," she said. "But I have to go." She started toward the door, but the woman rushed over to the stove, grabbed something from a cast-iron pan, and brought it back to her. It looked like a miniature loaf of bread, folded over, the edges pinched together. Pia wasn't sure she could eat anything, but she was feeling weaker by the minute. She couldn't collapse again. Maybe a little food would help her feel better. Trying to smile to show her gratitude, she took the bread. It was warm and crusty, topped with pepper and dark seeds. She took a bite and her mouth watered for more. Ground meat, spices, and some kind of cheese filled the inside. She couldn't remember the last time she'd eaten anything so delicious.

"It's wonderful," Pia said. "Thank you."

The woman clasped her hands together and raised her chin proudly. *"Pogaca,"* she said.

While Pia ate the meat-filled bun, the woman brought her a mug of warm tea. Pia took several sips, then drank it down. She hadn't realized how thirsty she was, her mouth and throat parched. "Thank you," she said. "For everything. But I really need to go. Please give the note to my father if he comes here."

The woman smiled and nodded, and Pia went out the door, closing it behind her.

Out in the hall, she took a deep breath, leaned against the wall, and tried to think logically. First, she'd check with the neighbors to see if anyone had found Ollie and Max, or if they knew what happened. She'd stop at every apartment in every building on Shunk Alley if she had to, until she found out the truth. *If* she could get people to talk to her.

With the rattle clenched in her fist, she went to the neighbor's door, knocked, and waited, chewing on her lip. When no one answered, she knocked again, harder this time.

"Mrs. Anderson?" she shouted. "It's me, Pia Lange. Please answer. I need help." Tilting her head toward the door, she listened for movement and voices. No sounds came from the other side.

Maybe Mrs. Anderson and her daughters and cousins were dead too. Maybe some other family had already taken over their apartment. She raised her hand to knock again when she heard footsteps running up the stairs. Praying it was someone she knew, or Vater returning home at long last, she ran to the stairwell and looked over the railing. Then she gasped and stepped back, a cold twist of panic tightening in her chest.

It was Miss O'Malley and the driver.

CHAPTER TEN

PIA

Struggling to break free of the rope binding her wrists to the sideboard, Pia sat cross-legged in the back of Miss O'Malley's wagon, the wooden wheels banging along the cobblestones, the splintered bed bouncing and shuddering, throwing her this way and that. The setting sun cast long shadows of buildings and lampposts across the empty thoroughfares and turned alleys into dark tunnels. Here and there, curtains pulled to one side, pale faces looked out, and the curtains dropped again. Pia shouted for help as loudly as she could, but Miss O'Malley hit her with a riding crop and told her to shut up.

With every passing mile, Pia berated herself for being so careless. If only she'd taken a minute to see who was coming up the stairs, instead of assuming it was someone she knew. If only she'd been more vigilant and not shouted at Mrs. Anderson's door, she might have gotten away. When Miss O'Malley and the driver rushed up the steps and cornered her in the hallway, she'd kicked and screamed and fought back like a wild animal, but it was no use. The driver was too strong. The scraggly bearded Hungarian in her family's apartment looked out to see what the commotion was, but the driver threatened him with a balled fist and he closed the door. She tried to jab the driver in the face with the rattle, but Miss O'Malley ripped it from her grasp, threw it on the floor, and stomped on it with one heel, fracturing the wood and breaking the twine. The bells fell off and scattered along the hall like marbles, jingling as they rolled. Pia cried out and tried to pick up the broken rattle, but the driver grabbed her again and put a sweaty hand over her mouth. Then he dragged her down the stairs, threw her in the back of the wagon, and tied her wrists to the sideboard.

Now there was nothing she could do but try to escape again. And apologize to the twins over and over in her head.

When two masked policemen appeared on a corner, she got up on her knees and yelled for help. Miss O'Malley whacked her with the riding crop and told her to be still. One of the policemen stepped into the street and raised a gloved hand. The driver pulled on the reins and stopped the wagon while Miss O'Malley cursed under her breath. The policemen came around the horse to talk to them, one eyeing Pia with concern.

"What's going on?" he said to Miss O'Malley. "Who's the girl?"

"Please," Pia shouted. "You have to help me!"

"Shut your bloody pie hole," Miss O'Malley hissed at her. Then to the policeman, she said, "The sisters at St. Peter's hired us to take her to St. Vincent's Orphan Asylum. As you can tell by her hollerin', she ain't keen on the idea."

"I'm not an orphan," Pia shouted. "My father is looking for me and my brothers."

One of the policemen held up a hand to quiet her, his eyes on Miss O'Malley. "Do you know where her father is?" he said.

"He's a soldier," Pia yelled.

"Well, if the nuns knew the answer to that, Officer," Miss O'Malley said, "I'd imagine they'd send her to him instead of an orphanage. He could be off on a bender for all I know."

"Shouldn't she be wearing a mask?" the second policeman said.

"She already had the grippe," Miss O'Malley said. "That's why she was at St. Peter's."

"And while I was sick my father came back from the war," Pia shouted. "The nuns didn't even try to find him. They just sent me away."

"Is that true?" the policeman said.

"Now, Officer," Miss O'Malley said. "Who are you inclined to believe? The good nuns at St. Peter's, or this wretched waif? I'm sure the sisters did the best they could. They were running out of room at the parish and they knew you didn't need another street urchin on your hands."

The policemen looked at each other and one of them shrugged. The one who had stopped the wagon addressed Pia. "Seems to me you'll be better off letting the nuns do what they think is best, darlin'," he said. "You're lucky you've got people willing to look after you."

She shook her head furiously. "No," she cried. "You can't let them take me. Please! I have to get back to my brothers! They're just babies. They need me."

"I'm sure someone's taking good care of them too," the policeman said. Then he patted the wagon and waved the driver on. "On your way."

"No," Pia cried. "Please. You have to help me!" She yanked on the ropes with all her might, trying to break free. It was no use.

The policemen started walking away. The driver slapped the reins across the horse's back and the wagon jerked forward, throwing her off balance. Her wrists twisted inside the rope and she fell back; her forearms felt wrenched from her elbows. Lying crumpled on her side, tears of frustration and pain filled her eyes. But she struggled upright again. She needed to pay attention to where they were going, needed to remember the names of streets and memorize buildings and other landmarks. That way, when she escaped the orphanage, she'd be able to find her way home.

After what seemed like forever, they reached the less populated area of the city and turned down what looked like a deserted country road. Eventually the wagon slowed, then traveled alongside a high iron fence topped with spear-shaped finials and copper ball caps. A brick four-story building with a bell tower and extensive wings sat inside the fence, centered in a vast yard lined with pine trees and willows. The driver steered the horse and wagon through the gate and up the long driveway. The building looked like a mansion at first, until they drew closer and the peeling window frames and broken porch spindles came into view. Lights came on behind the curtainless windows, and short figures moved behind the glass. When the wagon reached the sidewalk to the front entrance, the driver stopped the horse and secured the reins, then jumped out to help Miss O'Malley climb down.

Despair and anger twisted in Pia's stomach, and she started to tremble. "Please," she said. "You can't leave me here."

Miss O'Malley ignored her and marched up the steps. The driver untied Pia and waited for her to get down from the wagon, then grabbed her arm and dragged her up the sidewalk. Swallowing the sour taste of fear in the back of her throat, she rubbed her sore wrists and looked up at the orphanage. The pale faces of children drew close to the windows and peered out. Tall figures in black shooed them away from the glass, herding them backwards into the rooms. The front door opened and a nun appeared on the porch, her pale, wiry hands clasped in front of her habit, a heavy-looking cross dangling from a thick rosary around her waist. She peered at Pia over the top of round glasses, then addressed Miss O'Malley.

"Have you come from St. Peter's?" she said.

"We have," Miss O'Malley said.

"And you're positive this girl is no longer ill?"

Miss O'Malley shrugged. "That's what they said."

"Well, the good Lord knows we've had our share of the grippe here at St. Vincent's. We can't afford to take on any more sick children." The nun turned to Pia. "How are you feeling, child?" A thin smile stretched across her face, but her watery blue eyes seemed wary and cold.

"I'm fine, ma'am," Pia said. "But I shouldn't be here. I—"

"My name is Mother Josephina," the nun said. "You can call me Mother Joe. And you *are* here. So God had a reason to send you to us. Our job at St. Vincent's is to shelter those in need, not to understand the reason behind that need. The sisters at St. Peter's have sent you here and that's that. Now behave yourself and don't complain." She directed her attention back to Miss O'Malley. "Thank you for delivering her. You're free to go." Then she turned, opened the door, and held it for Pia.

Miss O'Malley shooed Pia forward, irritation pinching her face.

Pia stood rooted to the landing. Maybe she should make a run for it. Certainly she could outrun Mother Joe, and maybe Miss O'Malley, but the driver would catch her again. Besides, even if she could get away, where would she go? She had no home. No family. No money.

Miss O'Malley jabbed a finger in her back. "It's better than I had at yer age," she snarled, "Now get moving."

Pia shot her a bitter look, then gritted her teeth, stepped across the threshold, and entered the orphanage. Mother Joe started to close the door behind her, but Miss O'Malley put a hand out to stop it.

"Mother Joe?" she said. "I have a need to speak to you real quick, if I could."

"What is it?" Mother Joe said.

Miss O'Malley eyed Pia. "I have a message from one of the sisters at St. Peter's."

"Excuse us for a moment," Mother Joe said to Pia, turning her head to indicate she should move away.

Pia did as she was told, taking several steps into the high-ceilinged foyer. Mother Joe leaned out the door and closed it partway. Pia strained to hear what they were saying but couldn't make out the words. She looked around for a way out, but there were only two other doors, both of which looked like they went farther into the building. The smell of boiled potatoes and warm wood filled the air, along with a hint of smoldering incense and burnt matches. A gold-framed painting of Jesus surrounded by children hung between gas candelabras on one flocked wall, along with crosses and other religious paintings.

After Mother Joe finished talking with Miss O'Malley, she closed the door and led Pia across the foyer, her shoes clacking along the hardwood floor. When they reached the other side, she pulled an iron key ring out from beneath her scapular and unlocked one of the doors. Then she lit one of several oil lanterns on an end table and picked it up.

"Excuse me, Mother Joe?" Pia said.

Mother Joe raised an eyebrow at her, as if surprised she'd spoken. "What is it?"

"May I ask what Miss O'Malley said to you? Did it have anything to do with me?"

Mother Joe frowned. "You may ask," she said. "But that doesn't mean I'll tell you. It was official business, that's all you need to know."

Pia nodded and dropped her eyes to the floor. Annoying Mother Joe seemed like a bad idea.

Holding the lantern in one hand, Mother Joe opened the door and stepped over the high threshold, leading Pia into a murky corridor that smelled of urine and bleach. At the end of the corridor they turned down a narrow hallway, past rooms filled with rows of identical iron beds, the flickering lantern light revealing nothing but shadows inside. The place felt deserted, the air heavy, the silence as thick as a blanket. When they reached the end of a third hallway, Mother Joe opened a double door that led outside to a set of stone steps and a fenced yard.

A swing set, slide, and roundabout stood in the center of the lawn under the pink evening sky, empty except for scatterings of dry leaves and broken twigs. No orphans played on the playground. No children laughed or screeched or dashed about. Instead they sat cross-legged on the brown grass or walked the fence in quiet groups. A cluster of what looked like four- and five-year-olds sat on steps leading into another wing of the building, polishing what looked like hundreds of shoes. Other children stood around them in their socks and bare feet, waiting, all of them in ragged clothes that seemed either too big or too small. No one wore a jacket or scarf.

"Supper is in half an hour," Mother Joe said to Pia. "The sisters will come get you." Then she left her there.

Standing on the steps, Pia scanned the playground, hoping against hope to see Ollie and Max. Maybe whoever found them had brought them to this orphanage. Maybe it was a good thing Miss O'Malley had caught her. But to her dismay, all the children were older than the twins, the youngest being around two or three. Several of the bigger ones turned to look at her, no doubt wondering who she was, then turned back to the others. She sat down on the steps, blinking back tears, the cold stone seeping through her thin dress. The chances of her and her brothers being taken to the same orphanage were practically nonexistent. And she was a fool to think finding them would be that easy.

A little girl carrying a rag doll came over to the steps and smiled up at her with tired eyes. She looked to be about four years old, with dark hair that fell around her thin face in uneven curls. *"Halo,"* she said in a tiny voice.

Pia thought she'd said hello, but with an accent, or in a different language. Forcing herself to return the smile, she wished the little girl would go away. She was homesick and scared and sick to her stomach, and didn't feel like making friends. The only thing she wanted was to find a way out of there. She looked out over the playground, pretending to be busy watching the other children. But before she knew what was happening, the little girl climbed up the steps and crawled into her lap. Pia held up her hands, partly in surprise, mostly because she didn't want to touch her. The problem was, some of the others had turned to watch so she didn't want to tell the girl no or push her away. Making enemies within minutes of her arrival was the last thing she needed. She held her breath until the little girl got settled, then put her hands on the steps. One of the girl's bare legs rested against hers, but to Pia's relief, she felt nothing.

Proudly holding up her rag doll to show Pia, the little girl grinned again. Pia forced another smile and nodded. The girl patted the doll's worn head with a dirty hand, then clutched it to her chest, leaned against Pia's shoulder, and closed her eyes. Pia swallowed, bewildered. What was she supposed to do now? Hold her while she napped? Cuddle her? Clearly the little girl longed for affection and, for some reason, trusted Pia to give it to her. Just like Ollie and Max had trusted her. Overwhelmed with fear and misery and love, Pia's eyes filled and she wrapped her arms around the girl, rocking her back and forth, and trying not to cry. She had failed her brothers; she didn't have to fail this little girl. A hug was a small gesture that didn't cost a thing. Before long the girl was asleep, her small pink mouth hanging partway open. Looking down at her pale, dirty face,

Pia couldn't help wondering how she'd come to be in the orphanage. Had her parents died? Abandoned her? Just thinking about it made her chest ache.

An older girl with short, mousy braids strolled across the playground toward the steps. Pia wiped her eyes. She didn't want anyone to think she was weak. Being bullied again was the last thing she needed. The girl climbed up the steps and sat next to her, pulling her threadbare dress over her bony knees. A sprinkle of light freckles dotted her nose and checks. "Hi, I'm Jenny," she said. "Who are you?"

"Pia."

Jenny pointed at the little girl. "That's Gigi," she said. "We don't know her real name so we made one up."

Pia gave Jenny a weak smile, hoping she looked friendly.

Jenny pointed at another girl on the playground, this one with curly hair and long, knobby-kneed legs. "We call her Colette. She doesn't speak English either, but we knew what she meant when she said her name." She indicated several other children, girls and boys alike, and said the same thing about them speaking other languages. "And see that older, dark-haired girl over there, the one standing in the corner with the pinecone in her hands?"

Pia nodded.

"That's Iris. She's blind. Everyone says she came from another orphanage a long time ago, but she wasn't blind when she got there."

"What happened to her?"

Jenny shrugged. "Guess they were doing some kind of medical experiments on her, something to do with tuberculosis."

"Who was doing experiments on her?"

"One of the doctors at the other orphanage."

Pia's stomach turned over. She thought orphanages were supposed to keep children safe. "Do you think it's true?"

"Yeah, I believe it," Jenny said. "We're throwaways. They can do whatever they want to us. You'll see."

"What do you mean, I'll see? What about the nuns? I thought they were supposed to love and care about everyone."

"Just try to stay out of trouble," Jenny said. "That's all I can tell you."

Pia's eyes filled again. She felt like she was trapped in a nightmare, doomed to never wake up. If the people running St. Vincent's thought she and the other children were disposable, they'd probably think her brothers were disposable too. Why would they care about helping her find them?

"So what happened to your parents?" Jenny said, pulling Pia from her thoughts. "Did they catch the purple death?"

"The purple death?"

"That's what the nuns call the flu," Jenny said. "Because it turns people's skin purple. A bunch of us caught it and three girls died. Two of the nuns taking care of us did too. And I heard there's still some kids in the sick hall."

Pia's mouth went dry. For some reason, she'd thought isolated places like orphanages and asylums and jails would be safe from the flu. Knowing they weren't made her even more uneasy. Thinking about a deadly illness getting into a place with no escape made her skin crawl. "My mother had it," she said. "But my father is in the army, fighting in the war."

"Do you think he'll come back?"

Pia shrugged, her throat getting tight. Even if Vater came back, he'd never find her there. "Why were you sent here?"

Jenny gazed at the autumn clouds as if searching for something that wasn't there. "All I remember is my mother dressing my little brother and me in our Sunday clothes and dropping us off here. She used to visit sometimes and tell us she'd be back to get us. But then she stopped coming. That was two years ago."

Pia couldn't believe what she was hearing. How could a mother abandon her children on purpose? Then an image of Ollie and Max in the cubby flashed in her mind and she nearly cried out in agony and shame. Who was she to judge what any mother had done? Something cold and hard twisted in her stomach and she thought she was going to be sick. She clenched her teeth and took slow, deep breaths, trying to calm down. One thing was becoming more and more certain—she deserved to be punished.

"Pia?" Jenny said. "Did you hear me?"

Pia blinked and looked at her. "Oh," she said. "Yes. I'm sorry your mother never came back to get you. That's awful."

Jenny shrugged. "Yeah, I just wish I knew why. I don't know if something happened to her, or if she stopped coming because she didn't want us anymore."

Pia scanned the other orphans in the yard. "Which one is your brother?"

"He's not here," Jenny said. "After my mother stopped coming, he disappeared. Every day for months I asked the nuns where he was. Then Mother Joe told me to stop bothering the staff. I still don't know what happened to him."

Pia's heart squeezed in her chest. If they wouldn't tell Jenny what happened to her brother, they probably wouldn't tell her even if Ollie and Max *were* here. She almost told Jenny she understood how it felt to miss her brother, then stopped, cringing inside. Jenny didn't know what happened to her brother because of someone else's actions, but whatever happened to Ollie and Max was Pia's fault. She couldn't tell Jenny or anyone else at the orphanage what she'd done. They'd think she was a monster. And they'd be right.

"I'm sorry," she said again, because she didn't know what else to say. Then she had another thought. Jenny had been at St. Vincent's for two years; she had to know her way around. "Do you know if there are any babies here?"

"Of course there are," Jenny said.

Pia drew in a silent, sharp breath. "Where?"

Jenny shrugged one shoulder. "I don't know. I've never seen them."

"Then how do you know they're here?"

"Because sometimes at night I hear them crying."

Goose bumps rose on Pia's arms. Before she could ask more questions, a nun opened the door behind them and clapped her hands, making her jump.

"Come inside, girls," the nun shouted. "It's time for supper!"

The girls on the playground turned away from what they were doing or got to their feet and started toward the steps, moving in what seemed like slow motion. As they neared the building, they stared at Pia with a mixture of curiosity and sympathy. Pia dropped her eyes and stood, Gigi still asleep in her arms, then moved toward the doorway. The nun stepped outside, intentionally blocking her way.

"Put her down," the nun said. She was the tallest woman Pia had ever seen, with angry eyes burning in a hard-bitten face. Her wattled chin hung over the neck of her coif like flesh-colored cheese.

"I can carry her," Pia said. "She's sound asleep."

"And I suppose you're hoping to steal her supper?" the nun said.

Pia shook her head. "No, I—"

Without warning the nun yanked Gigi from Pia's arms, then set her on her feet and pushed her into the building, stumbling and disoriented. "What's your name, girl?" she said to Pia.

"Pia."

"Pia what?"

"Pia Lange."

"Well, Miss Lange, from now on you'll do as you're told. Trust me when I say it will make your time here a lot more pleasant."

Pia glanced at Jenny, who shook her head ever so slightly in warning. Pia looked back at the nun. "Yes, ma'am," she said.

"Yes, Sister Ernestine," the nun corrected her.

"Yes, Sister Ernestine," Pia repeated.

Sister Ernestine gave her another scowl, then turned on her heels and went back inside to wait. The girls lined up against one wall, silent and obedient, all facing the same way, their eyes straight ahead. Sister Ernestine and two other nuns split them into three groups, then Sister Ernestine took a lantern from one of the other nuns and ordered the first group, including Pia and Jenny, to follow her. Together they shuffled along the dim hall, Sister Ernestine's shadow marching along the ceiling like a giant bat. At the end of the hall, they clambered down a steep set of wooden stairs, planting their hands on the walls to keep from tumbling forward.

"Where are we going?" Pia whispered to Jenny, who was two girls in front of her.

"To the dining hall," Jenny whispered back.

"In the cellar?"

"Shhh," Jenny hissed over her shoulder.

At the bottom of the steps, they passed a coal bin as big as a trolley, then entered a long, narrow room with ductwork and rusty pipes running the length of the close ceiling. Something that looked like wet soot dripped down the brick walls, and the wooden floor was scuffed and worn. The air smelled like spoiled milk and cabbage. Metal bowls and spoons lined a long table surrounded by wooden stools. The girls sat down in an orderly fashion, Pia next to Jenny, then waited silently while a sweaty-faced nun ladled something that looked like runny stew into their bowls. Brown clots of the stew dripped from the ladle onto the floor, the stools, the table, the girls' shoulders and heads. No one seemed to notice.

"'Bless us, oh Lord, for these Thy gifts which we are about to receive from thy bounty through Christ Our Lord, amen,'" the sweaty-faced nun repeated over and over. Each girl said "Amen" after her bowl was filled.

Another nun followed the first with thin slices of bread. As soon as Pia's bread fell into her bowl, the girl opposite her snatched it away. Pia looked at Jenny, wondering what she should do, but Jenny was hunched over her bowl, already eating. Pia glanced down the line of girls to see if any of them saw what happened. Lantern light flickered off their weary faces and haunted eyes as they devoured their meager supper like a pack of hungry wolves. No one paid attention to anything other than the food. She had no appetite but knew she needed to eat and drink. She scooped up a spoonful of the stew and put it to her lips. It was runny and lukewarm and tasted like stale water mixed with a few mushy pieces of carrot, potato, and some kind of meat—either pork or chicken, it was hard to tell. It was all she could do not to gag when she put it in her mouth.

While the girls ate, Sister Ernestine walked up and down the table, telling them to hurry up so the next group could come in. A young girl with curly hair sat pouting and staring at her food, her arms crossed over her middle. Sister Ernestine came up behind her and pinched her nose shut. When the girl opened her mouth so she could breathe, Sister Ernestine shoveled a spoonful of stew in and let go of her nose. The girl gagged and the food came back out again, streams of stew and vomit dripping down her chin. Sister Ernestine held the girl's nose shut and force-fed her again.

"This will teach you to be ungrateful," she snarled.

Pia dropped her spoon and started to get up. She had to make the nun stop.

"Don't," Jenny hissed.

Several of the other girls shot her a warning look, their eyes wide with alarm. Pia sat back down, breathing hard, nauseated by anger and fear and disgust. Sister Ernestine repeated the process while the girl cried and gagged.

Pia's eyes filled. She didn't think she could finish eating. But she didn't dare stop. The other girls kept their heads down and did the same.

In a matter of minutes, everyone was done, with a few girls scraping their bowls, desperate to get every last drop. When another nun led the second group into the dining hall, Sister Ernestine ordered the first girls to put down their utensils and get up. Then she led them up two narrow flights of stairs to a room lined with what seemed like a hundred washbasins. The washroom was cold and damp, the wooden floor wet and slippery-looking. Next to each washbasin, a thin towel hung on a hook. Sister Ernestine grabbed a threadbare nightdress from a shelf and handed it to Pia.

"Clean yourself up, Miss Lange," she said. "And be quick about it."

The other girls had already taken off their shoes, stripped down to their undergarments, and were hastily washing their hands and faces. Pia went over to a washbasin and did the same. Searching up and down the row, she looked for Jenny but couldn't see her. After getting cleaned up as best she could with no washcloth and a thin towel, she slipped the nightdress over her head and hung the towel back on the hook. When everyone was done, they picked up their shoes and clothes, and followed Sister Ernestine out of the washroom into a dank corridor. At the end of the corridor, they climbed another staircase and came out in what seemed like an endless hall lined with doors and ceiling arches. Everything but the floor was painted white—the ceiling, the doors, the arches, the walls—but it did little to bring light to the space. Every time Sister Ernestine passed a ceiling arch, the yellow glow of her lantern went with her, casting shadows along the walls and leaving the girls at the end of the line in near darkness. Halfway down the hall, she held the lantern high and the girls filed into a narrow, brown-paneled room filled with rows of iron beds made up with gray sheets and lumpy-looking pillows. A mullioned window on the far end was shuttered from the outside, each thick pane dulled by grime. Pia stood near the door, waiting to be told what to do. Cold seeped up through the uneven plank floor, chilling her bare feet.

"Find your spot," Sister Ernestine said.

With that, the girls scrambled to the beds, some sitting two to a mattress. Pia moved down the center aisle and looked for an empty place. It was going to be hard enough being cooped up with so many other girls in one room, lying next to one would be unbearable. She didn't need, or want, to know if they were coming down with a cold, or had a stomachache, or God forbid, the flu. Just being in this dim, drafty room with all of them she could almost feel their pain, their longing for love and a place to call home. She didn't want to lie next to any of them when they cried at night, didn't want to feel the heavy ache of sorrow in their hearts. Then again, maybe what felt like the gut-wrenching emotions of all the other girls was just the weight of her own sadness and fear.

She could feel them watching her make her way down the aisle, waiting to see what she would do. No one spoke or moved. All the beds were full. Jenny was sitting on a mattress next to Colette, her head down, picking at her nails. No one wanted to be the new girl's first friend, and she wouldn't expect Jenny to give up her spot, anyway. On the last bed next to the window, Gigi sat smiling with her rag doll clutched to her chest. Pia turned around to face Sister Ernestine.

"May I sleep on the floor, Sister Ernestine?"

One of the girls snickered. "What's the matter?" she said. "You don't want to sleep with a wet-the-bed?"

The other girls laughed.

"Hush!" Sister Ernestine hissed. Everyone fell silent. "You'll share a bed with Gigi, Miss Lange, and you'll be grateful for it."

Gigi slid over to make room and Pia climbed in next to her, thankful at least that she'd already touched Gigi and hadn't felt anything amiss. Maybe once the rest of the girls went to sleep, she could get out of bed and lie on the floor between the bed and the window, where no one would see her.

"Hands on top of your blankets," Sister Ernestine said. "And no talking."

The girls got under the covers, making sure to rest their arms outside their blankets.

Sister Ernestine moved along the beds, checking to make sure everyone's hands were where she could see them, her wattled chin jiggling with every step. Once she was satisfied that everyone had obeyed, she went back to the door, turned, and said, "Who wants to tell Pia what will happen if she so much as whispers after I leave?"

A girl of about six raised her hand. Sister Ernestine pointed at her.

The girl gaped at Pia with frightened eyes. "The devil will come for you," she said.

"Say it again, louder, so everyone can hear you," Sister Ernestine said.

"The devil will come for you," the girl shouted.

A few of the older girls looked at one another and rolled their eyes. Sister Ernestine didn't seem to notice. "That's right," she said. "And because all of you come from fallen parents, you're easy prey for Satan. Remember that. Now say your prayers and go to sleep."

"Yes, Sister Ernestine," the girls said in unison.

Without another word, Sister Ernestine left and the room went dark. The door shut and the key turned in the dead bolt. The only sounds were her footsteps clomping down the hall and the night wind whistling through the cracks around the windows. After a long minute, the girls started whispering and giggling. Someone started humming. Someone else cried softly into her pillow. Gigi curled up beside Pia and put an arm around her, mumbling something Pia didn't understand.

"Welcome to ward six, Pia," a voice said in the dark. It sounded like it came from the next bed.

"What kind of name is Pia?" someone else said in a mocking tone.

A girl snickered, and another joined in.

"I was named after my great-grandmother," Pia said. She started to say her name was German, then stopped. Who knew what the other girls had been taught before they came to the orphanage?

"Well, don't thank your mother for that," the mocking voice said.

Some of the girls giggled.

"Don't listen to them," a third voice said. It sounded like Jenny.

Pia sat up on one elbow and looked around the room, trying to see her. It was too dark.

"Can we call you Pia piddle?" someone said.

"How about wee-wee?"

"Maybe her mother thought she was a real pisser."

More laughter.

"Stop it," Jenny said. "Her mother died from the purple death."

Several gasps sounded around the room and the laughter subsided.

"Did you see her die?" the first voice said.

"Yeah, tell us what happened," the mocking voice said. "Did her eyes bleed all over her face?"

"Don't say that," Jenny said. "You'll scare the littles."

"Oh, come on," the mocking voice said. "We all saw what happened to Sister Anne."

"That doesn't mean we have to talk about it," Jenny said. "I had nightmares for a solid week after she collapsed in the recreation room. So did Gigi."

"We all did," someone else said.

"I didn't see my mother die," Pia said. "When I woke up in the morning she was already gone."

"I'm sorry," a small voice said.

"Me too," someone else said.

"My mother is coming back to get me soon," the small voice said.

"No, she's not," the mocking voice said. "I told you a hundred times, Sister Ernestine is lying. She told you that so you'd stop crying. She tells all the kids that."

"She does not!" the small voice cried. "My mother is coming back! She told me she was!"

"Shhh," Jenny said. "Be quiet. Do you want to get punished again?"

Everyone stopped talking and the room grew quiet. Iron bed legs creaked and bodies moved on mattresses.

Then Jenny whispered, "Pia?"

"Yeah?"

"If Sister Ernestine catches anyone talking or crying after lights out, they get three lashes with a leather strap. And don't get scared if she comes into the room in the middle of the night to force us out to the outhouse. She does that sometimes, mostly when she's in a bad mood."

"Yeah," the mocking voice said. "And she makes us sit two to a hole and stay there until we go. Even in the winter." Whoever it was, she sounded sad and solemn now.

"Thanks for telling me," Pia said.

"Welcome," Jenny said.

Then the room went quiet again.

Pia turned toward the window and lay on her side, tears filling her eyes. Somehow, she had to get out of there.

Early the next morning, Sister Ernestine burst into the room a few minutes after sunrise with brooms and a wicker basket. She left them by the door and marched down the rows of beds, yanking the covers off and slapping anyone who didn't get up right away. Before she reached Gigi's bed, Pia shook Gigi to wake her, realizing at the same time that her nightdress felt wet. She lifted the blanket and looked underneath. Urine soaked the sheet and one side of her nightdress. The other girls were already up and making their beds. Pia jumped up, dragged Gigi off the mattress, and set her on her feet, half-awake and mumbling. Her small, wrinkled nightie hung yellow and wet around her thin legs. Trying to hide the stain, Pia pulled the blanket up to the pillow. Sister Ernestine stopped at the foot of the bed and glared at her wet nightdress.

"Strip the bed, Miss Lange!" she yelled.

Pia did as she was told, the stench of urine filling her nostrils. Sister Ernestine grabbed Gigi by the arm and dragged her into the aisle.

"You know what happens to wet-the-beds," Sister Ernestine snarled.

Gigi started to cry, struggling to break free of her grasp. Sister Ernestine pulled a leather strap from beneath her habit and lifted it in the air. Pia rushed toward her, one hand up to block the strap, the other reaching for Gigi.

"Stop!" she cried. "She didn't do it!"

Sister Ernestine froze, staring at her. "What did you say, Miss Lange?"

"I said she didn't do it."

"I heard that, but apparently you've already forgotten the proper way to address me."

"I'm sorry, Sister Ernestine. She didn't do it, Sister Ernestine."

A savage glee danced in the nun's eyes. "Then who did?"

"Me, Sister Ernestine," Pia said. "I did it."

Sister Ernestine let go of Gigi, who ran whimpering into Jenny's arms. "Come take your punishment then, Miss Lange."

"But it was . . . it was my first night here, Sister Ernestine," Pia said. "I was exhausted and scared and I didn't know if I was allowed to get up to relieve myself. And I don't know where to go. I tried to hold it, but I—"

"That's no excuse," Sister Ernestine said. She gestured for Pia to move closer, the leather strap hanging from one hand. The other girls stood silent, barely moving. A few of the younger ones started to cry. Pia did as she was told and closed her eyes, bracing herself. The leather strap hissed through the air and slapped against her wet nightdress, hitting the back of her thighs like a knife. Her knees gave out and she collapsed on the floor, her thighs on fire. It felt like her skin had split open. She turned over and held her arms up to protect herself, tears streaming down her hot cheeks. The nun lifted the strap again, ready to strike a second time.

"Please, Sister Ernestine," Pia begged. "I'm sorry. It won't happen again."

Sister Ernestine let the strap down. "It better not, Miss Lange," she said. "And I'm not talking about the mess. I punished you for lying. Gigi wets the bed every night. Now tell me, did you learn your lesson?"

Pia gritted her teeth against the pain and struggled to her feet. "Yes, Sister Ernestine," she managed.

"Good," she said. "Now don't forget it." She slipped the strap back beneath her habit. "I know you don't believe it now, but someday you'll thank me for being hard on you. The sooner you learn right from wrong, the easier your life will be." She looked around. "Isn't that right, girls?"

"Yes, Sister Ernestine," everyone said at the same time.

Sister Ernestine nodded, a satisfied look on her face, then marched toward the door, where she turned and waited. "Now get yourselves to work."

Some of the girls hurried to retrieve brooms and the wicker basket from the nun while the rest pushed the beds into the center of the room in a thunderous scrape and rumble, making the floorboards and windowpanes rattle. Pia limped over to her bed and slipped off her urine-soaked nightdress, her legs screaming in pain. She touched the tender skin on the back of her thighs and checked her fingers, expecting to see blood. To her surprise, there was none. Gigi watched with tears in her eyes, her rag doll crushed to her chest. The older girls swept behind the beds and dusted the windowsills, while others stripped the mattresses and put the sheets in the wicker basket. Jenny took off Gigi's wet nightdress, put it in the basket with the sheets, and told Pia to do the same.

"Are you all right?" she whispered.

Pia nodded and dropped her nightdress and the wet sheet in the basket.

"Sorry you had to sleep there. Sister Ernestine gets mad if we switch beds."

"It's not your fault," Pia said.

"She'll send you and Gigi down to the laundry to find fresh underwear," Jenny said. "But not until you've had to wear the wet ones all day." She gave Pia a weak smile and went back to helping the others.

Under the watchful eye of Sister Ernestine, two girls carried the wicker basket out of the room and set it in the hall. Once the beds were slid back into place, everyone got dressed and lined up to go to breakfast.

In the dining hall, Pia winced when she sat down, the pain in her legs almost unbearable. She moved to the edge of the stool to take her weight off her thighs, but it only helped a little. After eating bowls of cold, lumpy porridge, the girls lined up against the wall. Several nuns appeared to take them off to various jobs—some to the laundry or sewing room, others to the kitchen, some to clean rooms and halls. Pia had no idea if she'd be scrubbing floors, peeling potatoes, polishing shoes, or washing dishes. And she didn't dare ask Sister Ernestine.

A nun carrying a lantern came toward her. She was short and chubby, with a kind face and a wine-colored birthmark on one cheek.

"Hello, dear," the nun said. "I'm Sister Agnes. As you probably guessed, here at St. Vincent's everyone but the youngest among us is expected to do his or her share. And you're no different, you know."

Pia nodded. "Yes, ma'am. I mean, Sister Agnes."

"There's no need to be worried, dear. Mother Joe thinks she's found the perfect place for you." She crooked her finger at her. "Now follow me."

Pia trailed the nun up the steps and into the hall, trying to ignore the sharp pull and sting in her thighs. Sister Agnes walked faster than seemed possible for her size, her habit rasping along the floorboards like a black cape. She seemed to float down the corridor, leaving a pleasant-smelling cloud of lavender soap and something that smelled like cinnamon in her wake. Pia found herself wanting to move closer to her, to escape, however briefly, the heavy odor of urine and sorrow that seemed to emanate from every corner of the building. At the end of the hall, they took a right and started up a wide set of stairs. With every turn and junction, the orphanage felt more and more like a never-ending maze of hallways and rooms and staircases. How would she ever find a way out?

At the top of the stairs, they turned down a shadowy passageway that seemed to head away from the main building. It felt more like a tunnel than a hall. At the end, Sister Agnes opened a door and waited for Pia to go through. Pia stepped over the stone threshold into what looked a hospital ward filled with doll beds. When she realized what she was looking at, she gasped.

Row after row of iron cribs lined the high-ceilinged space, and babies of all ages and colors, some two and three to a mattress, filled every one. Some stood, red-faced and wailing, clasping the tall white crib bars in their small fists. Others cuddled blankets while lying on their backs or sides, or sat up drinking bottles or sucking their thumbs and fingers.

Immediately scanning the cribs for Ollie and Max, Pia blinked back tears, cursing herself for crying and making it harder to see. Most of the babies appeared peaked and thin, while some looked clearly ill. A toddler with patchy brown hair balanced on one leg, his other leg shrunken and crippled. Another little girl was blind, her lids half closed, her eyes milky and white. Sister Agnes continued down the center aisle, ignoring the small hands that reached out for her from between metal bars. Then she stopped and looked back at Pia, who stood frozen at the door.

"Are you coming, dear?" she said.

Pia nodded and started moving again, her heart thrashing in her chest, her watery eyes racing over every crib, every small face, every baby who looked the same age as her brothers. One baby was too thin, the next too bald. That one had dimples; this one had red hair. That baby's nose was too wide, the next one's cheeks too plump. Then she saw a blond head and blue eyes peeking out between the white bars of a crib, a baby boy sitting up and staring at her. She rushed over and picked him up, certain it was Ollie or Max. But her heart sank. It was a girl. Sister Agnes hurried back to where she stood, took the baby from her arms, and put her back in the crib.

"What are you doing?" she said. "You're here to help, dear, but you must follow the rules."

Pia dropped her flooding eyes. "Yes, Sister," she said.

"Come along now," Sister Agnes said. "There's no time to dawdle."

Pia swallowed the burning lump in her throat and followed the nun to the other end of the room, searching every tiny face for familiar features. When they passed the last of the cribs, a fresh flood of tears threatened to spill from her eyes. Her brothers weren't there.

In an open space at the end of the room, a pale-faced girl with a mop of brown curls changed a baby's diaper on a blanket-covered table. She looked to be a couple of years older than Pia, but shorter and sturdier. Her sleeves were rolled up, showing her thin, muscular arms, and she stood with her legs apart, as if to steady her stance. She pushed a clean diaper beneath the baby's bottom, pulled the front of it up and over, and pinned it together in one swift motion, like a factory worker who performs the same job over and over. Then she pulled the baby's nightdress down, picked her up, and placed her on one hip. Only then did she notice Sister Agnes and Pia.

"Edith, dear," Sister Agnes said. "This is Pia Lange. She's here to help you take care of our youngest charges."

"It's about damn time you found someone," Edith said. She brushed past them and put the baby girl back in her crib.

"Edith!" Sister Agnes said in a shrill voice. "How many times do I have to scold you about using that kind of language?"

Edith returned and glanced at the nun, an exhausted look on her face. "Sorry, Sister," she said. "It slipped out. I'll say ten Hail Marys and two Our Fathers." All the fire had gone out of her voice.

"Say ten of each," Sister Agnes said. "And when you're finished, mind your tongue. I don't have time to keep reprimanding you. Woe betide you if Mother Joe heard you talking like that!"

"Yes, Sister," Edith said. She pulled a diaper from beneath the table and trudged past the nun to get another crying baby.

"As I was saying," Sister Agnes said, watching Edith as she worked, "Miss Lange is here to help. She's old enough, and it's our understanding that she has experience with babies." She turned to Pia. "You had twin baby brothers. Isn't that right, dear?"

Pia went rigid and her heartbeat picked up speed again. "How . . . how did you know about my brothers?"

"Why, Mother Joe told me, of course. She told us all what happened. You poor thing, losing your entire family all at once."

The blood drained from Pia's face. "What . . . what do you mean?" she said. "What did Mother Joe say?" She started to tremble, her stomach growing tighter and tighter. Did the nuns know something she didn't?

Sister Agnes furrowed her brow. "She said you lost your parents and brothers to the flu."

Pia dug her nails into her palms, struggling to stay upright. "No," she said. "That's not what happened. I . . ."

"I'm sorry, dear," Sister Agnes said. "I didn't mean to upset you. Please forgive me."

"But why . . . How does Mother Joe know anything about my family? How does she know about my brothers?"

Sister Agnes shrugged. "Because that's what the woman who brought you here told her. Oh dear. Maybe I wasn't supposed to say anything. The good Lord knows I have a hard time keeping a watch on my heart and my words. Is there any chance the woman was confused?" She made a move to put her hand on Pia's arm, but Pia pulled away, shaking her head.

"No. I mean, yes," she said. "She must have been confused. I lost my mother, but my father is in the war, and my brothers might . . . they might still be alive. I just don't know where they are."

Sister Agnes crossed herself. "Oh dear, I'm so sorry. I didn't realize . . . I'll pray for them."

"I thought Ollie and Max might be here," Pia said. "But I don't see them. Do you know if anyone dropped off four-month-old twins in the last week or so? They have blond hair and blue eyes and—"

"No, dear," Sister Agnes said, her eyes sad. "I'm afraid we haven't had any twins come in, girls or boys."

Pia opened her mouth to say more, but Edith appeared and handed her a baby.

"He's wet," she said, and went to get another.

Pia stood frozen, holding the wiggling baby, his legs dangling. The infant was naked, except for his wet diaper, and her hands were wrapped around his tiny bare chest. She was still reeling from the shock of what she'd just been told, her mind spinning with questions, and for a moment she forgot about avoiding skin-to-skin contact. Then the baby started to wail and she knew she had to act. Fighting the urge to hand him to Sister Agnes, she took him over to the table and started changing his diaper. Whether she liked it or not, she had to get used to touching babies because working in the baby ward was the only way she'd ever know if someone dropped off Ollie and Max. She took off the baby's wet diaper and reached for another. Were her hands shaking because of what Sister Agnes said, or because something was wrong with the baby? When she finished changing him, she dressed him in a clean sleeping gown, lifted him up, and instinctively bounced him up and down.

Sister Agnes smiled at her. "I can already see that Mother Joe was right about you," she said. "It certainly looks like you know what you're doing. Your brothers were very lucky to have a big sister to help take such good care of them."

Pia chewed on the inside of her cheek, gazing at the baby to avoid the nun's kind eyes. *No, they weren't,* she thought, *they weren't lucky at all. And if you knew what I did to them, you wouldn't let me anywhere near the baby ward. In fact, you'd probably have me arrested.*

"Goodness me," Sister Agnes said. "I've upset you again. I'm sorry. I thought—"

Pia looked at her. "Do you know anything about Miss O'Malley?"

Sister Agnes's brows rose in surprise. "Miss O'Malley?"

"The woman who brought me here," Pia said. "Do you know her?" The baby whimpered and laid his head against her shoulder. She rubbed his back with a gentle hand, surprised that he already seemed to trust her. Then tears stung her eyes. She could feel his small shoulder blades and tiny ribs through his skin. And there was something else too, something shuddering and twitching inside his thin torso.

"No," Sister Agnes said. "I've never seen her before. Mother Joe had never met her either, until this horrible sickness took hold of the city and she began dropping off children."

"Do you know if she's dropped off children anywhere else?"

"I have no idea."

"Can you find out?"

"Whatever for?" Sister Agnes said.

"I'm wondering if she knows anything about my brothers. Maybe she took them somewhere, to a different orphanage or something."

Edith trudged past her with another baby girl and went over to the changing table. More babies started to wail.

"I suppose I can try," Sister Agnes said. "But I'm afraid we've got more urgent matters to attend to at the moment."

Pia looked around at the frightened faces and small hands reaching out between the metal bars, and the horrible ache in her chest grew heavier.

Edith went by her again. "Are you here to help or just look around and feel bad?" she said.

Pia wanted to hold the baby boy longer, to give him what small measure of comfort she could provide, but the others needed to be looked after too. She handed him to Sister Agnes. "There's something wrong with him," she said. "He needs a doctor."

Sister Agnes took the baby and put him back in his crib. "I'm sure he does," she said. "They all do. But people are still dying from the flu. And there aren't any doctors to check on orphans right now. The only thing we can do is ask our sisters in the sick hall to examine him. And pray God will take care of his precious soul."

Weak shafts of sunlight filtered in through the three narrow windows in the baby ward, cutting through the dimness but doing little to ward off the chill. Pia sat in a rocking chair feeding a bottle to a frail baby girl, wishing she had a warm blanket to cover them both up, and that there was a cushion on the hard seat. Ever since getting lashed with the leather strap on her first day at St. Vincent's ten days ago, she slept on the floor between Gigi's bed and the window, making sure to get up before Sister Ernestine came in to wake them. Gigi gave her their pillow, but the wood floor was hard, making her hips ache, and she shivered every night from the cold. In the wee hours when she couldn't sleep, she listened to the sounds coming from elsewhere in the orphanage, drifting up through the splintered planks—wailing voices, singing voices, frightened voices, young voices crying into the night. Sometimes she couldn't tell if she was awake or dreaming.

She set the bottle down, put the infant on her shoulder to burp her, and watched Edith move along the rows of iron cribs. One by one, Edith lifted babies out of their cribs, put them in with others, turned over their soiled mattresses, then put the babies back again. She worked like a machine, never stopping to comfort the crying children or smile at others who begged for attention with pleading eyes. Pia didn't understand how she could ignore them. Maybe she'd been working there so long her heart had turned to stone. Either that or her indifference was a means of survival. Hopefully Pia wouldn't be there long enough to find out.

Sister Agnes entered the baby ward and marched toward Pia, her chin high, the skirt of her habit twisting around her legs.

"Good morning, dear," she said. "I have news." She smiled, absentmindedly rubbing the birthmark on her cheek.

Pia sat up straighter and tried to reply, but the words froze in her mouth. Was the nun about to tell her what happened to her brothers?

"I wanted to let you know Mother Joe spoke with the nun who took care of you at St. Peter's parish," Sister Agnes said.

Pia nodded. Maybe she should hand the baby to Sister Agnes before she said another word. If Ollie and Max were dead, she wasn't sure what would happen. She might faint. Or fall over. Or drop dead. She pressed her elbows into the arms of the chair, bracing herself.

"The nun informed Miss O'Malley that you'd lost your family because you cried out for them in your sleep while you were recovering," Sister Agnes said. "She said you called for your mother and father, and for Ollie and Max, who you said over and over were only babies. No one has proof one way or another what happened to them. So you see, it was only a matter of hearsay. The nun at the parish told Miss O'Malley what she believed, and Miss O'Malley told Mother Joe."

Pia slumped back in the chair, weak with relief. The baby in her trembling arms suddenly weighed as much as a ten-year-old, but she kept patting her back, unable to do anything else. "Thank you, Sister Agnes," she managed.

"You're welcome, dear," Sister Agnes said, and turned to leave.

Pia sat up again. "Wait," she said. "Do you think Mother Joe would be willing to help me find out what happened to my brothers?"

Sister Agnes frowned sympathetically. "I'm afraid not," she said. "St. Vincent's can barely keep up with the care of the children we have now, let alone spare the time or resources to look for more. Besides, we wouldn't even know where to begin."

"What about letting me leave so I can look for them?"

"Heavens no," Sister Agnes said. She shook her head so hard her cheeks jiggled. "Like it or not, dear, it's up to us to keep you safe now. And Mother Joe takes her job, and the reputation of St. Vincent's, very seriously. She'd never let you loose on the streets of

Philadelphia, where there are all manner of ways a young girl could find herself in serious trouble, not to mention people are still dying from the purple death."

"Do you think she could find out if my father has returned from the war?"

Sister Agnes put her hands on her ample hips. "Look around you, dear. Do you believe we have the time or resources to search for the parents of any of these poor children?"

Pia's cheeks grew warm. "No, Sister Agnes," she said. "I suppose not."

CHAPTER ELEVEN

PIA

Two weeks before Thanksgiving, Pia stood at the narrow, mullioned window on the fourth-floor room of ward number six, looking out over the Delaware River outside St. Vincent's Orphan Asylum. It was a late Sunday afternoon, a few minutes before suppertime, and a gathering of gray clouds hung low and ominous in the sky. It had been raining all day, and the swollen river churned swift and deep, the bare trees on the opposite shore like black fingers reaching out of the rocky banks. Upstream, a stone bridge crossed the water into a jumble of brick buildings and towering smokestacks. The orphanage play yard stretched out toward the water, the brown, fenced-in lawn filled with gray puddles and soggy grass, the empty iron swing sets and slide like the skeleton of some half-buried beast. Despite the dreary weather, she would have given anything to open the locked window, to rid the room of the stench of fear, loneliness, and urine that seemed as thick as the paneling on the walls. She wondered if the other eighteen girls, talking and whispering on the ten beds behind her, felt the same way. She would have asked, but they probably wouldn't answer.

Had she known what their reaction was going to be, she never would have admitted she didn't like touching people when one of the girls asked her to braid her hair a few days ago. She would have lied and said she didn't know how. Instead she'd told the truth, and now they watched her from the corners of their eyes and kept the younger girls—including Gigi—away from her, as if she were someone to be feared. Even Jenny avoided her. It felt like school all over again. She told herself she didn't care, that she was used to being shunned and the only thing she cared about was leaving, but it hurt more than expected. Maybe because they all had something in common, being unwilling prisoners of this place, and she'd thought that would make a difference. But she was wrong.

Every day she wondered how many people were still dying in the city, and if Ollie, Max, and Vater were out there somewhere. She'd overheard the nuns talking about the end of the war a few days earlier; how, despite the lingering threat of flu, thousands of Philadelphians had gathered around the replica of the Statue of Liberty on Broad Street to celebrate. Fear and grief had kept many people home, but those who attended stood shoulder to shoulder, most still wearing masks, and cheered nonstop as flags flew from buildings and bands played. Since then, every time the ward door opened, and even though she knew it would take a miracle for him to find her in the orphanage, she prayed it was Vater coming home from the war. It never was.

Like the rest of the girls, her days consisted of making the beds and sweeping the floors, then prayer, meals, and work. Free time was spent in the fenced yard or, during inclement weather, in a large recreation room in the north wing. On Sundays, everyone attended church in a chapel in the back of the building and had a period of rest before dinner in the afternoon.

Pia worked in the baby ward seven days a week, with time off for sleep, meals, and an hour of recreation after supper. Edith was the only girl who would talk to her, and she hardly talked at all, other than what needed to be said while caring for the babies. Pia had to admit Edith scared her a little bit, like a tight lid on a simmering kettle, ready to explode at any second. One minute she was brooding silently, the next she was cussing out the girls from the laundry if they didn't put the basket of clean diapers in the right spot. Pia didn't want to get on her bad side, so she kept quiet and worked hard.

New babies came in nearly every week, some from the city, and others—with bottles of breast milk—from St. Vincent's Home for Unwed Mothers, which was next door. Sister Agnes once brought in an infant in a wicker basket with a note attached that read: *This infant was found on the sidewalk between 50th and 51st Streets.*

Another baby, a newborn, arrived with a letter that read: *Dear Madam, Knowing my little infant will get better care in your institution than I am able to give it, I for the present leave it in your charge. Born Monday 7 a.m. She has not been christened. I call her Mary. Yours ever truly, a poor mother.*

With every child that came in, Pia prayed it would be one of her brothers. It never was.

Now, blinking back tears as she stood at the window, she couldn't help thinking about last Thanksgiving, when Mutti was pregnant and her father hadn't enlisted yet. They had all been certain the war would be over soon, and life had seemed full of hope and possibility. They couldn't afford a turkey, but in an effort to fit in, Mutti had allowed Pia to join Finn as a Thanksgiving masker, which meant dressing up like a ragamuffin to "scramble for pennies" in the street and go door to door "begging" for treats. It was all in good fun, especially since everyone on Shunk Alley had so little to share, and no one cared if they got treats or not. But she and Finn tossed newspaper confetti in the air and followed the other kids, some in papier-mâché masks or giant hands, others wearing mops on their heads or their parents' oversize clothes. Pia and Finn didn't have masks, but they drew on their faces with coal and beet juice, and for those few hours, no one cared that she was German. It was the most fun she'd ever had, and she made Finn promise they'd do it every year, as long as they were able.

Now they were all gone. Mutti. Ollie and Max. Finn. Maybe Vater too.

And she was being kept in an orphanage.

How was it possible for life to turn into a nightmare so fast?

It was a Sunday when she tried to escape St. Vincent's after noticing a window slightly open behind the altar during Communion. She let everyone go ahead while they filed out of the chapel after the service was over, then looked around to make sure no one was watching and crawled under a pew to hide. Once the room was empty and quiet, she rolled out, ran behind the altar, and tried to open the window all the way. If she got out, she wasn't sure how she'd get through the fence surrounding the grounds, but she had to try. At first the window wouldn't budge, as if it were locked or painted shut; but she took a deep breath and tried again, grunting with the effort. Finally, it slid up partway, the swollen wood screeching against the frame.

Certain someone must have heard the noise, she glanced over her shoulder to make sure no one was coming, then tried to open it farther. It was no use. There was no moving it. She bent over and started climbing out, hands ready to brace her fall into the bushes below. It was going to be a tight fit, but she could make it. Her head and torso were out, her hips squeezing under the pane, when suddenly someone grabbed her ankles and yanked her back inside. Her chin bumped against the sill, her arms scraped along the wood, and she hit the floor hard, knocking the wind from her lungs. Gulping for air, she turned over and looked up, her heart like a train in her chest.

It was Mother Joe.

"What on earth do you think you're doing, Miss Lange?" she said, her voice shrill.

"I . . . um . . . I . . ." Pia said.

"Stand up this instant!"

Pia did as she was told, gasping for air and brushing off her dress. The skin on her chin felt scraped, her elbows bruised and sore. "There was a . . . a bird," she said. "A baby bird. He was stuck in the window and I—"

Mother Joe held up a bony finger. "Stop!" she said, making Pia jump. "Don't say another word, Miss Lange." She closed the window, then crossed her arms, pushed her gnarled hands beneath her sleeves, and regarded Pia with burning eyes. "Now I'm going to ask you some questions. And I want you to remember, God is listening."

"Yes, Mother Joe."

"Did you or did you not partake in the Holy Communion not less than fifteen minutes ago?"

"Yes, Mother Joe."

"And does that not mean that you, right now at this very moment, have the body and blood of Christ in you?"

"Yes, Mother Joe."

"And do you or do you not know that lying is a sin punishable by eternal damnation and whatever penalty I deem necessary to make sure you don't repeat the offense?"

"Yes, Mother Joe, I do."

"Very good, Miss Lange. Now think it through for a minute, then tell me again what you were doing hanging halfway out that window."

Pia dropped her eyes to the red carpet, chewing on the inside of her cheek.

"Miss Lange?"

"I was trying to leave," Pia said.

Mother Joe frowned. "Why would you try to do that? Are you unhappy here? Do we not take good care of you by giving you a place to sleep and food to eat?"

"Yes, Mother Joe."

"Then why, pray tell, didn't you go to the baby ward after the service was over like you were supposed to? Why did you try to climb out that window?"

"Because I think my brothers might still be alive. Sister Agnes told you about them, didn't she?"

"She did," Mother Joe said. Then she gave Pia a cynical look. "So you want to leave and search for these brothers of yours, is that it?"

Pia nodded. "Yes, Mother Joe."

"I see." She sighed and looked off to the side, thinking. After what seemed like forever she continued, "I suppose something can be arranged for you to take your leave of us. But not until we're certain the threat of flu has passed and the city has had time to recover from the resulting chaos."

Pia blinked, unable to believe what she was hearing. "Really?" she said. "I mean, do you mean it, Mother Joe?"

"I don't say anything I don't mean, Miss Lange."

Tears filled Pia's eyes and she nearly cried out. Finally, after all this time, she was going to be free to look for Ollie and Max. She almost wanted to hug the old nun. "Thank you, Mother Joe."

"Yes, well, in the meantime, trying to leave without permission and lying to your superiors carries its own punishment, Miss Lange. Pull yourself together and come with me."

Pia followed Mother Joe down the steep staircase to the basement, a strange mixture of apprehension and relief twisting in her stomach. Would her punishment for trying to climb out the window be peeling potatoes or washing dishes? Scrubbing the dining room floor or cleaning urine-soaked sheets? Three lashes with a leather strap? Whatever the price, it was worth getting caught now that Mother Joe had agreed to let her leave. The only problem was, other than going home to see if Vater had gotten her note from the people who lived in her old apartment and seeing if she could find Finn, she had no idea what she'd do next or where she'd go. She had no money. No family. No home. But at least getting out of the orphanage was a start—hopefully the first step in finding out what happened to Ollie and Max.

In the basement, she and Mother Joe crossed the dining room and entered the kitchen, a brick-walled room that felt like an oven and smelled like cold dirt, spoiled milk, and raw onions. Two red-faced nuns stirred oversized kettles on a coal stove and a third sliced loaves of bread on a wooden table with the longest knife Pia had ever seen. Three boys of about five or six years old sat in a corner peeling a mountain of potatoes, their shoes nearly buried in brown skins. Another boy poured milk into mugs lined up on a bench. He glanced up at Pia and accidentally spilled milk over the edge of one mug, dripping a little on the wood. The nun slicing the bread reached over and swatted him on the ear, making him jump, and scolded him for not being more careful. After the kitchen, Pia followed Mother Joe down a narrow hall, past a room filled with piles of dirty linens and empty washtubs. Pia couldn't imagine where Mother Joe was taking her. If washing dishes or working in the laundry wasn't going to be her punishment, what was?

"Excuse me, Mother Joe," she said. "But may I ask where we're going?"

"You'll see soon enough," Mother Joe said. "Remember, patience is a virtue, Miss Lange."

At the end of the hall, Mother Joe stopped at an ancient-looking door with rusty hinges and an iron latch. She pulled her ring of keys out from under her scapular, unlocked the door, and led Pia into a passageway with a rock floor and hulking archways. Closed doors lined the walls, each with a square hole in the center. A cavelike odor of mold and wet stone filled the space, and cobwebs dangled from the uneven ceiling. It looked like an old part of the building, one that hadn't been used in ages.

"What is this place?" Pia said, her voice trembling.

"We use it for quarantines and isolations. Over the years we've had outbreaks of typhoid, tuberculosis, yellow fever, polio, numerous cases of insanity. And more recently, of course, the purple death."

Nausea stirred in Pia's stomach. "You keep children down here?" she said.

"If the need arises," Mother Joe said.

Pia wrapped her arms around herself, goose bumps prickling on her skin. Being ill was bad enough; being kept in this cold, eerie chamber on top of that had to be torture. How many poor souls had suffered and died in this awful place? And why had she been brought down there? To take care of a sick child being kept in one of the rooms?

At the end of the hall Mother Joe stopped in front of a black iron door. It looked like the entrance to hell. "You'll be staying in here until you've learned your lesson."

Fear and panic clutched Pia's stomach. She thought about turning and running, but where would she go? Back upstairs? To her ward? To the playground? There was no way out, no escape. If she tried to run and got caught again, her punishment would only be worse.

"For how long?" she said.

"Until it's long enough."

"But I—"

"Don't try to argue with me, Miss Lange, or your stay will only get lengthier. We have an agreement, remember? Once I feel it's safe for you to leave St. Vincent's, I'll arrange it. But first, you must pay the price for your sins."

Pia shivered, her breath growing shallow and fast. "Yes, Mother Joe."

Mother Joe nodded once, then searched for the right key on her ring. When she found the one she was looking for, she unlocked the door and pulled it open, the hinges screeching like a wounded cat. An iron bed with a straw mattress sat against the back wall of the stone room, its legs bolted to the floor.

Mother Joe motioned her inside.

Pia edged forward, her legs like water. The musty space was no bigger than her parents' old bedroom, with crumbling walls and a tiny, recessed window near the sagging ceiling. She'd never seen a dungeon but imagined they looked and felt like this, the sour air thick with the memories of human suffering, the walls stained with black mold and something that looked like clots of blood. How many children had been locked in this room? How many had died? She turned to look at Mother Joe, praying this was only a threat, or a warning.

"Please, Mother Joe," she said. "You don't need to leave me here. I promise I've learned my lesson."

"I'll send down your meals," Mother Joe said. "And you can use the bucket to relieve yourself. I strongly suggest you use this time to pray, Miss Lange, to ask God for forgiveness for your sins and to help you be a better Christian."

Pia's mouth went dry as dust. She tried to think of something to say, but words escaped her. Her tongue felt like stone.

Mother Joe fixed critical eyes on her for a long moment, then left the room and slammed the door behind her, the dull clang of iron echoing in the empty passageway. Pia stared at the door, frozen and in shock. The key rattled and turned in the lock. Then Mother Joe's footsteps banged along the stone corridor, went through another door, and disappeared. Something about the sounds—the heavy clank of iron, the clack of shoes on cold stone, the silence that followed—reminded Pia that if anyone found out about the things she'd felt and the things she'd done, she'd spend the rest of her life in a place like this, either a prison or an insane asylum. Maybe she deserved to be locked up. Being in this cramped, cold room, she imagined how Ollie and Max must have felt in the dark cubby, frightened and confused, wondering where the people who loved them had gone, why no one had come to save them. She lay down on the bed and curled into a ball on the moldy mattress. A flood of fearful tears came first, then crushing guilt and grief. She closed her eyes and tried to remind herself that Mother Joe had agreed to let her go. Then she could begin searching for her brothers in earnest. And she wouldn't stop until she learned the truth. She owed them that at least.

Hopefully Mother Joe wouldn't forget she was down there.

CHAPTER TWELVE

BERNICE

December 1918

Watching the city slowly come back to life from the third-floor window of her new residence on Philadelphia's West Side, Bernice squinted at the winter sun peeking over the row houses across the way, long pink rays stretching over snowy rooftops and black water towers. According to the papers, over 47,000 Philadelphians had contracted the flu and over 12,000 had died during the first four weeks after the Liberty Loan parade. By the second week in November, deaths from influenza and pneumonia were a quarter of what they had been the prior week and—against the wishes of the State Health Department—churches, schools, vaudeville houses, and saloons began to reopen. However, the end of the war caused a resurgence of the flu due to Armistice Day celebrations and the release of soldiers, so the Committee of the American Public Health Association encouraged shops and factories to stagger their opening and closing hours, and advised people to walk to work when possible instead of using public transportation to avoid overcrowding. Streetcars, doctors warned, were "seed beds" for the flu.

Now, it seemed, many Philadelphians had taken the message to heart. On the short stretch of slush-covered sidewalk below Bernice's room, men in long coats and black hats hurried to their jobs with newspapers and lunch pails under their arms, some still wearing masks. A beggar woman in a ratty dress stood on the corner, holding out a dirty hand. The men ignored her, giving her a wide berth.

Astonished that the world could return to normal after everything that had happened, Bernice knew that, for her, nothing would ever be the same. Her beloved husband and son were gone, never to return, along with the naïve part of her that had believed in hope and happily ever after. For reasons she'd never understand, God had taken everything good and precious from her. Some days she still felt paralyzed by her loss, her chest filled with the sinking weight of the absence of her child. She didn't recognize herself in the mirror anymore, and wondered if she might shatter beneath the heavy burden of grief. Not one minute passed when she wasn't aware Wallis was gone. But the twins gave her a reason to wake up every day, and she reminded herself that from now on, if she wanted life to turn out a certain way, she needed to be the one who made it come about. All the prayers and begging in the world wouldn't get you what you wanted or deserved, no matter how good a Christian you tried to be.

She turned and looked at the boys, asleep side by side on her bed. With regular nursing and more solid food, their cheeks had begun to fill out and a rosy glow had returned to their skin. They settled down easier at bedtime and became more content with every passing day. She had named them Owen and Mason—Owen after her late father, and Mason because she liked the sound of it. They were good names, strong and solid and true, like real American names should be. And even though it was still hard to tell the twins apart sometimes, she grew more and more fond of them as time went on.

Their new home consisted of only one room, with just enough space for a dresser, bed, and chair. But it was far enough away from the Fifth Ward that no one would recognize her or the babies. And that was all that mattered. When she saved enough money, they would move to a bigger place, but for now it was perfect. She couldn't believe her luck when she found it—the older couple had been putting up the Room for Rent sign on the building's front door just as she was walking by, and it helped that they were immediately smitten with the twins. When she told Mr. and Mrs. Patterson she was a war widow and a nurse who was trying to start over, they readily agreed to give her the room without a deposit. Not only that, but they offered to watch the boys so she could go back to work. It seemed too good to be true. So far, everything was working out in her favor, which was further proof that taking the twins had been the right thing to do. It helped, too, that the Red Cross had asked "true American" women to open their homes to the many unfortunates orphaned by the epidemic. Because she certainly was a true American.

If only she could stop thinking about abandoning Wallis. The guilt of leaving him felt like a boulder in her chest, making it hard to sleep and breathe and eat. By now someone had seen the two ribbons on her old apartment door—white for Wallis and black for herself. By now they had found him and the dead nurse and taken them to the morgue. She'd left ribbons on the Langes' door too—four of them, black for Mrs. Lange and white for Pia and the twins. No one would suspect that the Lange children were alive unless Pia had returned and found the boys missing. Even then, there was nothing Pia could do about it, nor any way she could figure out who took her brothers. Bernice had never spoken two words to the girl. Not to mention that during and after the chaos and commotion caused by the flu, with so many deaths happening so quickly and new cases still being reported, no one would have time to look for two small boys, anyway.

Still, she had nightmares about what she'd done—dragging the nurse's corpse into her bedroom and putting her in the bed she'd shared with her late husband, struggling to put one of her own nightdresses over the nurse's head. She could still see the woman's blood-clotted nose and twisted mouth, her blue face and staring eyes rimmed with blood. She could still picture Wallis lying motionless and cold beside her, a woman who was not his mother. Did he know his real mother had deserted him and left him alone with a stranger? Would he and the nurse be buried together as mother and son? The thought was almost more than she could bear.

She pushed the image away and wiped her eyes. She had done what was necessary, to save the twins and to save herself. The nurse would have died from the flu, anyway. A little rat poison hadn't made a difference one way or the other. And Wallis would be reunited with his real mother in heaven someday. That was all that mattered, not where his body lay. Right now she needed to take Owen and Mason over to stay with Mr. and Mrs. Patterson. It was time to put on the nurse's uniform and go to work.

In the middle- and upper-class neighborhoods of northern Philadelphia, Bernice's plan to collect donations for the city's orphanages had turned out to be more profitable than she'd hoped. Perhaps surviving the epidemic had made those left behind more willing to help the less fortunate, or maybe her story about the orphanages and asylums being overcrowded with children who had lost parents during the flu tugged at their heartstrings. Whatever the reason, people's generosity, even if they could spare only a few coins, felt like more proof that taking the twins had been the right thing to do. Between that and the nurse uniform, she felt practically invincible.

Naturally there were times when the sight of her outfit filled people with fear and they told her to go away. But she understood they were scared of the flu, not her. More often than not, people seemed pleased and grateful to see her. Sometimes they asked her to come inside for tea and biscuits, or to check in on a sick loved one, more than a few with the flu or pneumonia. At first, she was reluctant to give medical aid, but once she realized those visits resulted in larger donations, she readily agreed to check for fevers, wipe brows, and recommend elderberry or peppermint tea for sore throats and stomachaches. In some cases, she dispensed drops of laudanum from the bottles she'd found in the dead nurse's bag, for earaches, the vapors, gangrene, measles, syphilis, epilepsy, and insomnia. On days when grief was the only thing she could feel, she prayed to God she'd catch a deadly illness so she could be with her son again. She loved Owen and Mason, but not like she loved Wallis. Something was missing that she couldn't quite put her finger on when it came to them, like a disconnect of the natural bond mothers felt so deeply for their children, or the savage maternal instinct that would have made her petrified of dying and leaving them behind. She wasn't willing to die for them, like she was for Wallis. She tried to feel the same way about the boys, wanted to feel it more than anything, but it couldn't be forced. If something happened to her, the twins would be fine with Mr. and Mrs. Patterson.

And after everything she'd been through and everything she'd lost, she had no remorse about using the donations to pay rent and put food on the table for Owen and Mason, especially money from those who were not native born. The number of immigrants living in big houses and nice neighborhoods both surprised and angered her. They had stolen jobs from real Americans and didn't deserve to be living the American dream. And according to the papers, the poorer sections of the city had been hardest hit by the epidemic, so it seemed only fair that the rich, no matter where they had been born, should help the poor. She just had to keep knocking on doors.

While canvassing a new neighborhood ten blocks south of the one she'd visited the previous day, she turned off the main thoroughfare and made her way past a barbershop and pool hall, then hurried along the sidewalk toward the residential area two blocks over. Feeling strong and enjoying the warmth of the sun in the winter sky, she couldn't help thinking about everything she wanted to buy the twins for Christmas: new clothes and shoes, wooden blocks, and Teddy bears. And if things kept going the way they were, they'd be able to move into a larger apartment as soon as one opened up in the building. Moving to another city so no one could find them had crossed her mind, but it'd be nearly impossible to find someone else to take care of Owen and Mason, especially for free. Right now she needed Mr. and Mrs. Patterson's help, at least until the twins were old enough to go to school. Besides, Philadelphia was her home. She belonged there more than most.

As she hurried past a recessed stairwell in front of a brick workshop, a flash of movement caught her eye. She stopped and looked over the iron railing, down the stone steps. A boy in a worn jacket and ripped pants sat at the bottom of the stairs, resting his elbows on his knees. He looked to be about seven years old, with a headful of greasy dark hair and dirty hands. *It's just another homeless immigrant,* she thought. The city was full of them. She started walking again, then had an idea. She turned around and went to the top of the stairwell.

"What are you doing down there?" she called to the boy. "Are you lost?"

The boy stood and spun around to look up at her. Anxiety furrowed his dirt-smudged brow.

She started down the steps. "Do you speak English?"

He moved backward, nodding. "Some."

"What's your name?"

He frowned.

She stopped halfway down the stairwell and pointed at him. "Your name?"

"Nelek," he said.

"Are you hungry, Nelek?" Using her hands, she pretended to eat.

He nodded again, harder this time, a hollow desperation widening his eyes.

She motioned for him to come up the stairs. "Follow me, then," she said. "I'll take you someplace safe, for a hot meal and a fresh change of clothes."

He shook his head, confused.

She smiled to prove she meant no harm. "It's all right. You're not in trouble. I'm going to help you." She waved him toward her. "I can get you food."

After a long hesitation, he finally followed her up the steps.

They walked for over thirty minutes, until she stopped in front of a brick building with row after row of curtainless windows. She'd noticed the building a while ago, during one of her donation outings, and she was relieved she'd remembered how to get there. To her surprise, Nelek had followed her the entire way without stopping or complaining. A painted sign above the double doors read: St. Joseph's Orphan Asylum.

The first time she'd seen the building, the horrible stories her brother had told about orphanages had come flooding back, and she crossed to the other side of the road. Now she couldn't believe she was going inside. Pushing away her fears, she took the steps up to the porch and smiled back at the boy. Suddenly, she froze, certain she couldn't follow through with her plan. Then she reminded herself that the city's problems were a direct result of too many immigrants; the overcrowded tenements filled with foreigners had contributed to the intensity of the flu epidemic—and ultimately the death of her son. She owed it to Wallis to do what she could to keep things from getting any worse.

Nelek stopped at the bottom of the steps and gazed warily up at the sign, his brows knitted.

"Come," she said, waving him up on the porch. "They will feed you here." She opened the door and waited for him, trembling with fear. What if the nuns could tell she wasn't a nurse? What if they called the police or tried to keep her there? What if they turned Nelek away? Maybe she should have taken him to an almshouse or an asylum instead. "It's all right. No one is going to hurt you." She wasn't sure if she was trying to convince herself or Nelek.

He put his hands in his pockets and scuffed a holey shoe against the sidewalk, then finally clambered up the steps. They went through the entrance into a short hall lined with straight-backed chairs opposite a closed door. The musty smell of old wood filled the air, along with a powdery fragrance similar to lavender or talc, but tinged with the hint of something sour, like sweat or rotten fruit. At the end of the hall, a nun sat behind a desk. She looked up when they entered.

"May I help you?" the nun said.

Bernice cleared her throat and approached the desk on wobbly legs. She couldn't help but imagine starving children locked in back rooms, their skin thin and white, their desperate eyes sunken in their shriveled faces. An image of the nun forcing her to stay there with Nelek flashed in her mind and she almost turned and ran. Then she gritted her teeth, glanced down at her nurse uniform, and reminded herself why she was there. Except she had no idea what the procedure was for dropping off a child at an orphanage, or if they accepted immigrants. Maybe they'd lock her up for even trying.

"I found this boy on the street," she said, her voice tight. "Do you have room for him?"

"Is he healthy?" the nun said.

Bernice nodded. She had no idea if he was or not, and she didn't care.

"We're nearly overcapacity right now," the nun said, "but I'll check." She stood, came around the desk, and rapped on the closed door in the middle of the hall. Without waiting for an answer, she opened it and stuck her head inside. "We have a drop-off."

A voice on the other side mumbled something Bernice couldn't make out. The nun nodded, then closed the door and pointed to the chairs against the wall.

"Have a seat," she said. "Someone will be with you shortly."

Bernice led Nelek over to the chairs, amazed to think it might be so simple to get an immigrant off the street. He took a seat, his hands still in his pockets, and the nun went back to her desk. Bernice wasn't sure what to do. Should she sit down and wait, or go? Would they want to know her name or ask if she knew anything else about the boy? More than anything, she wanted to get out of the orphanage, to leave the horrible place behind, but departing now might look unprofessional. Nurses didn't walk out. Nurses stayed and faced their fears.

The nun reached into a drawer, then came around the desk again to offer Nelek a package of Necco wafers. He smiled and took it.

"Thank you, miss," he said, then yanked open the wrapper and popped a wafer into his mouth.

The nun regarded Bernice. "Don't worry, my dear," she said. "We'll take good care of him. Thank you for bringing him here, but there's no need to stay. I know you're needed by so many others, so feel free to go knowing the good Lord will surely bless you for helping this poor child."

Breathing a silent sigh of relief, Bernice only nodded because she didn't know what to say. Nelek gave her a weary smile, his innocent eyes filled with gratitude. She turned away and headed for the door, a pang of guilt tugging at her heart. He had no idea what was in store for him. Her brother had told her how nuns used candy to lure children into believing they were nice; now she had seen it firsthand. Then again, why should she feel bad? It wasn't her fault Nelek was on the street. Where were his parents? She'd heard stories about immigrants dying on their journey to America, so maybe something happened to them on their way here. And if that were the case, he would have eventually ended up in a poorhouse or orphanage, anyway. Maybe his parents should have thought of that before they tried coming here.

CHAPTER THIRTEEN

PIA

On a Monday afternoon a few days before Christmas, Pia was easing a sleeping infant into a crib when she looked up to see Sister Ernestine enter the baby ward and start toward her. She covered the baby with a blanket and waited for the nun to reach her, suddenly on edge. It was the first time she'd ever seen Sister Ernestine in the ward, and she couldn't imagine why she was there. Had Pia done something wrong? With Sister Ernestine it was hard to tell, and she didn't dare ask. The last thing she wanted was to be locked in the basement again.

Luckily, Mother Joe had let Pia out of the dungeon-like room after four days, but it felt like she was in there for an eternity. She'd never forget the dark shadows that had swallowed the cramped chamber as the weak light coming through the tiny window faded, leaving a blackness so complete she couldn't see her hand in front of her face. Even now, she could still see and hear the rats scurrying along the rock floor, and feel the bone-chilling cold. And no matter how many times she washed her hair with cold water and lye soap, she could still smell the stale urine and mold from the straw mattress wafting from her pillow like a cloying, phantom perfume.

She chewed the inside of her cheek, wondering what Sister Ernestine wanted. Sister Ernestine came to a halt a few feet away, stopping so abruptly her wattled chin shook. "Come with me, Miss Lange," she said. Then she turned and headed back to the door.

Pia glanced over her shoulder at Edith, who was in the rocking chair feeding a baby, to make sure she knew she wasn't abandoning her, and to see if she, too, was surprised by Sister Ernestine's appearance. Edith jerked her chin in the air to acknowledge what was happening, but as usual, her face was impossible to read.

Pia took a deep breath and followed Sister Ernestine out of the baby ward, down the long corridor, and into another hall. She couldn't imagine where they were going. When they turned left toward the front foyer instead of right toward the other wards, her heart beat faster. She hadn't been in the foyer since her arrival. Was Mother Joe finally going to release her? Was Vater there, waiting to take her away? Had someone found Ollie and Max?

Sister Ernestine unlocked the door to the foyer and held it open, her face a blank slate. Pia hurried through it and scanned the room, her eyes darting from the front entrance to the reception desk and back again. Vater was nowhere to be seen. Neither was Mother Joe. A nurse waited at the reception desk, her dirty blond hair neatly combed into a low bun behind her military-style hat. She had a baby in her arms. Pia gasped and ran toward her, an overwhelming mix of relief and terror rushing through her chest. Someone had found one of the twins! But where was the other one?

When the nurse saw Pia hurrying toward her, her eyes went wide. She took a step back and clutched the baby protectively to her chest. Pia reached for him, but the nurse pulled him away. Pia couldn't imagine what she was doing. Why wasn't she giving her the baby? She stood there, panting and fighting the urge to rip her brother from this stranger's arms.

"It's all right," Sister Ernestine said to the nurse. "Pia helps care for the babies here at St. Vincent's. You can give him to her."

"But I . . ." the nurse said. "I . . . She's just a child herself."

Sister Ernestine sighed long and loud. "I can assure you, Nurse . . ." she said. "I'm sorry, but you neglected to mention your name."

A strange expression distorted the nurse's features, as if she'd suddenly forgotten how to speak; then the odd look was gone as quickly as it appeared, replaced by something that resembled apprehension. "I'm sorry, Sister," she said. "Please forgive me. I'm Nurse Wallis."

"Well, Nurse Wallis," Sister Ernestine said, her tone short. "I can assure you it's perfectly fine to give the child to Pia. I wouldn't have brought her out here otherwise."

Nurse Wallis eyed Pia warily, then reluctantly handed her the baby. Pia gathered the warm bundle in her arms, a soft laugh escaping her throat. She looked down at his face and rubbed a hand over the top of his small head, her flooding eyes blurring her vision. Overcome with relief that one of her brothers was alive, she paused for a moment to take in this miracle before asking about the other one, to breathe in his sweet scent and feel the weight of his body in her arms. She blinked back her tears so she could see his features more clearly, to figure out if it was Ollie or Max. She went to kiss his forehead. Then she stopped.

A note pinned to the baby's blanket read: *The mother of this child died of the flu last night. She was a Romanian beggar.*

Pia gasped and examined the baby closer, her horror growing. His eyes were hazel, not blue, and the corners of his lids turned down. His nose was too wide and his chin too pointed. Her stomach dropped and her legs nearly gave out.

It wasn't Max.

And it wasn't Ollie.

She gaped at the nurse, panic-stricken. "This isn't my brother!" she said, her voice quaking with fury. "Who are you, and why would you play such a cruel trick on me?"

Nurse Wallis recoiled, staring at Pia as if she'd lost her mind.

"Miss Lange!" Sister Ernestine barked. "Apologize this instant!" She took the baby and addressed the nurse. The baby woke up and started to fuss. "I'm sorry, Nurse Wallis. I can guarantee you this is not our usual procedure. Sister Agnes is under the weather today, otherwise she would have been here to meet you and take the child. I thought Pia could manage it, but apparently I was mistaken." She gave Pia a withering glare.

Pia's eyes flooded again. "I'm sorry," she said. "I thought . . . I thought the baby was . . ." The words got stuck in her throat and she couldn't go on.

Nurse Wallis smoothed the front of her uniform and pulled at her collar with shaky hands. Then she straightened her shoulders and lifted her chin, trying to maintain her professional composure. "I apologize for the confusion," she said. "I only know the boy's mother was in the country less than a year and his name is Nicolai. I was asked to bring him here, and that's the extent of my involvement." She glanced down at her uniform again, as if gathering her courage, and cleared her throat. "But I have to say, I certainly never expected to be treated so rudely, especially by one of your orphans." She gave Pia a disgusted look.

"I understand completely, Nurse Wallis," Sister Ernestine said. "I have no idea what's gotten into Miss Lange, but I can assure you she won't misuse you again." She looked down at the baby in her arms and adjusted the blanket around him, her face red, her temples pulsing in and out. Pia couldn't tell if she was furious or embarrassed. And right now she didn't care. It took all of her strength not to fall to her knees and sob.

"Well, I should hope not," Nurse Wallis said. "Because I certainly don't deserve it. I'm leaving now. Good day, Sister." She started to turn away, as if about to storm out, then changed her mind. Her face had suddenly turned hard-bitten, her mineral-gray eyes full of cunning. "Before I go, I have to ask. Have you thought about having Miss Lange evaluated for a mental disturbance? She seems quite unstable to me, maybe even prone to violence. Perhaps she'd be better suited to an institution meant to help people like her."

Pia's mouth fell open and panic ignited her chest. Why would the nurse say such a thing? Was it possible she had learned about the strange things she felt when she touched people? Had the nurse discovered the horrible things she'd done? "No," she said, louder than intended. "I'm not crazy. I just thought . . ." She hesitated and lowered her voice, choosing her words carefully. "I'm sorry for shouting at you, Nurse Wallis. It's just, I don't know where my brothers are, you see. And I thought . . . well, it doesn't matter what I thought. I was mistaken and I hope you'll accept my sincere apology for my offensive behavior."

Nurse Wallis looked down her nose at Pia. "I suppose I will accept your apology," she said. "You're just an insolent child after all. But just so you know, more than likely I'll be coming back here to help other orphans at some point, and if I see another outburst like that I'll have no choice but to talk to Mother Joe about recommending you for a mental evaluation."

Pia dropped her eyes to the floor. "Yes, ma'am," she said. "Thank you for accepting my apology, ma'am."

"You're welcome," Nurse Wallis said. She pulled at her collar again and regarded Sister Ernestine. "Now, if you'll excuse me, Sister, I must be on my way. I hope next time we meet it will be under better circumstances."

"I'm sure it will be," Sister Ernestine said. "Thank you for bringing in this poor boy. We'll take good care of him."

Nurse Wallis nodded, then turned, marched across the foyer, and went out the door.

Sister Ernestine scowled at Pia, her expression murderous. "What in the devil is wrong with you, Miss Lange? You scared that poor nurse half to death. Haven't we taught you anything about proper behavior?" The baby in her arms woke up and started to howl.

"I . . . I'm sorry, Sister Ernestine," Pia said. "It won't happen again." She held out her trembling arms for the baby. "Here, I'll take him back to the ward."

Sister Ernestine made another disgusted face and passed the boy over to her with as little care as she'd give a sack of potatoes. "Get on with it, then," she said. "And if I hear so much as one more cross word out of you, I'll make sure Mother Joe sends you to the loony bin myself."

"Yes, Sister Ernestine," Pia said. "I'll behave from now on, I promise." She held the crying baby against her chest and turned to leave, struggling to stay upright, afraid she might fall into a sobbing heap on the floor. When she was alone on the other side of the foyer door, she buried her face in the baby's soft neck and wept with him, their forlorn wails filling the empty hallway.

CHAPTER FOURTEEN

BERNICE

Twenty blocks from her old neighborhood in the Fifth Ward, Bernice entered the foyer of a two-story row house, went into the hall, and knocked on the first door. Practicing what she was going to say, she ran her hands along her coat pockets and squared her shoulders. Since finding Nelek in the stairwell, she'd picked up six more homeless immigrants—three boys and a girl, ages four to ten, and a fifteen-year-old boy with his three-year-old brother—and dropped them off at different orphanages around the city. She had to admit separating the fifteen-year-old from his little brother before taking him to a Home for Industrious Boys was harder than she thought it would be, what with both of them crying and her having to lie about reuniting them someday. But it was the right thing to do. Boys aged fourteen and older were hard to place.

Remembering the three-year-old's tear-stained cheeks, she pressed a hand over her milk-filled breasts and thought about Owen and Mason, back home with Mr. and Mrs. Patterson. Were they sleeping? Eating? Crying? Hopefully they were happy and playing, and the Pattersons were watching them more closely now that they were reaching for things. They were also starting to babble and react to their names, and she couldn't wait until they started saying mama. At the same time, her heart ached knowing she'd never hear Wallis call her that. And if she was being honest, she didn't relish the fact that Mr. and Mrs. Patterson were trying to teach the twins to call them Gramma and Grampa, or that they got to spend so much time with the boys. But there was nothing she could do about any of it. She had no choice; she had work to do. And she couldn't afford to upset the Pattersons.

On top of it all, she was still reeling from the shock of seeing Pia Lange at St. Vincent's when she'd dropped off the Romanian baby. Just thinking about the headache she'd had for days afterward was enough to make her stomach turn. When Pia ran toward her at first, Bernice thought the girl had recognized her, or remembered her from the Fifth Ward. Then she reminded herself that Pia hadn't witnessed the angry words she'd exchanged with Mrs. Lange, and she certainly didn't know Bernice's real name. Pia had never even made eye contact with her, let alone paid any attention to anyone besides that Duffy boy, who she looked at with dreamy eyes. When Pia wasn't with him or in school or inside her apartment, she sat on the stoop with her nose in a book. Maybe she wondered where she'd seen Bernice before but was too upset over the Romanian baby to care. Hopefully the threat of a mental evaluation had frightened her enough to make her steer clear if they crossed paths again.

She had to admit she'd felt a twinge of remorse when Pia reacted the way she did, crying out so pitifully when she realized the baby wasn't one of her brothers. But the feeling disappeared as quickly as it came, especially after Pia got cross and screamed at her. That was when Bernice remembered one of the reasons why she'd taken the twins in the first place, along with wanting to save them from their undesirable German heritage. Pia was too immature and unpredictable to take care of the boys; she'd proved that by putting them in the cubby and leaving them there. Just because she was their big sister didn't mean she deserved them. Whatever happened to her afterward was her own fault. If anything, she deserved to be punished.

Bernice had to admit something else too, that she was surprised by how easily ideas came to her, like threatening Pia with the mental evaluation and using her son's name when the nun asked who she was. Sometimes it felt like other, more mysterious forces were at work, helping her do what she needed to do. She'd certainly never thought of herself as clever or cunning, but something had certainly changed. Now she was about to find out if her latest plan for rescuing immigrant children from their parents' bad influence was going to work. She'd chosen this neighborhood on purpose. If only someone would answer the door. She knocked again, starting to get annoyed. Finally, the handle turned and the door opened a few inches. A young, dark-haired woman with brown skin peeked out.

"Yes?" the woman said.

Bernice gave her a warm smile. "Hello," she said. "I'm with the Red Cross collecting donations to help the city orphanages, which, as I'm sure you've heard, have become overcrowded with children who lost their parents during the flu."

The woman looked Bernice up and down, her brows knitted together, then opened the door all the way. The rank, animal aroma of boiled mutton drifted out into the hall, along with something that smelled like warm dust. "I'm sorry," the woman said in heavily accented English. "But I cannot help. I have hard time taking care of my own children."

"I understand," Bernice said. "If you don't mind me asking, how many do you have?"

"Three. A girl and two boys."

"How nice. May I ask how old?"

"My daughter is three, my sons four and seven."

Bernice raised her eyebrows. "Oh my. It sounds like you have your hands full."

The woman looked slightly puzzled, but nodded anyway.

"I'm Nurse Wallis. And your name is?"

"Yasemin," the woman said.

Bernice put a hand over her heart, feigning delight. "Oh my goodness," she said. "What a beautiful name. How long have you been in the United States, Yasemin?"

Yasemin held up a finger. "One year."

"And your husband? He works?"

Yasemin dropped her eyes.

"Please, don't worry yourself," Bernice said. "Along with collecting donations, the Red Cross has given me permission to offer help to those in need. There are so many families struggling during these difficult times, we want to do our part whenever we can."

"My husband has job, but it pays very little."

"I understand," Bernice said. "And I know that can make things challenging. Would it make a difference if I could get you some extra food?"

Yasemin gave her an embarrassed nod, her eyes glassy.

"All right. I'm happy to help. Let me take your boys back to our Red Cross center, and I can get them a hot meal and some new clothes. After that I'll send them home with additional food, which has been donated by the city."

Yasemin chewed on her thumbnail and glanced over her shoulder.

Sensing her hesitation, Bernice gave her a reassuring smile. "If you'd rather not," she said, "I understand. You don't know me and I'm asking to take your children. But just so you know, I'm not sure how much longer the city will be helping in response to the aftermath of the epidemic. I'd bring some food back to you myself, but I have too many other families to visit before the day is over."

Yasemin stopped chewing her thumbnail and sighed, her shoulders dropping in submission. "I send my oldest with you," she said. "His name is Hasan."

"Very good," Bernice said. "But if you send both boys, they can carry twice as much food back home."

Yasemin shook her head. "No, the other is too young. Too little."

"I understand."

Yasemin called over her shoulder for Hasan, then looked back at Bernice. "How long he will be gone?"

"He'll be home by suppertime," Bernice said. "You have my word."

Standing in the well-appointed foyer of the Orphan Society of Philadelphia on Market Street, Bernice grew impatient waiting for someone in charge to take the Ukrainian boy off her hands. She had never waited this long at any of the other orphanages, and she was beginning to worry there was some kind of problem. There weren't any nuns here, which made her think she should come here more often, but not if it was going to take forever.

A child's muffled voice, soft and crying, and the firm voice of a woman floated down from upstairs. Bernice moved toward the staircase, straining to hear, but couldn't make out any words. She went back to where the Ukrainian boy sat on the floor playing jacks, oblivious to the fact that this might be his new home. His name was Sava and he was seven years old. His mother was back in their cramped rooms on Tasker Street, waiting for him to return with food and extra clothing. He looked up at her and smiled.

"Would you like to play?" he said.

She shook her head.

"Are you certain?" he said. "It is a new game to me and I like it very much. Maybe you will too."

She shook her head again and turned toward the window. Despite his dark hair, Sava's deep-set eyes, his masculine nose, even his dimpled chin reminded her of her late husband, and what she imagined Wallis might have looked like at that age. It was uncanny and more than a little unsettling. The sooner she was free of him the better. Otherwise she might change her mind and take him home. And how would she explain that?

Outside the window, a horse-drawn wagon full of children—girls and boys of all ages—pulled over to the side of the road and stopped. A boy wearing a newsboy cap stood in the wagon bed and looked up at the orphanage. An older girl held a toddler in her lap. Another boy had his arm around a little girl who looked like his sister. While the driver waited, a man climbed down from the passenger seat, motioned for the boy in the cap to sit down, and started up the sidewalk. He took off his hat and hurried through the door into the foyer, bringing with him the smell of burning wood and rank cigars. A door slammed upstairs, and footsteps clicked along the hall and started down the staircase. Bernice, Sava, and the man looked up the steps at the same time, waiting. A thin woman in a gray dress came down the steps with a boy of about ten wearing a starched white shirt, brown jacket, and pressed trousers.

He gripped a small, tattered suitcase with both hands, holding it in front of him like a shield. Tears glazed his red eyes and dampened his freshly scrubbed face. When they reached the bottom, the woman rested her hand on his trembling shoulder.

"Good morning, Mr. Kent," she said to the man.

"Good morning, Mrs. Cromwell," Mr. Kent said. "Are we ready?"

"Yes," Mrs. Cromwell said. "I've explained to Barry that a new family is waiting for him and he needs to be on his best behavior. Isn't that right, Barry?"

Barry bit his lip and nodded.

"Good," Mr. Kent said. "Let's be off then, shall we? The train leaves in thirty minutes." He put his hat back on and headed toward the door. Mrs. Cromwell gave Barry a gentle shove and he followed Mr. Kent across the foyer.

"Don't forget to mind your manners!" Mrs. Cromwell called after him.

After they were gone, Mrs. Cromwell approached Bernice with a warm smile. "May I help you?"

"Yes, please," Bernice said. She glanced over her shoulder at Sava. "But first, may we speak privately?"

"Of course," Mrs. Cromwell said, and led her to one corner of the room.

Bernice lowered her voice. "His mother asked me to bring him here because she no longer has the means to care for him. He's not aware he's staying."

Mrs. Cromwell nodded. "I understand."

"Do you have room for him?"

"Yes," Mrs. Cromwell said. "Your timing is perfect. As you just saw, one of our beds was recently vacated."

Bernice nodded. "If you don't mind me asking, where were the children in the wagon going?"

Mrs. Cromwell beamed proudly. "I'd be happy to tell you," she said. "A number of years ago, the Children's Aid Society started a wonderful program to help homeless, abandoned, and orphaned children by transporting them out of the big cities and placing them with rural farm families. The children in that wagon have families waiting for them out in Michigan. They'll be treated as natural-born children in the matter of schooling, clothing, and training, and given one hundred dollars when they turn twenty-one."

Bernice raised her eyebrows. "They have families waiting? How is that possible?"

Mrs. Cromwell clasped her hands at her waist. "Well, not all of them. Some arrangements were made ahead of time, of course, but posters have been put up to let the townspeople know the trains are arriving. Then an open house will be held, where families can choose from the rest of the children."

Bernice couldn't believe what she was hearing. It was one thing to put children in orphanages in an effort to get them away from the bad influences of their immigrant parents. Sending them away by train to rural farm families would be even better. "Babies too?" she said.

Mrs. Cromwell nodded. "Sometimes, yes."

Bernice glanced at Sava. "What about him?" she said. "Is there time to take him to the station before the train leaves?"

Mrs. Cromwell furrowed her brow. "No, not this time," she said. "But in the future, perhaps. Does he speak English?"

"Yes," Bernice said.

"That's helpful," Mrs. Cromwell said. "We only send white, English-speaking children on the trains. The less desirables are too hard to place."

Bernice tried to hide her disappointment. "I see," she said. Of course foreign children were hard to place, especially those who didn't look American. It made perfect sense, but she was hoping she'd stumbled upon an easier way to get immigrants away from their parents. She went over to Sava, who was still playing jacks. Mrs. Cromwell followed.

"Sava," Bernice said. "Say hello to Mrs. Cromwell."

Sava stopped playing and looked up. "Hello."

Mrs. Cromwell squatted beside him. "That's one of my son's favorite games," she said.

Sava grinned at her, his chestnut eyes dancing. "How old is he?"

"Ten."

"Maybe we can play together sometime," Sava said. "If I come to visit again?"

"Maybe," Mrs. Cromwell said. "But right now, I have a question for you."

"Yes?"

"Are you hungry?"

Sava nodded eagerly.

Mrs. Cromwell straightened. "Then come with me," she said. "We'll see what we have cooking in the kitchen today. I think it might be bean loaf. Do you like bean loaf?"

Sava shrugged, picked up his jacks, and pushed them into his pocket.

Mrs. Cromwell gave Bernice a quick wink, then headed toward a door at the back of the foyer.

Sava started after her, then stopped and looked back at Bernice. "You come too?" he said.

Bernice shook her head. "No, I'll wait here," she said.

Sava shrugged again and followed Mrs. Cromwell. Suddenly he stopped, ran back to Bernice, and held out his hand, offering his prized jacks. "You want to play with these until I come back?"

A thick lump formed in Bernice's throat. She tried to say "no thank you," but couldn't find her voice. Instead, she smiled and took the jacks. Sava grinned up at her, then hurried after Mrs. Cromwell, who was holding the kitchen door open for him. He waved at Bernice, then disappeared into the orphanage. When they were gone, Bernice set the jacks on a chair and ran out of the building.

CHAPTER FIFTEEN

BERNICE

Climbing the porch steps of the two-story brick house in the upper-class neighborhood of North Philadelphia, her third house of the morning, Bernice couldn't stop thinking about the problem she'd had with a Hungarian Jewish boy the previous day. Thanks to her uniform, sending immigrant children away by train had turned out to be easier than she thought. The conductors never questioned her story about the children being sent out for adoption, and for the most part, the children seemed excited about the adventure. If they were homeless, she told them they were being adopted and someone would be waiting for them on the other end. If they thought they were picking up food for their families and returning home, she told them their parents would be at the station when they got back. Doubling her efforts to collect donations to pay for the tickets had been the biggest problem so far, until yesterday, when she picked up a pair of Hungarian brothers, one ten and one six.

After a long walk through a cold, driving rain, she led the boys into the train station, looking forward to going home afterward, to dry clothes, the twins, and a hot cup of tea. She might even splurge and pay a hansom cab to take her there. Having memorized the departure schedule of any train that went to the same out-of-state towns that accepted the other orphan trains, she bought two tickets for train number six, leaving for Ohio in twenty minutes. As expected, the locomotive waited on the tracks, billows of steam hissing from the iron pistons. A wave of leaden smoke churned from the stack and collided with the low sky, cloaking the crowded platform in a sooty, damp haze.

"Why did we come to this place?" the older boy said. "Where is the food to take home to our parents?"

"It's at a farm outside the city," Bernice said, holding out their tickets. "They will have fresh milk, eggs, bread, and cold-storage potatoes, but you have to pick it up and bring it back."

The younger boy took the tickets and started toward the train, but the older one grabbed him by the shoulder, yanked the tickets from his grasp, and handed them back to her. "We will go nowhere," he said. "You told my *anya* we would be returning home right away."

Bernice clenched her jaw. It was the first time any of the children had questioned her, and she was in no mood to argue. "You will be," she said. "As soon as you get back from the farm."

The boy shook his head. "No," he said. "You said nothing to my *anya* about a train." He grabbed his brother by the hand and turned to leave, pushing his way through the crowd.

Caught between anger and panic, Bernice didn't know what to do. If the boy told someone she had picked them up and was trying to put them on a train, they might call the police. Plus, she'd already bought the tickets. "Wait!" she called after them. "Let me explain."

The boy stopped and glared back at her, anger darkening his features.

She caught up to them and made a sad face, feigning sympathy. "I'm sorry," she said. "I wasn't supposed to tell you this, but you need to get on the train if you want to see your family again. They're packing to move to Pittsburgh as we speak, and they'll pick you up at the station there."

The older boy's face fell, his anger replaced by fear and confusion. His little brother stared up at him with worried eyes.

"Someone is taking your parents by car," she continued. "They knew how much you boys would have wanted to ride in the automobile, but there wasn't enough room for both of you and their belongings too. And they didn't want to disappoint either of you, so they—"

"But the tickets," the older boy said. "We have no money to pay . . ."

"A donation from the Red Cross," she said.

He looked doubtful.

"If I were you," she said, trying to sound friendly. "I'd much rather ride the train anyway. Haven't you heard the saying, 'Keep away from the fellow who owns an automobile, he'll take you far in his motor car, too darn far from your pa and ma, if his forty horsepower goes sixty miles per hour, say goodbye forever, goodbye forever'?"

The boy shook his head, his mouth set in a stubborn line.

Her patience was growing thin. "If you don't get on this train," she said, "I'll have no choice but to take you to an orphanage until your parents can come get you. Do you think they'll have enough money to travel back here anytime soon?"

The boy's eyes grew glassy and he shook his head again.

"Then you'd better get on the train. You don't want to take the chance that you'll never see your mother and father again, do you?"

He gazed down at his little brother with concern, thinking and uncertain, then reluctantly took the tickets. Misery clouded his face. He glanced at Bernice one more time, then, without another word, led his brother over to a passenger car and climbed on.

Thinking about it now, Bernice wondered what the boy thought when the train kept going, past the Pittsburgh station, out of the state of Pennsylvania, and beyond. She pictured him watching out the window, his chest filling with panic, at the same time trying to act like nothing was wrong to protect his younger brother. It made her think about Daniel putting her in a box, how frightened she was about being sent away, how devastated to think her parents wanted to get rid of her. A twinge of quilt tightened in her chest when she thought about causing the same kind of pain. Then she reminded herself that the boys would be better off away from their immigrant parents. And surely one of the rural farm families would be happy to have two boys instead of one.

She shook her head to clear it and realized she'd been standing on the porch of the two-story brick house in a daze. How long had she been standing there? Had she knocked on the door yet? She looked around, trying to remember. A white porch swing hung from the rafters, swaying slightly in the cold breeze. Stone pots sat on each side of the door, filled with dirt and the dried remnants of flower stems. The name on the mailbox read: WINSTON. Bernice took a deep breath, reminded herself why she was there, and knocked on the door. Part of her hoped no one was home. Her feet hurt and she was already thinking about taking the rest of the day off. She'd certainly earned it.

Then the door handle turned and the door opened. A young couple stood looking at her, their red-rimmed eyes and pasty complexions suggesting they might be suffering from the flu. She hoped they weren't going to ask her to come in and take care of them.

"You're too late," the man said. "He's gone."

"I'm sorry," Bernice said. "But I'm not sure what you're talking—"

"What took you so long?" the woman wailed, her face contorting in agony. She leaned against her husband, one trembling hand over her mouth.

He wrapped an arm around her to hold her up. "It's not her fault, darling," he said in a gentle voice. "He was too sick. There was nothing anyone could have done."

"I'm very sorry, Mr. and Mrs. Winston," Bernice said. "But I have to ask, who was sick?"

"My baby boy," Mrs. Winston cried. "Our son. He's dead." She buried her face in her hands and started to collapse.

Bernice went rigid, the memory of losing Wallis slamming into her like a runaway train. The world went gray and she reached for the doorframe to steady herself. She had come to this middle-class neighborhood looking for money and had found death instead. More than anything she wanted to run. But nurses didn't run.

Mr. Winston half carried, half dragged his sobbing wife to a cushioned bench in the foyer, propped her up with a ruffled pillow, and knelt beside her. "I'm sorry you've come all this way for nothing," he said to Bernice. "No one can help us now."

Bernice swallowed, trying to find her voice. "My sincerest sympathy for your loss," she managed. "I know how hard it is to lose a child. I lost my son too."

Mrs. Winston lifted her head to look at Bernice, her eyes like bleeding holes in her skull. "We tried everything," she said in a weak voice. "We gave him Mrs. Winslow's Soothing Syrup, onion syrup, chloride of lime, kerosene, whiskey. Nothing helped."

Bernice took a deep breath and, on wobbly legs, went over to the bench and knelt in front of the distraught mother. "Is there anything I can do for you?" she said. "Someone I can get? A family member, perhaps? Or a priest?"

Mrs. Winston shook her head frantically, her chin quivering.

"Not yet," Mr. Winston said. "It's too soon. He only just left us, not ten minutes ago."

Mrs. Winston scraped the heels of her hands across her eyes, leaving red marks on her cheeks. "He was so beautiful," she said, beaming through her tears. "So perfect."

Bernice nodded, forcing a sympathetic smile. "How old?"

"Only three months," Mr. Winston said.

"Oh dear," Bernice said. "I'm so sorry." She had to get out of there. Had to get up and go. But she couldn't. Her legs suddenly felt useless, her insides like gelatin. She started to straighten, to say goodbye, but Mrs. Winston seized her hands.

"I want you to see him," Mrs. Winston said. "I want you to see how beautiful he is before they take—"

"No," Bernice said, louder than she intended. "No, I can't. I'm sorry, but I need to—"

"Please," Mrs. Winston begged. She stood, pulling Bernice up, and started to drag her by the hands across the foyer. "I want you to see our boy. He needs people to see him, to remember him like he is now."

Mr. Winston grasped his wife by the shoulders and tried to slow her progress. "It's all right, darling," he said. "She doesn't have to if she doesn't want to. She lost her son too, remember?"

With that, Mrs. Winston stopped and let go, her face falling as if she'd had a sudden realization. "I can't do this," she cried. "I can't live without him. I want to die! I want to go with him!" Then her legs buckled and she fell on the floor howling, her knees and elbows cracking on the tile.

Tears flooded Bernice's eyes. She knew exactly what Mrs. Winston was feeling; an anguish so overwhelming it felt like a giant hand had ripped out her insides. Every wail from the poor woman pierced Bernice's chest. She wanted to go home, to get as far away from this shattered mother as possible. If she stayed any longer, the fragile pieces of her broken heart would fall apart again too. Then she looked at Mr. Winston standing there helplessly, watching his wife shudder and scream on the floor. No matter how hard it was for her to see this grieving couple, she couldn't abandon them yet.

"Do you have any whiskey left?" she said.

He nodded and went to get it.

She knelt and rubbed Mrs. Winston's quaking back, perfectly aware it provided no comfort but doing it anyway. "It's going to be all right," she said. "I know it doesn't seem possible right now, but you're going to get through this. It will take time, trust me, but you're going to pick yourself up and keep going because your husband needs you. And because your son would want you to stay strong." Saying those words reminded her that Wallis would have wanted her to stay strong too, and she wondered again if, somehow, he was behind her finding the twins, the nurse showing up at her apartment, and her seeing Mr. and Mrs. Patterson's Room for Rent sign. Her life had been completely turned around since he left this earth. There had to be more to it than luck.

Mr. Winston returned with the bottle of whiskey and knelt in front of his wife. Bernice got the woman up on her knees and he held the bottle to her lips. At first, Mrs. Winston turned away and shook her head, her eyes closed. Then she grabbed the bottle with both hands and drank a good number of generous swigs, barely stopping long enough to breathe between swallows. Bernice let her drink quite a bit, then pried the bottle from her grasp and gave it back to Mr. Winston, who took a few swigs too. Mrs. Winston slumped over and lay sobbing in Bernice's lap, her tears falling on her nurse uniform. Bernice rubbed her convulsing shoulders, fighting her own flood of emotions.

Mr. Winston leaned against the wall and eyed Bernice gratefully. "Thank you for helping us," he said.

"I wish I could do more," she said.

Then she had an idea.

Following the chubby nun with the birthmark down the shadowy hallway of St. Vincent's Orphan Asylum, Bernice couldn't help thinking about how easy it had been to convince Mother Joe to give her a baby. All it had taken was a piece of paper with the name and address of the adoptive parents, and her reassurance that they were a suitable family of high moral standing. The fact that she'd dropped babies off at St. Vincent's before certainly helped, but she wouldn't have been able to do any of it without the nurse uniform. In fact, she was dropping off a child now, a ten-month-old Irish girl whose mother was living on the streets. After that, she was going to choose a white baby for Mr. and Mrs. Winston, who recently lost their infant son.

It was the first time she'd been taken to the baby ward, and when she entered, she slowed, shocked to see row after row of white cribs in the high-ceilinged room. Babies of all ages filled every mattress, napping, wailing, drinking bottles, sucking thumbs, and cuddling blankets. She stopped at the first crib, her hand on her hammering heart. A newborn swaddled in cotton gauze lay on his back blinking up at her, his velvety pink mouth in a tiny O. He reminded her of Wallis and the twins.

The Irish girl on her hip peeked into the crib too. "Baba," she said.

Bernice wanted to scoop the baby boy up and take him home with her. But she couldn't. She already had her hands full with the twins. Plus, she was here to look for a baby for Mr. and Mrs. Winston. Maybe he could be their new son. Noticing she'd stopped, the chubby nun turned to look at her.

"The Lord has blessed that little one," she said. "His new family is picking him up tomorrow."

"How wonderful," Bernice said. "Will he be staying in the city?"

"Yes," the nun said. "In a lovely big house with his two big sisters."

Bernice smiled. At least the infant would have a home. And in Philadelphia, no less. They needed to keep babies like him here. "I had no idea you had such a large number of babies in your care. Why are there so many?"

"Because of the sin of this world, Nurse Wallis," the nun said. "And more recently, of course, because of the flu. We're not sure yet how many children were orphaned in the city during the epidemic, but hundreds, certainly. Maybe thousands." She turned and kept going. Bernice followed, thinking again about how grateful she was that Wallis would never have to live without her.

At the other end of the baby ward, a pale girl stood folding diapers while another rocked and fed an infant. Bernice swore under her breath. She recognized the girl in the rocking chair.

Was there no escaping Pia Lange?

CHAPTER SIXTEEN

PIA

Christmas came and went at the orphanage, with a short, bedraggled tree put up in the recreation room by the nuns, extra church services, and gifts for each child, either a book or small toy, donated by the parishioners of St. Vincent's. Pia received a stuffed rabbit with pink ears and gave it to Gigi.

A week later, Pia looked up from feeding Nicolai and saw Sister Agnes enter the baby ward and march down the center aisle, the cross around her waist swinging back and forth. Pia sat up straighter, hoping the nun was coming to tell her Mother Joe had finally approved her release. Then she noticed a nurse behind her with a baby girl on one hip, and her stomach twisted. It was the nurse who threatened to have her sent for a mental evaluation, Nurse Wallis. What was she doing there? The nurse stopped at a crib and viewed the baby inside, her hand over her heart. The girl on her hip looked to be around ten months old, with a headful of red hair that reminded Pia of Finn's mother. She was barefoot and bare-legged, in a dress that looked two sizes too big. Why hadn't Nurse Wallis left the baby at the front desk like last time? If only Pia could leave or hide instead of facing her again, but there was nowhere to go. All she could do was keep quiet and concentrate on feeding Nicolai.

Sister Agnes addressed Pia and Edith, who was folding diapers at the changing table. "Girls," she said, "this is Nurse Wallis. She's dropping off this poor child who was left outside the steps of a hospital, bless her heart. Not to mention along with her regular duties, she's recently found homes for three of our hard-to-place older children. Isn't that wonderful?"

"Yes, Sister Agnes," Edith and Pia said at the same time.

Sister Agnes turned toward the nurse. "Surely there's a special place in heaven for you, Nurse Wallis."

Color rose on Nurse Wallis's cheeks and she gave the nun an awkward smile. "It's my pleasure, Sister," she said. "I've always loved helping children."

Pia looked directly at the nurse for the first time since she came into the room. If she loved helping children, would she help her? More than anything, Pia wanted to ask if she'd run across twin baby boys during her visits to orphanages and hospitals. But what if she was still upset about their last encounter and followed through with her threat?

Sister Agnes took the baby girl from Nurse Wallis and directed her attention to Edith.

"Please show Nurse Wallis the youngest infant in our care," she said. "It seems she's found a lovely Christian couple willing to take one of our babies. Another blessing, to be sure."

"Yes, Sister Agnes," Edith said. She finished folding the diaper in her hands, then led Nurse Wallis into the sea of cribs.

With Nicolai fed and asleep in her arms, Pia stood and approached Sister Agnes and the redheaded baby girl. "She's beautiful," she said. The little girl seemed confused and frightened as she blinked and looked around with glassy hazel eyes.

"This is Alannah," Sister Agnes said, pushing a stray curl off the girl's forehead with a gentle hand. "It's a charming name, isn't it?"

"It certainly is," Pia said. She cupped Alannah's cheek in her hand and smiled at her, brushing her thumb across her soft skin and waiting. Thankfully, no pain throbbed in Pia's head, no nausea churned in her stomach. The girl felt healthy. Pia tickled her under the chin. "Hello, sweet Alannah. I know you're scared, but we'll take good care of you, I promise."

Sister Agnes beamed at Pia. "Bless you, child. You've certainly found your calling helping these destitute children. I'm sure there's a special place in heaven for you too, right next to Nurse Wallis."

Pia forced a weak smile. If Sister Agnes knew the truth about her brothers, she wouldn't think Pia had found her calling, or that she deserved a special place in heaven. Quite the opposite. And surely the nuns wouldn't let her take care of the babies at St. Vincent's. Shame crept up her neck, making her skin hot and itchy.

"Sister Agnes?" she said in a quiet voice.

"Yes, child?"

"May I ask you something?"

"Of course." Sister Agnes brushed another curl from the little girl's forehead and tried to push her hair behind her ears so it would stay out of her face.

"Do you think Nurse Wallis might know something about my brothers? Or maybe she'd be willing to look for them?"

"I have no idea," Sister Agnes said. "I suppose it wouldn't hurt to ask." She kept fussing with the baby, straightening the collar on her dirty dress, rubbing a smudge from her cheek.

"Could you ask for me?"

Sister Agnes looked at her then, surprised. "Whatever for? She seems nice enough and more than willing to help. There's absolutely no reason to be afraid of her. And you know what they say, child, 'The Lord helps those who help themselves.'"

Saying she had every reason to be afraid of Nurse Wallis was on the tip of Pia's tongue, but obviously Sister Agnes hadn't heard about the incident with the baby in the foyer. Pia was about to tell her what happened when Edith and Nurse Wallis came back down the aisle. Nurse Wallis had a baby boy in her arms, a three-month-old named Joseph who had arrived a few days ago. Sister Agnes put Alannah in a crib with another baby and hurried to meet them. Pia laid Nicolai in his crib and followed, trying to gather her courage. If it turned out to be the only chance she had to ask the nurse for help she couldn't waste it, no matter how scared she was. But she had to be careful.

Edith and Nurse Wallis were letting Sister Agnes admire Joseph.

"Nurse Wallis?" Pia blurted out before she lost her nerve. "If you don't mind, may I ask you something?"

The nurse looked up from the baby, her face unreadable. "Certainly," she said.

Pia did her best to act friendly. "Thank you," she said. "I was just wondering . . . I mean . . . Sister Agnes said you know a lot of people and you said you loved helping children, so I was wondering if you could help me find my brothers. They're twins, just four months old and . . . Well, almost seven months now . . . But anyway, they have blond hair and blue eyes, and they've been missing since October."

Nurse Wallis pressed her lips together, then gazed down at the baby again. She shifted him higher into the crook of one arm and adjusted the blanket around his head. "I suppose I can try," she said without looking up. "What part of the city are you from?"

Pia couldn't help noticing the way the nurse clenched her jaw after she answered, and how her temples pulsed in and out. Was she annoyed? In a hurry? Whatever it was, Pia couldn't let her reaction stop her. "The Fifth Ward," she said. "We lived on Shunk Alley. You might not know where that is because it's—"

"I know it," Nurse Wallis said.

Pia pressed her nails into her palms, trying to maintain her composure. She didn't want to seem too anxious, or upset the nurse again. She was the only person who might be able to help. "Have you been there since the flu started?"

"No," Nurse Wallis said. "I have no reason to go into that neighborhood."

"What about all the orphanages and hospitals you've been to?" Pia said. "Have you seen twin boys with blond hair and blue eyes anywhere?"

Nurse Wallis finally looked up at her and shook her head. "I'm sorry, but I haven't. Now if you'll excuse me, I really must be going." She started to turn away, then stopped and regarded Pia again. "I find it interesting that you said your brothers were missing. What happened to them? Did someone take them?"

Pia glanced at the floor and swallowed. "My mother and I got sick and—"

"And what?" Nurse Wallis said. She stared at Pia with hard eyes, almost as if she could read her mind.

Pia felt like she couldn't breathe. "I . . . I don't know," she said. "That's why I need your help."

Nurse Wallis sniffed dismissively. "Well, if I hear or see anything, I'll be sure to let Mother Joe know." Clearly finished talking to Pia, she directed her attention to Sister Agnes. "Thank you again for helping me, Sister. I hope it comforts you to know this child is going to a wonderful home."

"No, thank *you*," Sister Agnes said. "The good Lord knows we could use more people like you in this city."

"I do what I can," Nurse Wallis said. She started to leave, then stopped and turned to Sister Agnes again. "Perhaps next time I find a nice family willing to take in a baby, you could bring a few of them to another room for me to choose from. It breaks my heart seeing so many at the same time, knowing I can't possibly help them all."

"Oh yes," Sister Agnes said. "Of course. I understand."

"Thank you," Nurse Wallis said. "I'd appreciate that." She gave Edith and Pia a quick nod, then started toward the door again.

"Wait," Pia called after her. "Could you ask the other nurses you work with if they've seen twin boys anywhere?"

"I will," Nurse Wallis called over her shoulder.

Pia started to follow her, hoping to say more, but Sister Agnes caught her by the arm. Pia pulled away before she could feel anything wrong with the nun.

"That's enough, child," Sister Agnes said. "It's all right to ask for help, but don't badger the poor woman. She said she'd keep an eye out for your brothers, so I'm sure she will. That's all she can do."

"Their names are Ollie and Max," Pia shouted after Nurse Wallis.

Sister Agnes gave her a hard look, shaking her head, then followed Nurse Wallis out of the baby ward.

After they were gone, Pia stared at the closed door, hopelessness falling over her like a shroud. Even if Nurse Wallis could help, Pia didn't think she would. Between what happened the first time they met, and the fact that she was busy helping so many other children, she probably didn't have the time or desire to get involved in Pia's problems. Pia trudged back to where Edith was changing Alannah into a clean nightdress. "I don't think Nurse Wallis likes me," she said.

"Who cares?" Edith said. "I *know* she doesn't like me."

"What makes you say that?"

"You heard her tell Sister Agnes she doesn't want to come in here again. It's because of me."

"How do you know?"

"Well, first off, she wouldn't even look at the girls. And second, she didn't want Yakov, even though he's the youngest boy here."

Pia frowned. "Why not? He's perfect."

"Because he's Turkish. She said the couple specified a white baby."

"Oh my God. What did you say?"

"I asked why she'd give any baby to a couple of bigots."

Pia gasped, then started to chuckle. "Good for you," she said. "I wish I were that brave."

For the first time since Pia arrived, Edith smiled.

A week after Nurse Wallis dropped off Alannah, Pia and Edith hurried through the door leading out to the play yard to get some fresh air before supper. The sun was out for the first time in weeks, and they couldn't wait to feel its warmth. Pia followed Edith down the steps and across the lawn toward the river, sidestepping melting snow and piles of slush. The other children walked around the yard, jumping over puddles and running sticks along the fence. Sister Ernestine stood guard at the door, ready to reprimand anyone who dared get dirty or wet.

Pia and Edith headed straight for the far edge of the yard, an unspoken understanding between them that they wanted to get as far away from the orphanage and the watchful eyes of Sister Ernestine as possible. When they reached the fence, Pia gripped the rails and gazed out over the river, wishing she could climb over to its rocky banks and follow the shores back into the city. The river looked deep and brown and cold, and the smell of muddy water hung in the air, equal parts iron and wet rock. She took a deep breath, closed her eyes, and turned her face toward the sun. Since Thanksgiving, the weather had been dreadful, with snow or icy rain every day. Sometimes it seemed as though the sun would never shine again. Then this morning, it had finally broken through the clouds. She and Edith had waited all day to get outside, and she intended to soak in its rays for as long as possible. Blue jays screeched in the pines bordering the yard, and a train whistled in the distance. Except for the chill in the breeze, it almost felt like spring.

She turned to Edith. "If I'm still—" she said, then stopped. She'd almost said, "If I'm still here this summer," but remembered she hadn't told Edith she'd be leaving.

She couldn't count the number of times she'd asked Sister Agnes if Mother Joe had mentioned releasing her, but she hadn't confided in anyone else yet because she didn't want to jinx it. Plus, it seemed like Edith had finally warmed up to her, and she didn't want that to change either. If she knew Pia was leaving, Edith might grow distant again. Then again, Pia wasn't sure it mattered anyway, because Sister Agnes's answer was always the same: When Mother Joe made up her mind to let her go, Pia would be the first to know.

She cleared her throat and started again. "When it gets warmer," she said to Edith, "maybe we can bring the babies outside for some fresh air. It would do them good to get out of that stuffy ward."

"They're only allowed outside on the hottest days," Edith said. "Because that's when the baby ward turns into an oven. And you know we can't open the windows."

Pia sighed. "Of course we can't."

We can't do anything, she thought.

"Hey," Edith said. "Who's that sitting on the swings? I've never seen him before."

Pia turned toward the yard.

It was an older boy, maybe aged fourteen or fifteen, with his head down, the heel of his shoe striking the slush and scraping it back into a wet pile, over and over again.

Pia gasped.

It couldn't be.

She started toward the swings, then stopped, squeezed her eyes shut, and opened them again. She couldn't believe what she was seeing. She squinted and studied the boy again. No. It wasn't him. The hair was too long and stringy, the face too thin. Maybe the stress of losing her family and being locked in an orphanage was making her see things that weren't there. Then he lifted his head and she knew. She ran over to him, her heart racing in her chest.

"Finn?" she said.

He looked up at her, misery darkening his features. Then his eyes went wide and he jumped to his feet. "Pia?" he said. "What are you doing here?"

Her legs nearly gave out. His voice was unmistakable, the accent, the way he said her name. "You're alive?" she said.

"I am," he said. "And I'm happy to see ye are too." He stared at her with that mischievous one-sided grin and those familiar hazel eyes. Yet despite his smile, sorrow lined his features, aging him beyond his years.

"But all this time," she said. "I thought you were dead!"

"Nay," he said. "Not yet."

She put her hand to her trembling mouth. "I can't believe this."

"It's me, lass. And I have to say, I can't believe it either. But I'm mighty glad to see ye."

She laughed and threw her arms around him, not caring what she might feel when they touched. The only thing that mattered was that he was alive. He hugged her back, his cheek against hers, his warm, quick breath on her skin. Thankfully she felt nothing but joy at seeing him alive, and the genuine depth of his warmth and affection. No weight on her chest or ache in her bones. No discomfort in her throat or head. His clothes and hair smelled like the city streets—automobile fuel and vegetable stands, wet cobblestones and electric trolleys. Unlike her and everyone else at St. Vincent's, he hadn't been in the orphanage long enough to absorb the cloying odor of old wood and cold porridge, or the ever-present stench of sorrow and fear. Afraid to find she was dreaming, she didn't want to let go. Tears sprang in her eyes. Then she realized Mutti was the last person she'd hugged. And even though she normally didn't want to be touched, embracing Finn felt like being covered with a warm blanket after months of being cold. She felt like she'd been wandering lost and alone for an eternity and now, finally, someone else was holding her up.

Then a strange sound, like a yelp, drew their attention toward the orphanage.

It was Sister Ernestine, thundering toward them, waving her arms and scowling. "Get away from her," she shrieked. "Move apart from each other this instant!"

Finn stepped back and put his hands in his pockets, and Pia let go of him, her empty arms aching.

When Sister Ernestine reached them, she was out of breath, her wattled chin quivering like wet cheese. "What on God's earth is going on here, Miss Lange? You know close contact with the opposite sex is not allowed!"

Pia braced herself for another chiding, or worse. Beads of sweat broke out on her upper lip. "Nothing's going on, Sister Ernestine," she said. "He's an old friend and we were surprised to see each other, that's all."

Sister Ernestine pushed them farther apart and eyed them up and down. "That better be all," she said. "Thirteen-year-old girls are perfectly capable of getting themselves into a delicate situation with boys, Miss Lange, so you have permission to talk, but no physical contact." She glared at Finn. "Keep your hands to yourself, understand, young man?"

Finn nodded.

Sister Ernestine stood there for a moment as if trying to decide whether or not to take further action, her narrowed eyes darting back and forth between their faces. Then, finally, she turned and marched back to her post near the doorway.

When she was gone, Pia let out a trembling sigh of relief.

"Holy Mother of Mary," Finn said. "She's a disagreeable one. And she's got a face like a blind cobbler's thumb."

As usual, he was trying to make her laugh, and she loved him for it. "You have no idea," she said. "She's got a leather strap hidden under her habit and she likes to use it."

"Aye, that's no surprise," he said. "She looks like she rules with an iron fist." Then he gazed at her, his face serious. "So tell me, how'd you end up in this bloody awful place?"

She lifted her chin and straightened her shoulders, trying to seem stoic. "You first," she said. "Where have you been, and how did you end up here?"

He let out a long sigh. "Remember the last day I saw ye, when me mam called me inside?"

She nodded, dread tightening her throat.

"Me brother had started coughing that morning. We took him to the hospital straightaway, but we couldn't get in. We waited and waited, but by midnight, he was dead."

"Oh no," Pia said. She wanted to hug him again, to let him know how much she cared, but Sister Ernestine was watching. "I'm so sorry."

"And before his worn-out body was even cold," Finn continued, "me mam and granddad insisted we leave the city to get away from the flu. I wanted to tell ye, to go back to Shunk Alley and make sure ye were all right, but Mam refused to let me go. Somehow my granddad secured a horse and wagon, and we left from the hospital that very night to go to my uncle's house on the Jersey Shore. By the time we crossed the state line, my granddad had died on the wagon. We left his body in front of a church, to save me, Mam said. The problem was, we took the damn flu with us. Everyone in the house was sick within a few days but me. Some of the neighbors caught it too."

"And your mother?"

Finn dropped his gaze and kicked the wet ground with the toe of his boot. When he looked up again, his eyes were glassy. "She didn't make it. Same as my uncle and his wife."

Pia's eyes filled too. "Oh no. That's horrible. I'm so sorry, Finn."

"What about your mam?" he said in a gentle voice. His tightly creased brow made it clear he already knew.

She bit her trembling lip and nodded. "She's gone." It was the first time she'd shared the news with someone who wasn't a stranger, and the past few months of grief and loneliness suddenly overwhelmed her, making her dizzy. She took a deep breath and let it out slowly, trying to stand steady. "I sent you a note," she said. "Like we used to on the clothesline, remember? You must have already left." Thinking about it now, sending a note seemed foolish. She should have done more. She should have done mountains more.

He shook his head, miserable, and started to reach for her, then stopped. "I'm sorry I wasn't there to help you."

"It's not your fault."

"What about your brothers?" he said. "Wee Ollie and Max?"

She shook her head, the swift return of guilt and grief devastating and raw. For a second she thought she might collapse. How could she tell him what she had done? That her brothers might be dead because of her reckless decision? She turned away to hide her face.

"Oh God," he said. "I'm so sorry, lass. I wish I could do something to make it all go away."

She swallowed her sobs and turned back to him, praying he wouldn't read the truth in her eyes. She wasn't ready to confess everything, not yet. "Tell me how you got back to Philadelphia," she said.

He put his hands in his pockets as if to keep from hugging her and sighed again. "I stayed at my uncle's as long as I was able, but when the landlord realized everyone else was dead, he kicked me out. I had nowhere to go, so I jumped a train and came back home. The first thing I did was look for you, but . . . I'm sorry to have to tell you this, but there's someone else living in your apartment."

"I know," she said. "Keep going. What happened next? Where have you been living?"

"On the streets. And I was getting along right well until yesterday, when the cops caught me stealing. Guess the lockup was full 'cause they sent me here instead." He lowered his gaze briefly, then fixed soft eyes on her. "I thought you were gone too, lass. Can't tell you how glad I am to find out you survived."

She hung her head. "Sometimes I wish I hadn't," she said.

He lifted her chin with a gentle hand. "Don't say that," he said. "I know you've suffered greatly and sometimes you feel like you won't make it another day. Trust me, I feel the same way." Then he gave her a half grin and jerked his chin toward Sister Ernestine. "But ye wouldn't want to leave me here all alone with Sister Congeniality, would you?"

She tried to smile, but her mouth twisted and her face folded in on itself.

"Oh, don't cry," he said. "Go on now, tell me what happened."

She swallowed the thickness in her throat and tried to find her voice, knowing she had to tell him the truth, praying he wouldn't think differently of her. "I came down with the flu too," she said. "But someone found me and took me to the . . ." She hesitated, not sure she could go on. He waited patiently, watching her with haunted eyes. She glanced around to make sure no one was listening, then, in halting words that burned her mouth and shattered her heart, she told him what happened. When she got to the part where the bedroom cubby was empty, her knees went weak and she had to sit on the slush-covered ground.

Finn swore under his breath and knelt beside her, a safe distance away.

"It's my fault," she wailed.

"The bloody hell it is," he said. "Ye were doing what you thought was best. I would have done the same thing. You couldn't let your brothers starve. You didn't know you were getting sick. And you sure as hell had no way of knowin' some nasty clod would go in and take them."

"But . . . I . . . I forgot to lock the door!"

He shook his head vehemently. "Doesn't matter. Whoever took the lads, if they were trying to help, they should have left a note saying where they were."

"They did leave a note," she cried. "It said, *May God forgive you for what you've done.*"

"Ah, Christ," he said, shaking his head. "I'm sorry, lass. That's just downright vile."

"But what if . . . what if they died in there?"

"Don't cut yourself up like that. Were they sick when you left them?"

She shook her head. "I don't think so . . . but even if they weren't, I was . . . I was gone for so long," she said in between sobs.

"Aye, but you don't know when they were found, right? Might have been the day you left, for all you know."

"I have to find out what happened to them. I just have to."

"Ye will," he said. "We'll do it together."

She wiped her eyes with trembling hands and gaped at him. "How? How are we going to do anything when we're locked up in here? Mother Joe said she'd release me when she thought it was safe, but I'm starting to think she only said that to make me behave."

He grinned and brushed a tear from her cheek. "Aye, lassie," he said. "I thought you knew me better than that. Ye ought to know they can't keep Finn Duffy locked up for long."

CHAPTER SEVENTEEN

BERNICE

Bernice stood in the doorway of a stone Colonial in an upper-class neighborhood on the north end of the city, at a loss for words. Seeing the dark-haired boy wearing a yarmulke next to the white woman in the foyer had taken her by surprise, and she didn't know what to say or do. If the boy were only visiting, why would he come to the door too, and in his stockinged feet? He looked to be around six years old and was holding a tin spinning top in one hand. The woman, in a stylish, high-waisted dress the color of peaches, stared at her, one manicured hand on the door, waiting to hear what she wanted. The boy stared too.

"I'm with the Red Cross," Bernice finally said. "And I'm collecting . . ." Then she suddenly remembered the Red Cross had asked true American women to take in children orphaned by the flu. That had to be why the boy was there. What other explanation could there be? She pulled herself together and gave the woman a warm smile. "I'm sorry. I'm so used to saying the same thing over and over, I nearly forgot what I was here for."

"I've already made a donation," the woman said. "And no one is sick in our home, so I'm not sure why you're here either."

Bernice glanced at the mailbox, desperate for a name. GRAHAM, it said, in copper letters. "I assume you're Mrs. Graham?"

"Yes," the woman said.

"Well, it's a pleasure to meet you, Mrs. Graham. Please forgive me for the confusion. I've visited so many houses and have repeated my speech so many times it's become automatic. But I'm here today to thank you for taking such good care of this unfortunate child who found himself without a home during the flu."

Mrs. Graham glanced down at the boy. "Oh," she said. "Well, it's been no problem at all. He's been a delight."

"That's wonderful to hear," Bernice said. "I'm glad it's been going so well. Your help has been very much appreciated. But the main reason I'm here is because I have some very good news. We've found a member of the boy's family, and they're willing to take him in."

Mrs. Graham drew in a sharp breath, placing a hand over her middle as if suddenly ill. "Oh my," she said. "I see. Well, that is good news. But I have to say it's a bit of a surprise. I didn't think it would happen so fast, if at all." She looked down at the boy again and gave him a warm smile. "Did you hear that, Tobia? You're going to have a new home soon." The boy frowned and moved closer to her. When she lifted her gaze and regarded Bernice again, moisture glazed her eyes. "I must ask. Have you met them? This person who claims to be his family?"

"Of course," Bernice said. "It's his great-aunt. She's perfectly lovely and she's looking forward to seeing him."

"Then why didn't she come with you?"

Bernice's cheeks grew warm. She hadn't expected to find the boy here, but she couldn't pass up the opportunity. And she thought she'd handled it well. So why was this woman questioning her? Why did she care what happened to a little Jewish boy? "She didn't come because she lives in New Jersey," she said. "I'll be taking him to her by train."

"When?" Mrs. Graham said.

"Why, now, of course," Bernice said.

Tears welled on the rims of Mrs. Graham's eyes, reflecting the light from the late-afternoon sun. "But he's not ready," she said. "I'd need time to pack his things and . . ."

"That's fine," Bernice said. "I'll wait."

Mrs. Graham bit her lip and gazed down at the boy again, blinking back her tears. He watched her with worried eyes. She knelt in front of him and straightened his collar. "Don't worry," she said. "We talked about this, remember? That you might have to leave someday? But you're going to be really brave, remember?"

The boy nodded, his chin starting to tremble.

Mrs. Graham hugged him hard, then straightened and regarded Bernice. "I tried to prepare him for this," she said. "But unfortunately I think I forgot to prepare myself."

"I understand," Bernice said. "These things are never easy. But try to take comfort in the fact that he'll be better off, you know, with his own . . . family."

Nodding, Mrs. Graham pulled a cotton handkerchief from her sleeve and wiped her nose. "Yes, of course. You're right." She glanced over her shoulder, as if unsure about what to do next. "He only had the clothes on his back when he came, so I bought him a few new outfits and some books and toys. It should only take a few minutes to get everything together." Then she turned to Tobia. "Put your on shoes, all right, sweetheart?"

Tobia nodded again, then gave Mrs. Graham the spinning top and did what he was told.

When he was finished putting on his shoes, Mrs. Graham took him by the hand. "I'm just going to let him say goodbye to everyone," she said to Bernice. "Then we'll be back with his things." She sniffed and started out of the foyer, Tobia by her side.

"All right," Bernice said. "I'll wait here."

When Mrs. Graham and Tobia were gone, she checked her watch. If Mrs. Graham didn't take too long packing the boy's things and Bernice hurried, she could make it to the station in time to put Tobia on the train to Virginia.

CHAPTER EIGHTEEN

PIA

January 1919

The days following Finn's arrival at St. Vincent's were cold and dreary, with sleet or snow every day and every night. The nuns said it was the longest storm they'd seen in years. No one was allowed outside, and the ward windows were coated with thin sheets of ice, making the orphans shiver even harder in their beds. Pia saw Finn only during free time, when she sat cross-legged on the plank floor in a corner of the recreation room, pretending to read or do cross-stitch while he sat a few feet away, drawing or playing solitaire. They spent the entire time whispering back and forth, trying to come up with a plan to escape. Edith glanced at them every now and then from the other side of the room, her face a blank slate. She'd become distant again since Finn's arrival, and Pia couldn't blame her. After all, they used to play cards during recess, or sit together reading books while the other girls whispered behind their hands and laughed at them. Now Pia spent all her time talking to Finn. She tried to convince Edith she still wanted to be friends, but she couldn't tell her the truth—that they were planning a getaway. It was too big a risk. Not that Edith would tell on them—Pia was certain she wouldn't—but she might ask to come too, and that would only make the planning more complicated. It wasn't like Pia wanted to leave just to be free. She was doing it for her brothers. Keeping the secret had cost Pia her friendship with Edith and made working together more difficult, but there was no other choice. Hopefully she'd have the chance to explain and say goodbye before she left.

Having been assigned to stoke the boilers when the orphanage was able to get coal delivered, Finn searched for a way out of the maze of connecting cellars beneath St. Vincent's, but so far had no luck. After the janitor caught him wandering off several times, he started keeping a closer eye on him, asking him what he was up to and making it harder for Finn to explore. When Finn wasn't stoking the boilers, he was mopping floors or washing dishes in the dining hall, making it difficult to memorize the nuns' routines or watch for opportunities and ways to escape.

On the other hand, Pia's days never changed. Working under the watchful eyes of Sister Agnes and the other nuns who helped in the baby ward while she and Edith ate and slept, she had no freedom at all to wander or search for unlocked doors. Still, she tried to determine the length of drops from windows and the likelihood that the ground below might eventually lead to an escape route. Finn thought they could climb over the play yard fence and scramble down the rocky cliff to the river, if only the weather would change so they'd be allowed outside. She reminded him that the fence was tall and topped with pointed black spires, but he said they could get over it if they found something, or someone, to give them a boost up. He could lift her onto his shoulders and help her over, but it would be impossible for him to follow, and the nuns would probably stop him before he could.

They talked about moving the slide or the roundabout over to the fence to climb on, but the slide was anchored to the ground and he was certain the roundabout was too heavy. They thought about getting the other boys to help lift them over the fence, but they might tell someone what they were planning, or would want to come too.

Then on a dark, dreary afternoon, while Finn was telling Pia about a back door in the kitchen that led out to the vegetable gardens, Sister Ernestine marched into the recreation hall and ordered the boys to line up against one wall. Certain someone had overheard her and Finn talking, Pia dropped her eyes and concentrated on her cross-stitch, her heart pounding. Chairs scraped over the floor and footsteps hurried across the room as the boys put down their toys and books, the older ones helping the younger ones move over to the wall. Pia got up and edged closer, sitting behind a group of other girls so she could hear what was going on.

"Stand up straight and smooth your collars," Sister Ernestine ordered the boys. She pointed at one boy's feet. "And tie your shoes!" The boy dropped to one knee and did as he was told.

Mother Joe entered the room with Nurse Wallis a few seconds later, her face pinched, her chin in the air. "Here they are, Nurse Wallis," she said, then stood waiting with her sinewy hands in her sleeves. "If I'd known you were coming, I would have made them clean up a bit first."

"They're fine, Mother Joe," Nurse Wallis said. "Thank you for accommodating me on such short notice." She started moving down the line of boys, studying each one up and down. Some of the boys smiled hopefully at her, while others stared with frightened eyes. Halfway down the line, she stopped in front of a gangly, dark-haired, green-eyed boy.

"What's your name?" she said.

"Kafka," the boy said.

"We call him Thomas," Mother Joe said.

Nurse Wallis nodded once to acknowledge Mother Joe, then said to the boy, "And your surname?"

The boy furrowed his brow and looked at the older boy standing next to him. "Your last name," the older boy said. "What's your last name?"

"Bobek," Kafka said.

Nurse Wallis gestured for him to step out of line, then kept moving. She stopped in front of a curly-headed blond in a button-up shirt who looked to be about five years old. "And your name?"

"Gerhard," the boy mumbled, staring at his feet.

"Gerald," Mother Joe corrected him.

Nurse Wallis asked the boy to step out of line. "Thank you for telling me the truth, Gerhard," she said to him. "Do you know your last name?"

"Nussbaum," the boy mumbled.

"Well, I have good news, Kafka and Gerhard," the nurse said. "I've found both of you new homes."

Kafka beamed at Nurse Wallis, but Gerhard started to cry. Nurse Wallis knelt in front of him, the hem of her long uniform jacket folding over on the floor. "What's wrong, little one?"

Gerhard turned and stretched one hand toward an older boy standing against the wall, fat tears sliding down his red cheeks. *"Mein bruder,"* he cried.

The older boy smiled at him with flooding eyes. He opened his mouth to say something, but Nurse Wallis chimed in.

"Your brother?" she said.

Gerhard nodded frantically.

Nurse Wallis straightened and crooked a finger at the older boy, smiling and telling him to come stand beside his brother. "It's all right," she said to Gerhard. "Don't cry. Your brother can come too."

The older boy ran over to Gerhard and put a reassuring hand on his small shoulder. Gerhard wrapped his short arms around his older brother's waist and squeezed, beaming through his tears.

Pia swallowed the lump in her throat and glanced over at Finn, who was at the end of the line. Did seeing the brothers so happy together tug at his heartstrings too? Certainly it reminded him of his older brothers, just like it reminded her of the twins. To her surprise, he was scowling, his eyes fixed on Nurse Wallis. Why was he looking at her like that? Was he scared, confused, angry? It was hard to tell. Then she had another thought, one that made her heart race. What if Nurse Wallis took him too?

When Nurse Wallis started herding Kafka, Gerald, and his brother toward the door, Mother Joe trailing behind them, Pia breathed a sigh of relief.

"We're so grateful for this, Nurse Wallis," Mother Joe said. "Surely God will hold a special place for you in heaven. And, of course, there's nothing that makes us happier than seeing our children find new homes. Bless you, my dear."

Nurse Wallis stopped and turned to face her. "Thank you for trusting me, Mother Joe," she said. "I'll return for more as soon as I can." She glanced back at the boys, all of them still standing ramrod straight along the wall. When her eyes landed on Finn, she faltered, a strange, startled look on her face. She quickly looked away and hurried into the hall, ushering Kafka, Gerald, and his brother out ahead of her.

Pia turned her attention to Finn again. He was staring at the door, watching the nurse leave, the peculiar expression still on his face. Why had he and the nurse looked at each other that way? It didn't make sense. She went back to the corner and sat down again, waiting for him to sit nearby so she could ask. But Sister Ernestine clapped her hands, announced it was time to return to the wards, and started ushering the boys from the room. Pia got to her feet and rushed to catch up to Finn, a strange tightness building in her chest. Something about the way he looked at Nurse Wallis made her nervous. If he was worried about her taking him, why did he still look unsettled when she left? She hurried past several of the other boys and reached out to tap him on the shoulder, but Sister Ernestine grabbed her by the arm and held her back.

"Keep your hands to yourself, Miss Lange," she snarled. "And no jumping ahead in line."

Pia pulled away from her grasp, but not before feeling a funny sensation in her chest, like a slowing of her heart. Something was wrong with Sister Ernestine, but it didn't feel urgent, like anything that would sicken her right away. It probably had something to do with her age, and Pia didn't care, anyway. She had more important things on her mind. She started toward the door again, but Sister Ernestine made her wait until the last orphan filed out of the room. By the time Pia reached the hall, Finn was nowhere to be seen.

The following day, the sun finally reappeared, and everyone was allowed outside for a few minutes after breakfast. Sister Ernestine stood shivering on the steps with her arms crossed, a sour look on her face. Pia walked across the yard toward the river, waiting for Finn to come outside with the rest of the boys. After lying awake most of the night worrying about Nurse Wallis taking him the next time she came back, she could hardly wait to see him.

Brown swaths of frozen grass lay bared by the wind, and mounds of snow leaned against the fence and playground equipment, one massive drift stretching through the back fence like a giant sand dune, nearly reaching the top of the high spires. If the drift had been made of dirt, Pia could have walked up and over it to the other side. She tested it to see if it would hold her weight. Her shoes broke through the thin, icy crust, but the snow beneath was firm. She took a few steps, holding her arms out for balance, and climbed higher. Her heartbeat picked up speed. This could be their chance. She jumped down and glanced around the yard, searching for Finn. The boys had come outside, but she didn't see him anywhere. Rubbing her hands together and pacing back and forth, she pretended she was trying to stay warm, when in reality she felt like she'd stepped inside a furnace, her nerves making her roast inside her coat. Her mind raced, thinking of everything they had to do when they were free. The first place they needed to go was her old apartment, to ask the people living there if Vater had returned. If he hadn't, they would knock on the neighbors' doors to see if they knew anything about the twins. After that, she wasn't sure what would happen. Hopefully they'd find her father right away. She plunged her hands in her pockets and checked the door again. She didn't see Finn anywhere.

Melting snow dripped from the trees and the bars of the swing set while great sheets of ice cracked and slid down the slide. A girl shrieked and ran away from a boy playing blind man's bluff, making Pia jump. She scanned the yard for what felt like the hundredth time. Why was Finn taking so long to come outside?

She clenched her jaw and went over to two boys playing kick the can near the slide. One was tall and lanky, with a big nose, and the other was short and muscular. Despite their size, they looked to be only about ten years old. When they saw her approach, they stopped playing.

"Do you know Finn Duffy?" she said.

The lanky boy put a protective foot on the can. "Yeah," he said. "He's from our ward."

"Do you know where he is?"

The boys glanced at each other, then looked back at her, puzzlement lining their faces.

"You didn't hear?" the muscular one said.

Pia's stomach knotted. "Hear what?"

"He's gone," the lanky one said.

Pia drew in a sharp breath. "What do you mean, he's gone? Gone where?" Panic beat against her rib cage like a trapped bird.

"When we woke up this morning his bed was empty."

"He wasn't at breakfast either."

Pia's heart dropped like an anvil in her chest. Finn had left without her. He had escaped and abandoned her. He'd said something once about going alone and coming back for her, that maybe it would be easier, but she didn't think he was being serious. How could he do that to her, especially without telling her first? A dull, empty ache gnawed at her stomach and she felt like she might be sick.

"Where do you think he went?" she managed.

"How are we supposed to know?" the lanky boy said.

"Did he say anything to either of you before he left?" she said. "Did he leave a message for me or anything like that?"

The boys shook their heads.

"Do you think he got out on his own?" she said.

"You mean escaped?" the lanky boy said.

"Nah," the muscular boy said. "If he escaped, we'd all be locked in our wards right now, and the nuns would be in running around like chickens with their heads cut off."

"I say he got adopted," the lanky boy said, "either that or he got sent to the Home for Industrious Boys. That's what happens when you're his age."

"Where is that?" Pia said.

"How the heck would we know?" the lanky boy said. "We only heard about the place, we ain't never been there."

Pia reached blindly for the edge of the slide, certain she was about to fall over. But her hand caught nothing but air, her feet slipped out from under her, and she landed hard on a patch of ice. Pain shot through her elbow and arm, and the sound of cracking bones exploded in her mind.

The muscular boy leaned over her, his shocked face blocking out the blue sky. "Holy shit. Are you all right?"

She closed her eyes, struggling to catch her breath, and cradled her throbbing arm in her hand. No. She wasn't all right. She didn't think she'd ever be all right again.

CHAPTER NINETEEN

BERNICE

Sitting at the Pattersons' worn kitchen table, Bernice sipped her coffee and leisurely read the newspaper while flecks of snow swirled against the backdrop of a white flannel sky outside the window, clinking against the glass like tiny pebbles. It was Sunday, the boys were napping, the Pattersons had gone to play bridge with their friends, and she relished the rare few hours of peace and quiet. The past two months had been exhausting, asking for donations and looking for immigrant children, not to mention walking farther and farther in the cold every day to make sure she didn't visit the same houses twice. As usual, she read the obituaries to see how many deaths were attributed to the Spanish influenza. The list contained fewer and fewer names every week, but apparently the terrifying sickness hadn't been completely eradicated. Every time she saw a child's obituary, she couldn't help thinking about taking little Joseph to meet Mr. and Mrs. Winston. Seeing the shocked looks on their faces when they'd opened the door had undoubtedly been the highlight of her month.

"Who is that?" Mrs. Winston had gasped when she saw the infant. Her eyes were still swollen from crying.

Mr. Winston frowned at Bernice, clearly wondering what the hell she was doing bringing a baby to their home.

"This is Joseph," Bernice said. "He was abandoned at the train station, naked except for a diaper and—" Before she could finish, Mrs. Winston stepped forward to take him.

"May I?" she said.

"Of course," Bernice said.

"I don't think that's a good idea, darling," Mr. Winston said.

Mrs. Winston ignored him and gathered the swaddled boy in her arms. "Oh my word," she said. "Look at this perfect little angel." With a gentle finger, she pulled the blanket down from Joseph's chin to get a better look. He blinked up at her, studying her face with curious blue eyes, his perfect pink lips in a tiny O. "Who could do such a thing to an innocent child?"

"Unfortunately, in a city this size," Bernice said, "babies are abandoned quite often."

Mrs. Winston gaped at her, shocked. "How dreadful," she said. "What happens to all of them?"

"Normally they're sent to orphanages, poorhouses, even asylums," Bernice said. "But since the flu started, the orphanages have become severely overcrowded, so several temporary houses have been set up to take in the extras. Even so, I'm sometimes asked if I know of anyone who can take in an orphaned or abandoned child. And when I saw little Joseph here, you were the first people who came to mind."

Mr. Winston opened his mouth to say something, but Bernice didn't give him a chance.

"I know you've only recently suffered the tremendous loss of your precious son," she said. "But I can tell you're good, honest folk who loved your child with all your heart. You're the kind of people who make wonderful parents. And babies as young as Joseph fare far better in a loving home than in an institutional setting. He's barely three months old and likely wouldn't see the age of one if he were left in an orphanage."

Mrs. Winston turned to her husband, her eyes flooding. "We can't turn him away," she said. "I'd never be able to live with myself."

A war of conflicting emotions—agony, confusion, fear—played over Mr. Winston's face. "I don't know, sweetheart," he said. "We don't know anything about this boy. What if he's sickly or has some kind of mental infirmity? I couldn't bear to see you suffer again."

"I'm going to suffer forever," Mrs. Winston said. "Forever. Nothing in this world or the next will ever heal my broken heart. But this poor boy had his heart broken too—and by his own mother, no less."

"I swear on my brother's grave there's no reason to be concerned about Joseph's health," Bernice said. "He's been examined by a doctor and is surprisingly healthy, considering what he's been through." She took a folded paper from her pocket and held it out to Mr. Winston. She had written it with her left hand to make it look like the scrawl of a witless woman. "This was pinned to his blanket."

Mr. Winston took the note and read it out loud. *"Please find my Joseph a good home. I got nothing and can no longer care for him. He don't fuss much and his appetite is good. Tell him I love him and he will be in my prayers."*

"Oh good Lord," Mrs. Winston said, her voice trembling. "That poor woman." She gazed down at Joseph, already bouncing him gently in her arms, as if he belonged there. "And you, you poor, sweet boy. You must have been so frightened." A tear fell from her cheek onto his face and she gently wiped it away, then looked at her husband again, a sad, wistful smile on her face. "Can't you see? He needs us. And we need him."

Mr. Winston let out a loud sigh and dropped his shoulders. "Are you certain about this, darling?"

She nodded. "Yes, I'm certain. He deserves to be taken care of, and looking after him will help keep my mind occupied. If something had happened to us, you would have wanted someone to take good care of our son instead of sending him off to an awful orphanage, wouldn't you? Besides, look at him." She softly caressed his cheek again. "He already knows me."

Mr. Winston edged closer and observed the baby, worry lining his brow.

"There's just one other thing," Bernice said.

"What is it?" Mr. Winston said.

"In exchange for the child, the orphanage asks for a donation to help cover the cost of his care until today, and to help the other abandoned and orphaned children still there."

Mr. Winston's eyes went dark. "You might have mentioned that sooner."

"I would have," Bernice said. "But your wife took Joseph from me so suddenly and I was so caught up in the immediate, obvious bond between them, I simply forgot. I do apologize."

"Whatever it is," Mrs. Winston said, "we'll pay it."

"Darling," Mr. Winston scolded.

"I couldn't bear to turn him away," Mrs. Winston said. "And I won't. Especially because of money."

Mr. Winston regarded Bernice, his face hard. "How much?"

Bernice clenched her jaw. She'd only come up with the plan a few days earlier and hadn't been sure it would work, so she hadn't decided on an amount. "Generally, one hundred dollars," she said, pulling a number out of nowhere.

Mr. Winston's mouth fell open.

Bernice continued before he could refuse. "I understand that sounds like a lot of money, especially during these difficult times. But I don't need the entire sum all at once. I can collect payments whenever you can spare something. I must tell you, though, if you're unable to make the donation, I'm afraid I'll need to find someone else to take Joseph. Rules are rules. And I don't make them. If I did, he'd be yours without question."

Mrs. Winston tightened her grip on Joseph, panic-stricken. The fear on her face nearly broke Bernice's heart. But, she reminded herself, she had to do what was necessary to take care of Owen and Mason. Not to mention that giving a God-fearing American couple a white orphan to turn into a contributing member of society instead of letting him end up on the streets someday would be good for the city. The country too. Surely any patriot would agree with that. She wondered why the people in charge hadn't thought of that already. Instead they were sending the white children away by train and keeping the foreigners here. It didn't make sense.

"We only just buried our son," Mr. Winston said. "And as you know, funerals are not cheap."

A stab of guilt twisted in Bernice's stomach, thinking of little

Wallis left alone on the bed beside the nurse. He had no pillow-lined casket or solemn church service, no flowers or prayers by his grave. Instead he'd been abandoned next to a strange dead woman—most likely buried in the same coffin with her too, for all eternity. For all she knew, it was possible, even likely, that they were interred in one of the mass graves in the potter's field. The very idea made her head swim. She took a deep breath and let it out slowly, counting to three and trying to maintain her composure. She couldn't fall apart now, not when she was so close to successfully completing her clever plan. "I understand," she said. "And I'm sure I can persuade the orphanage to take less, considering your circumstances. Would fifty dollars be a reasonable amount?"

"Yes," Mrs. Winston said before her husband could answer. "That's an acceptable amount. We'll give it to you straightaway."

Mr. Winston nodded once, then stomped away to get the cash.

Now that money, along with several other donations Bernice had collected earlier in the week, lay safely hidden beneath her mattress in the other room, where Owen and Mason lay napping. It was enough for two months' rent, groceries, and three more train tickets for immigrant children. But it wasn't going to last forever. She needed to do more.

Then she had an idea. She took another sip of coffee, opened the newspaper, and skimmed the obituaries again. Surely some other white, middle-class couple had lost a child this week.

CHAPTER TWENTY

PIA

Pia gritted her teeth, trying not to scream as Sister Maria from the sick hall examined her injured arm. The nun's hands were strong and calloused, and every squeeze between her thumb and fingers felt like a vise crushing Pia's bones. If there was anything wrong with the nun, Pia never would have felt it. Between the pain, the sudden loss of Finn, and any hope of escape gone with him, she couldn't stop crying. Sister Ernestine stood at the foot of the bed glaring down on her with an angry, disgusted face.

"Her forearm feels broken," Sister Maria announced.

"Does she need to be moved into the sick hall?" Sister Ernestine said.

Sister Maria shook her head. "No, it's a small fracture, she can stay here. But she won't be able to work for a few weeks. I'll splint it and fashion a sling out of a sheet."

"Thank you, Sister Maria," Sister Ernestine said.

When Sister Maria left to get the supplies for the splint, Sister Agnes entered the ward with Gigi, leading her in by the hand. Gigi's face was wet with tears, and she clutched the stuffed rabbit Pia had given her at Christmas to her chest.

"What's this?" Sister Ernestine said.

"She saw Miss Lange fall and, for some reason, she's been inconsolable ever since," Sister Agnes said. "I wanted to show her she was all right so she'd stop crying."

Gigi let go of Sister Agnes's hand and edged up to Pia's bedside, then gently laid the stuffed rabbit beside her, it's long pink ears on the pillow. Her eyes were swollen, her face crumpled with sadness. Pia hugged the rabbit under her chin and did her best to smile through her tears.

"Thank you, Gigi," she said. "He's already making me feel better."

Gigi smiled back, then reached over to gently pat Pia's injured arm.

Before Pia could say anything more, Mother Joe marched into the room and shooed Gigi away. Sister Agnes took Gigi by the hand and led her toward the door, leaning over and talking softly in her ear. Before she left, Gigi turned and waved, her face glum.

Mother Joe shoved her sinewy hands beneath her sleeves and stood over Pia, towering above her like a black wall. "It's my understanding that no one is quite sure what happened to you, Miss Lange," she said. "Did those boys push you, or intentionally harm you in any way?"

Pia pushed herself up on her good arm and rested on her elbow. "No, it was my own fault. Please don't punish them."

"We haven't yet."

"They didn't do anything, I swear," Pia said. "I was asking them about Finn Duffy and I fell on the ice. Do you know where he is, Mother Joe?"

"No need to worry about him, Miss Lange," Mother Joe said. "Right now you have bigger problems."

"Was he adopted? Did you send him to the Home for Industrious Boys?"

"That doesn't concern you, Miss Lange."

"But it does, Mother Joe. Please. You have to tell me where he is. Did he escape?"

Mother Joe glanced at Sister Ernestine and rolled her eyes, an exasperated look on her face. "Miss Lange," she said. "I won't say it again. If it doesn't have anything to do with you, what goes on at

St. Vincent's is none of your business. Now mind your manners and thank God for looking after you. I spoke to Sister Maria and she said you were very lucky. The break in your arm could have been much worse."

"What about releasing me like you said you would, Mother Joe?" Pia said. "Is that any of my business?"

Mother Joe's eyes went dark. "I suggest you use your head for more than a hat rack and stop worrying about anything except staying out of trouble and getting better, Miss Lange. You're certainly not going anywhere with a broken arm. So until it's healed, I don't want to hear another word about Finn Duffy or you being released. As a matter of fact, I don't want to hear another word from or about you."

Pia knew she should stop aggravating her, but she was desperate. "But you said you'd arrange something," she said. "You said you'd let me go."

"Not another word, Miss Lange. Or you'll spend your recovery down in the basement. Is that clear?"

Pia dropped her gaze, her eyes burning. "Yes, Mother Joe."

Mother Joe harrumphed, then turned and left the room, Sister Ernestine on her heels. Pia collapsed back on the bed, sinking into a pit of despair, the sharp pain in her arm throbbing with every hard beat of her broken heart.

Despite the fact that she could only feed and rock the babies, Pia was sent back to work in the baby ward a few days after breaking her arm. The pain had dulled somewhat, but it was always there, like the black boulder of grief inside her heart, ready to make itself known if she moved just right or tried to lift something using that hand. The minute she saw Sister Agnes, she asked about Finn.

"I wouldn't know the boy if I fell over him, dear," Sister Agnes said.

"Well, has Mother Joe said anything about one of the older boys being sent somewhere?"

Sister Agnes shook her head. "She doesn't tell us where every child goes. The sisters are much too busy trying to—"

"What if someone escaped?" Pia said. "Would she tell you about that?"

The nun's eyes went wide. "Mercy me, I would think so." Then she furrowed her brow, thinking. "On the other hand, Mother Joe is extremely proud of running a tight ship. If something like that happened, she wouldn't want word to get out that someone had pulled the wool over her eyes."

"Would you ask her for me?"

"Ask her what, child?"

"If someone escaped."

"Oh no, child. Woe betide the nun who questions Mother Joe about her competence."

"Could you ask her if a boy named Finn was adopted?"

"And who do you think she'll suspect of putting me up to that?" Pia sighed. "Me."

"That's right. Now take my advice before you get yourself into more trouble. I suggest you forget about your friend for now and worry about yourself."

"Yes, Sister Agnes," Pia said. But that was impossible.

On a Monday afternoon several weeks later, after Pia's splint and sling were removed, Sister Ernestine informed her that Mother Joe wanted to see her. Following the sister into a hallway she'd never seen before, Pia fought to stay calm. It was the first time she'd ever been summoned to Mother Joe's office, and she had no idea what was going to happen. Maybe Mother Joe was going to tell her something about Finn. Maybe she was finally being released. Maybe there was news about the twins or Vater. Whatever it was, it was going to be very good or very bad. Instead of giving herself the vapors imagining all sorts of scenarios, she concentrated on putting one foot in front of the other. Otherwise, she might trip and fall in a heap.

When they entered the office, Mother Joe put down her pen and gestured for Pia to take a seat on the other side of her desk. Pia did as she was told, sitting on her hands to keep them from shaking. Sister Ernestine stood near a set of bookshelves, her arms crossed over her chest. Black-and-white photographs covered the wall above Mother Joe's head—orderly congregations of children posing in the play yard, their faces dark and somber, and groups of nuns holding babies gathered on the front steps. Some of the photos looked faded and old, while others looked more recent. Pia shivered, wondering how many children had passed through St. Vincent's. How many had been beaten with leather straps, force-fed, or locked in a basement room? How many had died? How many had sat where she was sitting now, waiting to hear news that would forever change their lives?

"How is your arm, Miss Lange?" Mother Joe said.

Pia pulled her eyes from the haunting photos and tried to focus on the here and now. Part of her wanted to stop time, to give herself a moment to prepare for whatever happened next. The other part of her wanted to get this over with as soon as possible.

"Miss Lange?" Mother Joe said.

"Um . . . yes, Mother Joe," Pia said. "My arm feels fine." In truth, it still ached, and her wrist didn't seem as straight as it used to be, but there was no point in saying any of that. No one cared.

"Good. I'll get right to the point, then. Now that you're strong again we're sending you to Byberry to live with a Dr. and Mrs. Hudson. They're looking for help with their children and housework in exchange for room and board. You leave this afternoon."

Pia went rigid. "But I . . . I thought you were going to release me?"

"That's what I'm doing, Miss Lange. Orphans are bound out all the time, but we've been unable to do it for a while because of the epidemic. There are still a few flu cases cropping up here and there, but we . . ."

The rest of her words were buried beneath Pia's thunderous heartbeat. "No," she said, louder than she intended. "I can't go there. I won't."

Mother Joe frowned. "This is a good opportunity, Miss Lange," she said. "If you don't take it, I'll offer it to someone else."

Pia's heart raced, trying to figure out how to change Mother Joe's mind. But she couldn't string two thoughts together.

"I thought you wanted to leave St. Vincent's?"

"I do, but—"

"Well, Byberry is in the northeast section of Philadelphia. You should be thankful I'm keeping you in the city. Your only other choice is to go out West, to work for a family there. There's a train leaving for Kansas tomorrow, and Jenny and some of the other girls will be on it. One way or another, we need to make room for incoming children. It's your choice, Miss Lange."

Pia couldn't breathe. She couldn't leave Pennsylvania. She just couldn't. "How long would I have to stay at the Hudsons'?"

"Why, until you're an adult, of course."

A white blinding panic rushed through Pia's body, making her head and chest feel like they were going to burst. Tears filled her eyes, and she looked down at her pale hands in her lap, swimming like white fish in the brown sea of her worn skirt. All this time, she'd thought she was going to be let go, that she'd be free to look for Ollie and Max. Now she was just being sent to another prison. It was like being put in St. Vincent's all over again. She took a deep breath and tried to think straight. Maybe it'd be easier to escape from someone's house. She'd just have to come up with a new plan. "Yes, Mother Joe."

"Yes? What does that mean, Miss Lange?"

"It means I'll go to the Hudsons', Mother Joe."

"Wonderful. I think you've made the right decision." Mother Joe picked up her pen again. "Miss O'Malley and her driver will take you there following lunch."

Pia gritted her teeth. Not Miss O'Malley again. She stood on wobbly legs and turned toward the door.

"Oh, and one more thing," Mother Joe said.

"Yes, Mother Joe?" Pia said.

"Make sure you're on your best behavior at the Hudsons'. If they're not happy with your work or you try pulling stunts like you pulled here, you'll either be sent to a city almshouse or the Byberry Mental Hospital. After today, we no longer have room for you here at St. Vincent's."

Sitting cross-legged in the splintered bed of Miss O'Malley's wagon and hanging on to the wooden sideboards as it bumped along the cobblestones, Pia shivered beneath a threadbare blanket. She wasn't sure if she was shaking because of the cold, or because she didn't know what lay ahead. Not only would it be even harder for Vater to find her now, she had no idea what kind of people Dr. and Mrs. Hudson were or how she would be treated. It was hard to believe anyone who'd turn an orphan into a servant could be compassionate and kind. For all she knew, Mother Joe had purposely taken her out of the frying pan and put her into the fire.

Along with being scared, her heart ached knowing she'd never see the babies at St. Vincent's again. Edith had warned her not to get attached, but her eyes grew misty when she thought of Alannah, who clung to Pia as if she were her mother, and little Yakov, who never cried, even when he had a dirty diaper or it was past his mealtime. There were others she would miss too—every thin, sad face would forever haunt her dreams—but her bonds with Alannah and Yakov were the deepest. With only a few minutes to say goodbye to the babies and Edith, who said little except "you shouldn't have tried to escape" and "good luck," she felt like she was deserting them. It felt like abandoning Ollie and Max all over again. Maybe she deserved whatever happened next.

Despite her fear and heartache, she was grateful to be out of the orphanage and relieved to see the city coming back to life. Motorcars, horse-drawn wagons, and trolleys filled the streets, everyone hurrying to their next destination. Horns beeped, horses whinnied, men yelled, and policemen blew whistles. Many people still wore gauze masks over their noses and mouths, mostly women and young children, but otherwise it seemed the epidemic had finally come to an end. Breathing in the crisp air to clear her lungs of the smell of St. Vincent's—the disinfectant and urine, the thick, invisible layers of sorrow and fear—she couldn't help but feel envious of those who seemed to be returning to normal. Surely almost everyone had been touched by the flu in one way or another, but for many, the nightmare was likely over. Even if they'd lost loved ones to the disease, at least they knew what had happened to them. At least they could try to start over. She, on the other hand, felt like she was stuck in purgatory.

Taking care of the Hudson children weighed on her mind too,

and the possibility that she might discover they were sick or hurt when she touched them. At St. Vincent's she had hardened herself to the fact that there was little medical help available for the orphans, and tried to ignore her aches and pains unless they were severe. Even then, the nuns wouldn't find a doctor. The sickest babies were sent to the sick hall and never came back. The rest were nursed by her and Edith, who could do little more than give them onion or catnip tea, and make poultices out of coal oil or bread and milk. Sometimes bottles of Mrs. Winslow's Soothing Syrup were donated to the orphanage, but not often. And it didn't seem to help much anyway, other than making the babies sleep.

She'd never forget the time eight-month-old Ellis had come down with what Sister Agnes thought was the croup; how she had wiped his small body with a cool rag and held him for hours while he coughed, her own chest aching with each bark, only to find the next morning that he had passed away in the night. It was like losing her brothers all over again. She couldn't stop crying the rest of the day.

Another thing that worried her was that the father of the Hudson family was a doctor. He and his wife would never believe her if she sensed something was wrong with one of their children. Either that, or they'd think she was crazy and send her to a mental hospital like Mother Joe said. Just thinking about it made her stomach churn with nausea. And it went without saying that they could never find out what she'd done to her own brothers.

As the driver steered the horse around wagons and trolleys, each mile slogging into the next, Pia scanned the faces on the sidewalks, desperately searching for Vater, Finn, Ollie and Max. When she saw women holding babies or pushing prams, she got up on her knees to get a better look. Mother Joe had warned her to behave, but if she had spied the twins anywhere, she would have jumped out of the wagon without a second thought. Even the threat of being sent to an asylum couldn't have stopped her from doing that.

She thought she saw her father once, striding along the curb at the end of Goodwell Street, his hands deep in his pockets, his eyes on the ground. The man had the same dark hair, the same broad shoulders and trimmed beard. He even walked like Vater, with a lanky stride that made his legs look a hundred feet long. She opened her mouth to call out to him, but he stopped to look up at a pedestal clock, revealing his entire face. It wasn't him. She sank back in the wagon bed, tears misting her eyes. In this city of thousands, how would she ever find the four she needed most?

After what seemed like forever, the wagon turned onto a residential street lined with sidewalks, massive homes, and manicured front lawns. Each house seemed bigger and more elaborate than the last, with corner towers, high-peaked gables, and porches with spindles and turned posts. Four or five families could have lived in each one with room to spare. Here and there, tattered strips of crepe hung from doorways, but not nearly as many as she'd seen in the tenements and slums.

Finally, the driver stopped the wagon in front of a brick three-story with tall windows, ornamental trim, and white shutters. Gardens and bushes with winter-browned stems and blackened leaves filled the front lawn, and a stone path led up to the front porch. Pia trembled even harder. The outside of the house looked warm and inviting, but who knew what awaited her inside? Someone who would beat her for the slightest mistake? Someone who would send her away without a second thought if she didn't live up to their expectations? A cold bed in a locked basement room?

Miss O'Malley got down from the wagon and instructed Pia to do the same. Pia grabbed the blanket and climbed over the sideboard, shaking and trying not to fall.

"I won't be long," Miss O'Malley said to the driver. "Follow me, Miss Lange." She hurried along the path, went up a set of painted steps, and crossed the front porch.

Pia wrapped the blanket around herself, gathered it under her chin, and did as she was told, her stomach churning. Miss O'Malley glanced behind her to make sure she was coming, then marched back down the steps and yanked the blanket off her shoulders.

"This ain't yours," she snapped. "It belongs to the orphanage." She thrust the blanket at her. "Now put it back."

Pia returned the blanket to the wagon and went back to where Miss O'Malley waited, her arms wrapped around herself, her teeth chattering from nerves. She thought about turning and running, but what if Miss O'Malley and the driver caught her again? The next stop might be an insane asylum. For now, she'd take her chances with the doctor and his wife. Maybe she'd have a warm bed and good food to eat. Maybe the Hudsons would be kind and understanding. Maybe, by some miracle, the day would come when she could tell them about Ollie and Max and they'd help her look for them. Or at least give her the freedom to try.

"If ye pull anything like that here," Miss O'Malley said, "or try to run again, you'll find yourself sent away so fast it will make yer pretty little head spin. And wherever you end up will be a lot worse than St. Vincent's. Understand?"

Pia thought about saying she wasn't trying to steal the blanket, but it would be a waste of breath. Instead she nodded and said, "Yes, ma'am."

Miss O'Malley climbed the steps again, waited for Pia to follow, then eyed her up and down. "Put yer arms down and stand up straight," she hissed. "And look happy."

Pia dropped her arms and tried to smile. It felt more like a grimace. Miss O'Malley studied the mailbox. Above a nameplate that read HUDSON, a copper sign read: THE ENTRANCE TO DR. HUDSON'S OFFICE IS AT THE BACK OF THE HOUSE. A handwritten sign tacked to the front door read: *No Visitors.*

Miss O'Malley produced a piece of paper from her coat pocket and unfolded it. "'Tis the right place," she said to herself, then returned the paper to her pocket and knocked. On the other side of the door, heavy footsteps hurried along a hard floor. A lace curtain drew sideways in a sidelight window and sprang back. After some jostling on the other side, the handle turned and the door opened. A tall man with blond, side-parted hair and a pencil-thin mustache came out on the porch, closing the door partway behind him. Miss O'Malley and Pia stepped back to give him room. It was only then that Pia noticed his left forearm was missing, the bottom half of his jacket sleeve folded up and pinned.

"May I help you?" he said.

"I'm dropping this girl off from St. Vincent's," Miss O'Malley said. "Mother Joe sent me."

"Ah, yes," the man said. "I'm Dr. Hudson." He studied Pia for a moment, then returned his attention to Miss O'Malley. "The nuns were instructed to send someone healthy."

"Aye," Miss O'Malley said. "Miss Lange had the flu and survived. I took her from the infirmary to the orphanage myself. Mother Joe can tell ye."

The doctor looked at Pia. "Is this true?"

Pia nodded.

To her surprise and relief, he smiled at her, a warm, genuine smile that lit up his blue eyes. "Welcome, then, Miss Lange." He went back inside and held the door open. "Please, come in."

Pia entered the grand house, her face growing hot, then stepped aside to await further instruction. The foyer was as big as her family's old apartment, with a shiny wood floor and a marble-topped side table full of colored glass vases and photos of young girls in hair ribbons and white dresses. Pia had never seen such an elegant, bright room. It looked like it belonged in a castle. Miss O'Malley made a move to follow her inside, but Dr. Hudson blocked her way and she stopped short, shock and anger contorting her face.

"I'm sorry," Dr. Hudson said. "I don't mean to be rude, but we've got young children in the house and there's still a lingering threat of the flu. We've just learned of a small resurgence in the city, so we're not taking any chances. My wife would have a fit if I let you in."

"But I'm—" Miss O'Malley started.

"I'm sorry," Dr. Hudson said again. "Thank you for bringing Miss Lange to us. You're free to go now."

Hearing the doctor say there were more flu cases in the city, Pia felt ill. Was the nightmare starting up again? Did the thousands of people on the streets have any idea? Why wasn't it being shouted from the rooftops?

Just then, a red-haired woman swaddling an infant in her arms appeared at the other end of the foyer, her bottle-green eyes quivering with nerves. She was pretty and petite, with a delicate nose and thin pink lips. Her blue dress shimmered in the light, each seam straight and true, each fold smooth and even, in stark contrast to her disheveled hair and tired face.

"Who was it, darling?" she said. "Did you send them away?"

When she saw Pia and Miss O'Malley, she stopped short and clutched the baby to her chest, as if they'd come to steal him.

"It's fine, dear," Dr. Hudson said. "I sent for someone to help with the children."

The woman gave him a worried look. "But I thought we were going to wait until we knew it was safe to—"

"I know," he said. "But don't worry. I asked the orphanage to send someone healthy and they did. She had the flu and survived. I realize we planned on waiting, but you're exhausted and need to rest. I couldn't bear it if something happened to you."

The woman sighed and her face softened. "Oh, Dr. Hudson, you're such a dear," she said. "And you know what's best, of course." She edged closer, eyeing Pia. "Look at you, you poor thing. Where on earth is your jacket?"

Pia shrugged, a small measure of relief washing over her. So far, the doctor and his wife seemed pleasant enough. Maybe working for them wouldn't be as awful as she'd imagined.

Mrs. Hudson gave Miss O'Malley a disgusted look. "Why, pray tell, isn't this child wearing a coat, or at the very least wrapped up in a blanket? Aren't you supposed to watch over the children in your care?"

Miss O'Malley blanched. "I don't work at the orphanage, ma'am," she said. "I only do what the nuns pay me to do."

"Well, it's still winter out there. Shame on all of you for being so heartless."

"But I—" Miss O'Malley started.

Dr. Hudson started to close the door, forcing Miss O'Malley back across the threshold. "Thank you again for delivering Miss Lange," he said. "If we need anything else, we'll send a telegram to Mother Joe. Good day, miss."

Miss O'Malley harrumphed, then turned and marched across the porch.

Dr. Hudson closed the door all the way and winked at his wife, clearly amused.

Mrs. Hudson smiled warmly back at him, then reached out to put a dainty, fluttering hand on Pia's arm. Pia stiffened and instinctively drew back. Thankfully Mrs. Hudson didn't seem to notice. Instead she wrinkled her nose as if smelling something rotten and pulled her hand away. "What should we call you, dear?"

Pia looked down at herself. Did she smell bad? For the first time, she noticed the glaring difference between her clothes and the Hudsons'. Next to Mrs. Hudson's shimmering blue dress and the doctor's navy suit and tie, she looked like she'd rolled in mud and let it dry. Everything about her, from her dress to her leggings to her shoes, looked ancient and brown, like the sepia colors of an old photograph. Compared to her outfit, even the doormat seemed a dazzling shade of cranberry red.

"My goodness, child," Mrs. Hudson said, laughing softly. "Has the cat gotten your tongue?" More relaxed now, she swayed gently back and forth, rocking the baby in her arms.

"I'm sorry, ma'am," Pia said. "My name is Pia Lange."

"Well, despite my initial reaction, Pia," Mrs. Hudson said, "I'm glad you're here, and I'll be grateful for your help with the children." She gazed lovingly down at the baby boy, who looked to be barely two months old. He blinked up at her, perfectly content. "This is our youngest, Leonard James. We call him Leo. He's a really good baby, but with the others to care for as well, I'll admit I've been a little overwhelmed."

"He's beautiful, ma'am," Pia said. And he was, with strawberry-blond hair and his father's masculine chin. Remembering when Ollie and Max were that small, sorrow tightened her chest and she blinked back the tears forming in her eyes—partly from grief, partly from relief, partly from disbelief. Hopefully no one noticed.

"Will you be all right for a little while, darling?" Dr. Hudson said to his wife. "I need to return to the office, but I shouldn't be long."

"I'll be fine," Mrs. Hudson said. "Thank you, sweetheart." She gave her husband a peck on the cheek, then turned to Pia again. "I'm sure you're starving, but first things first. Before I introduce you to the girls, you need to get cleaned up. After that I'll fix you something to eat and we'll get you settled. Does that sound all right with you?"

Pia thought about pinching herself to see if she was dreaming.

From the second she'd learned she was being "bound out," she'd been angry at Mother Joe, thinking she only wanted to punish her further. But maybe she was wrong. Maybe the old nun knew the Hudsons would treat her well, and her chances of surviving here were better than out on the streets. Then again, maybe Mother Joe had no idea what kind of people the doctor and his wife were, and Pia had just gotten lucky.

"Yes, ma'am," she said. "It sounds more than all right."

"Come with me, then," Mrs. Hudson said, starting toward a door at the other end of the foyer. Then she stopped and looked back at Pia's shoes. "But please remove your footwear first."

Pia bent over and took off her shoes, her face burning with shame. The feet of her leggings were dirty and stained, and two grimy toes stuck through a jagged hole. Mutti would have been appalled. Surely Mrs. Hudson was too.

"Oh dear," Mrs. Hudson said, her forehead creased. Then she looked at Pia with sympathetic eyes. "Don't worry, I know it's not your fault. After we get rid of those wretched things and get you washed up, we'll make sure to give the floors an extra good scrubbing." She turned and started toward the door again.

Mortified, Pia followed Mrs. Hudson into a long hall with mullioned windows looking out over the side yard. Opposite the windows, doorways opened into rooms filled with shiny, carved furniture and decorative rugs. Floral tablecloths covered every table and sideboard, and embroidered throw pillows filled every couch and chair. Books and vases and porcelain figurines filled every shelf, and oil paintings and mirrors hung on every wall. Pia tried not to stare, but she'd never seen such a beautiful house or so many knickknacks and decorations in her life. Luckily, Mrs. Hudson didn't seem to notice her gawking.

"Our previous nanny, Miss Bainbridge, passed from the flu a week after the parade," Mrs. Hudson said. "Poor thing. I think she was about to leave us anyway, though. After all, she had just gotten engaged. But no one deserves to die that young. She wasn't here with the children at the time, thank goodness." Mrs. Hudson was talking fast, as if trying to explain everything before she forgot. "It's a terribly ghastly way to go, from what I've heard. Dr. Hudson didn't tell me the details, he tries to protect me from that sort of thing, but I heard bodies were backing up in homes, on porches, and in corners of rooms, and people were drowning in their own blood." Then she came to a halt and gaped at Pia, her eyes wide. "Oh my word. I never asked what happened to your parents. And here I am going on and on about . . ." She dropped her shoulders, suddenly forlorn. "Please tell me they didn't pass from the flu."

"My mother did, ma'am," Pia said. "My father was sent overseas. The last I heard from him, he was in France."

"And you haven't heard from him since the war ended?"

Pia shook her head. "I don't think he'd know where to find me, ma'am."

"Oh dear," Mrs. Hudson said. "You poor thing. I'm so sorry. Didn't the nuns at the orphanage try to find out what happened to your father?"

"No, ma'am," Pia said. She thought about asking Mrs. Hudson if she could help find Vater, but it was too soon. She had only just met the woman. "They said they didn't have the time or resources to search for the parents of every child who walked in the door."

Mrs. Hudson sighed. "Well, I suppose that makes sense. And I'd imagine they're scared to go out into the city, anyway. I hope you can forgive me for not asking about your parents sooner."

"I do, ma'am."

"I swear I can't remember a thing since giving birth to Leo." She waved a hand in the air as if swatting a fly. "It wasn't like that with the girls, though. After them I felt fine." She started walking again. "I don't know why that is."

Pia followed, relieved Mrs. Hudson hadn't asked if she had any siblings.

"Anyway," Mrs. Hudson continued. "After our nanny passed, I thought about replacing her, but I was so worried about the flu. What if someone applied for the job without realizing they were sick until it was too late? Of course, when I found out how fast the illness was spreading, I let the cook and the maid go too. Paul, I mean, my husband, Dr. Hudson, was still overseas at the time. That's how he lost his arm. A bullet hit him while he was on the front line taking care of the injured, and the wound became infected. He came home right after they, you know, removed it, and of course I was happy he wasn't gone long. He returned right after Leo was born, you see, but he could only do so much. And he agreed we couldn't chance bringing anyone into our home with the flu going 'round. He said more soldiers were dying from that than were being killed in battle. And money was tight too. Luckily, I had a substantial dowry when we married six years ago, but those things don't last forever you know, especially when you have children. First they need diapers and clothes, then toys and more clothes, and food and more food."

Pia did her best to listen to everything Mrs. Hudson was saying, but she was talking fast again and it was a lot to take in. She was surprised little Leo kept quiet through it all.

"That's why I was stunned when I saw you," Mrs. Hudson went on. "My husband has been adamant about not exposing the children to the flu. He doesn't want me to leave the house because he's worried I might bring it home with me. He still sees patients in his office, because he can't drive the wagon anymore, you know, with one arm, but he promised if anyone came in presenting flu symptoms, he'd sleep in his office until enough time passed to know whether or not he was ill. But bless his heart, he's been so worried about me, he figured out a way to find help for me too, despite his fears about the latest return of the epidemic. And here you are." She smiled at Pia with tired eyes.

Pia forced herself to return the smile, but desperation swelled inside her chest. The thought of another wave of the flu—and what it might mean for her brothers, Vater, and Finn, if they were out there somewhere—made her heart feel like lead. When they reached the back of the house, she followed Mrs. Hudson into a white-tiled kitchen with wide windows overlooking a jumbled yard filled with trellises and birdbaths. Mrs. Hudson put Leo in a crib next to the coal stove and tucked his blanket in around him. He yawned and looked around without fussing. Pia had never seen such a content baby. Probably because he had a full belly, a warm house, and both his parents.

"Oh, before I forget," Mrs. Hudson said. "I meant to ask about your name. It's very pretty, but so unusual. Do you know its origin?"

Pia glanced at the floor, heat crawling up her neck. Then she remembered her father always said it was important to look people in the eye when you spoke. It made them believe you were honest. Except Pia couldn't be honest right now. Healthy or not, if Dr. and Mrs. Hudson found out she was German, they might not be so kind. She shook her head a little too vigorously and looked Mrs. Hudson in the eye.

"I was named after my great-great-grandmother," she said.

"How lovely. And where was she from?"

"Holland. She came to the States with her parents years ago."

"Well, as long as it's not German," Mrs. Hudson said. "The war might be over, but I'll never forgive those people for what they did, especially to my husband, the poor dear. Also, and I ask this of all my potential help so don't worry about your answer, what neighborhood are you from?"

"Near South Philadelphia," she said. "In the Fifth Ward."

Mrs. Hudson put a hand to her chest. "Oh my. Is it true there's sewage and garbage strewn in the streets down there? And rats everywhere?"

Pia shrugged. "My mother always said the neighborhood could have used some cleaning up."

"Well, it sounds like your mother was a very clever woman, which I'm glad to hear because I could never have someone working here who doesn't understand the importance of cleanliness. Did your mother teach you to be clean and orderly?"

"Yes, ma'am."

"Then we should get along just fine," Mrs. Hudson said. "The Philadelphia Tuberculosis Committee released a list of precautions to avoid the flu, which we abide by strictly in this house. Always use a handkerchief or napkin when you cough or sneeze, sterilize dishes and silverware after use, and do not share drinking cups or towels. It's very important for you to remember those rules, Pia. Do you think you can do that?"

"Yes, ma'am," Pia said.

"Good," Mrs. Hudson said. She turned and started out of the kitchen and Pia followed. "Little Elizabeth is napping right now. She's just shy of two years old. And Sophie and Margaret are in the children's room playing. At least I hope that's what they're doing. With those two you never know. The last time I thought they were playing nicely together I found them in the garden with mud up to their knees. It was an awful mess. I had to throw out everything they were wearing, including their shoes." She shivered at the memory. "I'm warning you, they're a handful, those two. Always getting into something they shouldn't."

Pia nodded, trying to look agreeable, although she never understood why mothers had such an aversion to their children getting dirty. Making mud pies after a rainstorm used to be one of her favorite things to do when she was small, and she remembered how Vater used to laugh when Mutti swore under her breath while scrubbing her filthy clothes. He said playing in the dirt was good for children, and it was nothing a little soap and water couldn't fix. That was when Mutti used to throw a wet shirt or sock at him, and they'd chase each other around the washtub, laughing. Pia's eyes grew moist just thinking about it.

From the kitchen Mrs. Hudson led her into a short hallway, her shoes clacking on the shiny floorboards, then took her into a wallpapered room with tasseled drapes, stained-glass windows, and strange-looking furniture.

"This is the water closet," Mrs. Hudson said with pride. "Brand-new last year." She moved toward a rectangular wooden box lined with what looked like porcelain next to one wall. A brass spigot and matching handles stuck out of one end. "This is the bathtub." She pointed at another piece of furniture that looked like an oversize mixing bowl with a pipe coming out the top connected to another wooden box with a dangling handle. "And that's the lavatory."

"I'm sorry, ma'am," Pia said. "What's a lava . . . lavatory?"

Mrs. Hudson grinned. "The toilet," she said. "And that's the foot bath and the sink." She reached into the bathtub and turned one of the brass handles. To Pia's surprise, water came out of the spigot. Mrs. Hudson ran a hand under the flow. After a moment, curls of steam rose into the air.

Pia's mouth dropped open. "Is that . . ." she started.

"Yes, it's hot water," Mrs. Hudson said, a pleased look on her face. "Dr. Hudson must have stoked the boiler in anticipation of your arrival." She pointed to a painted shelf beside the sink. "There are fresh towels and washcloths over there, and help yourself to a new bar of lavender soap. When the tub is halfway full, just turn the handle to shut off the water. And leave your clothes on the floor. I'll have Dr. Hudson burn them later. In the meantime, I'll see what I can find for you to wear."

Pia didn't know what to say. It all seemed so strange and wonderful at the same time. Like something you only read about in books. On one hand, she was beyond relieved to be treated so kindly; on the other, she didn't deserve any of it. "Thank you, ma'am," she said.

"Just be sure to wash your hair thoroughly and check it for fleas," Mrs. Hudson said. "If there's one thing I won't tolerate beside sloppy habits, it's personal uncleanliness."

"Yes, ma'am."

"I'll be right back," Mrs. Hudson said, then bustled out of the room and closed the door.

Pia stared into the steaming bath, her thoughts whirling like the water below the spigot. Being in this beautiful house with such kind people didn't seem right when everyone she loved and cared about had suffered so much. Vater had struggled so hard to provide for and protect his family, and he was sent off to fight in a war. Mutti did everything for everyone, including sick neighbors and strangers who needed help, and she had died a horrible death. Then there were poor little Ollie and Max, loving and innocent and new, whose older sister locked them in a cold cubby and left them there, crying and hungry and scared. Not only had they lost their entire family, but who knew what horrible fate they'd endured? And it was all her fault. She was the one who had abandoned them when they needed her most. Maybe being in the orphanage was the start of her penance for what she'd done. Maybe taking care of babies who reminded her daily of Ollie and Max was part of it too. Except this didn't feel like punishment. This felt like a reward. Then again, the only true reward would be having her family together again. And that was never going to happen. She hung her head, the horrible, heavy ache in her chest growing tighter and tighter.

The sound of footsteps on the other side of the door pulled her from her thoughts. She held her breath, waiting to see if Mrs. Hudson was coming back, but the footsteps grew fainter and disappeared. She shook her head to clear it. Nothing she felt mattered anymore. The only thing she could do was keep going and do the next thing, even when she didn't have the strength or desire to go on. She undressed, shut off the spigots, and got into the tub, the hot water slipping like silk over her dry, grimy skin. She picked up the bar of lavender soap and put it to her nose. The flowery, clean fragrance reminded her of climbing hills back in Hazleton, when the spring trillium and violets sprang through the damp ground. A wave of homesickness swept over her, so powerful she nearly cried out, and hot tears squeezed from her eyes. What she wouldn't have given to be back in that wooden, coal-stained washtub next to the coal stove in her parents' rundown shack, when everything seemed so simple and she didn't have a care in the world. Then she pushed the thought away, berating herself for giving in to her emotions again. She didn't deserve her own pity.

Someone knocked on the door. "Pia?" It was Mrs. Hudson.

"Yes, ma'am?"

"I found some clothes for you to wear. It's an old outfit of mine, but I think it will fit just fine. And I have several more that will work too. No need to get out of the tub, I'll just slip it in through the door."

"Thank you, ma'am," Pia said.

The door opened a few inches and a neat stack of folded clothes topped by a pair of pointed boots slid in on the floor. "Take your time getting cleaned up," Mrs. Hudson said. "And meet me in the kitchen when you're finished."

"Yes, ma'am."

After scrubbing layers of dirt and the desperate smell of the orphanage from her body and hair, Pia lay back in the hot, soapy water, surprised that she could nearly stretch all the way out. She could have stayed in the warm cocoon for another hour, but didn't want to keep Mrs. Hudson waiting. She climbed out and dried off with the thickest towel she had ever felt, then picked up the boots and stack of clothes by the door. Cotton bloomers, a silky chemise, and a pair of knee socks lay folded on top of a lilac-colored dress with an ivory sash; the boots looked brand-new, with leather buckles and cloth-covered buttons. She put on the undergarments, pushed her bare legs and calloused feet into the stretchy socks and boots, then slipped the muslin dress over her head. Not only was the dress beautiful, but it fit almost perfectly and the material didn't itch. It felt strange to be comfortable, her arms and legs covered and snug. She'd never worn anything like it in her life, and she was delighted by how luxurious it felt; at the same time it only added more weight to her guilt.

When she entered the kitchen, Mrs. Hudson and Leo were nowhere to be seen. Waiting next to a row of floor cupboards with a long, wooden top and what seemed like a hundred drawers, she felt strange and out of place, like a beggar at a masquerade ball. Laughter and the high, tinkling of little girls' voices filtered down from somewhere upstairs. She looked up at the ceiling. What would it feel like to be one of those girls, living in this beautiful house with your siblings and both parents? What would it feel like to know you were safe and you'd always have enough food and enough clothes and enough money? Back when she was too young to know the difference between rich and poor, hunger and starvation, want and need, she'd felt the same way she imagined the Hudson girls did now. The sky would always be blue, her parents would always take care of her, and they'd be together forever. Now, no matter how hard she tried, she couldn't remember that feeling; it was as elusive as a forgotten dream. And those days were long gone.

And what were the Hudsons going to expect of her? Did being "bound out" make her a prisoner here, or would she be allowed to leave the house when she wasn't taking care of the children? Would she have to wait until Dr. Hudson said the flu was no longer a threat? Then she had another thought and her heart started to race. She could leave right now. She could leave and no one would know until it was too late. She could go home and ask the strangers living in her family's old rooms if her father had returned. She could scour the city for other orphanages and see if her brothers were there. As far as she could tell, the house she was standing in was a normal one, with unlocked windows and unlocked doors. This wasn't St. Vincent's. This was her chance to be free.

Four different doorways led out of the kitchen, but she had no idea where they led. When she'd first arrived, she'd been too nervous to pay attention, and now she could only guess which one went back to the front door. She took a deep breath and tried to think rationally. If she left, she'd be homeless and on her own, with no food, no money, and nowhere to go. What if the police picked her up? She'd seen her share of homeless children getting dropped off at St. Vincent's. The last thing she needed was to get sent to another orphanage. Or worse. Maybe she should wait and see what happened. At the Hudsons', she'd have a roof over her head and food to eat. Maybe when she wasn't working, she'd be free to do as she pleased and could look for her brothers. If not right away, then someday. Maybe, after she earned Dr. and Mrs. Hudson's trust by taking good care of their children, she'd have the courage to tell them the truth. And maybe, just maybe, they would help.

Footsteps suddenly sounded on the plank floors, getting closer and closer. The decision had been made for her. It was too late to run now. She smoothed the front of her dress, stood up straight, and tried to relax. Mrs. Hudson appeared in an open doorway.

"I've put Leo down for a nap in the upstairs nursery," she said. "How do the clothes fit?"

"Everything fits fine," Pia said. "Thank you, ma'am."

"The boots too?"

"Yes, ma'am." In truth, they were a little loose, but Pia wasn't about to complain.

"Wonderful. I wore that dress when I was your age. I hope it's not too old-fashioned."

"Oh no, ma'am. I've never worn such a pretty dress in my life."

"Well, it's yours now. Let's go up to the playroom, shall we? While Leo is napping I'll introduce you to his sisters."

"Yes, ma'am."

Pia followed her out of the kitchen, along another hallway, and up a wide flight of stairs covered with a cushioned, decorative runner. At the top of the landing, they turned down the main hall, part of which ran along a railing above the staircase. Somehow, the upstairs looked even bigger than the downstairs, with what seemed like a dozen doors. Mrs. Hudson stopped at the first room, put a finger to her lips, and slowly opened the door. Two white cribs with lace bed skirts sat on either side of a changing table, and a rocking chair sat beneath a round window centered in the back wall. Leo lay swaddled in a blue blanket, sound asleep in one of the cribs, and a chubby-cheeked toddler napped in the other, her diapered buttocks in the air, her socked feet tucked beneath her tummy. She looked like one of the Christmas angels Pia had seen in store windows, with golden ringlets and chubby cheeks.

Mrs. Hudson pointed at the little girl and whispered, "That's Elizabeth. She's twenty-two months old."

Pia smiled and nodded.

Mrs. Hudson watched Elizabeth for a few moments, her face soft with love, then looked in on Leo and tiptoed out of the room. Pia had seen the same loving look on Mutti's face a thousand times. It seemed like a lifetime ago. With a lump in her throat, she followed Mrs. Hudson into the hall and waited while she quietly closed the door. Then they went to the end of the corridor, where little girls' voices floated out a half-open door, like the delicate notes of flutes on the wind.

The children's playroom was twice as big as the nursery, with high white ceilings and light gray walls. A red hobbyhorse with a yellow mane sat in one corner, his painted mouth in a perpetual smile. A dollhouse filled with miniature furniture and straight-backed dolls sat opposite a bookshelf overflowing with story and picture books. Porcelain dolls and cradles and blocks and wooden tops littered the plush carpet. Two little girls sat at a child-size table in the center of the room, pouring pretend tea into china cups; the other two chairs were occupied by an oversize Teddy bear and a giant stuffed rabbit. The girls looked up when Mrs. Hudson and Pia entered, then went back to giggling and serving pretend cookies.

Pia's breath caught in her chest. They were twins.

Mrs. Hudson started picking up toys and tossing them into the toy box. "Please excuse the mess," she said. "I don't know how I'll ever keep up when Leo starts getting into everything."

"No need to apologize, ma'am," Pia said. "I've never seen such a beautiful house in my entire life."

Mrs. Hudson smiled and went over to the table. "Sophie, Margaret," she said. "This is Pia. She's going to help look after you."

The girls glanced at each other, then set down their teacups, got out of their chairs, and stood next to their mother, studying Pia with wary eyes. One of them hid behind Mrs. Hudson's skirt. They were beautiful girls, with porcelain skin and auburn ringlets that fell past their waists. Mrs. Hudson put a hand on the shy one's head and stroked her hair.

"This is Sophie," she said. "Our second oldest. She's three. Margaret is four. They're fifteen months apart."

Pia let out a silent sigh of relief. She wasn't sure she could bear taking care of twins without thinking of Ollie and Max even more than she already did. "Hello," she said, doing her best to sound friendly. "It's very nice to meet you. I love your hair and your pretty dresses."

"I'm four and a half," Margaret said. "I'm going to be five on my next birthday." She approached Pia and tugged on her skirt. "Will you play with us?"

"Oh, my darling little love," Mrs. Hudson said. "Not right now. Pia only just arrived, and I haven't shown her where she'll be sleeping yet."

"Can she stay in our room?" Margaret said. "We can play games and tell stories!"

Sophie peeked out from behind her mother's skirt with hopeful eyes. "I wanna do that," she said in a quiet voice.

Margaret jumped up and down, excited. "Can we, Mother?" she said. "Pretty please?"

Mrs. Hudson shook her head. "Good heavens, no," she said. "She's just come from a filthy orphanage and who knows—" Then she realized what she was saying and gave Pia a nervous glance. "I mean, once we get to know Pia a little better, there will be plenty of time for fun and games."

Pia was puzzled, starting to wonder if Mrs. Hudson was as tolerant as she seemed. She had just taken a bath and changed into fresh clothes. Not that she wanted to stay in the girls' room—in truth she was exhausted and couldn't wait to have some time alone—but maybe it was going to be more important to watch her step than she'd thought. Thank goodness she hadn't admitted to being German.

"Well, now that you've met the children," Mrs. Hudson said, "shall we get you something to eat?"

Pia nodded. "Thank you, ma'am."

"All right, my darlings," Mrs. Hudson said. "You need to play nicely for a few more minutes; then I'll send Pia back up to fetch you."

"Yes, Mother," Margaret said, pouting. She crossed her arms and made her way back to the table. Sophie followed, giving her big sister a comforting pat with a chubby hand.

The sound of Leo crying drifted in through the door behind them. Mrs. Hudson hurried out of the playroom, padded along the hall, and slipped into the nursery. Pia followed and stood at the open door, not sure what to do. Mrs. Hudson scooped Leo up and whisked him out of the room, closing the door partway behind her.

"Is Elizabeth awake too?" Pia whispered. "Do you need me to get her?"

Mrs. Hudson shook her head. "I swear," she whispered. "This child doesn't like to eat or sleep." She snuggled Leo against her shoulder and patted his back. He settled down and stopped whimpering. "Elizabeth, on the other hand, would sleep half the day if I let her. And, sadly, sometimes I do because I don't have the energy for all four of them at once." She sighed and started toward the stairs. "There are times when I feel like I'll never have the energy to leave this house again. If I'm ever *able* to leave this house again."

Then she stopped and looked at Pia with miserable eyes. "I agree with my husband's concerns, and I'd never do anything to risk the health of my children. I'm scared to death of the flu. But to tell you the truth, sometimes I worry I'll never be able to have lunch with my friends again. Does that make me a terrible mother?"

Pia shook her head, surprised by the confession and that Mrs.

Hudson would care about her opinion. "I don't think so, ma'am. My mother used to say the only time she got any rest was when my little brothers were sleeping, and the only time she felt sane was when she could go to the market alone."

Mrs. Hudson gave her a weak but grateful smile. "You know what? I'm starting to like your mother more and more. I bet we would have been fast friends."

"I'm sure you would have, ma'am," Pia said, wondering if she would have felt the same way if she knew where Mutti was born.

Back in the kitchen, Mrs. Hudson pulled a chair out from beneath the table, told Pia to sit, then stood rocking Leo gently back and forth. "Have you had much experience with young children?"

Pia nodded. "Yes, ma'am. I worked in the baby ward at St. Vincent's. And I . . ." She bit her lip to stop herself from mentioning her brothers, hating herself for becoming careless. "I liked it very much."

Thankfully, Mrs. Hudson seemed unaware of her hesitation. "That's wonderful," she said. "I was afraid they'd sent someone who'd never handled babies before." She moved closer and held Leo out to her. "I guess you might as well get to know each other."

Pia clenched her jaw and gathered the baby in her arms, tucking the blanket around his little legs. She forced a smile at Mrs. Hudson, then looked down at his tiny face, her heart pounding. He cooed and lifted one arm from beneath the blanket.

"Oh, how precious," Mrs. Hudson said, laughing. "He wants to hold your hand."

Pia couldn't let Mrs. Hudson see her reluctance, so she let him wrap his tiny hand around her finger.

"While you two get acquainted," Mrs. Hudson said, "I'll fix you something to eat. Would you like a cup of tea?"

"Yes, please," Pia said, trying to keep her voice steady as she waited to see if she'd feel anything strange. "Ma'am."

Mrs. Hudson scurried about the kitchen like a little bird, lighting the fire under the teakettle, reaching into cupboards for cups and saucers and plates, putting tea bags into cups. She took a loaf of bread from a drawer and began to unwrap it.

"Today is a little different because I was surprised by your arrival," she said. "But normally I like to stick to a strict schedule. Well, I had a better one before, when I had help. Now that you're here, though, I'm determined to get back to it because the best thing for children is routine. The girls are to be woken up and dressed while Dr. Hudson and I have breakfast and read the paper; then you can bring them down to the kitchen to eat their morning meal. I'll prepare all the food. After breakfast, they can play either upstairs or in the backyard, depending on the weather, of course, and then . . ."

Pia tried to listen, but a strange sensation had come over her, as if she hadn't eaten for days. She felt weak and a little shaky but couldn't figure out why. Perhaps it was fatigue, or maybe she was hungrier than she thought. She'd been too upset to eat much of anything before she left St. Vincent's. Then, with growing dismay, she realized the sensation was coming from Leo. He wasn't sick, but he wasn't as strong as he should have been either. Not for his age. Even orphan babies who'd been abandoned and half-starved felt stronger than he did. Maybe he was coming down with a cold, or perhaps he'd been born too early and was still catching up. She wanted to ask but didn't think it was a good idea to pry into such personal matters. Not yet, anyway. She wrapped the blanket tighter around his little body and held him close, hoping it wasn't anything serious.

Mrs. Hudson returned to the table with a cup of hot tea and two slices of brown bread spread with marmalade. "Is this all right?" she said. "The bread is fresh this morning. I can warm up some leftover cream of spinach soup too, if you'd like."

"No, thank you, ma'am," Pia said. "This is plenty."

"Good," Mrs. Hudson said. "I must tell you, I have little tolerance for picky eaters."

Pia almost laughed. She couldn't remember if she'd ever had a slice of fresh bread spread with marmalade. When her family could afford bread, it was always two or three days old, purchased from a peddler who sold bakery leftovers. And they'd never had enough money for marmalade. Her last cup of tea was before Vater had left for the war, made from tea leaves that had already been used three times. The bread on the plate in front of her smelled delicious, all yeasty and warm, and the marmalade looked sugary and sweet. But how could she eat such wonderful food when she had no idea if her brothers were being fed, or even if they were alive? She didn't deserve it.

Mrs. Hudson put cream and sugar on the table, took the baby, and sat down across from her. For the first time since Pia's arrival, Leo started to fuss. Mrs. Hudson kissed his forehead and bounced him gently up and down on her arm.

"It's almost time to nurse," she said. She put the tip of her little finger in his mouth and he quieted down. "I just don't seem to have as much milk for him as I had for the girls. Maybe it's because he came right after Elizabeth." She smiled and rubbed her nose softly against his. "But that's all right because we couldn't be happier to finally get our sweet little boy."

Pia sat with her hands in her lap, wishing she could be honest with the doting mother, who was smiling and oblivious to the fact that something might be wrong with her baby.

As if sensing Pia's discomfort, Mrs. Hudson said, "Please, go ahead and eat so I can get you settled."

Leo spit out her finger and started to whimper.

Mrs. Hudson stood. "Oh dear," she said. "It looks like you'll have to excuse me for a few minutes. It's the gosh-darnedest thing, he doesn't nurse for very long, but he wants to eat quite often."

Pia pressed her lips together, her fear for Leo's well-being growing.

Mrs. Hudson nodded toward the stove. "Help yourself to more hot water if you'd like. And bread too. When I come back, I'll show you to your room."

"Thank you, ma'am," Pia said.

When Mrs. Hudson left the kitchen, Pia looked down at her plate, a sinking feeling in her stomach. Then she remembered Mrs. Hudson saying she didn't tolerate picky eaters. She picked up a piece of bread with marmalade and took a bite. It had no taste.

CHAPTER TWENTY-ONE

PIA

Sitting on opposite ends of the linen-covered table beneath a sparkling chandelier, Dr. and Mrs. Hudson made small talk between bites of roast beef and sips of wine. Pia sat next to Margaret, the oldest girl, and across from Sophie, trying to mimic the way the adults put their napkins in their lap and held their silverware. Elizabeth sat picking at her food in a wooden high chair beside her mother, and Leo lay swaddled in a cradle next to the fireplace. Behind Mrs. Hudson, platters of meat and barley biscuits lined the sideboard, along with bowls of carrots, peas, and scalloped potatoes. Pia had never seen so much food in her life.

Chewing slowly on a small mouthful of biscuit, she couldn't help but think about Ollie and Max—how they had known nothing but hunger since the day they were born; how she'd watered down broth and cut mold off of old bread to keep them alive; how they very well might have starved to death inside the bedroom cubby. Guilt tightened her throat and she could barely swallow. It didn't help that Mrs. Hudson, after fixing her husband's plate and cutting his meat while he watched with a mixture of irritation and embarrassment, had insisted on giving Pia extra servings. She was already struggling to eat what was in front of her, and every whimper from Leo set her on edge.

Earlier that day, Mrs. Hudson had taken her upstairs to show her where she'd be sleeping, and between that and the staggering amount of food on her plate, she felt like she was in a foreign country. Having expected to stay in the servants' quarters, which Mrs. Hudson had explained were only accessible by a separate staircase behind the pantry, Pia was surprised to be taken into a bedroom with a double poster bed made up with an eyelet quilt and flowered bed skirt, just down the hall from the nursery. A dark oak dresser sat between two wingback chairs below a tall window with tasseled curtains, and the rug felt as thick as a goose-down pillow beneath her feet.

"There's a closet too," Mrs. Hudson said, hurrying around the foot of the bed to show her. "I've already hung up the rest of the clothes I found for you. I even dug out another pair of shoes that should fit."

Pia stood in the middle of the bedroom, stunned and embarrassed and uncomfortable. "I'm sorry, ma'am," she said. "But I can't stay in here."

Mrs. Hudson's brows shot up. "Why on earth not?"

"I don't mean to be rude, ma'am, but I don't need . . . I mean . . . it's too fancy for me."

"Don't be silly," Mrs. Hudson said. "No one else is using it. Plus, I can't imagine what you went through in that orphanage. You deserve to be comfortable." She slapped the quilt, raising a small cloud of dust, then smoothed it flat with both hands.

"I appreciate it, ma'am," Pia said. "I really do. But I don't deserve anything." As soon as the words left her mouth, she wished she could take them back.

Mrs. Hudson waved a dismissive hand in the air. "Of course you do." Then she looked at Pia with a furrowed brow, suddenly realizing the weight of her words. "Is that what they told you in that place? Well, they're wrong. You deserve good food and a warm bed just as much as anyone else. If it makes you feel better, I want you to sleep here to be close to the children, and because you won't be much use to me if you don't get adequate rest."

Pia let out a silent sigh, relieved Mrs. Hudson hadn't asked why she'd said such a thing. And being close to the children made sense. Not that she had a choice in the matter anyway. "All right, ma'am," she said, "Thank you."

Now, sitting in the Hudsons' fancy dining room and trying to eat to be polite, all she could think about was how little food the orphans at St. Vincent's had, and how much longer she and her brothers could have survived on her plate of meat and vegetables alone. Finn was right when he said whatever situation you were born into was a matter of luck. But it didn't seem right or fair that some had so little while others had more than they could ever need. If she and her brothers had access to even half the bounty on the sideboard, they could have lived on it for weeks. And she wouldn't have had to leave them in the cubby.

"Is the food to your liking, Pia?" Mrs. Hudson asked. She fed a spoonful of potatoes to Elizabeth, who opened up like a baby bird as soon as she saw the food coming.

Pia wiped her mouth with her napkin, hoping no one noticed the tears in her eyes. "Yes, ma'am. It's delicious. Thank you."

"No need to be shy," Dr. Hudson said. "Eat up. I'm sure you didn't get this kind of food in the orphanage."

"No, sir," Pia said. "I didn't." She wanted to tell him about the thin stew and cold porridge she'd eaten day after day after day, but didn't think it was a good idea. What could he do about it? Instead, she picked up her knife, cut a thin slice of meat off the massive slab on her plate, and put it in her mouth, hoping she'd be able to chew and swallow without choking.

"What's an orphanage?" Margaret said.

"Never mind, Margaret," Mrs. Hudson said. "It's not anything you need to know about. Now sit up and eat your dinner, or there's no dessert." She fed Elizabeth a spoonful of carrots, then regarded her husband with a worried look. "Have you heard anything? Do you have any idea how long it will be before . . . you know . . . things start getting better?"

Dr. Hudson took a long sip of wine and set his glass back down, his forehead furrowed. "They're fairly certain a third wave has started. And this February cold keeps everyone inside buildings and crammed together on trolleys, which doesn't help."

Mrs. Hudson put down Elizabeth's spoon, pulled a handkerchief from her sleeve, and dabbed her eyes.

"I'm sorry, darling," Dr. Hudson said. "I know it's difficult staying cooped up in the house all the time. But it's for the best. We have everything we need right here, and anything we don't have, we can get delivered. You'd never forgive yourself if one of the children got sick."

Mrs. Hudson sniffed and wiped her nose. "Of course, you're right. I'm worried more than anything. I just wish you'd stop seeing patients again. At least for a little while."

"Tato," Elizabeth said, patting the wooden tray of her high chair. "Tato."

Mrs. Hudson fed her another spoonful of potatoes, still blinking back tears.

"I understand," Dr. Hudson said. "But I have to do my part, even if I can't do everything I used to do." He glanced at the stub of his arm, irritated, then looked at his wife again. "We all have to make sacrifices right now. And we need the money, remember?"

Mrs. Hudson stuffed the handkerchief back in her sleeve with trembling fingers. "Of course, dear," she said. "It just makes things more difficult worrying about that too, that's all."

"I know," Dr. Hudson said. "But as I assured you, if anyone comes in presenting with symptoms, I won't come into the house until I'm sure I haven't been infected."

Mrs. Hudson held his gaze for a long moment, nearly vibrating with nerves. "But if you do get infected . . ." She paused and dropped her eyes, fidgeting with her napkin. "It was hard enough worrying about you during the war, and now this—"

"What's infected?" Margaret said.

"It's not anything you need to worry about, sweetheart," Dr. Hudson said.

"Daddy's right," Mrs. Hudson said. "You don't need to fret about a thing." She picked up Elizabeth's spoon again, her face pinched, and went back to feeding her youngest daughter.

Dr. Hudson regarded Pia. "'Not leaving the house' includes you too, Pia. We still don't understand why this particular flu is so virulent, or how it's spread. And we don't know if surviving it means you can't get sick again. My guess is you aren't apt to, but we can't be one hundred percent sure. So we can't allow you to take the children to the park, or anywhere else, for that matter, until this latest wave has passed completely. If the weather is fair, they can play in the back garden for a little while, but they're not to set foot outside the fence."

"Yes, sir," Pia said. The news that she wouldn't be allowed to leave was no surprise, but it sounded like she might be able to eventually. When the time came, *if* it came, searching for her brothers with the children in tow would be difficult, if not impossible, but it was better than nothing. And right now she was grasping at any straw.

After a dessert of cranberry tapioca was served and eaten, Mrs. Hudson stood and clapped her hands. "Come along now, girls," she said. "You too, Pia. It's time to get ready for bed."

Nerves tightened Pia's overly full stomach, making it ache even more. Getting the girls ready for bed meant touching them—helping them change into their nightclothes, washing their faces, and brushing their hair. But she had no choice. Taking care of them was why she was there. She got up from her chair and pushed it beneath the table.

Mrs. Hudson wiped Elizabeth's face and took her out of her high chair. Elizabeth reached toward Leo's cradle with one arm, her hand opening and closing.

"Eo," she said. "Want Eo."

"Not right now, my darling love," Mrs. Hudson said. "Daddy will bring Leo upstairs in a little bit."

Sophie, the middle girl, padded over to her father, stood on her tiptoes to kiss him good night, then started out of the room. Margaret slumped in her chair, pouting and pushing her leftover peas around with her fork.

"You too, Margaret," Dr. Hudson said.

"But I'm not tired," Margaret whined.

"Listen to your father now," Mrs. Hudson said. "I need you to help me teach Pia our bedtime routine."

With that, Margaret perked up and put down her fork. "Do I get to pick the bedtime story?"

"Of course," Mrs. Hudson said. "And I'm sure Pia would be happy to read it to you."

Delighted, Margaret jumped down from her chair, ran over to her father, and gave him a kiss.

Mrs. Hudson edged closer to Pia and whispered, "You do know how to read, don't you?"

Pia nodded and tried to smile. Reading would be the easiest thing she'd have to do. Suddenly Margaret darted around the table and grabbed her wrist with both hands.

"Come on, come on," Margaret said, tugging and pulling her toward the door. "I want to show you my favorite book."

Fighting the urge to pull away, Pia allowed Margaret to drag her out of the room, waiting for a stab of pain or sense of heaviness somewhere in her body. To her relief, she felt nothing. Hopefully it would be the same with the other girls.

In the girls' bedroom, Mrs. Hudson showed Pia where the clothes were kept, in the dresser and armoire, then demonstrated how dresses and skirts and blouses were to be taken out and put away in an orderly fashion. Pia did her best to pay attention while she helped the girls change, but between worrying about what she might feel and the girls wanting her assistance at the same time, it was nearly impossible. When she knelt beside Sophie to help her step out of her leggings, Sophie's foot caught in the material and she grabbed Pia's arm to keep from falling. Pia tensed for a moment, but thankfully felt nothing. It was the same when she brushed the girls' hair and helped them into their nightdresses. No pain in her chest, no ache in her arms or legs or torso. Even Elizabeth felt perfectly happy and healthy. Unfortunately, their younger brother was another story.

Pia put gentle hands on little Leo every day, touching his head and chest, trying to figure out what was wrong with him, or if he was getting any worse. Strangely, she always felt the same thing— shakiness and a slight weakness in her legs. Other than that, he smiled and cooed, and looked to be completely normal. After a while, she convinced herself that Mrs. Hudson was right: She wasn't making enough milk. There was no reason to suspect he was anything other than a little underfed. Part of her wondered why Dr. Hudson hadn't suggested adding Mellin's Infant Food to his diet. But maybe, like Mutti, he and his wife believed nursing was best. If she ever felt brave enough, she would ask if that was the case. In the meantime, instead of worrying about something she had no control over, she decided to concentrate on taking care of the Hudson children as best she could.

Similar to her time at St. Vincent's, her days were filled with the everyday routine of taking care of children, dressing and washing, feeding and playing, wiping up spills and changing diapers—minus the church services, the cold rooms and hard beds, and more importantly, the fear of punishment. At the Hudsons' there was enough food for everyone and more. They all had clean clothes, hot baths, and warm beds. There were books and Lincoln Logs and crayons and laughter. And there was love. In the mornings, when the girls and their parents first laid eyes on one another and their faces lit up with delight and affection, it made Pia tear up, remembering when she'd had a family too.

If the weather was nice in the afternoon, she bundled up the children and took them outside to play in the fenced-in backyard, which was more like a forest with its tall trees, bushes, flower beds full of dried stems and brown petals, and a wintered-over vegetable garden full of dead weeds and black vines. While the girls played hide-and-seek and hopscotch on the stone paths, giggling and running and chasing one another, Pia stayed with Leo on the terrace. She wanted to play with the girls, or pull out the withered plants and clean up the ragged vegetable patch like she used to do with Mutti back in Hazleton, but Mrs. Hudson insisted she keep the baby out of the breeze, even though he was safe and warm in his pram, swaddled beneath layers of clothes and soft blankets. And no matter how warm it was, Mrs. Hudson called them inside after an hour, for fear they'd catch cold and compromise their ability to fight off the flu.

Thinking back to the mining village where she'd spent as much time as possible outside no matter the weather, catching crayfish, building snowmen, climbing hills and trees, making miniature houses out of sticks and pebbles, Pia couldn't understand Mrs. Hudson's reasoning. Vater always said it made children strong and healthy to play in the forest, to get dirty and wet and "blow off the stink." But Pia didn't make the rules, so instead of stewing about something she couldn't change, she tried to be grateful for the occasional hour of fresh air.

Every night at dinner she eagerly awaited Dr. Hudson's answers to his wife's questions about the latest wave of influenza, hoping against hope that things were getting better. To her dismay, his answers were always the same. New cases of the Spanish flu were being reported every day, and it was impossible to tell if there was an end in sight. Despite Mrs. Hudson's determination to protect her children at any cost, her weariness showed in her creased brow and sagging shoulders. Her husband reminded her that she should be grateful there was no need to go out because, once a week, groceries and other supplies were delivered and left outside on the porch. And when the delivery boy was gone, Pia and Mrs. Hudson carried everything in and put it away.

Pia couldn't help wondering if the rest of the city was behaving the same way, or if the Hudsons were being overly cautious. Of course she also worried about her father and brothers. And Finn, wherever he was. She glanced at the newspapers left on the breakfast table every morning, but only saw headlines about prohibition, taxes, and the Grand Canyon becoming a national park. Nothing about the flu, or another quarantine.

Then, on a Sunday morning in early March, a few weeks after her arrival, she lifted Leo from his crib and her heart sank. Something had changed. Her back felt like she was standing too close to a coal stove, and her lower abdomen ached as if someone had punched her with a hard fist. Leo smiled at her like always, his sweet little face lighting up, but something was different about his eyes, like the shine had been scrubbed off. Checking to make sure the sensations were coming from him—that she wasn't getting a cold or had hurt her back lifting the girls—she lay him down again.

As she feared, the pain disappeared. And when she picked him up again, it returned. She carried him over to the changing table, took off his nightclothes, and, with shaking hands, examined his legs and torso and back. There were no bruises or red spots, no rashes or injuries. His skin was rosy and smooth. She dressed him, then stood frozen next to the changing table, trying to decide what to do. If she told the Hudsons what she felt, they'd think she was crazy. At the same time, she couldn't sit by and do nothing.

She leaned over him and looked into his eyes, caressing his cheek with the back of her fingers. "What's wrong, little one?" she whispered. "Do you have a bellyache, or is it something else?"

He grinned and reached for her nose. She handed him his pewter rattle and he immediately put it in his mouth, covering it with drool. He kicked and lifted his arms, laughing when the rattle made noise. He seemed fine, like a normal three-month-old. And yet, she couldn't shake the feeling that something was wrong.

She checked the clock on the dresser, sitting next to a brown Teddy bear and woolen lamb on red wheels. It was six thirty-five, over twenty minutes before she was due to take the children down for breakfast. And the girls were still sleeping, Elizabeth with her butt in the air in the other crib. She picked Leo up and held him close, his cheek on hers. The heat and pain returned, even stronger than before. This couldn't wait.

Tiptoeing out of the nursery, she took him downstairs to the kitchen, where Dr. and Mrs. Hudson sat reading the newspaper and having their morning coffee.

Dr. Hudson looked up when she came in, his eyebrows raised. "What is it, Pia?"

Mrs. Hudson set down her coffee and turned in her chair. "Where are the girls?"

"Still sleeping, ma'am," Pia said, hurrying over to them. "Excuse me for interrupting, but I think something is wrong with Leo."

Mrs. Hudson jumped up and took the baby from her, nearly knocking over her chair. "What do you mean?" she said. "What's wrong with him?"

Dr. Hudson stood and felt Leo's forehead. "What makes you think something's wrong? He doesn't have a fever."

Pia twisted her fingers together, her hands clasped at her waist. "I . . . I . . ."

Mrs. Hudson cradled Leo in one arm and examined him, lifting his nightdress and running unsteady fingers across his head and arms and legs and chest.

"I don't think it's anything serious, darling," Dr. Hudson said. "There's no need to be alarmed." He turned to Pia. "Did he vomit? Any coughing?"

Pia shook her head.

"Was he sneezing?"

"No, sir," Pia said.

"Did he have a convulsion or a fit of some kind?"

She kept shaking her head, her fear mounting.

"What is it, then?"

"I don't know how to explain it, sir," Pia said. "He just doesn't . . . he doesn't look right to me. His eyes and—"

Dr. Hudson started toward the back door. "Bring him into my office so I can examine him more carefully," he said to his wife.

Mrs. Hudson went with him, her face contorted in fear, her son clutched to her chest. Dr. Hudson put his arm behind her as if protecting her and Leo from invisible intruders. Then he stopped and looked back at Pia. "Not a word of this to the girls," he said. "We don't want to frighten them."

"Yes, sir," Pia said.

Then they were gone and she was alone in the kitchen, the only sounds the ticking of the hot stove and the Hudsons' frantic footsteps hurrying down the back hall. Steam curled from their coffee cups on the table. Half-eaten muffins sat on plates next to bowls of baked pears and Cream of Wheat. If only she had time to sit down, to think about what had just happened. Dr. Hudson seemed to doubt what she was saying, but he was going to examine Leo anyway. Had he believed her in some small way, or was he just being cautious? More than anything she wanted Leo to be all right, but if Dr. Hudson didn't find anything wrong, he might think she was trying to start trouble. Or worse.

She went back upstairs to wake the girls, unease swimming in her stomach. While getting them dressed, she felt their backs and foreheads and shoulders to see if she sensed anything similar to what she'd felt in Leo. No heat or pain came from them, no shakes or queasiness. They seemed perfectly fine. When the girls were ready, she lifted Elizabeth onto her hip and, on watery legs, led the older two downstairs, dreading the news that something was wrong with their little brother. And what would happen if something wasn't?

When she and the girls entered the kitchen, Dr. and Mrs. Hudson were at the table, finishing their breakfast as if nothing had happened. Leo lay quietly in a cradle near the coal stove. Dr. and Mrs. Hudson greeted the girls with smiles and good mornings while Pia put Elizabeth in her high chair and settled Margaret and Sophie in their places.

"How are all of you on this beautiful morning?" Dr. Hudson said cheerfully.

"We're fine, Daddy," Margaret said.

Sophie mocked her older sister, then giggled.

Pia chewed on the inside of her cheek. Dr. Hudson looked relaxed, and Mrs. Hudson's eyes were dry, her brow soft. Had she been wrong about Leo? For his sake, she hoped she was, but what would the Hudsons think about what she'd said?

Mrs. Hudson got up to get the girls' breakfast from the stove, and Pia went over to help. Leo was sound asleep in the cradle, his arms splayed above his head, his hands curled into tiny fists. The picture of health. Mrs. Hudson bent over and tucked his blanket in around him.

"Is he all right, ma'am?" Pia whispered.

"Yes," Mrs. Hudson whispered back. "Dr. Hudson found nothing wrong, thank God." She handed Pia the kettle of oatmeal and gave her a stern look. "You scared the daylights out of us."

"I'm sorry, ma'am. But I had a strange feeling—"

"Feelings aren't able to recognize illness," Mrs. Hudson said. "That's what doctors are for. Why, if I took every one of my feelings for cash money, they'd lock me up in the loony bin."

Pia dropped her eyes to the floor.

"It's all right," Mrs. Hudson said quietly. "I'm not upset with you. In fact, I'm pleased you're keeping such a close eye on the children. Just do me a favor, next time you're worried about one of them, please let us know with a little less drama."

"Yes, ma'am," Pia said.

That night, Pia ran out of her bedroom and followed Mrs. Hudson's screams, her legs heavy as stone as she raced toward the nursery with her lantern. Dr. Hudson appeared in his bathrobe at the top of the stairs, his eyes wide with fear, his hair wild. He flew down the hall into Leo and Elizabeth's room, ignoring the slipper that fell from his foot. Pia followed, fear squeezing her heart against her ribs. When her lantern light fell into the nursery, it revealed Elizabeth on her feet in her crib, gripping the rail and wailing. Pia set the lantern on the accent table next to the door, fumbled for the room lantern, lit the flame, and replaced the globe with shaking hands. Dr. Hudson was on his knees next to Mrs. Hudson, who was howling in a heap on the floor next to Leo's empty crib. Leo lay in her trembling arms, his face bone-white, his body limp.

"Dear God!" Dr. Hudson cried. "What happened?"

Pia's heart went black. *No,* she thought. *This can't be. It just can't be.* She went over to Elizabeth's crib, the floor pitching beneath her, horror filling her throat like oil. She picked up Elizabeth and held her tight, shushing her and telling her everything would be all right. The sensible thing to do would have been to take her out of the room, away from the tragic scene, but Pia couldn't move. She had to know what happened.

Mrs. Hudson gaped up at her husband, her eyes red as blood in her ashen face. "I came up to check on him," she wailed. "And . . . and . . ." Anguished sobs swallowed her words.

Dr. Hudson lifted his son from her grasp, listened for a heartbeat, then crushed him to his chest, his shoulders convulsing. With gulping moans, Mrs. Hudson sat up and together they cradled Leo in their arms, their heads bowed together, caressing the pale cheeks of their lost child. Pia wanted to run out of the room, out the front door, and down the street, never to look back. She couldn't bear another second of the overwhelming agony that filled the room like a living, breathing thing. But she couldn't leave either. For a hundred reasons.

Margaret and Sophie appeared in the doorway in nightdresses and bare feet, their faces crumpled in fear. When Sophie saw her parents on the floor, she wrapped her arms around her older sister's waist and pressed her face into the folds of her nightdress. Margaret stood frozen, staring and confused and starting to cry. Pia went to them and knelt down, Elizabeth whimpering against her shoulder.

"It's all right," she said, her throat thick and hot. "Everything's going to be all right. Come on, let's go back to your bedroom."

She picked up her lantern, ready to herd them back into the hall, but Margaret rushed past her into the nursery and fell against her mother, crying. Mrs. Hudson wrapped an arm around her and kissed her forehead.

"Go with Pia, darling," she said in a raspy voice. "I'll come see you in a few minutes, I promise."

"What's wrong with Leo, Mommy?" Margaret said. "Does he have a hurt?"

Mrs. Hudson nodded. "Yes, sweetie, he does. A very bad one."

"Do you want me to get a bandage?" Margaret said. "I know where they are."

Mrs. Hudson shook her head and looked at Pia with pleading eyes.

Pia went over and put a gentle hand on Margaret's head. "Come on, sweetheart," she said. "We'll read a book or play a game while we wait. You get to pick."

Margaret sniffed, let go of her mother, and allowed Pia to coax her out of the room. Sophie was sitting in the hallway, tears streaming down her cheeks. With Elizabeth still sniffling against her neck, Pia led the girls toward their room as Dr. and Mrs. Hudson's tortured sobs followed them down the corridor, echoing like a hundred mourners' wails throughout the grand house.

White ribbons hung from every door of the Hudson home, crepe covered every mirror, and the hands of the clock had been stilled. Despite the fact that Dr. and Mrs. Hudson had decided not to have a wake lest someone paying their respects bring in the flu, Mrs. Hudson insisted they carry out the formalities of one. Now she stood like a statue over her tiny son in the small, open casket in the center of the parlor, a black handkerchief pressed to her mouth. Wearing his never-used christening dress and bonnet, Leo lay on a white silk pillow, his eyes closed, a pewter rattle in his hands. On the settee behind Mrs. Hudson, in matching navy dresses with pleated skirts, Margaret, Sophie, and Elizabeth kept worried eyes on their mother. It was the first time she'd been out of bed in two days, and no doubt they wondered if she might leave them too. Pia had wondered the same thing when she'd knocked on the Hudsons' bedroom door the morning after Leo died, to ask if she could do anything to help. Dr. Hudson opened the door, the whites of his swollen eyes webbed with red, and Mrs. Hudson lay motionless beside Leo on the bed behind him, her eyes closed, her face white as bone.

Pia swallowed, trying to find her voice. "Is she going to be all right, sir?" she said.

"I hope so," he said.

"Can I get either of you anything? Some tea and honey? Maybe a sandwich or a biscuit?"

He shook his head. "No, thank you. If I want something, I can get it." He glanced over his shoulder at his wife. "And Mrs. Hudson won't care about eating for a while. I've given her laudanum to help her sleep."

"All right, sir. But if there's anything I can do, please let me know."

"Thank you, Pia," he said. Then, to her surprise, he came out into the hall and closed the door behind him, his face grave. He bowed his head and lowered his voice. "I'm trying to understand how you knew something was wrong with my son."

She twisted her fingers together behind her back. How could she explain what she'd felt without looking like a raving lunatic? "I . . . I don't know, sir," she said.

He studied her with tortured eyes. "What do you mean you don't know? There must have been something. Some clue I didn't see or . . ."

"He looked a little pale to me, sir, that's all."

"Are you sure?" he said. "You seemed so certain. But I couldn't find anything, not a hint of a fever, no swollen glands or tender spot.

I'm sure it wasn't the flu. Did you see something? Feel something? A lump or a bruise . . . anything?"

She shook her head.

"Is it possible you accidentally dropped him? Or bumped his head on something?"

She drew in a sharp breath. It'd never crossed her mind that they might suspect her of harming Leo somehow. "No, sir," she said, louder than she intended. "I swear, I didn't do anything to him. I never would have hurt him. Never. And if something had happened by mistake, I would have told you. You can ask Sister Agnes at St. Vincent's. I took care of babies all the time and I never—"

He raised his hand to quiet her. "It's all right, Pia," he said. "You can tell me. Accidents happen sometimes, even when you know what you're doing."

"I swear on my father's life," she said, her eyes flooding. "It wasn't anything like that, sir."

He stared at her, long and hard, as if judging her innocence or guilt by the color of her eyes. "Then what was it?"

Panic pounded inside her head. If he thought she'd caused Leo's death, who knew what would happen? Then again, maybe that was why she'd been sent here. Maybe it was all an elaborate trick to throw her off guard and show her a comfortable life before she finally got what she deserved. She hung her head. "I don't know, sir. I just . . . I just knew. I can't explain it."

"But how? How did you know?"

"When I held him, sir."

"Are you saying you could feel he was ill when you touched him?"

She lifted her head, stunned by his words. Was he testing her to see if she was crazy? Or did he know something about the strange feelings that had bewildered her all her life? Either way, no matter what, she couldn't let him think she'd had anything to do with Leo's death. She looked him in the eyes. It was now or never. "Yes, sir," she said. "That's exactly what I'm saying."

He took a deep breath and let it out slowly. "I've heard of situations like that, but I . . . Has anything similar ever happened to you before?"

She nodded, holding his gaze. "Yes, sir, it has. Many times."

"I see." He glanced at the floor and shook his head slightly, his face lined with confusion and doubt. "And when did you first start sensing these things?"

"As far back as I can remember, sir. I wasn't sure what it was for a long time, but it grew stronger after the flu started. Then, when my mother got sick and died, I knew what I was feeling was real."

"Why didn't you tell us before now?"

"Because I . . . I didn't want you to think I was . . . unstable."

He pinched the bridge of his nose and squeezed his eyes shut, as if suddenly suffering an excruciating headache. Was he frustrated, trying not to cry, or wondering how he had hired a crazy person to take care of his children? Maybe he was trying to decide between calling the police to arrest her or a doctor to commit her to an asylum. The hallway seemed to shrink as her panic grew. She had to prove she was telling the truth. But how?

Then she had an idea.

She reached up and gently took his hand away from his face, praying it would work. He opened his eyes, surprised, but let her take it. She wrapped her hands around his and waited for something to come to her, some inkling or sensation, even the slightest pain of an aching tooth or the tight thud of a headache. Hopefully she'd feel something more specific, but nothing that would threaten his life. She closed her eyes, pushed away her misery and fear, and tried to concentrate. His hand was twice the size of hers, with warm skin and a calloused palm. And then she felt it. A deep throbbing in her forearm. And a burning sensation in her groin.

She let go and looked at him. "You can still feel where the bullet hit your missing arm," she said. "And you have pain when you . . . when you urinate."

His mouth fell open. "How did you . . . ? I haven't even told Mrs. Hudson about—"

"I felt it, sir."

He gaped at her, clearly stunned. "That's extraordinary," he said. "I've been treating myself for the urinary infection and it's getting better, so I'm surprised you could still . . ." He paused, scrubbed his hand down his face, and sighed loudly. "I just wish you had trusted me sooner, Pia. I worked with someone like you on the front lines once."

The hair on the back of her neck stood up. "You did?"

He nodded. "A nurse who somehow knew if gangrene was setting in before I could tell. She had a kind of sixth sense that could locate lodged bullets and bleeding veins. At first I thought the stress of everything she'd seen and experienced had taken a toll on her and she was imagining things, but after working with her for a while, I realized nine times out of ten she was right. I saved a lot more men because of her."

Pia felt like weeping. All this time she'd thought she was the only one on earth who had such strange feelings—that she'd be locked up in the loony bin if she told the truth. She couldn't believe what she'd just heard.

"What I'm trying to say is," Dr. Hudson continued, "I believe you. I don't know if I could have done anything for Leo even if you'd told me, but from now on, I'll take you seriously if you feel something might be wrong with any of my family members. And most of all, I'm sorry for doubting you."

She could only nod, afraid she might start crying and never stop. Losing Leo was too big a price to pay, but having someone validate and believe her felt like a miracle.

Now, Dr. Hudson stood beside the settee during his son's wake, gripping the carved crest rail as if to keep from falling, his lips pressed together in a hard, thin line. Having brought the girls down from the playroom a few minutes prior, Pia awaited further instruction on the other side of the parlor, her watery eyes fixed on poor little Leo. No one spoke or moved.

While her heart broke for the Hudsons, she was helpless, it seemed, to stop picturing her own family at a wake for the twins— Mutti standing over Ollie and Max, Vater looking on with a tormented face. She imagined her parents finding out what she'd done, their disappointment and anger, their heartache and grief, and the blame aimed at her for her brothers' deaths. She'd deserve every bit of it, and more. Just thinking about it, something cold and hard twisted in her chest and she bit her lip, swallowing the sobs that threatened to wrench from her throat.

As if noticing her for the first time, Mrs. Hudson gazed at her with haunted eyes. "How did you know?" she said in a weak voice.

Pia didn't know what to say, or if she should say anything at all. Instead, she looked at Dr. Hudson, hoping he'd answer for her.

He stepped forward and put his arm around his wife. "Pia and I have talked about that," he said. "And I believe what she said."

"And?" Mrs. Hudson said. "What did she say? That she knew my baby was sick?"

"Yes, darling, but—"

Mrs. Hudson grimaced and pushed him away. "Then why didn't you do something?" she cried. "Why didn't you save him?"

Dr. Hudson put his hand to his chest. His face, filled with agony, looked shattered. "It wasn't like that," he said, nearly choking on his tears. "She knew something was wrong, but she didn't know what exactly. And I couldn't find anything. You were there. He seemed fine. Sometimes these things just happen, sweetheart. It might have been a physical defect he was born with, something we don't understand yet. You know better than anyone that if there had been anything I could have done to save him, I would have done it. I would have laid down my life for my son." He looked at the girls. "I'd lay down my life for every one of you."

With that, Mrs. Hudson's face folded in on itself. "I'm sorry," she sobbed. "I know it's not your fault. It's just . . . I miss him so much I don't know if I can bear it." She buried her face in her hands.

Dr. Hudson gathered her to him, kissing her cheek and forehead. "I know, darling. I know. I miss him too." He motioned the girls over, and they got up from the settee and put their small arms around their parents' legs, crying with grief and fear and relief. Pia lowered her flooding eyes and edged toward the door, ready to slip out of the room.

"Wait," Mrs. Hudson said. "Don't go."

Pia stopped and pressed her nails into her palms. More than anything, she wanted to get out of there, to go hide in her bedroom, where she could fall apart in private. "Yes, ma'am?"

"I'm sorry I doubted you," Mrs. Hudson said. "Even if nothing could have been done, somehow you knew something was wrong with my Leo. I'm his mother and I . . ." She hesitated and swallowed, her chin trembling. "I'm his mother and I didn't even know. I realize you were only trying to help, and I appreciate that. I truly do."

"Thank you, ma'am," Pia said. "I'm very sorry about Leo and I . . . I'm sorry I couldn't do more for him."

Mrs. Hudson nodded, fresh tears filling her eyes. Then she turned back to her grieving family, shoulders convulsing. Pia left the room, slowly closing the door behind her. She started down the hall, trying to walk quietly, then ran the rest of the way upstairs, her hand over her mouth to stifle her sobs.

CHAPTER TWENTY-TWO

PIA

Despite Dr. Hudson's multiple offers to take Leo to the undertakers himself to be buried in the family plot outside the city, Mrs. Hudson insisted her only son be interred in the backyard, in the far corner between her prized rose beds. She didn't want to send him away, to let some stranger bury him in a cemetery overflowing with flu victims. Other people had graves in their backyards, she reasoned, and with the number of flu victims in the city over the past six months, certainly backyard burials had been happening even more frequently. She didn't care that their yard was smaller than most. Only after she agreed to move his casket to the family plot outside the city when, or if, the third wave of the flu was ever over, did Dr. Hudson let her have her way.

After marking his grave with an angel statue borrowed from the dining room curio cabinet, Mrs. Hudson retreated to her bedroom for another four days while Pia took over the cooking and housecleaning along with looking after the girls. In between running after Margaret and Sophie, changing Elizabeth, keeping the house from complete disarray, trying to make sure everyone got fed, and delivering meals to Mrs. Hudson—who, despite her husband's coaxing, ate little more than a few bites of toast or a mouthful of soup—Pia was exhausted. Now she understood why Mrs. Hudson had needed help in the first place.

Five days later, when Mrs. Hudson finally emerged from her bedroom, she was dressed, but her skirt was askew on her hips and her cheekbones jutted out from her haggard face. Snarled strands of dirty hair hung from the heavy pins holding her bun, and her skin looked thin as rice paper. She entered the playroom, gliding through the door like a ghost, and the girls ran to meet her with delighted cries, their arms outstretched. Mrs. Hudson knelt and kissed their faces and foreheads and cheeks, giving them a weary smile as they all talked at once.

"Are you feeling better, Mommy?" Margaret said.

Mrs. Hudson caressed her oldest daughter's cheek. "Yes, sweetheart. Mommy is still sad, but I'm getting better, I promise."

"I missed you," Margaret said.

"I missed you too, darling," Mrs. Hudson said.

"Is you hurt all done?" Sophie said.

Mrs. Hudson nodded. "Yes, baby girl, my hurt is almost gone."

Elizabeth started to climb into her mother's arms, nearly knocking her over.

Pia hurried over to help. "Hold on, little one," she said, and held her back.

Mrs. Hudson got up, sat in a chair, and patted her lap with both hands. "All right," she said. "Come here, my loves."

Pia picked Elizabeth up and placed her in Mrs. Hudson's lap, then moved out of the way so the other girls could get close to their mother. Mrs. Hudson hugged Elizabeth tight, her nose buried in her downy hair, and Margaret and Sophie lay their cheeks against her skirt.

"Is there anything I can get for you, ma'am?" Pia said. "Some hot tea? A little something to eat?"

Mrs. Hudson looked up, one pale hand on the back of Elizabeth's small head. "Some tea would be lovely, Pia, thank you."

"My pleasure, ma'am," Pia said. "Will you be taking it downstairs, or would you like me to bring it up here to the playroom?"

"Downstairs will be fine," Mrs. Hudson said. "Will you please get a snack for the girls too? Maybe some fruit muffins or dried apricots?"

"Of course," Pia said, and turned to leave.

"Pia," Mrs. Hudson said.

"Yes, ma'am?"

"I don't know what we would have done without you here. Thank you."

Heat crawled up Pia's cheeks. "I'm glad I was able to help."

Just then the doorbell rang downstairs and Mrs. Hudson sat up with a start, her eyes wide. "Who in heaven's name could that be?" she said. "Did someone take down the No Visitors sign?"

"No, ma'am," Pia said. "It's still there as far as I know, unless it fell off. I'll see who it is and send them away."

"Please do," Mrs. Hudson said. "I don't want anyone coming into this house."

Pia hurried out of the playroom, along the hall, and down the stairs, her irritation growing. What kind of person would ignore the sign on the front door, not to mention the white crepe? Whoever it was, they had to be rude or dim-witted, or both. The doorbell chimed several more times, a little longer with each ring, until the bell sounded like it would shatter. When she reached the foyer, Pia drew back the sidelight window curtain to peer out, ready to give the doorbell ringer a piece of her mind. But then she saw who it was, and she gasped and stepped back.

Nurse Wallis stood on the porch with what looked like a medical bag in one hand. What was she doing there? Had she come to take her to an asylum, or send her away on a train? No, that didn't make sense. Mrs. Hudson wouldn't get rid of her. She had just thanked her for taking care of the girls and helping out. Then she remembered what Mrs. Hudson had said, about not knowing anything was wrong with Leo even though she was his mother. Maybe Pia's presence made her feel guilty. Maybe she couldn't stand to look at her one more day.

"I know someone's in there," Nurse Wallis said from the other side of the door. "I saw you peeking out the window." She pressed the doorbell again, this time leaving her finger on the buzzer.

"Can't you read the sign?" Pia said. "It says no visitors." Then she had another thought and her heart leapt in her chest. Maybe Nurse Wallis had found Ollie and Max. Maybe Mother Joe had sent her here to tell her the news. She fumbled with the lock and yanked the door open.

When Nurse Wallis saw who answered, her brows shot up in surprise. "Oh," she said. She started to say something else, but paused, as if rethinking her words, then raised her chin. "I wondered what happened to you."

Pia's shoulders dropped. Nurse Wallis wasn't there about the twins. She had no idea Pia even worked there. "Mother Joe sent me here to help with the children," she said.

"I can see that. Lucky you."

"I was hoping you were here because you had news about my brothers."

Nurse Wallis glanced behind Pia, trying to see into the house. "No, I haven't heard or seen a thing about them."

"Did you talk to anyone? Did you ask about them at other orphanages? What about the hospitals?"

"I already told you, I didn't find anything. And I'm not here to see you anyway. I've come to check on Mrs. Hudson. Her husband sent for me."

Pia clenched her jaw. Why was she being so heartless? Either she didn't care about the twins, or she hadn't looked for them. Even if she was still upset about Pia yelling at her the first time they met, her indifference seemed strange for someone who claimed to love helping children. But regardless of the reasons behind her behavior, Pia needed to decide whether or not to allow her inside. Mrs. Hudson would be upset if she did, and if Dr. Hudson sent for her, he might be upset if she refused.

"Well, are you going to let me in, or just stand there looking confused?" Nurse Wallis said.

Pia wasn't sure what to do. Dr. Hudson had sent for help with the children without his wife knowing, so maybe he'd sent for Nurse Wallis too. She should run into his office and check. She stepped back and opened the door all the way. "You'll have to wait in the foyer while I let Dr. Hudson know you're here."

"There's no need for that," Nurse Wallis said. She entered, set down her bag, and proceeded to take off her coat. "His instructions were very clear. I'm to meet with Mrs. Hudson while the nanny, that would be you, occupy the children."

"But I—"

"Is she still in bed?"

"No, she was getting ready to come down for tea when you rang."

Nurse Wallis smoothed the front of her uniform and picked up her bag again. "Very well, then. Where is she taking it?"

"In the kitchen, I think. But she doesn't want anyone in the house. I'll get Dr. Hudson. I'm sure he'll want to speak to her first, to tell her what's going on."

"That won't be necessary," Nurse Wallis said. "I can deal with Mrs. Hudson. Trust me when I say she doesn't know what's best for her right now. Dr. Hudson, on the other hand, does. He told me about their son, and what a hard time his wife has been having since he passed. She needs someone to talk to, someone who understands. Now show me to the kitchen, then you can fetch Mrs. Hudson."

"I don't think that's a good idea," Pia said. "I don't want to go against her wishes."

Nurse Wallis scowled. "Why don't you let me do my job and I'll make sure you can keep doing yours. Otherwise, I'll tell Dr. Hudson how uncooperative and troublesome you were at St. Vincent's and recommend you be sent away."

Pia blanched. Why was she being hostile? Surely the Hudsons wouldn't appreciate her acting that way. She took a deep breath and gathered a small measure of courage. "He won't believe you," she said.

"Are you sure?" Nurse Wallis said. "I heard you tried to escape St. Vincent's several times. And Sister Ernestine didn't have one good thing to say about you. Have you even told Mrs. Hudson about your missing brothers?"

A hot flush of fear and frustration crawled up Pia's neck. She couldn't risk the nurse talking to Mrs. Hudson about Ollie and Max. Mrs. Hudson might wonder what else she was hiding, especially after the incident with Leo. Dr. Hudson and his wife were some of the nicest people she'd ever met, but they'd never understand what she'd done to her brothers, especially so soon after losing their baby boy. Maybe she would tell them someday, but not now.

With the heavy weight of resentment like a boulder on her chest, she reluctantly showed Nurse Wallis the way to the kitchen, then went up to the playroom to get Mrs. Hudson. After explaining the situation and apologizing numerous times, she was relieved to hear Mrs. Hudson say it wasn't her fault, that she was upset with her husband for sending for the nurse, not with her. After Mrs. Hudson told the older girls to stay in the playroom, then put Elizabeth, who had fallen asleep in her arms, in the nursery, she and Pia went back downstairs.

When they entered the kitchen, Nurse Wallis was at the table, pouring hot water into two teacups. She set the teakettle down on a hot mat and smiled at Mrs. Hudson, her hands clasped at her waist.

"May I help you?" Mrs. Hudson said, her voice curt.

"I hope you don't mind," Nurse Wallis said. "But your daughter said you were getting ready to have tea and I thought I'd help out. May I join you?"

Pia frowned. Why was Nurse Wallis acting like she didn't know who she was? Maybe she was the one who needed a mental evaluation.

"My daughter?" Mrs. Hudson said. Then she realized who the nurse meant and she ran a hand along the back of Pia's arm, surprising her and making her stiffen at the same time. "Oh, this isn't my daughter, she's . . ." Mrs. Hudson hesitated and regarded the nurse with wary eyes. "I'm sorry. Who are you again? Pia said my husband sent for you, but he didn't tell me you were coming. I'm sure he would have told me something that important."

Nurse Wallis gave her a smile that was both kind and condescending. "Forgive me, Mrs. Hudson, but that was a little white lie. I knew Pia wouldn't let me see you otherwise."

Pia gaped at the nurse, anger flushing her cheeks.

Mrs. Hudson's face went dark. "What's this all about, then?" she said. "What are you doing in my house?"

"First, let me say how very sorry I am about your son, Leonard," Nurse Wallis said. "One of my nurse friends read about his passing in the newspaper and told me about it. Such a tragedy. She says your husband is a wonderful doctor and she thought I should stop by because I—"

"You work at the hospital?" Mrs. Hudson said. Fear edged her voice.

Nurse Wallis shook her head. "No, I'm a visiting nurse. I visit people in their homes when they're sick."

Mrs. Hudson gasped and took a step back.

"Oh no," Nurse Wallis said. "There's no need to worry. I promise I haven't been around a new flu case in weeks. And I'd never take the chance of bringing sickness into your home when you've already lost so much. I was only hoping I'd be able to talk to you. To offer my sincere condolences about your boy, and to help you get through this difficult time."

"No one can help me," Mrs. Hudson said. "Especially someone I don't know. Now, if you don't mind, I'd like you to leave."

Nurse Wallis came around the table, a sympathetic look on her face. "You're right, you don't know me, but I've helped many women get through the death of a child, and I know what you're feeling. I know you've suffered a tremendous loss and have a hard time thinking clearly right now. I know you're in the deepest, darkest pit of despair you ever imagined. And I know your heart is shattered. Most of all, I know you're not sure you can keep living with such unspeakable pain."

Tears flooded Mrs. Hudson's eyes and her face twisted in anger. "How could you possibly know what I'm feeling?" she said. "You don't know anything about me. And you certainly don't know anything about my son."

"I know because I've been where you are," Nurse Wallis said. "I lost my baby boy too, when he was only four months old."

Pia drew in a sharp breath. She had no idea.

"I know what it's like to feel so heartbroken and alone you think you'll go mad," Nurse Wallis continued. "Like no one else will ever understand the devastation you feel. I know what it's like to want to die, and if you go on living, to wonder how you'll ever eat or laugh or smile again. But I also know you have other children to live for, which is something I didn't have. You owe it to them to get through this, Mrs. Hudson. Just think what would happen to them if they lost you too, how awful it would be for them to have that much tragedy in their lives. They need you to stay strong."

Mrs. Hudson pressed her trembling fingers over her mouth, stumbled over to the table, and sat down, shoulders convulsing. Nurse Wallis laid a comforting hand on her arm, and Mrs. Hudson reached over and squeezed it hard, her fingers turning red, as if the nurse were a lifeline in a storm. Pia gritted her teeth and blinked back tears. She wasn't a mother yet, but she knew the horrible, heavy heartache of grief; the jagged, aching hole in your chest that could never be fixed. Losing a child had to be a thousand times worse. And seeing Mrs. Hudson break down again made her think of her own mother, who would have been equally shattered to lose one of her children. To think she could be responsible for that kind of pain was almost too much for Pia to endure.

"I'll go check on the girls and give you some privacy," she said. Before anyone could protest, she slipped out of the kitchen.

Maybe Nurse Wallis was right. Maybe Mrs. Hudson needed to talk to another grieving mother. It couldn't hurt and might even help. When she reached the end of the hall, playful voices and soft giggles floated down the stairway. The girls were on the top steps, starting to come down. Pia hurried them back up again, with promises to play hide-and-seek. The last thing they needed was to see their mother fall apart again.

The next afternoon, Nurse Wallis came by to talk to Mrs. Hudson again while Pia kept the girls occupied upstairs. Following routine, she put Elizabeth in the nursery for her nap at two o'clock, then went down to the pantry to get Sophie and Margaret an afternoon snack of plum pudding or fruit farina. When she got to the bottom of the stairs, she overheard the women's voices drifting out of the parlor and down the empty hall. Mutti always said it was wrong to eavesdrop, but she couldn't help straining to hear, one hand on her stomach, ready to run if someone came out of the room. She listened partly because she was worried Nurse Wallis might tell Mrs. Hudson about Ollie and Max, and partly because she hoped the nurse would say something to help ease her own grief. No one, not the nuns at St. Vincent's or sweet Sister Agnes, had ever talked to her about losing her family. No one had ever tried helping her through her heartache and sorrow. Sometimes the depth of her misery frightened her, and she worried she really might lose her mind.

"I'll never be the same," Mrs. Hudson said, sniffing. "My heart will be broken forever. Sometimes I feel so desperate I want to die just so I see his face again."

"I understand," Nurse Wallis said. "Truly I do. I felt the same way. The only thing that helped me carry on was helping women like you, and helping orphans find new families."

"I commend you for helping orphans. But I'm not sure I could do that without bringing them all home with me."

Nurse Wallis chuckled. "Oh, trust me, there have been a number of times I've wanted to do just that. The conditions in the orphanages are dreadful. They're dirty and overcrowded, and some of the people in charge really don't care about the children at all. Sometimes I wonder if God took my son to lead me to my true calling, helping those in need, especially children. I know that sounds strange, horrible even, but there's something about putting myself aside and seeing the gratefulness in their eyes that's makes life worthwhile."

"Well, if that's the way He works," Mrs. Hudson said, "He's not the God I thought He was."

Pia had to agree with Mrs. Hudson. If God loved everyone so much, why would He purposely cause them so much pain? She wanted to listen longer, but Sophie was in the upstairs hall, calling her name. She grabbed the snacks and hurried back up the steps, moving as quickly and quietly as possible.

By the third day, it seemed as though Nurse Wallis's visits were actually helping Mrs. Hudson. She started combing her hair again and took over the cooking. Pia didn't think the nurse had said anything about her or her brothers yet, and she hoped it would stay that way. Still, she kept thinking about telling Mrs. Hudson the truth before Nurse Wallis could. And now that Mrs. Hudson had a relationship of sorts with the nurse, maybe she could talk her into really looking for Ollie and Max. Maybe Dr. Hudson could help and, between the two of them, they could find out something, anything to lead her in the right direction. But it was too soon after Leo's passing to say anything. And she always lost her nerve at the last minute anyway.

On the nurse's fourth visit, Pia noticed her medical bag sitting outside the parlor. Why did she always bring it if she was just there to talk? Made of black leather, it had a metal clasp and worn handle, and a thin book, like a ledger, stuck out of a side pocket. Pia's heartbeat picked up speed. Maybe it was a list of nuns and orphanages in the city. Maybe it was something that would help her find her brothers. She edged closer to get a better look.

In the parlor, a spoon clinked against the sides of a china cup as someone stirred their tea. Pia held her breath to listen, making sure no one was about to come out into the hall.

"I'm sorry, but we're all out of lemons," Mrs. Hudson said.

"This is fine," Nurse Wallis said. "Thank you."

Pia moved closer to the bag, then bent over and slowly eased the ledger out of the side pocket. The ledger was made of leather too, but newer than the bag, and it was bound shut with a large rubber band. When she pulled it all the way out, three ten-dollar bills slipped out from behind it and floated to the floor. More bills hung halfway out of the pocket. She swore under her breath, clamped the ledger under her arm, knelt down, and, with trembling hands, quickly picked up the bills and shoved them back in the pocket. When she started to straighten, the ledger slipped from under her arm and hit the floor with a loud slap.

"What was that?" Nurse Wallis said.

"I have no idea," Mrs. Hudson said.

Chairs creaked and footsteps clacked across the parlor floor.

Pia grabbed the ledger, shoved it back in the bag, and sprinted down the hall on her tiptoes. When she reached the kitchen, she stood out of sight, breathing hard.

"Pia?" Mrs. Hudson called out.

Pia bit down on her lip, not sure what to do. If she didn't answer they might come into the kitchen and wonder why she was hiding. She edged toward the pantry, then went back to the door, and looked out. "Yes, ma'am?" she said, trying to sound casual. Nurse Wallis stood beside Mrs. Hudson in the hall, her hands on her hips.

"Oh, it's just you," Mrs. Hudson said. "We heard a noise and didn't know what it was."

"I'm sorry," she said. "I was getting the girls' snack and I dropped something." She hoped Mrs. Hudson wouldn't ask what.

"Is everything all right?" Mrs. Hudson said.

"Yes, ma'am. Of course."

Mrs. Hudson turned to Nurse Wallis. "It's nothing," she said. "Let's finish our tea, shall we?"

Before following Mrs. Hudson back into the parlor, Nurse Wallis glanced down at her bag and frowned. It was only then that Pia noticed the ledger was nearly falling out of the pocket and a ten-dollar bill still lay on the floor. Nurse Hudson reached down to pick up the money, pushed the ledger back in the pocket, and lifted the bag, suspicious eyes locked on Pia the entire time.

Pia forced a smile, then turned to go back to the pantry, a hot flush of fear crawling up her neck. If Nurse Wallis thought she'd gotten into her bag, there was no telling what she might do. It would be her word against Pia's if she said something was missing. But what was a nurse doing with all that money, anyway?

The next day, she came downstairs to get the girls' snacks and heard something that made her stop in her tracks.

A baby crying.

She tiptoed down the hall and stood outside the parlor door, listening. The cries sounded like those of an infant, maybe even a newborn. Why would Nurse Wallis bring a baby into the house? Was she trying to torture poor Mrs. Hudson?

"No," Mrs. Hudson said, her voice trembling. "I can't do it."

"Of course you can," Nurse Wallis said. "It will be the best medicine for both of you. And it'll help you stop thinking so much about Leo."

"I don't want to stop thinking about Leo," Mrs. Hudson cried. "I don't *ever* want to stop thinking about him."

Pia clenched her jaw, fighting the urge to march into the parlor and stand up for Mrs. Hudson. Of course she didn't want to stop thinking about her lost son, no more than Pia wanted to stop thinking about her mother and father and brothers. Not to mention it was impossible. How could Nurse Wallis say such a thing?

"Oh no," Nurse Wallis said. "Please forgive me. That's not what I meant. Of course you don't want to stop thinking about Leo. And you won't. Ever. It's just that you and this baby need each other, that's all. What better way to honor your son's memory than helping a destitute child? If you think about it, it makes perfect sense. God works in mysterious ways, Mrs. Hudson."

Pia gasped, cupping a hand over her mouth. She couldn't believe what Nurse Wallis was asking Mrs. Hudson to do, especially so soon after Leo passed.

"Please," Mrs. Hudson said. "Just take him and go."

"All right," Nurse Wallis said. "But if you turn him away I'm not sure what will happen to him. I can check the orphanages to see if they have room, but there's so much sickness and neglect in those places it wouldn't be the ideal choice for any baby. I've seen it first-hand and it's truly inconceivable. And he's so young, I don't know how well he'd fare—"

"But he has a mother," Mrs. Hudson said. "Perhaps she'll get better and—"

"If that were the case I wouldn't have brought him here," Nurse Wallis said. "His mother was sent to the lunatic asylum last night. The doctor said it's very likely she'll spend the rest of her days there."

"But he . . . he must have other family," Mrs. Hudson said. "An aunt or grandmother to take him in."

"If he does, I have no way of locating them. His mother was out of her mind when they found her, and she doesn't speak English."

The baby's cries grew weaker, as if he were getting tired.

"Oh God," Mrs. Hudson said. "I can't bear it. The poor dear." The sofa creaked and her shoes clicked on the parlor floorboards, back and forth, back and forth. "Well, there must be something else we can do besides . . . besides . . ."

Listening to the baby whimper, Pia's eyes filled. It was all she could do not to go in there and take him, to find out what was wrong and comfort him as best she could.

"If there was something else I could do," Nurse Wallis said, "I would have done it already. I understand how hard this is for you, Mrs. Hudson. I truly do."

"I'm not sure you do. Otherwise you never would have brought him here. Even if I wanted to take him in, Dr. Hudson would never allow it."

"You might be surprised what a man will allow if it makes his wife whole again."

Mrs. Hudson's footsteps stopped. "No, I won't do it," she said. "It wouldn't be right. Leo has only been gone a little over a week. My arms still ache for him. My heart screams for him. It's . . . it's too soon."

"Well, then do you have any leftover formula in the house?" Nurse Wallis said.

"No, I . . . I nursed my son. My husband and I believe a mother should suckle her children. I know it's considered old-fashioned by many, but—"

"Take him," Nurse Wallis said. "Just for a few minutes."

"No, I can't. I just can't." Mrs. Hudson's footsteps resumed pacing, then stopped again. "Can't you find a wet nurse for him?"

"I could, but they're either immigrants or colored. And wet nurses cost money. Who would pay for it? Besides, this poor boy needs to be fed now."

Mrs. Hudson started to say something else, but the baby started crying in earnest again, the loud, high-pitched wail of a hungry newborn.

"Please, Mrs. Hudson," Nurse Wallis said. "I'm not sure when he ate last."

Pia could barely stand listening to the baby carry on, each cry a little louder and more desperate than the one before, each wail and intake of breath more frantic. She thought she might scream if they didn't do something for him soon. Maybe she should go find a bottle to fill with water, anything to ease the poor child's hunger. Were they just going to let him shriek? And if Nurse Wallis really cared about the baby, what difference did it make if the wet nurse was an immigrant or colored? She said his mother couldn't speak English, so she must have been an immigrant too. It didn't make sense.

Finally, after what felt like forever, little by little, the baby calmed down. He made several muffled, nuzzling sounds, then went quiet.

Pia let out a long, silent breath. Nurse Wallis must have had a bottle of formula with her all along. So why had it taken her so long to give it to him? Had she been trying to pressure Mrs. Hudson into taking the boy by letting him cry and playing on her emotions? Anger swirled in Pia's stomach. The more time she spent around Nurse Wallis, the more her distrust grew. She started to turn away and retreat down the hall, relieved at least that the baby was being fed.

Then she heard Mrs. Hudson weeping.

"I'm sorry, Leo," Mrs. Hudson said, her voice raspy and quivering. "But I have to help this poor, hungry boy. Please, please forgive me. I promise, my sweet baby, I'll love you with all my heart until the day I die."

CHAPTER TWENTY-THREE

PIA

Pia was sitting on the rug in the playroom playing tiddlywinks
with the girls when Mrs. Hudson came in with the baby boy swaddled in her arms, her eyes swollen from crying. Sophie and Margaret looked up from their toys and froze, confusion pinching their
innocent faces. Immersed in her own little world and humming
to herself, the youngest girl, Elizabeth, continued playing with
her blocks. Mrs. Hudson regarded Pia with a fretful expression,
as if worried what she might think. Pia feigned surprise and got
up from the rug to greet her. It had been only a few minutes since
she'd heard Nurse Wallis leave, and she wasn't sure if she'd taken
the baby with her or not, so in truth, she *was* surprised. But if she
were being honest, she was relieved Mrs. Hudson had agreed to
take care of the boy. Because if her brothers were alive, she hoped
someone had shown them the same kindness. She brushed off her
dress and gave Mrs. Hudson a slight smile to show she wasn't taken
aback. Sophie and Margaret stared at the baby in their mother's
arms.

"It's all right," Mrs. Hudson said to the girls. "We're only looking after him for a few days, until Nurse Wallis can find him a permanent home." She sat in the rocking chair and the two older girls

got up and gathered around her. Sophie gently pulled the blanket away from the baby's face to get a better look

"Where did he come from?" Margaret said, suddenly sounding older than her four years.

"His mother is very sick," Mrs. Hudson said. "And we can't find his daddy. So Nurse Wallis brought him here because he doesn't have a home."

"Oh, Mommy," Margaret said in a high, desperate voice, sounding like a little girl again. "That makes me want to cry."

"I know, sweetheart," Mrs. Hudson said. "It makes me want to cry too."

Wondering what all the fuss was about, Elizabeth pushed herself up on her feet, toddled over, and peeked over the arm of the rocking chair. When she saw the baby, she grinned, reached out with one arm, and plopped her chubby palm on his head as if patting a ball.

"Careful," Mrs. Hudson said, protecting the baby's head with a trembling hand.

Elizabeth laughed and said, "Eo."

Mrs. Hudson's eyes filled. "No, precious girl, this isn't Leo. This is a different boy. He's not your brother."

"Eo!" Elizabeth said again, delighted. "Eo, Eo, Eo." She clapped and jumped up and down, bouncing on her tiptoes.

Mrs. Hudson's face crumpled in on itself and she hung her head.

Pia moved closer. "May I hold him for a minute, ma'am?" she said.

Mrs. Hudson gave her a grateful look and lifted the baby into her waiting arms. Pia gazed down at his pale, thin face and he observed her sleepily, his chestnut eyes blinking. He was a beautiful baby, with a headful of dark curly hair, the complete opposite of blond Leo and the rest of the Hudson family. Using the tips of her fingers, she softly caressed his cheek and forehead to see if she felt anything worrisome. Because despite what Mrs. Hudson said about taking care of him only until he found a new home, Pia knew Nurse Wallis wanted Mrs. Hudson to keep him. And the last thing the Hudsons needed was to take in a sick baby. Dr. Hudson would probably examine him even if they didn't keep him, but Pia wanted to check him over, anyway. Luckily, she didn't feel anything other than a weary sensation, as if she were overtired and hungry. Of course it made sense that the baby would be both of those things, considering what he'd been through, and that his ailing mother likely hadn't taken care of him properly. Giving in to her soft touch, he closed his eyes and started to doze off. She looked up to see Mrs. Hudson watching with anxious eyes.

"Does he feel healthy to you?" she said.

Pia nodded, surprised and pleased to be asked her opinion. "He's very tired. But other than that, I think he's well, yes."

Elizabeth crawled into her mother's lap, put a thumb in her mouth, and snuggled into the folds of her blouse. Mrs. Hudson wrapped her arms around her youngest daughter and started rocking the chair, trying not to cry.

"Can we keep him, Mommy?" Margaret said. "We miss Leo so."

"Uh-huh," Sophie said. "We want him to stay wif us. Pretty please?"

Mrs. Hudson closed her eyes, her features twisting in agony, and buried her face in Elizabeth's golden hair.

"Come along now, girls," Pia said. "Why don't you go back to your toys? Your mother needs some peace and quiet."

Mrs. Hudson lifted her head and wiped away her tears. "It's all right," she said. "I'd like to stay here with them for a little while." She looked at the baby. "Is he asleep?"

Pia nodded.

"Would you mind putting him down for a nap?"

"Of course not," Pia said. "I'd be happy to." She turned toward the door, then stopped. "Um . . . where would you like me to put him, ma'am?"

Mrs. Hudson pressed her lips together for a few seconds, then said, "In the nursery, I suppose."

"Are you sure?" Pia said. "I could put him in my room or—"

"No, it's fine. Really."

Pia watched her for another moment to make sure she wasn't going to change her mind.

Mrs. Hudson nodded once to let her know it was all right.

"Yes, ma'am," Pia said, and went to put the baby in the nursery.

When she came back into the playroom a few minutes later, Mrs. Hudson was on the floor playing dolls with the girls. "Is there anything you'd like me to do for you, ma'am?"

"Play with us!" Margaret said.

"I can't think of anything at the moment, Pia," Mrs. Hudson said. "Thank you. Just come sit with us."

Pia went over and knelt between the girls. Mrs. Hudson was helping Margaret dress a doll with brown ringlets and painted-on shoes, but a lost, faraway look dulled her eyes. Clearly, her mind was elsewhere.

"You be dis one," Sophie said, giving Pia a doll in a ruffled dress.

Pia took the doll, ran her fingers through its snarled hair, and eyed Mrs. Hudson. "Are you feeling all right, ma'am?"

Mrs. Hudson nodded. "When the baby wakes up, I'm going to take him into the office to meet Dr. Hudson. So I might need you to start dinner, something simple, like ham toast and baked beans. I'm not up to cooking an elaborate meal this evening."

"Of course, ma'am," Pia said. She thought about telling Mrs. Hudson she shouldn't worry about what her husband was going to say, but didn't feel like it was her place. Because from what she could tell, he was one of the most compassionate men she'd ever met. He'd never turn a needy child away. She often thought that if and when she ever felt brave enough to tell the Hudsons about her brothers, she might tell him first. Plus he worshipped the ground Mrs. Hudson walked on. If there was one thing Nurse Wallis was right about, it was that Dr. Hudson would agree to anything if it helped make his wife whole again.

Pia had no idea what transpired when Mrs. Hudson took the baby into her husband's office, but other than the usual mealtime chatter about passing the salt and reminding the girls to use their manners, Dr. and Mrs. Hudson spoke little at dinner. It had been the same way since Leo passed once Mrs. Hudson rejoined them, somber and bleak and uncomfortable, but another feeling seemed to pulse in the air, like a strange mixture of anxiety and anticipation. Judging from the girls' faces when they glanced at the baby sleeping in the corner, the exhilaration was coming from them. The adults, however, seemed preoccupied. No one corrected Elizabeth when she smiled at the baby, clapped her hands, and said, "Eo." Maybe they didn't notice. Pia could hardly wait for the meal to be over.

Later that night, when she got up to do her usual check on the children before turning out her light, Pia found Mrs. Hudson asleep on the nursery chaise, the baby boy sleeping on her chest. Elizabeth was in her usual position in her crib: butt in the air, feet tucked under. Pia brushed a curl from the little girl's forehead. Did she have any idea how lucky she was to have such loving parents? When Pia turned to leave, she startled. Dr. Hudson stood in the doorway, watching his wife with tender, watery eyes.

The next day, after Nurse Wallis's normal visiting time came and went, Pia brought Elizabeth down from the nursery and found Mrs. Hudson looking out the parlor window with a furrowed brow, the drape pulled to one side. Sitting on the floor, Margaret and Sophie were taking turns rocking the sleeping baby in Leo's cradle.

"Do you think something happened to her?" Mrs. Hudson said to Pia.

Pia put Elizabeth down on the rug and repositioned the bow in her nap-flattened hair. "I don't know, ma'am."

Mrs. Hudson let the curtain drop. "Maybe she's bringing someone to pick up the baby." She tugged on the drapes to straighten the folds, smoothed the front of her dress, then sat down in one of the wingback chairs, her fingers tapping the flowered arm. "Do you think she could have found someone to take him so quickly?"

"I'm not sure, ma'am," Pia said. "It's possible, I guess."

Mrs. Hudson told the girls to stop rocking the cradle, then knelt and put a gentle hand on the baby's chest to make sure he was breathing. "Dr. Hudson said he seems healthy, but he's so thin and pale, I . . . I wish Nurse Wallis would come get him. I couldn't take it if—"

"I'm sure he'll gain weight with more food and proper rest," Pia said.

"Oh Lord, I hope you're right," Mrs. Hudson said. "The poor darling. What he must have gone through. It would break my heart to think he was unwell."

As afternoon turned into evening and there was still no sign of Nurse Wallis, Mrs. Hudson grew more and more nervous. After Pia tucked the older girls into bed, she stuck her head into the nursery, where Mrs. Hudson sat with the baby cradled in her arms.

"I can take care of him for a while if you'd like," Pia said. "Maybe you should get some rest."

"Do you think Nurse Wallis is sick?" Mrs. Hudson said. "I shouldn't have let her in the house. Do you think that's why she hasn't come back?"

"I don't know, ma'am."

Mrs. Hudson looked down at the baby with anxious eyes. "What if she has the flu? Do you think he'll get sick too? Will he be the first to fall ill, or will it be me? I shouldn't have let the girls near him. I'll never forgive myself if—"

"I'm sure she'll be back," Pia said. "Try not to worry, ma'am. Why don't you give him to me and go lay down for a bit." In truth, Pia had her own doubts that the nurse would return, but there was no point in telling Mrs. Hudson that. The nurse had convinced the Hudsons to take the boy in, and maybe that was all she wanted. Maybe she thought her job there was done. Pia couldn't help berating herself for not telling Mrs. Hudson about her brothers so she could have asked the nurse for help before she disappeared. Then again, after the incident with the ledger and the bag, Nurse Wallis probably had even less desire to help. Pia reached out to take the baby and Mrs. Hudson placed him gently in her arms.

"Does he still feel all right to you?" she said.

Pia put a hand on his forehead. "He feels perfectly fine, maybe even a little stronger than he did at first."

"Really?"

"Yes, ma'am," Pia said. She wasn't sure if the baby was healthier or if he just had a full belly for the first time in a while, but if saying he was stronger kept Mrs. Hudson from having a nervous fit, she didn't regret the little white lie.

By the time Nurse Wallis returned two days later, Mrs. Hudson was nearly beside herself.

"Where have you been?" she said when the nurse walked into

the kitchen at lunchtime. She handed Pia the bread she'd been slicing and wiped her hands on her apron. "I was worried you'd fallen ill."

Pia went over to the table and divided the sliced bread between the girls' plates, avoiding eye contact with Nurse Wallis. It was the first time they'd seen each other since the incident with the bag, and Pia didn't know what to expect. Hopefully the nurse had forgotten about it, but somehow Pia didn't think she had.

"I'm sorry," Nurse Wallis said. "But I'm fine. Thank you for your concern."

"I'm glad to see you're all right," Mrs. Hudson said. "But I've been extremely anxious and worried that you'd exposed me and my children to some type of illness."

"Well, I didn't mean to frighten you," Nurse Wallis said. "I'm a very busy woman and I've been looking for someone to take the baby."

Mrs. Hudson's hand flew to the collar of her blouse, her fingers fluttering nervously over the ruffled edge. "And? Did you find someone?"

Nurse Wallis shook her head. "No. One couple was interested, but when I inadvertently mentioned the mother's lunacy, they worried her affliction might be passed along to the boy."

"Is that a concern?" Mrs. Hudson said.

"Not at all," Nurse Wallis said. "Dr. Henry Cotton from the New Jersey State Hospital recently discovered that insanity begins with a focal sepsis, or infection, of the teeth. The boy doesn't even have teeth yet."

"I hadn't heard that," Mrs. Hudson said.

"It was in the papers a few months ago," Nurse Wallis said. "You should ask your husband, I'm sure he knows about it."

"I will," Mrs. Hudson said.

"I inquired at the orphanages too," Nurse Wallis said. "And presently the only one with room for an infant is one of the poorest, most overcrowded institutions in the city."

"Oh no," Mrs. Hudson said. "You can't put him there." She went over to the cradle, picked up the baby, and held him to her chest.

"I'm afraid it's the best I can do," Nurse Wallis said. "I've talked

292 • *Ellen Marie Wiseman*

to every headmaster, nun, and nurse in the city and they all said the same thing."

"And what was that?" Mrs. Hudson said.

"That the best thing for him would be for you to keep him."

At the kitchen table, Margaret and Sophie clapped their hands. "Hooray!" they yelled at the same time.

"He gets to stay!" Margaret said, beaming. "Oh, Mommy, that makes me so happy I want to cry!"

Bouncing the baby in her arms, Mrs. Hudson gaped at her daughters, her face a curious mixture of confusion, fear, and relief.

Pia agreed the best thing for the baby was for Mrs. Hudson to keep him, but she'd never say so out loud. It wasn't her place. Besides, she would have been sad to see him go, and it seemed as though having him around helped Mrs. Hudson feel better. But now that Nurse Wallis was back, Pia wondered if she should ask her for help one more time, before she disappeared again. Except she still hadn't told Mrs. Hudson about her brothers, and she couldn't just blurt it out. Not to mention Nurse Wallis suspected her of getting into her bag.

Just then, the back door opened and Dr. Hudson came into the kitchen. When he saw the look on his wife's face, he hurried over to her side. "What is it, dear?" he said. "What's happened?"

"Nurse Wallis can't find anyone to take the baby," Mrs. Hudson said, her eyes filling. "She said she has to put him in an orphanage."

Dr. Hudson put his hand on her shoulder. "There, there, darling. Everything will be all right."

Sophie got down from her chair, hurried over to her parents, and wrapped her arms around their legs. "Please, can he stay wif us?" she cried.

Margaret did the same. "Don't let her take him," she wailed. "We love him and we'll help take care of him. We promise."

Dr. Hudson smiled lovingly and touched their heads, stroking their hair.

Elizabeth slapped her high chair tray and rocked back and forth in her seat. "Get 'own," she said. "Get 'own." Pia lifted her from the high chair and put her on the floor. She toddled over to join her sisters, circling her family and hugging them one by one, giggling. "Momma, Dada, 'ophie, 'arget, 'eo." Then she went over to Pia, reached up for her hand, and tried pulling her over to join them. "Pia," she said, plain as day.

A burning lump formed in Pia's throat. The gesture touched her deeply, but Elizabeth was a toddler who loved everyone. She didn't know any different. Pia shook her head, hoping Elizabeth wouldn't get upset if she didn't go with her. The last thing she wanted to do was ruin this happy moment. Then Mrs. Hudson gave her a weak smile, nodding to let her know it was all right, that Elizabeth was allowed to bring her into the circle. Heat crawled up Pia's face and she went with Elizabeth to stand awkwardly next to Mrs. Hudson, her head bowed. The idea that they might consider her part of their family made her eyes burn.

Mrs. Hudson gazed at her husband, smiling through her tears, a question on her face.

"It's up to you, darling," he said. "Whatever decision you make, I'll stand behind it."

Mrs. Hudson nodded and buried her nose in the baby's neck, her shoulders convulsing. "All right, yes," she cried. "I wouldn't be able to give him up, anyway."

Nurse Wallis tented her hands under her chin, looking pleased. "That's wonderful," she said.

"Well done, Nurse Wallis," Dr. Hudson said. "It seems as though you've found this boy a new home."

"I think you've made a very wise and compassionate decision," Nurse Wallis said. "Congratulations to all of you."

Margaret and Sophie jumped up and down, laughing and clapping and repeating over and over, "The baby can stay! The baby can stay!"

Mimicking her older sisters, Elizabeth did the same.

With regular feedings, a warm house, and clean clothes, the baby's thin face and scrawny legs filled out, and his pale skin turned a healthy pink. Dr. and Mrs. Hudson named him Cooper Lee, and within a couple of weeks, Mrs. Hudson started smiling and bustling around the house again. The spirited gleam in her eyes had been forever dulled, but she laughed on occasion, happily played with her daughters, and beamed when she held Cooper in her arms. And she slept in the nursery every night.

Having Cooper in the house also gave Pia hope that Ollie and Max, if they were still alive, had found a family to take care of them too. She told herself that was the case anyway, and it helped loosen the black chains around her heart. Except as she feared, once the Hudsons decided to keep the baby, Nurse Wallis stopped coming. Pia hated herself for not having the courage to tell the Hudsons about her brothers before the nurse left for good, but she still worried they wouldn't understand or forgive her. Especially because their grief over Leo was still so fresh. And what she'd done was so horrible.

Then one day, out of the blue, Nurse Wallis came back.

It was a Thursday and Pia was in the nursery, getting Elizabeth up from her nap. As usual, Elizabeth rolled over and grinned, her eyes bleary, her lips wet with drool. She was a happy child who rarely cried or fussed, and that day she acted no different. Pia changed her diaper as she lay in the crib, then put her back in her dress, leggings, white sweater, shoes, and crocheted bonnet. When Pia was finished, Elizabeth stood, wrapped her arms around Pia's neck, and pressed her cheek to hers, waiting to be picked up. It was their usual routine, and Pia always said "upsy-daisy" to make her laugh. This time, though, when their faces touched, pain exploded in Pia's ear and traveled down her jaw. She untangled Elizabeth's arms from around her neck and set her back down in the crib. The second she let go, the pain stopped. Brushing Elizabeth's soft blond hair out of the way with gentle fingers, Pia examined her ear. The skin looked normal and healthy. Elizabeth giggled and bunched up her shoulders as if being tickled. She seemed perfectly fine. Still, worry settled like a stone in Pia's stomach.

"What's wrong with you, little one?" she said. "Please tell me you're not getting sick."

"'Eo," Elizabeth said. "Want 'eo. And 'arget." She grinned and wrapped her arms around Pia's neck again.

Trying to ignore the throbbing ache in her ear and jaw, Pia picked her up, set her on her hip, and started out of the nursery.

"Margaret's in the playroom with Sophie," she said. "And Leo's not here anymore, remember? You want to see Cooper?"

"'Eo," Elizabeth said, grinning.

With dread building in her chest, Pia carried her toward the staircase. She didn't look forward to telling Mrs. Hudson something was wrong with Elizabeth. Halfway down the hall, she heard female voices drifting up from downstairs and stopped to peer over the railing, wondering who was there. Mrs. Hudson and Nurse Wallis stood on the first floor next to the steps, speaking in hushed tones. Mrs. Hudson sounded angry. Pia had never heard her talk like that. Even from above, her shoulders looked bunched, her face pinched. Then she handed Nurse Wallis what looked like a large sum of money.

"My husband can't know anything about this," Mrs. Hudson said.

Nurse Wallis put the money in her bag. "I understand," she said. "You have my word. And you'll have the rest for me next month?"

"Yes, but I still can't fathom why you didn't tell me sooner. It seems to me that you forgot on purpose."

"Would it have affected your decision?"

"Of course not," Mrs. Hudson said. "But you should have been honest with me from the beginning. And I certainly don't appreciate being threatened."

Pia straightened, her heart suddenly pounding. Hopefully, the women hadn't seen or heard her. She hadn't meant to eavesdrop. Not this time, anyway. She wanted to keep listening, to figure out what was going on, but she couldn't chance getting caught. Then, before she could stop her, Elizabeth grabbed the railing with her chubby hands and peered over it, nearly pulling herself from Pia's arms.

"Mommy," she shouted. "Want 'eo."

Pia pried Elizabeth's hands from the railing and turned back toward the nursery.

"Pia?" Mrs. Hudson called up the steps.

Pia stopped in her tracks, her stomach knotting. "Yes, ma'am?"

"Come to the top of the stairs, please," Mrs. Hudson said.

Pia did as she was told, Elizabeth squirming in her arms. Mrs. Hudson and Nurse Wallis looked up at her from the bottom of the staircase.

"Were you eavesdropping, Miss Lange?" Nurse Wallis said.

Mrs. Hudson gave the nurse an irritated look. "With all due respect, Nurse Wallis, this is my house and I'll handle Pia the way I see fit."

"But she was listening to our conversation," Nurse Wallis said.

Mrs. Hudson ignored her and looked up the stairs again. "Is everything all right, Pia? Do you need something?"

"I was bringing Elizabeth down to see you, ma'am."

"Take her to the playroom with the other girls," Mrs. Hudson said. "I'll be up shortly."

"I'm afraid this can't wait, ma'am."

"Why? What is it?" Mrs. Hudson said.

"I'm not sure, ma'am," Pia said. "I'm worried she might be getting sick."

Mrs. Hudson grasped the banister, anxiety instantly creasing her brow. "Bring her to me, please."

Pia carried Elizabeth to the bottom of the staircase, avoiding Nurse Wallis's penetrating glare. Mrs. Hudson put a gentle hand on Elizabeth's forehead and cheeks.

"She doesn't feel feverish," she said. "What do you think is wrong?"

Pia swallowed. She wasn't sure what was wrong and she couldn't say what she felt in front of Nurse Wallis, but she had to tell Mrs. Hudson what was happening, for Elizabeth's sake. "She acts like her ear is bothering her, tugging on it and such."

Mrs. Hudson gathered Elizabeth into her arms. "Does your ear hurt, baby doll?"

Elizabeth grinned and shook her head, her wispy blond curls bouncing back and forth.

"What about your throat?" Mrs. Hudson said, touching her daughter's small neck. "Does it feel sore or scratchy?"

Elizabeth bunched her shoulders and giggled, then tickled her mother's ears as if they were playing a game.

"She seems perfectly fine to me," Nurse Wallis said. She scowled at Pia. "Are you sure you're not using her as an excuse to hide the fact that you were caught eavesdropping?"

Mrs. Hudson shot the nurse another cross look. "Pia would never do such a thing. She's a good girl."

"Are you sure about that?" Nurse Wallis said.

Pia kept her eyes locked on Elizabeth, her mind racing. What was Nurse Wallis trying to do? Why was she trying to cause trouble?

"Of course I'm sure," Mrs. Hudson said. "She always has my children's best interest at heart, no matter what. If she thinks something is wrong with Elizabeth, I believe her."

Nurse Wallis let out a frustrated sigh. "Well, maybe the child has a new tooth coming in. Do you have any of Mrs. Winslow's Soothing Syrup?"

Mrs. Hudson's eyes went wide and she clutched Elizabeth to her chest as if someone were trying to snatch her away "Goodness, no," she said. "Dr. Hudson says that so-called medicine is nothing but poison that kills babies! I'd think you'd know better, being a nurse and all. Now if you'll excuse me, I need to take Elizabeth over to my husband's office right away."

"Do you mean to tell me you're taking this lying German's word over mine?" Nurse Wallis said. "She was spying on us!"

Pia went rigid, her fingernails digging into her palms. Her head suddenly felt like it weighed a hundred pounds. Why did Nurse Wallis hate her so much?

Mrs. Hudson started to say something else, then stopped and gave the nurse a puzzled look. "What makes you think Pia is German? You don't even know her. And come to think of it, how did you know her last name? As I recall, you thought she was my daughter the first time you were here."

Panic flickered behind Nurse Wallis's eyes and she glanced at the floor. Then she regarded Pia, her temples moving in and out. Pia held her breath. How *did* Nurse Wallis know her last name? And how did she know she was German?

"The head nun at St. Vincent's told me," Nurse Wallis said.

"So you knew all along who she was," Mrs. Hudson said. "You knew all along she was an orphan."

Nurse Wallis shook her head a little too vigorously. "Not at first," she said. "When I mentioned your situation to Mother Joe while searching for a home for Cooper, she told me about sending Pia here."

"Why would she do that?" Mrs. Hudson said. "What concern is it of yours?"

Nurse Wallis shrugged. "I don't know. I wondered the same thing."

"I see," Mrs. Hudson said. She directed her attention back to Pia, her brow creased.

Pia could hardly look at her, waiting to be asked why she'd been dishonest about being German. At the same time, she was amazed at how quickly Nurse Wallis told lies. Between that and the money in her bag, what else was she hiding? Had she looked for her brothers at all? It was hard to believe, especially now that she'd admitted to hating Germans. Except, except . . . calling the nurse a liar was like the pot calling the kettle black. She'd done nothing but lie since she arrived at the Hudsons'. Right then and there she made up her mind that as soon as possible, she would tell Mrs. Hudson everything.

After what felt like forever, Mrs. Hudson's eyes softened and she turned to Nurse Wallis again. "Well, regardless of how you found out," she said, "I don't appreciate you calling Pia a liar. I truly don't care if she's German, and I'm sorry I said anything to make her think otherwise." She gazed tenderly at Pia. "My children love her, and my husband and I appreciate everything she's done for our family. We're extremely grateful to have her here, and this is her home now."

Relief loosened Pia's shoulders and her eyes flooded with gratitude. She couldn't believe what she was hearing. One of her secrets was out of the way, and Mrs. Hudson didn't care.

"She didn't tell you, did she?" Nurse Wallis said with a satisfied smirk. "See? You can't trust Germans. They lie about everything. She's even trying to make you think your daughter is sick to cover up the fact that she was listening to our conversation. I wasn't going to tell you this, but she tried to steal from me once, while you and I were visiting in the parlor."

"That's not true!" Pia said.

"Stop lying," Nurse Wallis snarled at Pia. "It was the day before I brought Cooper here." She turned to Mrs. Hudson again.

"Remember that time we heard a noise out in the hall? It was her, trying to get money out of my bag."

Hurt and confusion lined Mrs. Hudson's face. She held Elizabeth even tighter, making her squirm.

"That's not what I was doing," Pia said to her. "I swear on my life, ma'am. I wasn't trying to steal anything. I was trying to look at her ledger because . . ." She twisted her fingers together, trying to gather her courage. Her mouth felt dry as dust. She had to tell her about Ollie and Max. Now. There was no other choice. "I was trying to look in her ledger because my baby brothers disappeared after my mother died of the flu. When I saw Nurse Wallis at St. Vincent's, I asked her to look for them, but I don't think she did. I know she doesn't like me because I'm German and because I upset her the first time we met, but there's nothing I can do about that except apologize. I needed her help, but she acted like she didn't care. I was hoping the ledger had a list of the orphanages and other nurses in the city. That's the only reason I was looking in her bag."

Mrs. Hudson went pale, her eyes wide. "Oh, Pia," she said. "You poor thing. Why didn't you tell me about your brothers?"

"Because it's a long . . ." Pia paused, not sure how much more she should say in front of Nurse Wallis. "It's a long story and I was afraid you wouldn't understand." She held her breath and waited for more questions, but thankfully, Mrs. Hudson turned to Nurse Wallis again.

"Can't you help her?" she said.

Nurse Wallis stared at Pia for what seemed like forever, her pitiless eyes boring into her as if trying to read her mind. It was hard to tell if she was angry or trying to come up with another lie. She rubbed her right temple with her fingers, like she had a headache or was thinking too hard. When she finally spoke, her face was unreadable. "Were your brothers sent to St. Vincent's with you?"

Pia shook her head. "You know they weren't."

"Why not?" Nurse Wallis said.

Pia's face grew hot. Why would she ask her that? And what difference did it make? "I don't know. I got sick and when I was released from the hospital, they were gone."

"So your mother passed while you were ill?" Nurse Wallis said.

Pia swallowed and nodded, praying they couldn't read the truth in her eyes. She'd tell Mrs. Hudson the rest of what happened. But not here. Not now. Not in front of Nurse Wallis.

"Did you go to the police?" Mrs. Hudson said.

Pia shook her head. "I never got the chance because the nuns sent me to St. Vincent's."

Mrs. Hudson gaped at her, stunned. "How dreadful," she said. "I'm so sorry, Pia."

"I'm sorry too," Nurse Wallis said. "But I'm afraid I can't help you. Thousands of children have been orphaned by the flu. Trying to find your brothers would be like looking for a needle in a haystack."

"But you helped the babies at St. Vincent's," Pia said.

"And Cooper," Mrs. Hudson said.

"That's different," Nurse Wallis said. "I'm not a detective and I don't have time to be one. I'm sorry." She picked up her bag, getting ready to start for the door.

"Please," Pia said. "I'll do anything. Someone has to know something, even if . . ." She nearly choked on the growing lump in her throat. "Even if . . . they're dead."

Nurse Wallis turned to face her again, her features dark and intimidating. "Like I said, I can't help you. Especially when you're still lying. If your brothers are anything like you, it's just further proof that the world is better off without more Germans, anyway." She spat the words out with contempt.

Mrs. Hudson gasped. Then her face went hard and she glared at Nurse Wallis. "How dare you say such a horrible thing to Pia, or anyone else, for that matter." She repositioned Elizabeth onto her hip, marched over to the door, and yanked it open. "Please leave before I say something I shouldn't."

"After everything I've done for you?" Nurse Wallis said. "This is how you treat me?"

"I'll keep up my end of our agreement," Mrs. Hudson said. "But I won't have you insulting Pia and her family, especially her poor little brothers. I'm shocked you would even think such a thing, let alone say it. I have to say, it's been an enormous disappointment to learn you're not the person I thought you were."

"Me?" Nurse Wallis said. "Pia's the one who didn't tell you the truth about herself."

"And you said you didn't know her," Mrs. Hudson said. "So you weren't being honest either."

"But I—"

"I've heard quite enough for today, Nurse Wallis," Mrs. Hudson said, holding the door open. "Good day."

Nurse Wallis shot Pia one last disgusted glance, then lowered her head and left.

When she was gone, Mrs. Hudson shut the door and leaned against it, breathing hard and pressing Elizabeth's head protectively to her chest. Pia stood frozen at the bottom of the stairs, not knowing what to do or say. If Nurse Wallis had no intention of helping, why had she asked when Pia's mother died? Why had she asked if her brothers were sent to St. Vincent's? More importantly, how did she know she was lying? Did she know something she wasn't telling her? And what did Mrs. Hudson think after everything she'd just heard? She looked at her, waiting for the questions to start.

Mrs. Hudson straightened and opened her mouth to say something.

Then Elizabeth started to cough.

Standing opposite Mrs. Hudson on the other side of the examining table, Pia put one hand on the back of Elizabeth's leg, the other on her small shoulder blade. Elizabeth lay on her belly wearing only a diaper, whimpering and trying to get up. Her face was red and covered with tears and snot, and with every cry, she choked and coughed, a hollow, barking sound that sent shivers up Pia's spine. Somehow, she'd gotten worse in only a few minutes, from the time Nurse Wallis left until Dr. Hudson was finished with his previous patient. Pia could feel the congestion in her lungs, the pain in her ears, and rawness in her throat. Dr. Hudson said she had a double ear infection and a bad chest cold. Pia prayed that was all it was.

"Get down," Elizabeth sobbed. "I done. I doooone."

"Just a little while longer, sweetheart," Mrs. Hudson said, trying to soothe her. "Daddy's almost finished. Then you can have a cookie and I'll read you a book." She looked up at Pia with flooding eyes, then glanced over at Sophie and Margaret, who were standing in the doorway with their arms around each other, watching with frightened faces. Cooper was in a cradle in the waiting room behind them, thankfully asleep. "Everything's going to be all right, girls. Don't worry."

Dr. Hudson held a glass cup upside down over the burning, alcohol-soaked cotton balls on the metal table next to him, then quickly placed the cup upside down on Elizabeth's bare back. Her skin pulled and puckered, drawn into the glass by some unseen force, and making her howl. It was the last of six cups on her back, lined up like spikes on a caterpillar.

"That's it," Dr. Hudson said. "Now we just need to keep her still for about ten minutes."

"Her skin is starting to bruise," Mrs. Hudson said, misery and fear shaking her voice.

"It's the sickness leaving her body," Dr. Hudson said.

"Do you think it's going to help?" his wife said.

Dr. Hudson nodded. "I believe so, otherwise I wouldn't put her through it." He patted his wife's arm. "Try not to worry, darling. She's young and strong."

"Daaaaddyyyyy," Elizabeth cried. "Owie. Ooowieeeeee."

Dr. Hudson stroked her hair, his brow lined with concern. "I'm sorry, baby girl," he said. "Daddy's just trying to help you feel better. We're almost done, I promise."

Mrs. Hudson bent over her tiny, frightened daughter, put her lips softly next to her ear, and started to sing.

> *Hush little baby, don't say a word,*
> *Mama's gonna buy you a mockingbird.*
>
> *And if that mockingbird won't sing,*
> *Mama's gonna buy you a diamond ring.*

Listening intently to her mother's soft voice, Elizabeth finally started to settle, her breath hitching in her chest, her chin quivering. Pia blinked back tears, remembering how Ollie and Max used to do the same thing when Mutti sang to them. She couldn't wait for this to be over, for Elizabeth's sake as well as her own. And for Margaret and Sophie, who were surely scared they might lose another sibling. If only she could take them out of the room to save them from seeing their little sister suffer, but Dr. and Mrs. Hudson needed her help.

Trying to push away the jumbled, swirling thoughts about her brothers, Nurse Wallis, Elizabeth, and the girls, she skimmed the room and took note of the cotton balls, the wooden tongue depressors, and the shiny, sharp objects in the glass-faced cabinet. She studied the device used for looking in ears hanging from a hook, the brown bottles of tinctures and medicines on the wooden shelf. There were so many ways to treat illness—goose-grease poultices, sulfur fumes, onion syrup, chloride of lime—but the flu had been stronger than them all. And now, some other invisible illness was trying to take beautiful little Elizabeth. No wonder Mrs. Hudson never wanted to leave the house.

CHAPTER TWENTY-FOUR

PIA

"I know we haven't had time to talk since Elizabeth got sick," Mrs. Hudson said to Pia. "But I'd like to know why you didn't tell me about your brothers until the incident with Nurse Wallis the other day."

They were sitting in the parlor in the wingback chairs, Cooper napping in the cradle and the girls on the floor playing with dolls and blocks. After the cupping in Dr. Hudson's office, and three days and nights of bread and milk poultices, elderberry blossom tea, and laudanum drops in her ears, Elizabeth's fever dropped and her chest and nose cleared. Now, thankfully, she laughed and played with her sisters as if nothing had ever been wrong. During that time, Mrs. Hudson had talked little, and never about anything that didn't pertain to her sick child. Until now.

Pia studied the floral pattern on the rug, hesitant to look her in the eye. Since the confrontation with Nurse Wallis, the heated exchange had gotten mixed up in her desperate mind, and she was starting to have doubts that the nurse knew anything about Ollie and Max. Maybe Nurse Wallis was torturing her on purpose because she didn't like her. Maybe she was getting revenge for the first time they'd met, when Pia had screamed at her and accused her of playing a cruel trick. Or maybe imagining Nurse Wallis knew something about her brothers was just wishful thinking. Still, despite her uncertainties, Pia was relieved Mrs. Hudson had started the discussion. She needed to tell her the truth once and for all, no matter what her reaction might be. Especially before Nurse Wallis came back to pick up the rest of her money.

"I was worried you'd send me away, ma'am," she said.

"Why on earth would I do that?"

"Because when I tell you what happened to my brothers, you might not want me around your children."

"I trust you with my children," Mrs. Hudson said. "But now you're scaring me. Please tell me so I can stop thinking the worst."

Pia took a deep breath and, somehow, told Mrs. Hudson the truth, even while her heart shattered into a million pieces for the hundredth time. With every turn in her story, Mrs. Hudson's eyes grew wider and wider.

"No one would help me," Pia said. "They were afraid to answer their doors, and I don't blame them." The memory of those helpless moments—the awful realization that something was dreadfully wrong before she collapsed, the grip of panic that seized her heart when she woke up six days later, the horror of finding her brothers gone—came rushing back, washing over her in alternating waves of terror and guilt. Tears blurred her vision.

"My God," Mrs. Hudson said. "You poor dear. I'm so sorry. I can only imagine what you must have gone through." She got up and knelt in front of her on the rug, in her drop-waist charmeuse dress and satin shoes, and laid a handkerchief in Pia's lap. Pia took it and wiped her eyes, waiting for her to tell her to leave, or worse. Maybe she'd call the police.

"If I'd known what was going to happen," Pia said. "I swear I never would have left the twins alone. They had to be so scared."

Mrs. Hudson gazed up at her with a tired, kind expression. "I understand," she said. "But you need to stop blaming yourself. When the flu first broke out, it was a horrible, terrifying time. It felt like the world was coming to an end. You did the best you could under dreadful circumstances, and that's all we can ask of ourselves. Not to mention, you're only a thirteen-year-old girl. I'm a grown woman with everything I need right here, and I'm still not that brave."

"But whatever happened to them is my fault," Pia said. She sniffed and dried her cheeks again. "That's why I don't deserve everything you've done for me." She hadn't expected to cry, and she hated herself for it. She didn't deserve anything, let alone anyone's pity or compassion. "If you want me to leave, I understand."

"Don't be silly," Mrs. Hudson said. She glanced over at the girls to make sure they weren't listening. Margaret and Sophie were busy changing their dolls' clothes, and Elizabeth was stacking blocks. She lowered her voice. "Is it my fault Leo got sick and died?"

"Of course not."

"What about your mother? Is it her fault she caught the flu?"

Pia looked down at her lap and shook her head, crumpling the handkerchief in her fist.

"Then how can it be your fault you got sick and couldn't make it back to your brothers?"

Pia shrugged and unraveled the handkerchief, pulling it apart with trembling fingers.

"You do realize you would have gotten sick no matter what, don't you? Even if you'd stayed home, you would have collapsed. You said yourself you were only gone a few hours."

Pia shrugged again. "I guess."

"So whatever happened to your brothers might have happened anyway. And instead of sitting here talking to me, you'd probably be dead."

Pia gazed up at Mrs. Hudson, stunned by her words. She was right. In the cubby or not, Ollie and Max probably would have been alone in the apartment when she got sick. And if she'd died, which would have been likely, who knows how long it would have been before someone found them? But that didn't lessen her remorse about leaving them. And yet, she felt like she could take a deep breath for the first time in months. She wiped her eyes and managed a weak smile. "Thank you, ma'am."

"For what?"

"For trying to make me feel better, and for not asking me to leave."

"Thank you for being honest with me," Mrs. Hudson said. "I just wish I had known sooner. I hate to think of you carrying such a heavy burden on your young shoulders. It must have been awful to be so scared and worried all this time with no one to confide in." She got up and returned to the other chair. "No more secrets, all right?"

"Yes, ma'am." Pia twisted the handkerchief between her fingers. Maybe she was pushing her luck, but she had to know. "May I ask you something, ma'am?"

"Of course, Pia, anything."

Pia hesitated, unsure if she should continue.

"Please," Mrs. Hudson said. "Tell me what you were going to say. No more secrets, remember?"

Pia nodded. "Well, I . . . I didn't mean to, but I overheard you and Nurse Wallis talking and . . . I saw what you gave her."

Mrs. Hudson shifted in her chair, picking imaginary lint from her skirt. "It was a donation," she said. "For the orphans."

"Then why don't you want Dr. Hudson to know?"

Color bloomed on Mrs. Hudson's cheeks. When she finally met Pia's gaze again, she said, "Because he'd be angry if he knew the truth."

"I swear I won't tell, ma'am. I'm only asking because I feel like Nurse Wallis might know something about my brothers."

Mrs. Hudson frowned. "What makes you say that?"

"Because of the things she asked me, and because she kept saying I was lying. How did she know I wasn't being honest?"

"I don't know. That's a good question."

"I'm sorry to keep prying, ma'am, but what's the truth about the money you gave her?"

Mrs. Hudson leaned forward and lowered her voice, her face taut with guilt. "It was a finder's fee."

"I'm sorry," Pia said. "But I don't know what that is."

"It was a payment for finding Cooper. Nurse Wallis said she finds babies for people who lost children or can't have their own, then charges a fee to help with the expenses. I didn't ask her to find Cooper, but she said I had to pay her anyway, so she could help other children. Otherwise . . ." She paused, misery contorting her features.

Pia clenched her jaw, waiting for her to finish. The more she learned about Nurse Wallis, the more she wondered if she was telling the truth about anything. "Otherwise what, ma'am?"

"Otherwise, she'd have to find someone who *could* pay."

Pia drew in a sharp breath. In that moment, her understanding of Nurse Wallis seemed complete. She cared nothing about children, least of all two young German brothers. Every kindness and thoughtful gesture, every smile and act of sacrifice, were nothing but a disguise. Maybe Pia's suspicions about her were right after all. An image flashed in her mind—the look on Nurse Wallis's face when Pia had asked her to help find Ollie and Max, both at the orphanage and at the Hudsons'. She looked like she'd seen a ghost. "Excuse me for saying so, ma'am, but that doesn't seem right. It sounds like . . ." Pia hesitated, unsure if she should say what she was thinking.

"It sounds like what?" Mrs. Hudson said. "Please, finish what you were saying."

"It sounds like she's selling children, ma'am."

Mrs. Hudson froze, aghast.

"When I tried looking at her ledger," Pia said, "there was quite a lot of money in her bag and I wondered where it came from." She started to say more but suddenly had another thought. Her heart skipped a beat and she sat up straighter. "Maybe that's why she won't look for Ollie and Max. Maybe she knows where they are because she sold them to someone."

Mrs. Hudson's fingers fluttered to her collar. "Oh dear." She moved to the edge of her seat. "But if that's what she's doing, where does she . . ." She swallowed as if trying not to get sick.

"Where does she what, ma'am?"

"Where does she get the children? Where did she get Cooper?" She gaped at Pia with panic-filled eyes. "What if she took him from someone?"

Pia shook her head. "I don't think that's how she's getting them," she said. "When I was at St. Vincent's, abandoned babies came in all the time. And I saw her picking up older kids there too. Her story about Cooper might be the one thing she's not lying about."

"Good Lord," Mrs. Hudson said. "Well, I hope you're right." She let out a trembling breath and sat back in the chair, her face pale.

"When do you think she'll come back to get the rest of the money?"

"I don't know."

"Did she happen to tell you where she lived?"

Mrs. Hudson shook her head. "No, otherwise the way I'm feeling right now, I'd be tempted to send the police after her."

Pia was unsure how to pose her next question, scared of saying the wrong thing, more scared of being told no. But there was no other choice. She had to ask before she lost her nerve. "I know it's a lot to ask, ma'am, but do you think Dr. Hudson could find out more about her, and maybe look for my brothers at the same time? Maybe he can search hospital records and talk to other doctors and nurses?"

Mrs. Hudson sat up, nodding. "Of course. I'll ask him this evening."

Pia let out a sigh of relief. "Thank you, ma'am," she said. "I hate to ask for more help, but do you think it might also be possible for him to find out if my father came back from the war?"

"I'll see."

"Thank you. You have no idea how much that means to me, ma'am."

"After everything you've done for us, the very least we can do is help you try to find your family."

Pia chewed on the inside of her cheek, scared to keep asking for more but knowing she had to try. "Forgive me for being so needy, ma'am, but what about allowing me to go to our old apartment to see if the people living there now have any news?"

Uncertainty pinched Mrs. Hudson's face, her eyes glazing over with exhaustion and worry. She seemed torn between fear and trying to help. "Let me talk to Dr. Hudson," she said. "You know how we feel about the possibility of the flu still being around. If he thinks it's safe and he can support your search, I'll make sure he takes you there himself."

A burning lump formed in Pia's throat. Finally someone was willing to help. "Thank you, ma'am," she said again, her voice catching.

The next morning, after Pia told Dr. Hudson everything, he said he'd take her to her family's old apartment on his next day off, which was the following week, as long as the number of reported flu cases kept steadily dropping. In the meantime, as soon as he was done seeing patients for the day, he'd telephone the head nun at St. Vincent's to ask about Nurse Wallis. It would take him a few days, but he'd also make phone calls and send telegrams about her brothers to every doctor he knew, the rest of the orphanages in the city, and the heads of the hospitals too. He warned her he might not find any answers but promised he'd try his best. And to her that was all that mattered. Finally, someone of importance was listening, someone was willing to help. Finally, she had hope. Her only regret was not confiding in the Hudsons sooner.

That night, when Dr. Hudson took his chair at the head of the dinner table, it was all Pia could do to sit still. She fidgeted with the silverware and fussed with the napkin in her lap, wishing she were brave enough to ask if he'd talked to Mother Joe yet. The telephone was in his office, so she had no way of knowing if he'd called her like he promised. But she didn't want to appear pushy or ungrateful. The only thing she could do was hope Mrs. Hudson was anxious to hear if he'd spoken to her too.

While the corn fritters and veal loaf were passed around the table, and Mrs. Hudson cut her husband's meat, Pia felt like she might jump out of her skin. After everyone's plates were filled, Mrs. Hudson sat down in her chair, put her napkin on her lap, and started feeding Elizabeth. Pia stared at her, mentally willing her to ask her husband if he had made the phone call.

Finally, Mrs. Hudson said, "Did you have a chance to call St. Vincent's, dear?"

Dr. Hudson nodded, chewing. "Yes, I spoke to a Mother Joe."

Pia's throat seemed to close around the meat she was swallowing. She put down her fork and knife, picked up her napkin, and wiped her mouth.

"Does she know Nurse Wallis?" Mrs. Hudson said.

He nodded again. "She said she was a saint. Couldn't sing her praises high enough. Said she's helped more orphans in recent months than she could remember anyone else doing, both babies and older children."

Pia and Mrs. Hudson exchanged a knowing glance. They'd only told Dr. Hudson that Nurse Wallis might know something about Ollie and Max, not about their other suspicions. Mrs. Hudson planned to tell him, but not yet. Not until she saw how much he could find out.

"Did Mother Joe know about Nurse Wallis bringing Cooper here?" Mrs. Hudson said.

"No, I didn't tell her anything about him. Why would I?"

"I was just wondering if Nurse Wallis asked Mother Joe if they had room for him at St. Vincent's," Mrs. Hudson said. She looked nervously at Pia, realizing she'd almost told him more than she planned, then quickly asked him another question. "What about Nurse Wallis's address? Does Mother Joe have it?"

Dr. Hudson shook his head. "They don't keep information like that on non-staff members. It's not like she's on the payroll or anything."

"Excuse me, sir," Pia said. "But did Mother Joe know if Nurse Wallis had visited the orphanage recently?"

"She said she hasn't seen her in about a week. But I asked her to get her address if she stopped in again, and to give me a call when she did."

"What about the hospitals?" Mrs. Hudson said. "Would anyone there know how to find her?"

"Maybe, maybe not," Dr. Hudson said. "During the epidemic, any able-bodied woman with or without nursing experience was called on to help, which means a lot of untrained women joined the nursing ranks. Some continued to practice, others didn't. Some went to work for hospitals or doctors, some went to work on their own, visiting needy families. So there's no way of knowing if she ever worked at a hospital or not."

"But she had a uniform, sir," Pia said. "Someone must know who she is."

"I'll check with the Red Cross," Dr. Hudson said.

"Did you ask Mother Joe if she knew anything about Pia's brothers?" Mrs. Hudson said.

"Yes, she didn't remember taking in twins after the first outbreak, either boys or girls. But she also admitted their record-keeping was disorderly at best, especially during the first months of the epidemic."

"So there's still a chance my brothers might have gone through St. Vincent's," Pia said.

"Or any of the other orphanages or poorhouses in the city," Dr. Hudson said. "When I told Mother Joe we were looking for two baby boys, she said thousands of children were orphaned by the flu, and the orphanages were so overcrowded the Children's Bureau asked people to open their homes to them. Others were being kept in groups in rented houses. A few remained in the homes they were sent to, but most were eventually sent to orphanages or other families outside the city."

Pia's heart dropped like an anvil in her chest. How would she ever find Ollie and Max amongst thousands of orphans, especially if some had been sent away?

"Would they have records of all those children?" Mrs. Hudson said.

"Possibly," Dr. Hudson said. "But certainly a good number of them fell through the cracks."

Pia pushed the food around on her plate, what little appetite she had, gone. The situation seemed hopeless. And no matter how painful it was—even if she was right about Nurse Wallis, even if they could find her, even if they could search the names of all the children orphaned by the flu—she needed to remember there was still a chance Ollie and Max might not have survived being left in the cubby in the first place.

Two days later, a Saturday, Pia was on her way to wake Elizabeth from her nap when the doorbell rang, long and loud. She went back down the stairs and hurried to answer it, hoping against hope it would be someone Dr. Hudson had talked to over the past couple of days—either the head of the Red Cross or one of his doctor friends—coming to tell her Ollie and Max had been found. The No Visitors sign was still on the door, so whoever had rung the bell must need something important. But when she reached the foyer and put her hand on the doorknob, she hesitated. What if it was Nurse Wallis?

She braced herself and pulled the sidelight curtain aside to look out. A young woman in a brown coat stood on the porch, loose corkscrews of straw-colored hair hanging around her forehead, the rest pulled back in a frizzy ponytail. She looked to be about eighteen, with a pale face and dark rings under her blue eyes.

"May I help you?" Pia said through the door.

"Mother Joe sent me," the young woman said.

Pia's heart started to race. Maybe Mother Joe had called Dr. Hudson with news about Nurse Wallis but couldn't get through. Maybe she sent someone to deliver a message in person instead. She opened the door with shaking hands.

The young woman smiled and held out a brown paper package wrapped up in string. "I found this on the porch," she said brightly.

The package was addressed to Dr. and Mrs. Hudson. Pia took it and said, "You said Mother Joe sent you?"

"That's right. She said your mother was looking for help with the children."

Pia frowned, confused. Why would Mother Joe say Mrs. Hudson was looking for help with the children? Did Dr. Hudson tell her that was the case? Had Mrs. Hudson changed her mind about keeping her there? Maybe being honest about Ollie and Max had been a mistake after all. She swallowed the rising panic in her throat. "I'm sorry," she said, "but you must have the wrong house."

"Then why did you take the package?" The young woman pointed at the name on the letterbox. "It says this is the home of Dr. and Mrs. Hudson."

Before Pia could respond, Mrs. Hudson came into the foyer behind her, wiping her hands on her apron.

"Who's there?" she said. "Is it Nurse Wallis?"

Pia stepped aside so Mrs. Hudson could see who was at the

door, her heart in her throat. Would she be surprised to see the girl, or did she know she was coming?

When Mrs. Hudson saw her, she stopped halfway across the foyer, her forehead lined with concern. "What can we do for you, miss?"

"Good day, Mrs. Hudson," the young woman said. "It's a pleasure to meet you. My name is Rebecca Stillman. Mother Joe at St. Vincent's sent me. She said you might need help around the house."

Mrs. Hudson shook her head. "I'm sorry, but there must be some mistake. I'm not employing anyone right now."

Pia's shoulders loosened in relief. They weren't getting rid of her after all.

"But I can do anything, ma'am," Rebecca said. "I'm good at cleaning, cooking, gardening, taking care of children, whatever you might need."

"I don't need anything," Mrs. Hudson said. "And I have someone to take care of the children. Perhaps you can come by again in the spring when the garden needs planting."

"Please, ma'am," Rebecca said. Her chin suddenly trembled and she looked ready to cry. "I'm begging you. Just give me a chance. I don't need room and board or anything troublesome like that. I have a place to stay. I just need a little money to take care of my son." She wiped her flooding eyes. "He's fresh born, just a few weeks old, and if I don't find work soon, they'll take him away from me."

"Oh dear," Mrs. Hudson said. "How dreadful." She looked at Pia, her brows knitted, then directed her attention back to Rebecca. "I wish I could help you, I truly do. But I can't allow just anyone into our home. Not with the flu still making the rounds."

"I understand completely, ma'am," Rebecca said. "But you don't have to worry about me. I'm healthy as a horse, and honest too."

"You might be today," Mrs. Hudson said. "But who knows what might happen down the road."

"I beg your pardon, ma'am, but I already had the flu, last year when I was in New York. The doctors said I got over it faster than anyone they'd ever seen. Been strong and well ever since."

Mrs. Hudson studied Rebecca, nervously looking her up and down and fingering the lace on her collar, clearly torn between worry and wanting to help. "Well, I certainly wouldn't want you to lose your baby."

"Please, ma'am," Rebecca said. "If you hire me, I promise you won't be sorry. Mother Joe told me to tell you so."

Mrs. Hudson pressed her lips together, thinking. She smoothed the front of her apron and fidgeted with her collar again. Rebecca glanced at Pia hopefully, as if she could help. Finally, Mrs. Hudson said, "Do you know how to iron and do laundry?"

Rebecca brightened. "Yes, ma'am. I surely do."

"Well, all right," Mrs. Hudson said. "Can you come for a few hours in the morning, then? Monday is normally laundry day, but with four children we can hardly keep up. Perhaps you can start tomorrow morning, around eight?"

Rebecca clasped her hands together under her chin, her eyes glistening with gratitude. "Yes, ma'am. Of course."

"All right," Mrs. Hudson said. "We'll try that for a few days and see how it goes."

"Thank you so much, ma'am," Rebecca said. "I can't begin to tell you how much this means to me and my boy."

"You're welcome," Mrs. Hudson said. "We'll see you tomorrow, then."

"Yes, ma'am," Rebecca said. "I'll be here at eight sharp." She moved backward across the porch, pumping her clasped hands up and down. "Thank you again, ma'am. You won't regret it, I swear." Then she hurried down the steps and disappeared along the sidewalk.

When she was gone, Pia closed the door and gave the package to Mrs. Hudson. "She found this on the porch," she said.

Mrs. Hudson took the package, gazing at Pia with doubtful eyes. "Do you think I did the right thing?" she said.

Pia shrugged. "I have no idea, ma'am," she said. While it was no surprise that Mrs. Hudson would help a mother keep her child, Pia didn't care one way or another if she hired Rebecca. In truth, it would be nice to see and talk to someone new. At the same time, she wondered why Mother Joe had sent Rebecca to the Hudsons, of all places. "But one thing's for sure, we certainly need help with the laundry."

Mrs. Hudson chuckled. "Truer words have never been spoken, Pia," she said. Then, in a serious tone, "In any case, I couldn't let them take her baby away from her, could I? That would be horrible."

Pia agreed. She'd seen enough of mothers and children being separated to last her a lifetime. "No, ma'am," she said. "You couldn't. But why do you think Mother Joe sent her here?"

"I don't know," Mrs. Hudson said. "Maybe she thought there was a problem because Dr. Hudson called asking questions."

"Maybe," Pia said. "Or maybe Mother Joe thinks I'm not doing my job properly."

"Don't worry, Pia. It doesn't matter what Mother Joe thinks. When I said this was your home, I meant it. Mother Joe can't do anything about that."

Pia smiled, her eyes suddenly burning. "Thank you, ma'am," she said. "That means more than you know."

When Pia took the girls down to the kitchen for breakfast the following day, Rebecca was already there, filling a washtub with dirty linens. Her curly blond hair was piled on top of her head like a bunny tail, all fluffy yellow and cotton-soft. Mrs. Hudson was at the stove, stirring a kettle of Cream of Wheat with a wooden spoon. When Rebecca saw the girls shuffling over to the table rubbing their sleepy eyes, she wiped her wet hands on her apron and hurried toward them, beaming.

"Well, good morning," she said. "Who are these beautiful little ladies?"

"This is Margaret, Sophie, and Elizabeth," Pia said, patting the tops of their heads.

Rebecca did a small curtsy, then addressed each girl, calling them Princess Margaret, Princess Sophie, and Princess Elizabeth. "I'm delighted to meet you all. My name is Rebecca."

The girls stared at her in silence, likely surprised to see someone new in the house.

"Now don't forget your manners, girls," Pia said. "It's polite to speak when spoken to, remember?" She lifted Elizabeth into her high chair, picked up her milk cup from the table, and placed it on the tray.

"Hello," Sophie and Margaret said at the same time, climbing into their chairs.

"I'm the oldest," Margaret said. "I'll be five on my next birthday."

"Oh my goodness," Rebecca said. "You're getting so big."

"And I'm going to be four," Sophie said.

"How wonderful," Rebecca said.

Elizabeth picked up her toddler-size cup with two hands and started drinking, droplets of milk running down her chin. Pia wiped the drips off with a napkin, then helped the girls get started on their steamed prunes and fruit muffins. While Rebecca smiled and stared, Mrs. Hudson brought over the kettle and started ladling Cream of Wheat into the girls' bowls.

Pia finished cutting Sophie's muffin in half, then wiped her hands on her apron. "Shall I see if Cooper is awake?" she asked Mrs. Hudson. "Or would you like me to stay with the girls while you get him? I think I heard him stirring in the nursery on my way down."

"Yes, please get him for me," Mrs. Hudson said. "I need to show Rebecca how to use the mangle."

When she was certain the girls were settled and eating, Pia went upstairs to get the baby. He was lying on his back in his crib, watching the shadows of leaves flutter on the ceiling.

"Good morning, precious boy," she said.

He smiled at her, cooing and putting his small arms in the air.

She reached in and started to lift him from the mattress, then froze. A wooden rattle lay in one corner of the crib, an exact replica of the ones Vater had made for Ollie and Max. Her heart skipped a beat, and for a moment everything went out of focus. She lay Cooper back down in the crib and picked up the rattle to examine it more closely. It was definitely homemade, with a piece of twine holding four brass bells on each side of the smooth handle. Dr. Hudson couldn't have carved it, not with one arm. She shook it and tears filled her eyes. It sounded the same as her brothers' rattles, like sleigh bells at Christmas. She looked at the bottom of the handle. The wood was rough and worn, as if it'd been rubbed against something hard, but she could still make out the blurred remnants of a single initial.

M

She gasped and dropped the rattle, just missing Cooper's head. It was Max's rattle. But where did it come from? And how did it get here? She started out of the nursery, trembling and trying to stay upright. She had to ask Mrs. Hudson where it had come from. Then she stopped and went back to the crib. Cooper needed to come too. She couldn't just leave him there. But she had to hurry. She had to know where the rattle came from before her heart burst from her chest. She reached in for the baby with shaking arms, then paused and rested her hands on the crib railing. Had she lost her mind? There had to be hundreds of homemade rattles, and even more babies with the initial *M*. Maybe it was Cooper's rattle. Maybe his real name started with an M. Maybe Nurse Wallis had given it to Mrs. Hudson, and Mrs. Hudson finally felt comfortable giving it to him. She took a deep breath and tried to think clearly. Just because the rattle had an *M* on the bottom didn't mean it was Max's. It could be a coincidence. She picked it up and looked at the handle again, rolling it between her thumb and finger. The *M* turned into a *W*. It could have been either one. And yet, the similarities between this rattle and her brothers' were unnerving.

Just then, Cooper started to fuss, breaking her trance. She set down the rattle, picked him up, and took him over to the dressing table. She was going to ask Mrs. Hudson about the rattle, but it could wait a few minutes. Cooper grinned up at her as she took off his nightclothes and changed his diaper. She smiled mechanically down at him and tickled his warm neck with gentle fingers, her mind elsewhere.

"Are you a happy boy today?" she said. "I think you are."

He rubbed his small fist across his mouth, trying to suck on his knuckles.

Forcing herself to concentrate on the task at hand, she finished changing him, got him dressed, then went back downstairs. In the kitchen, Mrs. Hudson was at the sink washing dishes. Rebecca was bent over a tub of steaming water next to the stove, sweat dripping from her red face. When she saw Pia and Cooper, she dropped a wet sheet on the floor and rushed over to get a closer look.

"Oh my word," she gushed. "Would you look at him? He's so handsome, he reminds me of my little Simon. And he's not even crying." She clasped her hands together under her chin. "I've always adored babies. May I hold him for a moment?"

Ignoring the feeling that she might scream before she found out about the rattle, Pia regarded Mrs. Hudson with a question on her face. Did she want to let Rebecca hold Cooper?

Mrs. Hudson shook her head slightly, wiped her hands on a dish towel, and started toward them. "Rebecca," she said. "I hired you to do the laundry, not play with the children. If there's time after your work is finished, you can spend a few minutes with Pia and the children then. And you might do well to remember that this is the first time in months I've allowed anyone into our home. I'm sure you'll understand why my husband, myself, and Pia are the only people allowed to hold Cooper right now."

Rebecca dropped her arms, her hands slapping against her wet apron. "Yes, ma'am," she said, clearly disappointed, and went back to the steaming washtub.

Pia gave Cooper to Mrs. Hudson. "He's changed and clean."

"Thank you, Pia," Mrs. Hudson said. She kissed Cooper's forehead. "Good morning, my beautiful boy." Then to Pia, "I'll feed him in the other room. Will you keep an eye on things for a few minutes?"

"Of course," Pia said. More than anything, she wanted to ask about the rattle, but Cooper was hungry. It would have to wait.

While Mrs. Hudson fed Cooper, Pia sat with the girls to make sure they ate their breakfast without squabbling or getting food on their fresh clothes, her leg bouncing up and down beneath the table. Rebecca kept busy scrubbing clothes and diapers on a metal washboard, every once in a while giving Pia and the girls a friendly smile. If nothing else, she was a hard worker. And even though Pia had looked forward to having someone else to talk to, right now she was relieved Rebecca wasn't trying to start a conversation. She was too preoccupied to chat with anyone, let alone a stranger.

When Mrs. Hudson finally came back into the room, she lay Cooper in the cradle next to the stove, covered him with a blanket, and went back to the sink to dry and put away dishes. Pia got up and went over to her, glancing over her shoulder to make sure Rebecca wasn't listening. Rebecca was squeezing water out of a sheet, her back to them.

Pia lowered her voice. "If you don't mind me asking, ma'am, where did the wooden rattle in the nursery come from?"

"That old thing?" Mrs. Hudson said. "It was in the package Rebecca found on the porch yesterday."

Pia's mouth went dry. "Do you know who sent it?"

Mrs. Hudson returned a white serving dish to the counter, grabbed a dry dishrag to wipe her hands, and crooked a finger at Pia, motioning for her to follow her into the pantry. When they were out of earshot, she whispered, "It's the strangest thing. There was no return address, no note, no anything. I wasn't going to give it to Cooper at first, but Dr. Hudson said maybe his mother had it with her when she was committed, and someone from the asylum sent it to us. So if there's a chance it's from his mother, it would have felt wrong not to give it to him."

"What about the initial on the bottom? Do you have any idea what it stands for?"

"I assumed it was for Cooper's real name," Mrs. Hudson said.

Pia clenched her jaw. She'd thought the same thing but was hoping Nurse Wallis had told Mrs. Hudson Cooper's given name. Now there was no way to know if it was his initial or not. Except why would anyone working at an asylum care about an old homemade rattle, let alone pay the postage to have it delivered? And why not use a return address? Then a sudden realization hit her and her heart started to race.

"I don't think it came from an asylum," she said.

"Why not?"

"Because if it belonged to Cooper, whoever mailed it had to know he was here. And if Nurse Wallis is doing what we think she's doing, she wouldn't tell anyone where he is."

Mrs. Hudson's eyes went wide, shining with surprise and nervous energy. Then she jerked her chin toward the kitchen. "What about Rebecca? She said she found the package on the porch."

"We can ask her, but I don't think she had any idea what was in it."

"Why not?"

"Because that rattle is exactly like the rattles my father made for my brothers, with the initial on the bottom and everything. I think Nurse Wallis sent it here."

Mrs. Hudson put the dishrag to her forehead. "Oh my word."

"I don't know for sure, ma'am, but it makes sense. And I have a strong feeling I'm right."

"Like the feeling you had about Leo and Elizabeth?"

Pia nodded. It wasn't the same, but if saying it was made Mrs. Hudson take her seriously, she'd agree to anything.

"Maybe it's time to tell Dr. Hudson what's going on," Mrs. Hudson said. "Maybe he'll know what to do."

Pia nodded again. She wasn't sure how telling the doctor would help, but anything was worth a try. Except she'd go crazy if they had to wait until he was done working for the day. "May I go talk to him now, ma'am?" she said.

"Now?" Mrs. Hudson said.

"Yes, please. I'm not sure I'll be able to stand it if I don't try and figure this out soon."

Mrs. Hudson furrowed her brow, thinking; then she started out of the pantry. "I suppose we could check to see if he has a few minutes to spare between patients."

Pia followed, relieved Mrs. Hudson believed her and wanted to get to the bottom of it too. When they came out of the pantry, Rebecca was next to Cooper's cradle, kneeling on the kitchen rug and singing softly. The minute she saw them, she got up and went back to her work. Mrs. Hudson hung the dishrag over the drying rack and untied her apron.

"Rebecca," she said. "We were just discussing the package you found on the porch. Where was it, exactly, when you first saw it?"

"Why, it was sitting right next to the front door, ma'am," Rebecca said.

"So you didn't see the postman drop it off?" Pia said.

Rebecca shook her head. "No, it was there when I came up the steps." She regarded Mrs. Hudson with a worried look. "Is there a problem, ma'am?"

"No," Mrs. Hudson said. "We're just wondering where it came from, since there was no return address."

"I'm sure I don't know, ma'am," Rebecca said.

Mrs. Hudson glanced at Pia, like she was about to say something to her, then regarded Rebecca again. "Will you watch the children for a few minutes, please? I need to take Pia over to my husband's office. I'll be right back."

Rebecca's face lit up. "Of course, ma'am, I'd be happy to."

"If the girls are finished eating," Mrs. Hudson said, "they can help you clear the table."

"Yes, ma'am," Rebecca said. "Take your time." She wiped her damp brow on the back of her wrist and went over to the girls.

"I won't be long," Mrs. Hudson said. "But if you have any problems at all, the office is through that door and just down the hall. Even if Cooper starts to fuss, don't pick him up. Just come get me, understand?"

"Yes, ma'am," Rebecca said. "We'll be fine. Don't you worry."

Mrs. Hudson gave her a quick nod, then started out of the kitchen toward her husband's office. Pia followed, her heart in her throat. After waiting a few minutes while Dr. Hudson finished up with a patient, Mrs. Hudson asked if Pia could speak to him. She intended to go back to the kitchen immediately, but once Pia started explaining everything, she couldn't pull herself away. Dr. Hudson was shocked by what Pia said, of course, and angry at first that his wife hadn't confided in him about the money. But he forgave her once she explained how frightened she was when Nurse Wallis threatened to find another home for Cooper if she couldn't pay.

"I think Pia is correct about him being abandoned or taken from an orphanage," he said. "Because, as far as I know, no kidnappings have recently been reported in the city. Some older children have gone missing, but no infants that I'm aware of. Either way, what Nurse Wallis did was wrong."

"So you no longer think the rattle came from his mother?" Mrs. Hudson said.

He shook his head. "Not after what you've told me."

"Do you think it's possible to find out if Nurse Wallis sent it?" Pia said.

"I don't see how," he said.

"Could you ask the postmaster or the letter carrier?" Mrs. Hudson said.

"Do you know for sure it was mailed?" he said. "Did it have stamps and postmarks on it?"

Mrs. Hudson's shoulders sagged. "I don't remember," she said. "And I burned the paper."

"I don't either," Pia said. "Maybe she just dropped it off herself."

"Well, if it was from her," Dr. Hudson said, "that's a possibility. And if she's really selling children, that's a police matter. But they'll need proof to start an investigation."

"She threatened to take Cooper if I didn't pay," Mrs. Hudson said. "Isn't that proof enough?"

He shook his head again. "That would be your word against hers. Not to mention, we don't even know where she is, so how can we send the police after her?"

Pia looked at Mrs. Hudson with flooding eyes.

"I'm sorry, Pia," Mrs. Hudson said. "We'll talk about this again at dinner, all right? I'm sure we'll figure something out, but right now, we need to get back to the children. I've already left them longer than I'd intended."

Pia nodded and followed her out of the office, nearly swallowed by despair. How would they ever find out if Nurse Wallis knew anything about Ollie and Max if they couldn't find her? All she could do was pray the nurse would come back for the rest of her money. But even then, what would they do if she did? Force her to confess? Tie her up until the police arrived? It didn't seem likely.

Back in the kitchen, Elizabeth was out of her high chair and standing on the table, Cream of Wheat smeared on her hands and dress and her hair. Margaret was jumping up and down on a chair, singing "I've Been Working on the Railroad," and three-year-old

Sophie was in her seat balancing a prune-smeared plate on her head. Rebecca was nowhere to be seen. Mrs. Hudson gasped and rushed over to Cooper's cradle, shouting at Margaret to get down from the chair. Pia picked up Elizabeth and took the runny plate off Sophie's head, anger and shock lighting up her chest. How could Rebecca leave the children unattended? And where was she?

Then Mrs. Hudson cried, "He's gone!"

The hair on the back of Pia's neck stood up. "What?" she said.

"Cooper is gone!" Mrs. Hudson yelled.

"Margaret," Pia said, her voice high and tight. "Where did Rebecca go? Tell me right now."

Still standing on the chair, Margaret pointed at the door leading out to the front hall. "She went upstairs because Cooper needed a clean diaper. She said he made a doodoo." She giggled. "What's a doodoo, Mommy?"

Mrs. Hudson sighed in relief and put a hand to her forehead, swaying slightly. Then she went over to the table to help Margaret down from the chair. "She wasn't supposed to pick him up," she said. "And she certainly wasn't supposed to leave you girls alone." Her voice cracked with anger.

Pia put Elizabeth back in her high chair and wiped the Cream of Wheat from her face. "I'll go see what they're up to," she said.

"Please do," Mrs. Hudson said. "And send her back down here right away. I need to have a word with her." She took Sophie over to the sink to wash the prune juice from her hair.

Pia hurried out of the kitchen and down the hall, unease swirling in the pit of her stomach. Cooper's diaper had just been changed. And even if he'd dirtied it again so soon, Rebecca had been told not to pick him up. If she needed this job as badly as she claimed, why would she disobey Mrs. Hudson? It didn't make sense. She padded quickly up the stairs and rushed toward the nursery, her apprehension growing with every step. What if Rebecca had lied to Margaret about the diaper? What if she wasn't upstairs at all? When she reached the nursery door, she stopped in her tracks, stunned by what she was seeing.

Rebecca sat in the rocking chair, her face wet with tears, her blouse unbuttoned, Cooper at her naked breast. When she looked up and saw Pia, she put a gentle hand on his small head and held him closer.

Pia flew across the room and reached for the baby. "Give him to me," she demanded.

Rebecca shook her head. "No," she said in a quiet voice. "Not yet."

"Have you lost your mind?" Pia said. "Give him to me now."

"No, I won't," Rebecca said. "My milk is coming back."

"He's not your baby," Pia said, fury twisting in her chest. "He's not Simon."

"I know," Rebecca croaked. "I know he's not my son." Misery flooded her eyes.

Pia tried to take him, but Rebecca tightened her grip. They struggled for a moment, but Pia let go, afraid of hurting him. "Let me have him," she said through clenched teeth.

Just then, footsteps pounded down the hall and Mrs. Hudson came into the nursery with Elizabeth on her hip, Sophie and Margaret on her heels. When she saw Cooper suckling at Rebecca's breast, she came to a halt, the blood draining from her face.

"What in God's name are you doing?" she cried. She thrust Elizabeth into Pia's arms and went to take Cooper from Rebecca. "Give him to me!"

At first Rebecca resisted, but then she let go. Mrs. Hudson snatched the baby and backed away, staring at her like she was a raving lunatic. Rebecca's hands went limp in her lap, a thin drizzle of milk leaking from her breast onto her powder blue blouse, creamy wet blotches growing gray.

"Sophie and Margaret," Mrs. Hudson said. "Go to your room. Now."

"But, Mommy," Margaret started. "We just—"

"Don't make me tell you again," Mrs. Hudson said. "Go to your room this instant. Pia will come get you in a few minutes."

The girls turned their lips under, pouting, but they moved away from the door and did as they were told.

"I'm sorry, ma'am," Rebecca said. "But he was starting to fuss and I . . . I couldn't help myself."

Mrs. Hudson pointed a trembling finger at the nursery door.

"Get out of my house," she said, her words rattled by rage. "And don't ever come back."

"Please, ma'am," Rebecca said. "I'll never do it again, I promise. It was a mistake."

"A mistake?" Mrs. Hudson said. "A mistake is tearing a sheet or dropping a plate. This was not a mistake. You need to get out of my house now, before I have my husband send for the police."

Rivers of tears spilled down Rebecca's cheeks. "Please," she cried. "I'm sorry I lied to you earlier, ma'am, but . . . my baby . . . my precious Simon . . . he passed away right after he was born. His father promised marriage, but then he left, and I . . ." She leaned forward and buried her face in her clawed hands. "I just miss my baby boy so much."

Mrs. Hudson held Cooper to her chest, her eyes filling. "I'm sorry about your son, I truly am, but you can't . . . you shouldn't have . . . Cooper is *my* baby. He's *my* son."

Rebecca straightened, scraping her fingers down her cheeks. "I know he's yours, ma'am," she said. "You're right. He's your son. And I had no right to . . . I just . . ." She pushed herself up from the rocking chair and buttoned her blouse with shaking fingers, swaying like she'd had too much whiskey. "I just hope you know how lucky you are to have so many children, and to have the means to take care of them all. Not every mother is so blessed."

"I know how lucky I am," Mrs. Hudson said. "I don't need you to tell me."

Rebecca nodded, then half walked, half staggered toward the door, her bloodshot eyes blinking as though she'd just woken up from a nightmare.

Mrs. Hudson watched her stumble out of the nursery, tears wetting her face, then handed Cooper to Pia. "Please go take care of the children," she said. "I need to make sure she leaves."

"Do you want me to get Dr. Hudson?" Pia said.

"No," Mrs. Hudson said. "I can handle this on my own."

The following Sunday, after announcing that the number of flu cases had dropped sufficiently over the past week, Dr. Hudson told

Pia he'd hired a hansom cab to take them to her family's old apartment in the Fifth Ward. Mrs. Hudson insisted they wear masks on the trip, and Dr. Hudson agreed they shouldn't take any chances despite the promising reports that the flu might finally be coming to an end. Pia didn't care either way, she only hoped against hope that she'd find news about her brothers or Vater. It had been months since the war ended; surely he'd found his way home by now.

Staring out the cab window, she felt like she'd been let out of prison. How long had she been holed up at the Hudsons'? With everything that had happened, she'd lost track of time. Days blurred into weeks and weeks blurred into months and the months felt like years. As usual, she searched the sidewalks for familiar faces, for Ollie and Max, Vater and Finn. And, of course, Nurse Wallis. At least if she saw someone she knew this time, Dr. Hudson would make the driver stop and let her out.

When they arrived in front of her old row house, she got out of the cab on shaking legs. If she found her father, how would she explain what had happened to Ollie and Max? Would he understand? Would he blame her and be angry? She gripped her elbows and stared up at the window to their old apartment, shivering while Dr. Hudson paid the driver to wait. To her surprise, she realized she'd never wanted to see the place again. Because other than the possibility of finding out what happened to her loved ones, never coming back here would have been fine. The cramped, dim rooms of 408 Shunk Alley held too many bad memories—Vater leaving for the war, Mutti dying of the flu, Ollie and Max inside the dark cubby.

"Are you ready?" Dr. Hudson said, making her jump.

She nodded, then swallowed and led him up the front steps.

Stepping around crumpled newspaper pages, a rusted bucket, and shards of broken glass, they made their way across the dim foyer and started up the stairs. Plaster and dirt gritted under their shoes, and the smell of boiled cabbage and fried onions filled the corridors. For a fleeting moment she remembered what it felt like to be returning home after school, looking forward to eating dinner with her parents and playing with Ollie and Max. The light, happy feeling of being carefree, before the world went dark and her life was turned upside down, flickered just within reach. Then it disappeared as fast as it came, replaced by the horrible, heavy crush of heartache and grief.

When they reached the fourth floor, she hurried to the door of what used to be her family's home, certain her heart was going to burst from her chest. What if a different family lived there now and she had to explain herself all over again? What if they didn't understand English either? What if they refused to answer the door? She took a deep breath, knocked, and glanced up at Dr. Hudson. He gave her a reassuring smile, but doubt muddied his eyes. Seconds seemed like hours as they waited for someone to answer. She bit her lower lip and knocked again. Finally, the handle turned and the door opened. A dark-haired woman with a tired face stood holding a baby on her hip. To Pia's relief, it was the same woman who was there before.

"Visszajöttél?" the woman said, smiling warmly. She gestured for Pia and Dr. Hudson to come inside.

Dr. Hudson took off his derby and followed Pia into the apartment. The two children who'd been on the bed the first time she returned looked up from where they were playing, the same doll and wooden top on the floor between them. The scraggily bearded man was nowhere to be seen, and she wondered what happened to him. After being in the Hudsons' beautiful house, the rooms she used to call home seemed even smaller and darker now, the floors and walls and cupboards and dishes peeling and coated with grime, the curtains and bedding dirty and ragged. She'd never understood how poor they really were until now. The difference between this home and the Hudsons' was like night and day, black and white, diamonds and dirt. Again she asked herself why God allowed such injustice. Why should some suffer based on matters of luck and circumstance and place of birth? On top of everything else, she felt like kicking herself. Why hadn't she asked Mrs. Hudson to send food and clean linens for these poor people? The Hudsons certainly had enough to spare. Maybe Dr. Hudson could give them some cash before they left. He looked dazed by what he was seeing.

The woman pointed at him, her eyebrows raised. *"Ez az apád?"*

Pia didn't understand her words, but she knew what the woman was thinking. She shook her head. "No," she said. "This isn't my father."

The woman cocked her head, frowning.

Pia made a writing motion with her hand. "Did Vater come back here? Did you give him my note?"

The woman shook her head, then went over to the dusty shelf above the table, reached inside the blue vase, and handed Pia a piece of folded paper. Pia's throat constricted. It was the note she'd left for her father, covered in a thin layer of soot. He hadn't come back yet. Then the woman pulled another piece of folded paper out of the vase. It was yellow. A telegram.

Pia's stomach twisted in on itself, a writhing coil of fear nearly bending her over. She glanced at Dr. Hudson to make sure he was still there, then took the telegram and opened it with shaking fingers.

WASHINGTON, D.C. JANUARY 7, 1919
MRS. AMELIA LANGE
SHUNK ALLEY, ROOM 408, PHILADELPHIA,
PENNSYLVANIA
DEEPLY REGRET TO INFORM YOU THAT
PRIVATE KARL LANGE IS OFFICIALLY REPORTED
AS KILLED IN ACTION OCTOBER 9, 1918.
HARRIS, THE ADJUTANT GENERAL

Pia doubled over, the black space in her heart expanding with a painful jolt. She dropped the telegram and crumpled to the floor, every muscle and bone aching with renewed grief. A few words written on a piece of paper had destroyed her last fragment of hope that her father might return. Now it was certain. She'd never see him again. He'd never be coming home to help her find the twins. She'd never be able to tell him she loved him again. Images flashed in her mind: Vater carrying her into the woods on one shoulder, patiently waiting while she picked pinecones from the evergreens; him teaching her how to sound out the words in the newspaper; and the happy smile on his face when he held his sons for the first time. Her mind raced back to the day he left for the army. Had she squeezed his hand twice like she used to, to make sure he knew how much she loved him? Surely she'd said it out loud. Surely she'd hugged him and made him promise to be careful. But had she told him in their special secret way how much she cared? She couldn't remember. Then a gruesome image assaulted her: her beloved father in an army uniform lying dead in a field, bloody bullet holes in his chest, his pale face covered in gore. *No!* her mind screamed. *This can't be real! He can't be dead!*

Burying her face in her hands, she wailed and shuddered, each violent sob wrenching the strength from her body. Reality hit with a final, crushing thud. Her parents were dead. And her brothers might be too. She really was an orphan now.

CHAPTER TWENTY-FIVE

PIA

1924

By the third week in November, it had been raining for three days straight. The wind gusts broke branches from trees and sent them whirling across lawns like they were made of paper. Muddy water ran along the sidewalks and pooled in the roads, making Pia's walk back to the Hudsons' feel like a jungle trek. Normally she enjoyed the leisurely stroll home after dropping off ten-year-old Margaret, eight-year-old Sophie, and seven-year-old Elizabeth at school, even when it snowed, but now she couldn't wait to get back to the warmth of the house. She clutched her jacket collar under her chin, blinking against the icy drops hitting her face like a hundred tiny bullets, and skirted around men wielding umbrellas and women pushing baby prams. Thankfully, she was wearing gloves, a habit she'd developed years ago, no matter the weather. Dr. Hudson thought wearing them might help dull unwanted sensations when she left the house, and luckily he'd been right. She was glad, too, that she hadn't brought Cooper with her today, given the five-year-old's inclination toward catching cold.

Along with making her cold and wet, the miserable weather seemed to mirror her mood. After helping Mrs. Hudson get breakfast ready while listening to Dr. Hudson read an article in the morning newspaper about the new immigration act signed by Calvin Coolidge limiting the number of southern and eastern Europeans, Arabs, and Jews allowed into the country—the purpose of which was to preserve the American ideal of homogeneity and stabilize the ethnic composition of the population—a feeling of sadness had come over her that she couldn't seem to shake. Maybe the new act reminded her of her parents and how they'd come here seeking a better life, only to find death instead. Or maybe it reminded her of Nurse Wallis's hatred for Germans, which, of course, reminded her of her lost brothers, and how every clue over the last five years had led to more dead ends.

They thought they'd found Nurse Wallis once, a few years ago when Dr. Hudson talked to a hospital payroll clerk who had a record of a nurse with the same last name. But when they went to the address on the other side of the city, the woman who answered the door was not the Nurse Wallis they were looking for, and she'd never heard of any other nurses by that name either. Dr. Hudson had called St. Vincent's numerous times to see if Nurse Wallis had been back to get more children, but no one had seen her since the spring of 1919. It was like she'd disappeared from the face of the earth, which only strengthened Pia's suspicions that she had something to hide. Where the rattle had come from remained a mystery too. No local asylum employees had ever seen it before, nor did they have any memory of an immigrant being brought in with an infant, and the postman didn't remember dropping the package off either. If only they'd questioned Rebecca further before sending her away. She'd lied about her baby, so who knew what else she'd been lying about?

The third wave of the flu epidemic had finally subsided during the summer of 1919, nine months after the terror began. Everyone said the aftermath was chaos and record-keeping had been a muddled mess, with children unaccounted for and families separated or wiped out completely. Hundreds of children, too sick or too small to remember their names after being picked up by visiting nurses, had been given to other people or sent away, some by mistake. Pia wondered how many times Nurse Wallis had taken advantage of the situation, how many times she'd made money off lost orphans and other children. And how many other people were like Pia, look-ing for vanished sons and daughters and siblings? No hospitals or orphanages or temporary homes had any information on Ollie and Max, so she still believed Nurse Wallis knew where they were. Her greatest fear, other than her brothers being dead, was that they'd been sent to another state on one of the orphan trains. But she'd heard promising stories too, stories that gave her hope—like the one about the mother who fell ill and came home to find her three children gone, then opened her door two years later to find one standing in the hall, clinging to a Red Cross worker's hand.

Everywhere she went, the open-air markets and trolleys, the al-leyways and crowded streets, she looked for little boys of about six; blond-haired twins with Mutti's blue eyes and Vater's strong chin. But like Nurse Wallis, it seemed Ollie and Max had disappeared off the face of the earth. And maybe they had. Maybe she was search-ing for ghosts.

Even now, she could still picture them sleeping in her parents' bedroom cubby, their little legs pulled up to their distended bellies, their soft-skinned faces, their long eyelashes like feathers on their pale cheeks. If she'd known back then what she knew now, she would have crawled in the cubby with them. The guilt of what she'd done and her failure to find out what happened to them felt like a bleeding wound inside her heart, constantly ripped open by the slightest poke or nudge. And today, for some reason, it had all come flooding back, bringing to the forefront all she had been through and all she had lost.

Realizing now that she would need to change out of her wet clothes before checking in with Dr. Hudson to see if he needed help, she walked faster. After her feelings about Leo and Elizabeth had proved to be accurate all those years ago, there'd been several more instances when she'd known something was wrong with a member of the family—Sophie with strep throat, Margaret with an eye infection, and even Mrs. Hudson, who came down with pneu-monia during the winter of 1921. Dr. Hudson believed that, like the nurse he'd worked with on the battlefront who helped him save soldiers, Pia had helped save his loved ones' lives by making it easier for him to figure out what was ailing them before things turned more serious. It didn't take long before he asked for help when he was stumped by some of his patients' symptoms, and over the years she'd assisted him in diagnosing kidney stones, impacted bowels, impending heart attacks, lung infections, swallowed objects, fractured bones, and more.

While she was glad to help him and his patients, at the same time she dreaded putting her hands on strangers, waiting for the first stab or twist or throb of pain to strike. After a while it seemed as though the patients' suffering had become part of who she was, like an invisible, heavy burden carried in her body and soul. Or maybe it was her shattered heart that weighed her down. She often wondered what an X-ray of herself would look like. Would it show the broken bones and ruptured masses, the enlarged organs and rotted membranes of all the ill and damaged people she'd touched? Or would it show the emptiness and sorrow she carried inside, like a black space in the night sky?

She'd never forget the time Dr. Hudson asked her to lay hands on a three-year-old girl, brought in by her frantic mother in the middle of the night. The child was curled up in a ball, howling in pain, her face covered in sweat, her lips blue. When Pia reached beneath her frilly pink dress and touched her tight belly, she fell to her knees, a violent cramp shooting up through her chest, her stomach muscles hollowing out. The mother screamed and grabbed her daughter, gaping at Pia as if she'd hurt her child. After Pia pulled herself together and stood, she asked to speak to Dr. Hudson privately. Whatever was wrong with the girl was going to take her life, of that she was sure. Two hours later, when Dr. Hudson came home from the hospital, he said the little girl had died of either gallstone colic or ptomaine poisoning, which was milk sickness brought on by drinking milk from a cow that had eaten snakeroot. Afterward, Pia cried all night, knowing how much agony the little girl had been in before she died, and trying to understand why God allowed children to suffer so. It felt like losing Ollie and Max all over again.

Still, despite her discomfort, she couldn't say no to Dr. Hudson after everything he and Mrs. Hudson had done for her, not to mention treating her like family and helping her search for her brothers. They'd even started paying her several years ago, along with continuing to supply free room and board. She had Christmas dinner and opened presents with them, and they gave her gifts and a cake on her birthday. Despite the fact that she didn't deserve their kindness and generosity, she was thankful for it. She cared about them and thought they cared about her, and she loved the children more than she would have thought possible. Margaret, Sophie, Elizabeth, and Cooper treated her more like an older sister than their nanny. And they needed her—at least she told herself they did. At the same time, she felt like she was living someone else's life. Perhaps that was her punishment.

Now her eyes started to burn and, as she'd done countless times before, she pushed the painful memories away and tried to think about something else. Remembering the new library book she had picked up the previous day, *Howards End* by E. M. Forster, she lifted her chin. Later, after the children were tucked in bed, she'd lie in her bedroom and read about three families in England: one wealthy, one poor, and one German. It was a small distraction, but it was something to look forward to, something to keep her from thinking too much. Every day she tried to remind herself that it was never too late for a miracle to happen, that someday she might find her brothers. Still, it would never erase what she had done. Nothing would.

When she turned the corner onto the next street and neared the Hudsons' house, she furrowed her brow. A strange man was at their front door. Visitors had been welcome again since the end of the epidemic, but most of them were friends, couples from church, or the mothers of the girls' classmates. The man at the door, in scuffed boots and a ripped vest, rain soaking his scraggly hair, didn't look like anyone from the Hudsons' close circle. Maybe he was looking for Dr. Hudson and hadn't seen the sign pointing to the office. She shoved her hands in her pockets and hurried up the sidewalk.

"May I help you?" she said.

The man spun around, grabbing the newsboy cap off his head. "Um, aye. I'm here to ask about a friend."

She went up the steps onto the porch. "Are you looking for Dr. Hudson?"

"Nay, I'm looking for a girl named Pia Lange."

Pia stiffened, her skin prickling. Who was this man, and what did he want with her? How did he know her name, unless . . . unless this was the miracle she'd been hoping for. Her heart went into her throat and it took a moment to find her voice. "Are you here about my brothers?"

His brows shot up. "Is it you, Pia?"

She wiped the rain from her eyes and squinted at him, trying to figure out how he knew her name. His bristled face looked familiar and strange at the same time, the hazel eyes and copper-colored hair, the deep dimple in his chin. And then she knew. His voice was deeper, more mature, but his accent and the way he said her name were unmistakable. Five years had changed her best friend into a man.

"Finn?" she said in a weak voice. Her legs and arms started to tremble. "What are you doing here? How did you find me?"

He threw his arms around her and hugged her tight, squashing her face against his damp collar. "They told me ye were here," he said. "But I figured you'd be gone by now. I thought I'd never see ye again."

She pulled away, trying to breathe normally. "Where have you been?" she said, surprised by her anger. "Why did you leave St. Vincent's without me?"

He frowned, his face going dark. "I didn't leave," he said. "Ye should know I'd never desert you like that. I was taken."

"What do you mean you were taken? By whom?"

Before he could answer, the front door opened and Mrs. Hudson appeared. Except for the fine lines around her eyes and a few light hairs streaking the hair above her forehead, she looked the same as she had when Pia first arrived—but this time, her hair was as neat as her dress, her eyes bright and lively. She regarded Finn, frowning as she took in his ragged clothes and dirty boots. "What are you doing out here in this miserable weather, Pia?" she said. "And who is this?"

"This is my friend Finn," Pia said. She felt breathless and confused, and more than a little overwhelmed. "We lived across from each other growing up, and we were in the orphanage together."

"Oh my goodness, yes," Mrs. Hudson said. Her displeasure at

his appearance vanished. "I remember you telling me about him. Well, bring him in out of the cold and damp. You'll catch your death out there."

Finn gave Pia a doubtful look.

"It's all right," Pia said, trying to smile. "You should have seen me the first time she let me in." She moved toward the door and motioned for him to follow, grateful but not surprised that Mrs. Hudson was inviting him in just because he was a friend.

"Come in, come in," Mrs. Hudson said. "You're letting in the chill."

Finn shrugged and followed Pia into the foyer, then stepped aside and stood dripping on the rug. He raked his fingers through his wet hair and gaped up at the vaulted ceiling, his mouth hanging open. Pia took off her gloves, put them in her jacket, hung it on the coat tree, and offered to take his.

He glanced down at himself. "I'm afraid I'm a right mess. I'm not dressed properly to come visiting."

"Nonsense," Mrs. Hudson said. "We don't care what you're wearing. If you're a friend of Pia's, you're welcome here."

Finn hesitated, looking at Pia with doubt-filled eyes. She nodded and he finally took off his jacket, revealing a ragged wool vest over a wrinkled, graying shirt with missing buttons. A length of frayed rope held up his trousers.

"Oh dear," Mrs. Hudson said.

"Forgive me, ma'am," Finn said. "I told you I wasn't—"

"No worries," Mrs. Hudson said. "I'll find a change of clothes for you. Dr. Hudson wears about the same size, and I know for a fact he has too many pairs of trousers and shirts." She turned to Pia. "Why don't you take him into the parlor while I see what I can come up with. And fix him a cup of hot tea while you're at it. He looks chilled to the bone."

"Yes, ma'am," Pia said.

"Thank you, ma'am," Finn said. "But I don't want to impose. I only came here looking for Pia."

"Well, now that you've found her," Mrs. Hudson said, "you must stay a bit. I know she's happy to see you, and you have a lot of catching up to do." She gave Pia a wink and started out of the foyer, then stopped and spun around. "Oh, I don't mean to be rude, but please take off your boots before you go into the parlor. And don't sit on the furniture until you've changed. I'll be right back." Then she turned and disappeared.

Finn gave Pia a weak smile.

"Don't take it personally," she said. "She's always been like that."

"If you say so," Finn said. He took off his boots and put them side by side on the rug. Jagged holes riddled the toes and sides of the leather, and his socks weren't much better. "I'm sorry for shocking you like this, but I didn't know—"

"There's no need to be sorry," she said. "I'm just glad you found me. Come on in, I'll make some tea and you can tell me what happened."

In the kitchen, she put the teakettle on to boil and offered him a seat at the table. When he shook his head, she remembered what Mrs. Hudson said about changing his clothes before he sat down. Her thoughts were a jumble and she couldn't think straight. Standing on the opposite side of the table, equally as awkward and bashful as he was, she couldn't believe what she was seeing, that he was here, in the Hudsons' kitchen. A strange mixture of confusion and elation roiled in her stomach. Finn had grown into a man, and he was here, staring at her, a million questions on his face. That she was happy to see him was an understatement. At the same time, he was a stranger.

"I'm mighty disappointed ye thought I left without you," he said.

She put her hands on the back of the chair, squeezing so hard her knuckles turned white. "What was I supposed to think? One day you were there and the next you were gone."

"Believe me when I say it wasn't my idea."

"Where did you go?"

"Mother Joe said a family in Iowa wanted to adopt me so she was sending me on a train with a pack of boys from other orphanages. I put up a hell of a fight, but some big fella wrangled me into a cart and took me to the station. Except there weren't no bloody family waiting when I got off."

Pia gasped. "Oh my God. That's horrible." She started to ask him another question, but Mrs. Hudson came into the kitchen with a change of clothes, socks, shoes, and a wool overcoat.

"These should fit," Mrs. Hudson said. "You're welcome to use the water closet to clean up and get changed. I've put a shaving kit in there for you too."

"You're too kind, ma'am," Finn said. "But I have no money to pay you."

Mrs. Hudson pshawed and piled the clothes in his arms. "No need to pay me a thing," she said. "Just hurry along and tidy up."

Finn smiled at her, a smile that was both grateful and embarrassed, then did what he was told.

"How amazing that he found you after all this time," Mrs. Hudson said after he was gone.

"I know," Pia said.

"He must really care about you."

Pia nodded because she didn't know what to say. Her cheeks grew warm.

"Well, I'll be upstairs in the playroom with Cooper," Mrs. Hudson said. "But I expect you to tell me everything later." She chuckled and gave Pia another wink, then turned and left the kitchen.

While Finn was getting washed and dressed, Pia took a serving tray with a silver carafe and two teacups into the parlor and waited in one of the wingback chairs, thinking about what he'd said. All this time, she'd been wondering if he'd left St. Vincent's without her. And until she saw him on the porch, she hadn't realized how resentful she'd been, despite the fact that she didn't know what really happened. Maybe she couldn't imagine him letting a nun force him to do something against his will. She should have known better. He never would have abandoned her. And Mrs. Hudson was right. It was amazing that he'd found her after all this time. That *had* to mean something.

She got up and checked her reflection in the mirror next to the curio cabinet, suddenly remembering she'd been out in the rain and probably looked like a drowned rat. Running her fingers through her damp hair and pushing a few unruly locks behind her ears, her hands started to shake. What did he think of her now that she was a woman? Did he think she was attractive? At nineteen, she resembled Mutti in more ways than she could count, from her thin nose to her arched brows and cobalt-blue eyes. She thought that was a good thing—in her mind, Mutti was the prettiest woman she'd ever seen—but she'd never asked anyone's opinion. When she and Finn were younger, she hadn't cared. So what difference did it make now? She rolled her eyes and went back over to the chair to sit down, berating herself for being so foolish. They were only friends. For all she knew, he could be married now.

When he came into the parlor a little while later, he was wearing the clean shirt, vest, and trousers, his hair slicked back from his face, his cheeks scrubbed and red from shaving. She glanced up when he came in, then quickly looked away and started pouring the tea. For the first time since he arrived, she noticed the chiseled line of his jaw and cheekbones, the deep emerald of his kind eyes. Her best friend had grown into a handsome man. Maybe she should have changed out of her damp dress.

Keeping her eyes on the serving tray to hide her flushed face, she said, "So what happened when you got to Iowa and no one was waiting for you? What did you do?"

He sat in the opposite chair and sighed. She couldn't tell if it was a sigh of relief because it felt good to be clean and wearing fresh clothes, or a sigh of frustration because of her question. Likely it was a combination of both.

"I survived best I could," he said. "That's what I did. I found work on a farm and saved my pay until I had enough money to come back here. First thing I did was go to St. Vincent's to look for you."

She handed him a cup of tea, hoping he couldn't see the heat in her cheeks. "Who told you where I was?"

"Mother Joe. I wasn't sure she'd remember me, but she did after I told her that the bloody nurse who put me on the train lied about someone being on the other end."

Pia started to pick up her teacup, then stopped. "What nurse?"

"Remember the time we lads had to line up in the rec room and that nurse took Kafka, Gerhard, and his brother?"

Her heart started to race. He was talking about Nurse Wallis. She nodded.

"Well, later that night Sister Ernestine took me to Mother Joe's office and that same nurse was there waiting for me."

Pia could hardly breathe. "Nurse Wallis."

He took a sip of his tea, then set it down on the tray. "Nay, Bernice Groves."

She shook her head, confused. "What do you mean? The nurse who took Kafka and Gerhard was Nurse Wallis."

"Nay, it wasn't."

"Yes, it was. I know Nurse Wallis. She was the one who took Kafka and Gerhard. I'm certain of it. You must have her mixed up with someone else."

He frowned, his brows knitted. "Nay, I don't."

"Yes, you do."

"You don't remember Bernice? She lived two doors down from us in the same row house, and she was mean as a mule. My brothers and I called her Old Biddy Bernice because she used to call us dirty Irish boys and make smart-ass remarks about my mother's brogue."

She shook her head and picked up her tea. "No, sorry. I don't remember her."

"What d' ye mean you don't remember her? How could you forget? She was a real bucket of piss, that one. She's the woman who yelled at your mam about your father stealing her pa's job, said it put him in his grave."

She shook her head again, getting more and more perplexed. Why was he talking about this Bernice person? What did she have to do with anything? "I wasn't there when that happened. I only heard about it after it was over. And I had no idea who my mother was talking about."

"So you're saying ye didn't recognize her when you saw her at St. Vincent's, all dressed up in that nurse outfit? I did, right off. And I knew she weren't no nurse. She recognized me too. When she put me on the train that night, she said she was doing it to clear the city of riffraff and immigrants. But I think she did it so I wouldn't tell the sisters she was lying about who she was."

Pia suddenly went rigid, her body turning to ice. In that moment, everything clicked into place. Nurse Wallis's reaction when she first saw her at St. Vincent's the day she dropped off the Romanian baby, her refusal to help look for the twins, her anger, her accusations, her questions. She knew who Pia was because she used to live in the same neighborhood. She knew she was German because she had argued with Mutti.

And she knew Ollie and Max.

Pia started shaking, her teacup rattling against the saucer. She put the cup down and slumped back in the chair, dizziness sweeping over her.

Finn got up and knelt beside her. "What's wrong?" he said. "Are ye feeling ill?"

Pia shook her head, her eyes filling. "Bernice was the one who took Ollie and Max."

CHAPTER TWENTY-SIX

PIA

The day after Pia learned Nurse Wallis was really Bernice Groves, she sat next to Finn on the other side of Mother Joe's desk in the office at St. Vincent's Orphan Asylum. Being back in the orphanage was unsettling to say the least; it felt like she'd stepped back in time, to a part of her life she'd give everything to forget. Except she was an adult now and could leave whenever she wanted. That's what she had to keep telling herself, anyway. The office looked smaller some-how, but the smell of moldy wood, stale incense, and old potatoes still filled the air, as if the place had been locked up for a hundred years. The only difference was the number of group photos on the wall behind Mother Joe's head. There were more now, each new frame filled with the haunted, somber faces of children who had lost—or been deserted by—those who were supposed to love them most of all. Just looking at them made Pia want to cry. She pulled her eyes away and reminded herself why she was there.

"When was the last time you saw Bernice Groves?" Finn asked Mother Joe.

"He means Nurse Wallis," Pia said. "Wallis wasn't her real name. Does she come here anymore?" She waited for Mother Joe to reprimand her for not addressing her properly, but that didn't happen, which was a good thing. Pia might have laughed or told her to go to hell, and that wouldn't have gotten them anywhere. The old nun couldn't tell her what to do anymore. And she didn't deserve respect. But now was not the time to tell her that.

Mother Joe folded her age-spotted hands on the desk and blinked, thinking. The last six years had not been kind to her. One eyelid drooped lower than the other, sagging over one milky eye like a piece of dead skin, and her wimple looked two sizes too big, the rippled sides gaping around her shrunken face like a stretched rag.

"I'm afraid not," she said. "It's been years since Nurse Wallis came by. Like I told Dr. Hudson when he called, she just stopped coming one day, I don't know why. I assumed something had happened to her."

"I know Dr. Hudson asked you this before," Pia said. "But are you sure you don't know anything about her? You don't know her address or have any way to get in touch with her?"

"I'm sorry," Mother Joe said. "But I don't."

"What about one of the other nuns?" Pia said. "Like Sister Agnes or Sister Ernestine? Maybe they know something."

Mother Joe shook her head, the saggy wimple flopping against her sharp cheekbones. "Sister Agnes was assigned to another post nearly two years ago. And Sister Ernestine, bless her soul, went to be with our Father in heaven six months ago. We found her facedown in the play yard one day, the poor dear. The doctor said her heart just stopped."

The news about Sister Ernestine was no surprise—Pia remembered feeling her heart slow when she'd grabbed her. She wanted to ask Mother Joe why she thought someone like her deserved to go to heaven, and how she could pretend to be unaware of the horrible things she'd done. But she had more important things on her mind. At least Sister Ernestine wouldn't be beating children at St. Vincent's anymore. "I'm sorry," she said, because it was the right thing to say.

"What about the other nurses who come here?" Finn said. "Was Bernice . . . I mean, Nurse Wallis friends with any of them? Maybe they'd know where to find her."

"Oh no," Mother Joe said. "Nurse Wallis was truly one of a kind.

It's a rare thing for nurses to stop out here on their own. But she came here because she wanted to help our children, not to mention what she did for our unwed mothers."

"What did she do for the unwed mothers?" Pia said.

"Why, found good homes for their babies, of course."

Of course. Pia thought. Her stomach shriveled, thinking about Nurse Wallis taking and selling the babies of women and girls who were already scared and heartbroken. Did Mother Joe know about that too? The thought of it made her sick. But she had to stay calm. She couldn't afford to upset Mother Joe or accuse her of anything. Not yet, anyway. "You must have those records then," she said. "Maybe one of the unwed mothers would know how to get in touch with Nurse Wallis."

"Heavens, no," Mother Joe said. "Those records are sealed. I couldn't possibly share anything with you about the young women we assisted."

Pia sat forward in her seat. "But you have to help me," she said. "Nurse Wallis wasn't a real nurse, and I have reason to believe she stole my brothers."

Mother Joe's milky eyes grew wide. "That's a serious accusation, Miss Lange."

"I realize that," Pia said. "But she lived in my neighborhood and knew my family. Except I didn't know that until—"

"I'm sorry," Mother Joe said. "But I'm afraid I can't help you. In my heart of hearts, I don't believe Nurse Wallis would *steal* your brothers. Help them? Yes. But steal them and keep their where-abouts from you? I don't believe it. She was one of the kindest women I've ever met."

"Bloody hell," Finn said. "We're sitting here telling you she lied about who she was and you're defending her? I haven't even gotten to the part where she lied to you about me being adopted and put me on a train instead. What good reason would she have for doing such right awful things?"

"I'm sure I don't know," Mother Joe said. "But if anything you're saying is true, and I have a feeling you might be confused, I'm sure she had nothing but the best of intentions." With that, she pushed herself up from her chair, started around the desk, and shuffled toward the door. "Now if you'll excuse me, I have other matters to attend to."

"What about the finder's fees?" Pia said. "Did you know she was charging money for the babies she took from St. Vincent's? She told people it was a donation to help the orphanages."

Mother Joe stopped and turned to face them, her sagging lid almost all the way closed.

"Did she give you money for the children at St. Vincent's?" Pia said. "Or was she lying about that too?"

"As a matter of fact, she did," Mother Joe said. "They weren't sizable donations, but she gave us what she could spare. And if you had any idea how much money it takes to properly care for so many orphans, care of which you two were beneficiaries, I might add, you'd understand why we're willing to accept what any kind soul is willing to give." She started toward the door again. "Now, I suggest you pray for forgiveness for accusing Nurse Wallis of such horrible things, Miss Lange and Mr. Duffy. That woman is deserving of sainthood."

Pia and Finn looked at each other and stood, their faces lined with frustration.

"You're wrong about her," Pia said, blinking back angry tears. "And when I find out the truth, you're going to be the one asking for forgiveness for not helping me sooner. Doesn't the Bible say learn to do good and seek justice?"

"Yes, Miss Lange, it does. It also says you shall not bear false witness against your neighbor. You're welcome to come back and speak to me when, or if, you find proof about what you're saying. Until then, good day, God bless you, and take good care of yourself."

Pia wrapped her arms around herself and followed Finn out of the office, bewildered and stunned into silence by fury and despair. She'd thought for sure Nurse Wallis was still coming to St. Vincent's and that once she and Finn revealed their suspicions, Mother Joe would be willing to ask the nurse where she lived, or let Dr. Hudson know when she came in again. But the old nun hadn't seen her in years—and she didn't believe them, anyway. Either that, or she didn't care. Now Pia didn't know what to do.

She trudged down the hall beside Finn, each of them lost in their own thoughts. Like Mother Joe's office, the orphanage corridors seemed to have shrunk, but fear and misery still filled the air like a living, breathing thing. She couldn't wait to get out of there.

"Are you all right?" Finn said.

She nodded, swallowing the lump in her throat.

At the end of the hall, a door opened and a line of young girls with sad faces and ill-fitting clothes filed out and moved toward them. Pia and Finn stepped aside to let them pass. She couldn't help looking at their desolate, sunken eyes. What had led them there, to such a horrible place? Had their parents died? Abandoned them? Had they gotten lost at the open-air market and been snatched up by the police? Another door opened and two women in dark dresses and damp aprons came out, their sleeves rolled up to their elbows. Pia gave them a quick glance, then directed her attention back to the young girls. She wanted to rescue them all, to steal them from this prison and take them home, to feed them and love them and let them know they weren't alone. If Mrs. Hudson could see them, she'd feel the same way. Maybe Pia should bring her here. Maybe they could open their own orphanage and run it with kindness and love.

"Pia?" someone said behind her.

Pia turned, surprised to hear someone say her name. The woman's pale face looked familiar somehow, but Pia couldn't place her. Maybe it was a girl who'd been at St. Vincent's at the same time she was there, all grown up. Maybe it was Gigi. Or Jenny. No, the girl didn't look like either of them. Was it Edith? No, Edith had brown hair; this woman had blond corkscrew curls and blue eyes. Then she remembered.

"Rebecca?" she said.

"What are you doing here?" Rebecca said. She eyed Finn with suspicion, then gave Pia a worried look. "Are you in trouble?"

At first, Pia didn't understand what Rebecca meant. If she were in trouble, why would she come to St. Vincent's? Then she remembered St. Vincent's housed unwed mothers as well as orphans, and heat crawled up her face. Rebecca thought Finn was her boyfriend.

"No, I'm fine," Pia said. "We're just looking for someone."

"Who?" Rebecca said.

"No one you know." Pia started walking again and Finn followed.

Rebecca went with them. "Are you sure?" she said. "I've been working here ever since I left the Hudsons'. And I gave birth to Simon over at St. Vincent's home for unwed mothers. I've seen a lot and I know a lot."

Pia stopped and turned to face her. After what Rebecca had done with Cooper, she didn't think she could trust her to be honest about anything. But right now she'd take any help she could get. "Do you remember seeing any nurses picking up or dropping off children?"

"Maybe," Rebecca said.

"What about a Nurse Wallis? She was really tall, with dirty blond hair and pasty skin. Mother Joe said she stopped coming years ago, but maybe—"

"I'll never forget her," Rebecca said.

Pia's stomach clenched. She hadn't expected such a quick response. And even though Rebecca sounded sincere, how could Pia believe anything she said? She glanced at Finn, looking for reassurance, but his eyes were locked on Rebecca, waiting to see what she'd say next.

"Why do you say that?" Pia said.

"Because she took my son," Rebecca said.

Pia gritted her teeth. Rebecca was lying again. "You said your baby died."

Rebecca hung her head and clasped her hands together, squeezing until her knuckles turned red. Then she sighed and dropped her arms to her sides. When she looked up again, her eyes were wet. "I said he died because I couldn't tell you the truth."

"What truth?" Pia said. "You've changed your story so many times, how am I supposed to know if you're being honest now?"

"Because Cooper Hudson is my son. Nurse Wallis stole him and gave him to Dr. and Mrs. Hudson."

Pia gasped, her mouth falling open. It made perfect sense. That was why Rebecca had been desperate to work at the Hudsons', and why she was so enamored with Cooper. That was why she wanted to nurse him and hold him close. "Oh my God," she said. A hundred questions raced through her mind but she didn't know what one to ask first. Clearly Mrs. Hudson had been right to worry about where Nurse Wallis had found the babies she sold. Before she could put her spinning thoughts together and form a rational sentence, Rebecca continued.

"I wanted to work at the Hudsons' just so I could be near him," she said. "I knew I couldn't take care of him properly and I'd planned on giving him up, but she took him without telling me." Tears started down her cheeks. "I know what I did was wrong, but he was crying and I couldn't help myself. I'm his mother." She buried her face in her hands.

Pia started to say something when a sudden realization hit her. Her heartbeat picked up speed. "I'm sorry," she said. "I truly am. But how did you know where he was? Did Nurse Wallis tell you?"

Rebecca scraped her fingers under her eyes, trying to swallow her sobs. "No, she didn't tell me anything. He was underweight and a little sickly, so I thought the nuns were going to see if he'd survive before putting him up for adoption. But two days after he was born, I woke up and he was gone. The nuns said Nurse Wallis had already found him a good home. But I never got to say goodbye."

"Then how did you find out she took him to the Hudsons?" Pia said.

"Because I stayed on to work so I'd be there when she came back to get another baby. I told her I just wanted to see my boy one more time, just to say goodbye. I swore on my life I wouldn't cause her any trouble, and I'd do anything she wanted if she'd just let me see him. I said I'd be her housemaid for free or pay her anything she wanted. Anything. At first she refused, but a few days later she agreed to tell me where he was if I dropped off a package. That was it, just drop off a package."

Pia was confused. Why would Nurse Wallis want her to drop off a package? Then she recoiled as if slapped. "At the Hudsons'?"

Rebecca nodded. "I didn't know what was in it or anything. And I didn't care. I just wanted to see my boy. That was all that mattered to me."

"So she gave you the package and you took it to the Hudsons'?" Finn said.

Rebecca shook her head. "No, she didn't want the nuns to see her give it to me. I had to pick it up."

"Where?" Finn said.

"At her apartment."

Pia could hardly breathe. "So you know where she lives?"

Rebecca shrugged. "I knew where she lived five years ago, but I don't know if she's still there."

"Do you remember the address?" Finn said.

"I think I remember where the building was."

"Can you take us there?" Pia said.

Rebecca nodded.

CHAPTER TWENTY-SEVEN

PIA

With her heart in her throat, Pia followed Rebecca along the trash-littered alleyway, hoping they didn't have too much farther to go. It was early evening, the night air still and moist with coming rain, and a waning moon dimmed behind the gathering clouds. A train whistle sounded in the distance, hollow and lonely-sounding. Here and there, lights burned behind row house curtains, and a chorus of conversation, laughter, shouting, and the tinny music of a phonograph floated out from half-open windows.

Nerves churned in Pia's stomach, and she prayed she and Finn weren't being led on a wild-goose chase. Five years was a long time. Nurse Wallis could have moved to another building. Or another city. Or another state. And what was Pia going to do if she found her? How was she going to make her admit to taking Ollie and Max? Tie her up? Threaten her? Call the police? More importantly, what was she going to do if this turned out to be another dead end? She wasn't sure she could handle another disappointment. Not when it felt like they were so close.

"How much further?" she asked Rebecca. It seemed like they'd walked halfway across the city.

"We're almost there," Rebecca said. "Just one more block."

Pia glanced back at Finn, who shrugged and urged her to keep going. Rebecca had been more than willing to help, perhaps to make amends in some small way for what she'd done, but that didn't mean she remembered how to get to the right building. And what would Dr. and Mrs. Hudson think if they knew she and Finn were with Rebecca instead of going for an evening stroll like she'd said? She felt bad for the white lie, but wanted to make sure Rebecca could really help before telling them the truth about her.

At the end of the alley they turned left, walked another block, and crossed a busy thoroughfare. Pia had no idea what neighborhood they were in, but it was nicer than South Philly. Multistoried buildings lined the streets, with thick stone steps leading up to each door. Men in wool coats and women in wide-brimmed hats walked side by side along the sidewalks, which were swept clean of litter and trash. How was Nurse Wallis able to afford living in such a nice area? By selling babies?

At the corner, Rebecca finally stopped and pointed at a brick building across the road. "That's it," she said. "When I first got here she was outside with an older couple and two little boys. She kissed the boys goodbye, then the older couple put them in a pram like they were taking them for a walk. After they left, she took me up to her apartment and gave me the package."

Pia's heart pounded hard in her chest. She hadn't told Rebecca about Ollie and Max, only that it was vital she find Nurse Wallis. "Did you say two little boys?"

"Yes," Rebecca said.

"How old do you think they were?"

Rebecca shrugged. "I'm not sure, maybe six or eight months. They were bundled up in hats and coats so I didn't get a good look."

The sidewalk swayed beneath Pia's feet and she grabbed Finn's arm to keep from falling. It sounded like Nurse Wallis might have kept Ollie and Max. She might not have sold them after all. They might still be here. In Philadelphia. In that very building. She tried to find her voice. "Did they look like twins?" she managed.

Rebecca screwed up her mouth, thinking. "Yeah, I guess so. Although one seemed a little bit bigger than the other."

Pia's heart felt like it might explode. Ollie was two minutes older than Max, and he'd always been taller and heavier. Rebecca *had* to be talking about them. She had to be. Seeing Nurse Wallis with two little boys was too much of a coincidence. "Let's go," she said, and marched across the street toward the brick building. Rebecca and Finn followed.

"What are you going to do?" Finn said, trying to keep up.

"I'm going to knock on her door and ask her where my brothers are," Pia said.

"What if she doesn't live here anymore?" Finn said.

"Well, I'm not going to find out by standing out here on the street."

"What are you talking about?" Rebecca said. "Did Nurse Wallis take your brothers too?"

"Yes," Pia said, keeping her eyes straight ahead. She didn't have the time to explain.

"What if they're not Ollie and Max?" Finn said.

Pia ignored the question and kept going. The boys had to be Ollie and Max. They just had to be. Nurse Wallis never mentioned having other kids to Mrs. Hudson, only that she'd lost a son. And that she loved helping children. *Stealing* would have been a more appropriate word.

When Pia reached the building, she sprinted up the front steps two at a time, yanked open the door, and went inside. Flyers and notices shuddered on the walls of the shadowy foyer, blown about by the incoming breeze.

"What's her apartment number?" she asked Rebecca.

Rebecca's face grew pale, like a white plate floating in the gloom. "I . . . I'm not sure, I was so nervous waiting for her to tell me where my boy was I didn't pay attention. But I'm fairly certain it was on the second floor."

Pia peered up the staircase for a moment, gathering her courage, then grabbed the handrail and started up the steps. "I guess we'll just have to knock on every door until we find her."

At the top of the landing, she hurried over to the first door, pounded on it, and glanced around, trying to breathe normally. Four doors surrounded the stairwell. Four doors, one of which could reveal Ollie and Max. One of which could hold the answer to six years of searching. Finn and Rebecca stood behind her, silent and waiting. Pia couldn't look at them. If she did, she might cry. She lifted her chin, straightened her shoulders, and knocked again, then pressed her ear against the door.

"I hear something," she said, and took a step back.

After some jostling, the door opened. A tall woman stood in the doorway, frowning and clutching the collar of her thin dressing gown, her long blond braid over one shoulder. Her face was pasty white, and puffy bags hung under her tired, gray eyes.

It was Nurse Wallis.

Pia hesitated, frozen and unsure. It was as though she'd forgotten how to move or speak. Seeing Nurse Wallis out of uniform for the first time, in her nightclothes and wool stockings, made her seem younger and more vulnerable somehow. She didn't look like a criminal, or someone who could steal babies and sell them. She looked like a nice woman who would bake cookies and take soup to her ill neighbors. But Pia knew better. She took a step toward her, ready to push her way inside the apartment. Recognition transformed the nurse's face. She drew in a sharp breath and tried to shut the door.

Pia thrust her hands onto the door, and Finn jumped forward, shoving his foot in the way to stop it from closing. Together they pushed against it, straining with the effort, and Rebecca helped. Nurse Wallis was no match for the three of them. The door flew inward, knocking her backward. She stumbled and fell with a bone-jarring thud, her nightdress flying up her doughy thighs. They hurried into the apartment, and Finn slammed the door behind them.

Nurse Wallis rolled over and got up, scrambling to her feet with considerable effort. "What are you doing here?" she said, her voice shrill. "What do you want?"

"I want my brothers," Pia cried. "Where are they?" She scanned the room, searching frantically for Ollie and Max.

A copper teakettle sputtered on the coal stove, water boiling out of its fluted spout. Gaslights flickered on the dark-paneled walls. The place was clean and tidy—dishes arranged neatly on the shelves, a stack of linens folded on the table, a trio of cast-iron pans hanging on the wall. But there was no sign of her brothers. No small trousers hanging from the clotheslines or draped over the stove, no toys or little boots on the floor. Pia bolted past the nurse into a back bedroom.

"Get out of here before I call the police," Nurse Wallis yelled. "This is my home. You have no right to be here!"

"Ollie?" Pia cried. "Max? Are you in here?"

The bedroom was empty except for a single bed with a flannel blanket and an oak dresser against one wall.

"Have you lost your mind?" Nurse Wallis shouted. "You need to leave!"

Pia raced out of the bedroom, back across the kitchen, and into a parlor. A button-back davenport, a rocking chair, an end table, a secretary's desk, various potted plants, and other decorations filled the cramped space. But no wooden trucks or rubber balls littered the floor or end table, no blocks or children's books. No young boys played jacks or marbles on the rug. She returned to the kitchen and glared at Nurse Wallis, trying to catch her breath.

"Where are they?" she cried. "What did you do with the twins?"

Nurse Wallis stood holding her elbow and wincing in pain. "Get out of my apartment before I have you arrested," she yelled, spittle flying from her lips. "All of you!"

Finn and Rebecca stood guarding the door, eyes wide, waiting to see what was going to happen next.

"You're the one who's going to be arrested," Pia said. "Unless you tell me what you did with my brothers."

Nurse Wallis scowled at her. "I have no idea what you're talking about. Now leave this instant!"

"I'm talking about Ollie and Max," Pia said. "I know you took them." She pointed at Rebecca. "She saw you with them."

Nurse Wallis glanced at Rebecca, her face filled with disdain. "I've never seen that girl in my life."

"I suppose you never saw me either," Finn said.

Nurse Wallis shook her head. "Never."

Loathing welled like bile in Pia's throat. She wanted to grab Nurse Wallis by the neck and shake her until she confessed. "You're lying," she said. "You took Finn from St. Vincent's and put him on a train to get rid of him because you were afraid he'd tell Mother Joe who you really were. You stole Rebecca's baby and sold him to the Hudsons. And your real name is Bernice Groves."

Fear flickered across Bernice's face like the ripple of a stone thrown in a lake. She let go of her elbow and glanced around the room as if looking for an escape. Finn turned the dead bolt on the door.

"You knew my mother because you lived in the building across from ours," Pia continued. "You saw me leave after my mother died. Then you went over to our apartment and took the twins." She reached into her pocket, pulled out a faded piece of paper, unfolded it, and held it up. "And you left this." It was the note from the cubby.

Bernice shook her head. "You're insane," she said. "I have no idea who your mother was, where you lived, or who wrote that. And I certainly don't know anything about any twins."

Pia crumpled up the note and threw it at her. "What did you do with the babies you took from St. Vincent's? Did you sell them too? And what about Kafka and Gerhard and his brother? Did you get rid of them like you got rid of Finn?"

"I helped those babies," Bernice said. "I found them good homes, better homes. And the older children too."

"So you admit it," Pia said.

"I didn't do anything wrong," Bernice said. "Even President Coolidge knows we can't let immigrants take over the country. We're being overrun. I gave those children a chance to become regular Americans."

Pia couldn't believe what she was hearing. Not only was Bernice stealing and selling babies, she was prejudiced too. She balled her hands into fists, fighting the urge to scream and hit the woman. "And Ollie and Max? Did you find them a better home too?"

"I told you," Bernice said. "I don't know who you're talking about."

Pia reached into her coat pocket and pulled out the rattle. "Then how do you explain this? You had Rebecca deliver it to the Hudsons in exchange for telling her what you did with her son. It's my brother's rattle."

Bernice pressed her lips together as if trying to come up with another lie. But it was no use. She couldn't resist saying what was on her mind. Hate filled her eyes. "What kind of person puts babies in a cubby and leaves them there to die?" she sneered.

Pia drew in a sharp breath. All that time, all those years, the person who had taken Ollie and Max had been right in front of her. A thousand questions whirled in her head. Had she missed the clues somehow? Had she been blind to the evidence? She shook her head to clear it. Right now, she needed to stay calm. Somehow, she had to get Bernice to tell her what she did with the twins. "I left to get food so we wouldn't starve," she said, her voice shaking with rage. "I was coming back. Now tell me where they are."

Bernice shot her a spiteful smirk. "You're too late," she said. "They're gone."

"What do you mean they're gone?"

"Tuberculosis," Bernice said. "Three years ago."

Pia's heart went black. No. It couldn't be. She hadn't come all this way to lose them again. Bernice had to be lying. Pia would have known, would have felt it in her soul, if her brothers had died. She scanned the room for what felt like the hundredth time, frantic for proof Ollie and Max had been there, that they were still alive. No pictures hung on the walls. No colorful drawings done by small hands. She ran into the parlor again and looked around. The others followed. Somewhere, there had to be something to confirm what she knew in her heart.

"You're not going to find anything that belonged to them," Bernice said, her voice like ice. "I got rid of it all."

Pia ignored her, hurried over to the secretary's desk, and pulled it open. Envelopes, both new and used, filled the slots, along with flowered stationery, sheets of paper, and writing instruments stacked like cordwood. The small drawer between the slots held stamps and buttons, clips and a crochet hook, pennies, and a dried daisy. Bernice ran over and tried to push her away, to stop her from going through the desk, but Finn grabbed her by the arms and held her back. Pia shut the fold-out, opened the drawer below it, and pulled out skeins of yarn, knitting needles, a pincushion full of silver needles, a scuffed darning egg, and a basket full of other sewing materials. In the door below she unearthed folded aprons, yellowed doilies, boxes of old Christmas cards, and stacks of letters. She hauled everything out and threw it on the floor, then reached into the very bottom of the last drawer. There, beneath a folded tablecloth, lay a book held shut with a rubber band. She took it out. It was the ledger she'd seen in Bernice's bag all those years ago. She yanked off the rubber band and opened to the first page.

"You have no right to go through my things," Bernice yelled. She lunged forward and tried to rip the ledger out of Pia's hands, but Finn held on tight.

Names and dates and ages filled each line and column in the ledger. The first line read:

Francis . . . Age 6 months . . . boy . . . sold to Mr. and Mrs. Johnston

The rest of the lines on the page—more than thirty of them— were all the same: young babies sold to married couples. Pia scanned the names looking for Ollie and Max, her vision blurred by tears, but they weren't there. She turned the page and read the first entry.

Piotr (renamed Peter) . . . Age 6 years . . . boy . . . sent by train to Michigan

From there, the foreign names went on to the next page, every one changed into something more "American-sounding." Every one of them, boys and girls, had been sent away by train. One name in particular caught her eye.

Finn (renamed Fredrick) . . . Age 14 years . . . boy . . . sent by train to Iowa

Pia flipped through the rest of the pages. Another list of sold babies had been started, but the remainder of the ledger was blank, except for the fifty-dollar bills stuck between each page. She turned to Bernice, her face burning with fury. "What did you do with Ollie and Max?"

"I told you, they're gone," Bernice said.

"I don't believe you," Pia said. She looked at Rebecca. "Go get the police. Tell them we caught someone trying to kidnap a baby."

Suddenly Bernice lifted her foot and kicked backward, hitting Finn hard in the shin with her heel. He grimaced, startled, but held on. Then somehow she turned, yanked herself from his grasp, and ripped the ledger from Pia's hands. Pia grabbed it again and tried to wrestle it away, but Bernice pushed her, hard, and started toward the kitchen. Pia fell against the davenport, crashing into the wooden arm, and pain exploded in her back. She ignored it and scrambled to her feet just as Finn caught Bernice by the arm. But Bernice was too fast. She pulled away and bolted out of the parlor, fifty-dollar bills flying in her wake. They chased after her, but Bernice was already in front of the coal stove. She opened the door and pitched the ledger inside.

"No!" Pia cried, arms outstretched as if she could stop what was happening by sheer force of will. When she caught up to Bernice, she shoved her out of the way, pushing her to the floor, and reached into the stove. But the fire was too hot. The heat seared her skin. She yanked her hand out and watched helplessly as flames enveloped the ledger, the pages curling up, turning to ash, and disappearing before her eyes.

Beside her, Bernice struggled to get up, panting and red-faced.

Furious, Pia grabbed her by the wrist and wrenched her forward, pulling her off balance. She fell again and Pia gripped her arm with both hands, digging her fingers into her skin and refusing to let go. She wasn't about to let her run.

"You're not getting away with this," she said. "And you're going to tell me what you did with Ollie and Max." She started to say something else, but a sudden jolt of pain ripped through one side of her head, just above her right eye, like something had burst inside her skull. She let go and fell back on her haunches, suddenly dizzy and nauseous.

Bernice got to her feet and staggered over to the sink, her elbow bleeding, the hem of her nightdress ripped and hanging. When she turned around, lantern light reflected off the knife in her hand. "Get out," she said. "Now. Or so help me God I'll use this."

"Go get help," Finn said to Rebecca. "Hurry!"

Rebecca started toward the door.

"No, wait," Pia said. She put one hand on the floor to stop the room from spinning. "We're not going to need the police." She squeezed her eyes shut for a second, and as quickly as it had started, the pain and dizziness disappeared.

"What do you mean we don't need the police?" Finn said. "She's got a knife!"

Pia straightened and got to her feet, wary eyes fixed on Bernice. "She took my brothers," she said. "She took a lot of children. And she's going to pay for what she did, very soon."

"Is that right?" Bernice laughed, taunting her. "And how do you know that? You don't have proof."

"It doesn't matter," Pia said. "I know the truth. And you're dying as we speak."

"Jaysus, Pia," Finn said. "What are you doing? We need to get help."

"No," Pia said. "Not yet. She's not going to hurt us."

"The hell I'm not. If you don't . . ." Bernice paused, then coughed abruptly. "We can't go today."

Finn gaped at Pia, confused. "What the hell is she talking about?"

Pia held up a hand, telling him to wait. Panic played around the edges of her mind, but she pushed it away. She had to get Bernice to talk before it was too late. And she didn't have a lot of time. "She doesn't know," she said. "She can't think clearly right now."

"What do you mean she doesn't know?" Finn said. "What in the bloody hell is happening?"

Bernice lowered the knife and swayed. A thin sheen of sweat broke out on her forehead and upper lip. She furrowed her brow in confusion, then reached back and grabbed the edge of the sink to steady herself.

"You're not feeling well, are you?" Pia said. "We'll get a doctor, but first you have to tell me what you did with my brothers."

"I'm fine," Bernice said. "Now get out of here."

"No, you're not fine," Pia said. "You need to go to the hospital."

Bernice wiped her wrist across her forehead, the knife quivering in her hand. "No, I don't," she said. "Just go. Leave me alone. I need to get ready for the party before . . ." She paused, puzzled by the words coming out of her mouth.

"You need to go to the hospital right now," Pia said again. "Or you're going to die."

She'd felt the same agonizing burst in her head while helping Dr. Hudson before, and had seen similar strange behavior. An older woman had come into his office with the worst headache she'd ever had, hoping to get something for the pain. One minute she made perfect sense, the next she had no idea who or where she was. Dr. Hudson took her to the hospital straightaway but the woman died of a brain hemorrhage later that day. Something similar was happening to Bernice, but at a faster pace.

"No, I'm not," Bernice said. "I'm just—"

"Getting caught was too much for you," Pia said. "Something ruptured in your head. I felt it."

Bernice put a trembling hand to her temple and started to say something else, but her mouth twisted and she dropped the knife, just missing her foot. It fell to the floor, the sharp blade gouging the plank surface before clattering over on its handle. Bernice's arm went limp and hung at her side, useless. Then she fell to her knees and made a muffled sound, like the grunt of a burrowing animal.

Pia picked up the knife and handed it to Finn. He regarded her with a worried look while Rebecca stood behind him, staring and about to cry. She seemed scared yet fascinated, like she wanted to leave but couldn't. Pia wanted to explain what was going on, but there wasn't time.

"Does your head hurt?" she asked Bernice.

Bernice nodded, fear burning in her bloodshot eyes. She grimaced and spittle oozed from one side of her mouth, then she slumped to the floor, curling up on her side.

"Tell me what you did with my brothers and I'll send Rebecca to get help," Pia said.

Straining with the effort, Bernice turned her head to gaze up at her, her face knotted with determination. The fight hadn't left her yet. "I put them on a train," she mumbled. "An orphan train."

Pia cursed under her breath. For the first time ever, she prayed

Bernice was lying again. Otherwise she'd never find Ollie and Max. "Where was the train going?"

"Don't remember," Bernice said. A cruel smile twisted across her face. "It was in the ledger."

"I don't believe you," Pia said.

Bernice clenched her jaw and squeezed her eyes shut in agony.

"Tell me where they are," Pia said. "Or we won't get a doctor."

"I'm not . . . telling you . . . anything," Bernice said. "I'm ready . . . to die. I've been . . . waiting years to be with my son . . . my precious Wallis."

Pia went rigid, as if the air had frozen in her lungs. Bernice wanted to die. She wasn't going to tell her anything. The rush of panic returned, plowing through Pia at full force. How could she frighten someone who had nothing to lose?

"Maybe I should get help," Rebecca said

Bernice opened her eyes and glared at her. Blood rimmed one lower lid. "No," she croaked. "I . . . I want . . . to go."

Pia didn't know what to do. If Bernice wanted to die, threatening to let her was pointless. She had to try something else. She shouted over her shoulder at Finn and Rebecca. "Go tell the police a woman needs to go to the hospital right away. Tell them to send for an ambulance!"

"I'll go," Finn said. His heavy footsteps pounded across the floor and he hurried out of the apartment.

Pia knelt over Bernice, pushing her face close to hers. "Rebecca saw Ollie and Max with an older couple. Who were they? Your parents? Do they live in this building? Where are the twins? If you don't tell me, I won't let you die. Finn went to get the police to take you to the hospital. The doctors will keep you alive, but you'll never talk or move again. Tell me the truth, or you're not going to be with your son for a long time."

"Pia," Rebecca said in a gentle voice. "You don't know for sure those babies were your brothers."

Pia turned and glared at her, pain and frustration burning in her eyes. A miserable clutch of fear settled in her stomach. If Bernice died, all would be lost. She was the only person on earth who knew where to find Ollie and Max. "Yes, I do," she said. "It was them. It had to be. You said yourself they looked like twins. She took them and she's going to tell me where they are." Then she looked back at Bernice, fighting the urge to strangle the last bit of life out of her. But it was too late.

Bernice was already dead.

When Finn returned with a policeman, Pia and Rebecca were waiting in the foyer, Rebecca sitting on an iron bench with her head down, staring at the floor. Her hair was disheveled and her face was red and streaked with tears. Finn gaped at them, confused. Pia shot him a warning look, signaling for him to play along.

"I'm sorry, Officer," Pia said. "But it's a false alarm. She's feeling much better now, thank goodness." Glancing down at Rebecca, there was no need to pretend being distraught. Finally finding Bernice and coming so close to learning the truth about her brothers was almost more than she could bear. Her legs felt like water, and her stomach churned with nausea. Maybe she should have played the part of the sick person instead of Rebecca. It wouldn't have been much of an act. "Isn't that right, Rebecca?"

Rebecca lifted her head and nodded, pretending to mope. "Yes," she said. "I'm sorry for making such a fuss."

The policeman knelt in front of her, his leather boots creaking. "Are you certain, miss? This young man made it sound quite urgent. I can get you to a hospital right away if you need to go."

"No, I'm fine, Officer," Rebecca said. "I was feeling rather light-headed for a few minutes, but I'm better now, really."

"She's just getting over childbed fever," Pia said. "And she's been having the vapors recently."

The policeman straightened, his brow furrowed. "I see," he said. Then he eyed Finn, his chest out, one thumb hooked over his utility belt. "I understand you're mighty worried about her, son, but next time make sure it's an emergency before you get the law involved."

Finn gave him an apologetic nod. "Aye, Officer," he said. "Sorry to be a bother."

"Do you all live in this building?" the policeman said to them.

Rebecca started to shake her head at the same time Finn and Pia nodded. Then Rebecca realized what she was doing and nodded too. Pia pushed down a swallow. The air turned thick as sludge. It was only a small lie, but what if the officer read the truth in her eyes? There was a dead woman upstairs. And even though Bernice probably would have died from whatever ruptured in her brain anyway, there was a high chance Pia had something to do with it happening sooner rather than later. And explaining why they were with her when she died but hadn't told anyone yet would be difficult to say the least. She had no proof Bernice had taken her brothers. Not yet, anyway.

"Well, perhaps you should take your friend back to her apartment so she can rest," the policeman said to Pia.

"Yes, Officer," Pia said. "Thank you so much for coming."

The policeman tipped his hat at them. "No problem," he said. "Have a good day." Then he left the building.

After he was gone, Finn gaped at Pia, eyes bulging. "In the name of all that's holy, what is going on? What happened?"

"Bernice is dead," Pia whispered.

"Bloody hell," Finn said. "Did she tell you anything? Did she confess before she—"

"No," Pia said. "She didn't say anything." Thinking about the way Bernice had smiled at her right before she died, the cruel, satisfied smirk on her twisted face, a fresh bolt of fury flashed through Pia. She turned and started up the staircase.

"Where are you going?" Finn said.

"To search her apartment," Pia said, taking the steps two at a time. Her determination clearly surprised Rebecca as much as it did Finn. Instead of protesting, they followed her up the steps without a word.

Back in Bernice's apartment, Finn put a blanket over her body, then went into the bedroom to look for clues that the twins had been there. Rebecca explored the parlor while Pia searched the kitchen, gingerly stepping around Bernice's corpse and trying to ignore the feeling that she might jump up and grab her at any second. Her arms and chest ached from trying to wrestle the ledger away from her, and her back hurt from falling on the davenport. Worst of all, grief and disappointment weighed her down, making every movement seem slow and difficult. The only person who knew what had happened to Ollie and Max was dead. It would take a miracle to find them now. But imagining the worst was easy, and she wasn't willing to give up yet.

After examining every nook and cranny, combing through every notebook and letter and greeting card, they found nothing—no paperwork, no children's clothes, no toys, no photographs. When they were finished searching, Finn lifted the blanket off Bernice and put it back in the bedroom. Pia stared at her crumpled body, wondering if she was, at long last, where she yearned to be—in heaven with her son. It didn't seem fair or likely, given what she'd done, but Pia wasn't sure what to believe anymore.

After Finn came out of the bedroom, they left the apartment and stood in the hallway trying to figure out what to do next.

"We need to tell someone she's in there," Finn said.

"We will," Pia said. "But not yet. I'm not ready to give up looking for clues. Someone in this building had to know her. Someone had to see the twins."

"What are we going to say happened to her?" Rebecca said.

"We'll say we stopped in for a visit and she collapsed," Pia said. "Which is the truth. But when we go to the police, we have to make sure we don't talk to the same officer Finn brought here earlier." She started toward the neighbor's door, gesturing for them to come too.

"I can't," Rebecca said. "I have to go back to St. Vincent's. I'm sorry but I'll get locked out if I'm not back by curfew."

"That's all right," Pia said. "Thank you for helping me get this far."

"You're welcome," Rebecca said. "To tell you the truth, I really wanted her to get arrested so she could pay for everything she's done."

"Me too," Pia said.

"Will you let me know if you find your brothers?"

Pia nodded. "Of course."

Rebecca gave them a weak wave and started down the stairs, worry and something that looked like fear lining her features. When she was gone, Pia started toward the apartment door next to Bernice's.

"Wait," Finn said. "I have to ask ye something."

She turned to face him. "Now?"

He nodded. "I wanted to wait 'til we were alone."

"What is it?"

"When we were with Bernice. What did you mean when you said you felt something break inside her head?"

Pia sighed. She hadn't thought about him hearing that. It was no wonder he was confused, and eventually she'd explain it to him, but not here, not now. Her nerves wouldn't allow it. "I'll tell you later, all right? I promise."

"Aye. Sure."

She turned and knocked on the neighbor's door.

"What are ye going to say?" he said. "You can't tell them what happened."

"I'm not going to," Pia said. "But we didn't do anything wrong. She was going to die, anyway. We probably made it happen sooner by upsetting her, but we didn't do it on purpose. We didn't know."

"But we could have helped her," he said. "Instead we let it happen. We could have gotten someone sooner."

"I know," she said. "And that's my fault. But I honestly don't think it would have made any difference. It happened too fast. Besides, you heard what she said. She wanted to be with her son." Blinking back tears of misery and frustration, she kept her eyes straight ahead and knocked on the door. She had failed at everything, from keeping her brothers safe to making Bernice pay for what she'd done. And now Finn probably thought she was crazy. And heartless.

"Are you all right, lass?" he said, his voice tender.

She nodded, clenching her jaw.

Behind the door, a male voice shouted something she didn't understand. Footsteps got closer, the lock and handle shook, and the door opened. An elderly man with a gray mustache as thick as a scrub brush stood looking at them, one crusty-looking hand resting on the doorframe. The heavy smell of pipe tobacco and fried onions wafted out from behind him into the hall. He eyed them with suspicion through thick, black-framed glasses.

"Yes?" he said.

"We're sorry to disturb you," Pia said. "But we're looking for two missing children. They're little boys, about six years old."

"How can I help?" the man said.

"May I ask you a few questions?" Pia said.

The man looked behind her, his dark eyes scanning the length of the hall. "I guess so," he said.

"Thank you," she said. "First, how well did you . . . do you know your neighbor?"

"Which one?" the man said.

Pia and Finn answered at the same time. "Nurse Wallis," Pia said. "Bernice Groves," said Finn.

Pia glanced nervously at Finn, twisting the sides of her skirt around her fingers, then tried again. "The nurse," she said. "How well do you know the nurse next door?"

The man pushed his glasses back on his nose, furrowing his brow. "What's this about? I thought I heard shouting coming from her apartment earlier. Is everything all right?"

Pia weighed her words. Surely this man didn't suspect his neighbor of anything criminal. And what if they were friends?

"May I ask how long you've lived in this building?" she said.

"Since my wife and I married forty years ago," the man said. "But what has that got to do with—"

Pia swallowed. He must have seen Ollie and Max at one point or another. "Do you remember your neighbor, the nurse, ever having two little boys? It would have been around five or six years ago, when they were babies."

The man shook his head, then moved his crusty hand from the doorframe to the door, closing it just the slightest bit. Someone else might not have noticed, but Pia did. Her heart thumped hard in her chest. He knew something.

"I don't recall," the man said. "Why don't you go over there and ask her yourself?"

"We tried knocking," Finn said. "She didn't answer."

Pia wrapped her arms around herself and shivered, only partly pretending. "May we come inside for a few minutes?" she said. "It's quite chilly out here in the hall."

The man glanced over his shoulder. "I'm sorry," he said. "But the wife and I were just getting ready to have dinner and now it's getting cold. I don't know about you, but I don't like my soup luke-warm." He chuckled, trying to act friendly and humorous, but his expression looked forced.

Pia pretended to laugh too, and started to step over the thresh-old. "Well, maybe your wife could help us. Sometimes women are better at remembering things, especially when it comes to children."

The man held up a hand, frowning. "Please," he said. "She isn't feeling well. And I don't think we can help you anyway. Now if you don't mind, I've got to get back to—"

"Who is it, dear?" a woman said behind him. She came to the door and stood beside him, wiping her hands on her apron and smiling at Pia and Finn. She was a petite woman, with wispy gray hair and a shiny, smooth face, the skin at her temples marbled with tiny blue veins.

"I don't know who they are," the man said. "But they're asking about the twins." As soon as the words left his mouth, he cringed.

The hair on the back of Pia's neck stood up. He said *the twins*. "So you know who I'm talking about," she said.

The man gazed at the woman with troubled eyes, the shadow of regret clouding his face.

The woman gave his arm a comforting pat and grinned sadly at Pia. "I'm sorry," she said. "My husband is getting a little forgetful in his old age. Perhaps you can tell me what we can do for you."

"Who did he mean when he said *the twins*?" Pia said.

The woman raised her eyebrows and smiled a little too brightly. "I'm not sure. Did you say something to him about twins perhaps? Like I said, he gets easily confused."

Pia tried to stay calm. "No, I didn't," she said, her voice trem-bling. "But my twin brothers have been missing since they were babies. And I have reason to believe your neighbor stole them after my mother died during the flu epidemic."

The woman's face fell and her smile disappeared. She stared at Pia in disbelief, her thin lips pressed into a hard line. It was impos-sible to tell if she was shocked or angry.

"A friend of mine saw her with them," Pia continued. "She said an older couple took them for a walk in a baby pram. Do you remember if Bernice ever had twin boys?"

"I'm sorry," the woman said. "But I don't know anyone named Bernice. Perhaps you're in the wrong building." Her voice had turned hard, her eyes glassy.

"She meant to say Nurse Wallis," Finn said.

The woman swallowed and glanced at her husband, bewilderment and something that looked like fear passing between them.

"Yes, I meant your neighbor, Nurse Wallis," Pia said. "Her real name is Bernice Groves."

The man shook his head and dropped his watery gaze to the floor. Either he didn't believe them or he was ashamed; it was hard to tell. The old woman grasped his hand, her face suddenly filled with misery. She searched Pia's eyes as if looking for the truth there. Pia thought she might scream before the woman said something.

"She broke our hearts," the woman finally said.

The man nodded, sniffing, and wiped his wrist under his nose.

"What do you mean she broke your hearts?" Pia said. "How?"

"Those boys were like grandchildren to us," the woman said.

Pia's breath caught in her chest, a rush of emotions surging through her like a thousand lightning bolts. If Finn hadn't been standing right beside her she would have fallen over. These people knew the twins. They knew Ollie and Max!

"That's right," the man said. "The good Lord never saw fit to give us children of our own. So when she and the boys showed up out of the blue, we thought our prayers had been answered. They lived with us for a while. We even watched the twins while she went to work. And we were starting to think of her as a daughter, until—"

"We never understood how a mother could give her children away so easily," the woman interrupted. "Or why she wouldn't tell us where they were, especially when she knew how much we loved them." Tears filled her eyes. "But if what you're saying is true, maybe she didn't care about them as much as we thought."

Pia's heart instantly dropped, her elation replaced by despair. No. This couldn't be another dead end. It just couldn't be. The hallway felt like it was closing in, getting ready to crush her. She struggled to find her voice. Finn slipped his hand into hers and gave it a squeeze. She barely felt it. "It's true," she managed.

"Are you saying you don't know where the boys are?" Finn said.

The woman regarded her husband, a question on her face, her chin trembling.

"Tell them," her husband said.

CHAPTER TWENTY-EIGHT

PIA

After introducing themselves as Ben and Louise Patterson, the elderly couple invited Finn and Pia inside. They sat in the parlor, Ben in an overstuffed chair, Louise wringing her hands on the edge of an ottoman, and Pia next to Finn on the davenport. Louise had offered them tea and biscuits, but Pia politely declined. Between waiting to hear what the Pattersons were going to say about her brothers and picturing Bernice dead on the floor just a few feet away on the other side of a wall decorated with oval-framed portraits, the Lord's Prayer in cross-stitch, and a vase filled with peacock feathers on a shelf, she felt like she might get sick. The dark eyes of the people in the photographs seemed to bore through her, judging her as if they knew what she'd done.

"We'd never seen her act that way," Louise said. "It just came out of the blue one day."

Shaking his head in disgust, Ben dug a pipe from his vest pocket and cupped it in his wrinkled hand like a baby bird.

"She came home that day close to hysterics," Louise said. "We still don't know why. But we almost called a doctor because she kept saying she had to get rid of the twins, that she couldn't do it anymore."

Ben nodded and put the pipe between his teeth, searching his pocket with one finger for tobacco.

"Couldn't do what anymore?" Pia said.

"Take care of them," Louise said. "She said it was too difficult and she was going to send them away on an orphan train."

Pia's stomach twisted in on itself. *No. Please, God. Not when I'm this close.*

"She said people out West were willing to take in children," Ben said. "Said someone would be happy to have twin boys and she wouldn't have to worry about them anymore."

"We begged her to give them to us, but she refused," Louise said. "We even offered her money, but she wouldn't take it."

"Not at first, she wouldn't," Ben said. He stuffed his pipe with tobacco and lit it. "But we doubled our offer."

Pia swallowed the lump in her throat. "I'm confused," she said. "Are you saying she took your offer?"

"Yes," Louise said. "But that only guaranteed she wouldn't send the boys away on the train. We still couldn't have them."

"And you agreed to that?" Pia said. On top of everything else, she was getting dizzy. She glanced at Finn to make sure he was still there. He took her hand and held on tight. She tried concentrating on the warmth of his skin, the width of his palm, anything to distract her from having the vapors. It was no use. She started shaking.

"It was the only way we could get her to promise she'd keep them in the city," Louise said. "But only if we agreed not to ask where they were or try to find them."

Pia bit her lip, trying not to scream. The Pattersons were her only link to Ollie and Max, and they had been nice enough to invite them in and answer her questions, but she could hardly believe what she was hearing. "How did you know she didn't send them away anyway?"

Louise shrugged. "We didn't."

Pia stood and started to pace, frustration and nerves boiling from her chest into her head. "So you have no idea where they are," she said. Her tone was hard, but she couldn't help it. "You have no idea what Bernice did with them."

"We didn't say that," Ben said.

Pia turned to face him, her vision blurred by tears. "Then what are you saying? Please, tell me before I go mad."

CHAPTER TWENTY-NINE

PIA

Wearing her favorite crepe dress and high heels, Pia hurried around the table in the Hudsons' dining room, putting cloth napkins at each place setting and straightening the silverware. After working with Mrs. Hudson in the kitchen all afternoon, peeling potatoes and making biscuits for the beef stew, stirring the cranberry tapioca, and keeping an eye on the buttered beets, she'd finger-waved her hair and put on a little lipstick and rouge, hoping it would make her look more approachable. Now she picked up a water glass and polished it with an extra napkin, her hands unsteady. Upstairs, the children ran through the house, laughing and playing and shouting.

She tried not to think about whether or not Ben and Louise Patterson would be able to keep their promise, but it was hard not to hope. If they couldn't follow through with it, more than likely she'd fall apart—for a little while anyway, until she figured out what to do next. Either way, she wasn't about to give up, not when she was this close to finding Ollie and Max.

When she'd told Dr. and Mrs. Hudson who Nurse Wallis really was and everything she'd been doing, they were shocked and appalled. Dr. Hudson promised to let the orphanages and poorhouses know too, with the hopes that, in the future, they would be more vigilant about who took their children. He also met with the police and, after an autopsy proved Bernice had suffered a massive brain hemorrhage, made sure her remains were taken to the nearest funeral home. The Pattersons offered to pay for her burial because she had no other family that they knew of, and because, despite what she'd done, she was the closest thing to a daughter they'd ever had. Louise said you could still love people despite their faults, but Pia wasn't sure someone like Bernice deserved to be loved. Not only had she gotten away with taking Ollie and Max without being punished, she had sold babies, and was so filled with hate that she'd sent children away on trains because they were immigrants. Some things were too evil to forgive. Then again, Mutti always said God made the final judgment on them all, so maybe Bernice was getting what she deserved anyway.

"You look nice," someone said behind her.

She startled and spun around, almost dropping the water glass. It was Finn, in a new jacket and fresh-pressed trousers. His face was clean-shaven, his hair slicked back from his handsome face.

"You scared me half to death," she said. She set down the glass and swatted him with the napkin.

He caught it and drew her toward him, grinning. "I meant to," he said.

She pulled away. "What if I'd dropped the glass?"

"I would have picked it up," he said.

"Ha ha," she said. "Very funny. I'm about ready to have the vapors and you're making jokes. What if the glass had broken and I had a mess to clean up on top of everything else?"

He ran gentle fingers along her forehead, pushing a stray piece of hair from her eyes. "Try to relax, lass, there's no reason to be so nervous."

She sighed and rested a hand on his arm. It felt wonderful, after all this time, to finally enjoy human contact. She was surprised by how pleasant it could be. Luckily Finn hadn't been frightened off when she explained what Dr. Hudson called her sixth sense. In fact, he thought she was courageous for using her gift to help other people and said it only proved what he knew all along, that she was special.

"What if they don't come?" she said.

"They will."

"How can you be so sure?"

"Because Mr. and Mrs. Patterson said they were nice people. I'm sure after they hear what happened they'll—"

"Either that, or they'll leave town."

"They won't do that."

"All right. But what if they don't like me?"

"Don't be silly," he said. "Of course they'll like you. What's not to like?"

Just then, Dr. and Mrs. Hudson came into the room, her in a blue two-piece dress, him in a tailored gray suit and black vest. Dr. Hudson had grown a full blond beard that reminded Pia of a Viking, and his hair had started to turn white over his temples. Even with a few gray hairs and added wrinkles, the Hudsons made a striking pair.

"Is everything ready?" Mrs. Hudson said.

"I think so," Pia said.

Dr. Hudson leaned out the door and shouted up the stairs. "Come along, children. We need to sit and get settled down while we wait for our special guests."

What sounded like a hundred footsteps pounded down the stairs and raced along the hall, punctuated by shouting and laughter. Sophie appeared first, a white bow askew in her hair, slowing to a walk when she reached the door. Then came Margaret and Elizabeth, their braids tied in matching ribbons, the waists of their ruffled dresses crooked and bunched. Cooper followed in an Indian headband with a single feather and carrying a bow and arrow. Mrs. Hudson chuckled and rolled her eyes, then plucked the headband from his head, took the bow and arrow, and started out of the room with it. Pia fixed Sophie's hair and straightened the other girls' dresses.

Then the doorbell rang, and she froze.

Cooper started toward the hall, anxious to see who was there. Dr. Hudson caught him by the collar and held him back. "I'll get it, young man," he said.

Mrs. Hudson stashed the bow and arrow in the sideboard instead of taking it out of the dining room and ordered the children to sit. "I want you on your best behavior, now," she said. "Pia is expecting some very important company, and I won't have you causing a ruckus."

"Yes, Mother," the children said in unison.

Pia waited next to Finn with her heart in her throat, giving him a nervous glance. He took her hand and gave it a squeeze.

"Don't worry," he said. "They're going to do what's right, I just know it."

She tried to smile to show her gratitude, but her lips trembled. It was all she could do not to cry. Dr. Hudson's voice traveled down the corridor, along with a woman's quiet muttering. Pia clenched her jaw and locked her knees. What if they didn't come? What if it was Mrs. Patterson coming to apologize? Then Dr. Hudson entered and stepped aside, his face giving nothing away. When Pia saw who it was, her shoulders dropped.

Rebecca stood in the doorway holding a brown paper sack. "I picked up some candy for the children," she said.

Berating herself for forgetting she'd invited Rebecca, Pia went over to her, took the bag, and led her into the dining room. "That was nice of you, thank you."

"Where are they?" Rebecca said.

"They're not here yet," Pia said.

"Are you sure they're coming?"

"No," Pia said. "I'm not sure of anything."

Rebecca hugged the children one by one, and gave Cooper an extra kiss on the cheek. He scowled and wiped it off. She laughed and ruffled his hair, then stood next to Finn.

Pia had to admit she'd been shocked when Mrs. Hudson agreed to allow Rebecca to visit Cooper after learning he was her son, but then again, the Hudsons had always been the kindest people she'd ever known. Cooper was never to know Rebecca was his mother, of course, but Rebecca was beyond grateful just to see him. The Hudsons even agreed to let her stop by on his birthday and holidays, treating her like an old friend. Pia marveled at their generosity and courage. She could only hope they weren't the only people with generous hearts.

"Who is coming again?" Sophie said. "I forgot."

"Why did we have to get all dressed up?" Elizabeth whined. "My collar itches."

"Stop fussing, girls," Mrs. Hudson said. "You'll just have to wait and see."

Pia scanned the faces in the room, her heart overflowing with gratitude and love for each and every one of them. She couldn't believe they were all here, ready to care for and help her, no matter what happened next. Dr. and Mrs. Hudson had been good to her all these years; Finn had found his way back home; and finally, with Rebecca's help, she had unraveled the mystery of what happened to Ollie and Max. Most importantly, she'd found out for certain that they were alive. Maybe that would have to be enough. Maybe tonight was asking too much. Maybe every person on earth had only a certain number of answered prayers and she had run out.

When the doorbell rang again, she nearly cried out. Despite her earlier decision to wait in the dining room to avoid looking too eager, she followed Dr. Hudson into the hall and out to the foyer. She couldn't just stand there and wait to see what happened. Her nerves wouldn't allow it. She hurried past Dr. Hudson, braced herself, and yanked open the front door.

Mr. and Mrs. Patterson stood on the porch, holding the hands of two young boys, each grasping a wooden truck. A young couple stood beside them, staring at Pia with nervous eyes.

Pia felt herself sway, slightly enough that no one else would have noticed, but enough to send a rush of panic through her. She couldn't faint. Not here. Not now. She reached blindly for the doorframe with one hand and her temple with the other. A loud noise pounded in her head; at the same time, she could hear the wind in the leaves outside and the birds squawking in the trees.

She would have known the boys anywhere.

She went down on one trembling knee and smiled at them, trying not to fall over or cry. She wanted to hug and kiss them and tell them how sorry she was, but she worried it would scare them away. It was too soon.

"Well, hello there," she said, her voice quivering. "What are your names?"

They looked at her with matching sets of cobalt-blue eyes. Mutti's eyes.

"Mason," the one on the left said.

"I'm Owen," the other one said. "Daddy says I'm the oldest."

Pia straightened and regarded the young woman, who was watching her intently. She looked to be about five years younger than her husband, with shiny auburn hair and rosy skin. Her face was kind.

"I know these boys," Pia said to her.

The woman nodded and her eyes filled. "I'm Prudence," she said. "This is my husband, Marshall."

Pia gave them a grateful, trembling smile. These were the people who had taken her brothers in, who loved them and cared for them, and were nice to the old couple who had approached them in a park to admire their newly adopted twins. These were the people who hadn't shied away when the old couple showed up at the playground every Sunday with toys and cookies and offers to help with the babies. These were the people who listened to the old couple recall their sadness about not having children, and who invited them into their home and family, to share Sunday dinners and the love of their sons. And these were the people who, by showing up today, proved they trusted the Pattersons—and more importantly, that they had room in their hearts for one more.

"I can never thank you enough for coming," Pia said.

Prudence and Marshall smiled back at her and nodded. There was no need for words. She could see the acceptance in their eyes. Prudence knelt next to the twins.

"Boys," she said. "I'd like you to meet your big sister, Pia."

The twins smiled up at her, happy, little-boy grins with lopsided lips and missing teeth.

"Can we come inside and play?" Max said.

Ollie held up his wooden truck. "I want to show you my new toy," he said. "Grandpa Patterson made it for me."

Pia swallowed the lump in her throat and nodded, her heart about to burst. "Of course," she said. "Please, all of you, come in."

AUTHOR'S NOTE

The Spanish flu came in three waves, the first coming from America, most likely in Kansas, when, in March 1918, soldiers and civilians around Fort Riley rapidly became ill. After the disease spread to other camps and port cities, it subsided that summer. But the flu was on the move, riding the troop ships to Europe and Asia. In late summer, the virus mutated and its most virulent strain returned on the same ships that took it to Europe, landing in Boston in September. It appeared in Philadelphia at the navy base and shipyard on September 18, and by the next day, six hundred sailors were sick, and civilian hospitals started receiving patients.

I chose Philadelphia as the setting for *The Orphan Collector* because the epidemic hit that city exceptionally hard after the Liberty Loan parade brought 200,000 people together on the streets on September 28, 1918. As a result, more than half a million people, in a city of almost two million, contracted the virus over the next six months, and more than 16,000 perished during that period. As the flu became more widespread, Philadelphia's nurses were not enough; student nurses and lay volunteers were quickly utilized. The nurses of the Visiting Nurse Society of Philadelphia were busy around the clock, going into homes and caring for the thousands who could not reach a hospital. A number of them gave their lives. In some neighborhoods, the nurses were hailed as saviors, while in others they were rejected due to their white gowns and gauze masks. Accounts from the nurses described entering houses where all members of a family were dead; some found both parents dead and the children starving. By the time the third wave of the flu finished ravaging the city in 1919, untold numbers of children, at least several thousand, had been orphaned.

While the courageous visiting nurses inspired the character of Bernice Groves, I have no knowledge of any nurses taking advantage of the people of Philadelphia during the epidemic, either by sending children away by train or selling babies. Bernice is purely a product of my imagination, as are the rest of the characters in this novel. To serve the story, creative license was used to move St. Vincent's Home for Unwed Mothers in West Philadelphia to the orphanage in Tacony. Also some street names were changed.

During the writing of *The Orphan Collector*, I read the following books: *People of the Plague*, by T. Neill Anderson; *The 1918 Spanish Flu Pandemic*, by Charles Rivers Editors; and *The Great Influenza: The Story of the Deadliest Pandemic in History*, by John M. Barry. I also relied on *The Encyclopedia of Greater Philadelphia* website (https://philadelphiaencyclopedia.org/archive/influenza-spanish -flu-pandemic-1918-19/).

FURTHER READING

Influenza: The Last Great Plague by William I. B. Beveridge

America's Forgotten Pandemic: The Influenza of 1918 by Alfred W. Crosby

The Plague of the Spanish Lady: The Influenza Pandemic of 1918-1919 by Richard Collier

The Devil's Flu: The World's Deadliest Influenza Epidemic and the Scientific Hunt for the Virus That Caused It by Pete Davies

A Cruel Wind: Pandemic Flu in America 1918-1920 by Dorothy A. Pettit

ACKNOWLEDGMENTS

Writing a novel is a lonely endeavor with many, many hours spent alone at my keyboard, one that would be impossible to accomplish without the encouragement and support from the beloved people who always believe in me. Once again, I'm delighted to offer my heartfelt thanks to those people, along with others who have cheered me on and helped me along during this sometimes bumpy ride.

First and foremost, I want to thank Louise Patterson for igniting the spark that led to the idea for this book. It was your suggestion that opened my eyes to the Spanish flu epidemic and the public nurses who risked their lives helping families and orphaned children during that horrific time. You have my eternal gratitude. I'm also beyond grateful to my good friend Debbie Battista for sharing a family story about twins that ultimately inspired the plot. Thank you for reading the first few chapters, for your endless enthusiasm, and for always supporting me, no matter what.

A special shoutout to booksellers, librarians, and my online friends and readers who joyfully help spread the word about my work and make social media a fun place to be—Andrea Preskind Katz, Nita Joy Haddad, Susan Peterson, Sharlene Martin Moore, Jenny Collins Belk, Barbara Khan, Kayleigh Wilkes, Lauren Blank Margolin, Melissa Amster, Kristy Barret, Tonni Callan, Linda Levack Zagon, LuAnne Rowsam, and fellow Kensington author Cathy Lamb. If I've forgotten anyone who happily promotes me and my books, either online or in the real world, I do hope you'll forgive me. Please know I truly appreciate each and every one of you!

Thank you to my family and friends for understanding my unpredictable schedule and for being patient when I'm getting close to a deadline. If you don't hear from me sometimes, just remember I still love you! A special thanks to my cosmic sister, Barbara Titterington, and my dear friends Beth and Steve Massey, for listening to me go on and on about my writing, for bolstering me when I need extra encouragement, and for dragging me out of the author cave when I don't know enough to take a break. As always, a thousand thanks to the people in and around my wonderful community who support me in too many ways to count and happily show up to fill our little library to the rafters at every book launch. You have no idea how much seeing your smiling faces means to me. It truly makes all the hard work worth it!

I'm indebted to my mentor, William Kowalski, for believing in me from the beginning and for teaching me how to be a storyteller. I'm so happy we finally got to meet! Thank you to my brilliant agent and trusted friend Michael Carr for your indispensible feedback on every book, and for your much-appreciated wisdom regarding my career. We've come a long way since I sent you that first email! Thank you to my marvelous editor, John Scognamiglio, for always being a pleasure to work with, for helping me make every book stronger, and for your continued confidence in my stories. To everyone at Kensington, I can never express my gratitude for everything you do for me, and for your hard work getting my books out into the world: Steven Zacharius, Lynn Cully, Vida Engstrand, Alex Nicolajsen, Jackie Dinas, Kristine Mills, and everyone else who works magic behind the scenes—thank you, thank you. I'm very fortunate to have you and the rest of the Kensington family on my side.

It goes without saying that I owe everything to the unconditional love of my family, especially my beloved mother, Sigrid; my husband and best friend, Bill; my precious children who make me proud every day, Ben, Shanae, Jessie, and Andy; and the treasured little people who fill my world with laughter and tremendous joy, my grandchildren, Rylee, Harper, Lincoln, and Liam. I never imagined I could cherish anyone as much as I cherish you. The sun rises and sets on you! Thank you all for loving and believing in me. You are, and always will be, my everything.

A READING GROUP GUIDE

THE ORPHAN COLLECTOR

Ellen Marie Wiseman

ABOUT THIS GUIDE

The suggested questions are included to enhance your group's
reading of Ellen Marie Wiseman's *The Orphan Collector*!

Discussion Questions

1. The influenza epidemic that swept the world in 1918–1919 infected one-third of the planet's population and killed an estimated 50 million people. Approximately 675,000 of those were in the United States, with around 28 percent infected by the virus, a horror that turned victims bluish black, then drowned them with their own body fluids. The victims would be fine one minute and incapacitated and delirious the next, with fevers rising to 104 to 106 degrees. Death was quick, savage, and terrifying. No other pandemic has claimed as many lives, not even the Black Death in the fourteenth century or AIDS in the twentieth century, yet the Spanish flu is seldom mentioned. Many people have never heard of it. For that reason, 1918 is called the year of forgotten death. Did you know about the pandemic before reading *The Orphan Collector*? If so, where did you first learn about it? Do you know of anyone who died of the Spanish flu? Did you lose any family members?

2. Despite warnings from the city's health officials to avoid crowds because of the Spanish flu, the Fourth Liberty Loan Campaign in Philadelphia, Pennsylvania, brought 200,000 people together on the city's streets on September 28, 1918. In *The Orphan Collector*, when the flu starts to spread during the parade, Pia is frightened to discover that she can feel illness in other people. Have you ever heard of or met anyone with that ability? Would you want to be able to tell when other people are sick before they know it themselves? Why or why not?

3. After her mother dies of the flu, Pia must take care of her twin baby brothers until her father returns from the war. But she lives in the poorest section of Philadelphia, the city is under quarantine, and everything, including schools,

churches, and markets, is closed. When she and the twins run out of food, she makes the difficult decision to leave her brothers in a bedroom cubby while she goes out to look for supplies. Do you think she could have come up with a different plan? Should she have taken her brothers with her? Should she have waited a little longer? What would you have done in that situation?

4. During the epidemic in Philadelphia, the hospitals and morgues quickly became overcrowded, with bodies piling up by the dozens, and many left for days in the streets. Carts traveled the city, their drivers calling for people to bring out their dead. Eventually five makeshift morgues were established to deal with the deluge of corpses. Highway workers dug huge trenches and filled them with victims. Relatives were persuaded to give up their loved ones with promises that the bodies would later be retrieved and reinterred, but most were never recovered. When the flu started, Philadelphia General Hospital was at its capacity of 2,000 patients and had to find room for 1,400 more, turning even larger numbers away. Parish houses and armories were turned into makeshift hospitals, and with the shortage of medical staff due to the war, volunteers were called from religious and civic organizations, and medical and nursing schools. In *The Orphan Collector*, Bernice's growing dislike for immigrants is cemented when her sick baby is turned away at an overcrowded hospital. She thinks it's bad enough that they can't speak English and probably brought the flu into the country, but taking medical attention away from true Americans is the last straw. Yet despite her loathing of foreigners and the fact that the Lange twins are German, she steals them and decides to bring them up as her own. What do you think was her motive? Do you think she wanted the baby boys because she lost her son? Was it revenge for Mr. Lange taking her father's job? Or was it something else?

5. During the time of the Spanish flu, people used all kinds of folk remedies to protect themselves from illness and help cure disease, many of which we now consider useless, strange, and even dangerous. Along with tying garlic around their necks, eating extra onions, and sucking on sugar cubes soaked in kerosene, they took formaldehyde tablets, morphine, laudanum, and chloride of lime, and gave whiskey and Mrs. Winslow's Soothing Syrup to babies and children, despite the fact that it contained morphine, alcohol, and ammonia. The American Medical Association called the syrup a "baby killer" in 1911, but it wasn't removed from the market until 1930. Can you think of any other strange things people did in the past to cure or protect themselves from illness? Were you ever given any peculiar "medicines" as a child? Do you think there are folk or natural remedies that actually work? Which ones? What current medicines or medical practices do you think will be considered unsafe or barbaric in the future?

6. Wartime restrictions on communication had deadly effects during WWI, including in the United States. President Wilson's Committee on Public Information and the Sedition Act passed by Congress both limited writing or publishing anything negative about the country. Posters asked the public to "report the man who spreads pessimistic stories," and to maintain morale, wartime censors curtailed early reports of influenza and mortality in Germany, Britain, France, and the United States. But the newspapers were free to report the epidemic's effects in Spain, creating the false impression that Spain was especially hard hit and leading to the nickname Spanish flu. In Philadelphia, doctors pushed for the Liberty Loan parade on September 28 to be canceled because they were concerned that the crowds of people would spread the flu. They convinced reporters to write stories about the danger, but editors refused to run them, or to print any letters from the doc-

tors. Consequently, despite their earlier warning to avoid crowds, the city's public health officials allowed the largest parade in Philadelphia's history to proceed. Two days later, the epidemic had spread, and over the following six weeks, more than 12,000 citizens of Philadelphia died. How much of a difference do you think it would have made if those stories had been printed in the newspaper? Do you think people would have stayed home or gone to the parade anyway?

7. Philadelphia was the American city with the highest, most rapidly accumulating death toll in the worst pandemic in recorded history, the Spanish flu. The increased demand for labor in its shipbuilding, munitions, and steel industries during the war only compounded matters. Though the disease knew no gender, racial, or ethnic boundaries, the city's immigrant poor suffered the worst, with the largest loss of life happening in the slums and tenement districts. Why do you think that was? What issues do you think contributed to it?

8. Besides feeling overwhelming grief and tremendous guilt, Pia is afraid to tell anyone the reason her brothers are missing—because she left them home alone to search for food. Do you think she should feel so guilty? Do you think it would have been helpful to tell the nuns at St. Vincent's? Why or why not? What about Dr. and Mrs. Hudson? Should she have told them sooner?

9. Even though she has no money and nowhere to go, Pia tries to escape St. Vincent's Orphan Asylum to look for her brothers. Considering the time, what do you think would have happened to her if she had been successful? Did you think Mother Joe was going to release her after letting her out of the basement room? Why or why not? After being sent to the Hudsons', should Pia have tried to flee? Would she have been better off or worse if she had gotten away? Do

you think she still would have found out what happened to Ollie and Max? Why or why not?

10. Disguised as a nurse, Bernice does a lot of horrible things to the immigrants in Philadelphia. She tricks parents into letting their children go with her to get food and clothing, then doesn't return them. She sends the older ones away by train and takes the younger ones to orphanages. Why do you think she keeps the younger ones in the city? What do you think is her worst crime? Do you think she paid for what she did? Were you satisfied with the way her story ended?

11. After Finn shows up at St. Vincent's Orphan Asylum, he and Pia try to hatch a plan to escape. But before they can carry it out, he disappears. Pia has no idea if he was adopted, sent away, or if he left without her. The nuns refuse to tell her anything. Before you found out the truth, what did you think happened to him? Did you figure it out, or were you surprised?

12. When Pia knocks on her neighbors' doors looking for food, no one will answer, or they tell her to go away. Likewise, Dr. and Mrs. Hudson refuse to let anyone leave or enter their house until the last wave of the flu is over. But unlike the people in Pia's neighborhood, they have plenty of supplies and money for more to be delivered when needed. Would you have answered the door if Pia knocked looking for food? What would you do if you were a poor immigrant in that situation? How would you make your provisions last? What other precautions would you take to keep your family safe?

13. When Bernice is finally confronted by Pia, she says the twins passed away from tuberculosis. Then she says she sent them out West on an orphan train. Finally, after talking to Bernice's neighbors, Pia discovers the truth. Why do you think Bernice ended up doing what she did with the boys?

21982319584219

Do you think it had anything to do with the fact that she kept running into Pia? Do you think she was worried about getting caught?

14. How did you feel about Bernice when you first met her? When did your perception of her change? How and why did it change?

15. How do you think Pia changed over the course of the novel? What were the most important events that facilitated those changes?